MW00720884

THE CLOCK STRIKES MIDNIGHT

Joan C. Curtis

MuseItUp Publishing
www.museituppublishing.com

The Clock Strikes Midnight © 2015 by Joan C. Curtis

MuseItUp Publishing
14878 James, Pierrefonds, Quebec, Canada, H9H 1P5

Cover Art © 2014 by Carolina Bensler
Edited by Lea Schizas
Layout and Book Production by Lea Schizas
Print ISBN: 978-1-77127-743-3
eBook ISBN: 978-1-77127-599-6

To Isabelle

Acknowledgements

This book has been a long-standing project. I'd like to thank the many people who stood by me in the process as well as those tireless readers of many drafts.

My husband read this story in so many renditions, he hardly recognized the final version. My thanks go to him. I also want to thank Terri Valentine not only as a reader and editor but also as one who encouraged me throughout the writing-to-publishing journey.

I wish to thank MuseItUp Publishing and especially Lea Schizas for her editorial help as well as her willingness to take this book on.

To all my friends who have listened to me tell this story in one fashion or another, I just want to say, we did it together! Thank you all.

PART ONE

Chapter One

"It's a fast growing tumor, Miss Knox," Dr. Mills told Janie. "Hard to detect early, I'm afraid."

His words—chemotherapy, death, prognosis—collided in her head and buzzed around as if lost.

She had done some wicked things in her life. *It serves me right to die young.*

"How much time do I have?" She swallowed the heaviness in her throat. *Stay focused. Don't panic.*

He fiddled with the stethoscope around his neck. "That's hard to say."

How they must hate telling people they're going to die. "Listen, doctor, I need to know. I've got things to do."

"Unfortunately, I can't be too precise. We do have counselors who can help you put things in order, if that's what you mean." He reached for the prescription pad.

"Can't you give me some idea?"

"These things are hard to predict. Some people live as few as three months, and others make it longer, maybe even a year."

She stared at the wall behind him where he had hung his diploma, illegible from her vantage point. Her life with Sue Anne had been too good. This was God's punishment for all the bad things. Three months. "And there's nothing you can do?"

"We could operate, but to be honest—and you asked me to be honest—it might just add a few more months, maybe guarantee you a year. Or, there is the risk of dying in surgery." He paused and shook his head. "Personally, I wouldn't recommend chemo, not at this stage. I'm sorry. You can always get a second opinion, though. I'd be glad to make a referral."

"That won't be necessary."

He scrawled something on his pad. "Is there anyone you'd like me to call?"

She got up, surprised her legs held her. "No, thanks."

He handed her the prescription. "This will help with the pain."

She left the doctor's office and drove directly to the drug store on the corner. While waiting for the prescription, her mind played out what she had to do. Go home. Pack. She couldn't face Sue Anne, who would insist on knowing everything. Janie had things to take care of. Things she had put off for too long. *Three months,* the voice in the back of her head said. *My God! I need more time.* She took the bag of meds from the faceless pharmacist and raced home.

Once there, she pulled down the hidden staircase and climbed into the attic where cobwebs stretched across the beams above her head. Her flashlight shone on the rows of boxes, a Lava lamp, and an old black and white TV she and Sue Anne had stowed when they moved in nearly twelve years earlier. Such a beautiful day that had been.

Brushing the cobwebs from her face, she edged her way toward a container the size of a shoebox. She had hidden it there while Sue Anne was busy unloading the van and arguing with the movers. She blew off a thick layer of dust—twitching her nose to keep from sneezing—and lifted the lid. She rummaged inside until her hand caught hold of the gold-inlaid music box she was looking for, turned it upside down, and peeled off the adhesive holding a flat, narrow key.

Ten minutes later, she tossed an overnight suitcase and the music box into the trunk of her bright red Honda Accord and took off.

In her rearview mirror she watched the wide beach fade in the distance. When she and Sue Anne had found their house on Tybee

Island, it had been in shambles but less costly than those in historic downtown Savannah. With their joint incomes, they could barely afford putting a bid on the house. Over the years when their incomes expanded —Sue Anne with a thriving interior design business and her own multiple beauty salons—they had fixed up the place, replacing faulty pipes and painting the rooms with bright colors. Her body tensed with regret as the world she loved grew smaller in the distance.

In the four-hour drive from Savannah to Atlanta she considered what Dr. Mills had told her. She was going to die. Her time was running out. Everything she thought about doing someday, she must do now. She let out a long, tired sigh. *I'm not making excuses for what I've done in my life. I just want to sort it all out and right some wrongs before it's too late.*

She reached for a cigarette, put it in her mouth, but didn't light it. She had stopped smoking ten years earlier but never tired of the feel of a cigarette between her lips. The smell of tobacco triggered memories long ago buried—Mom sitting at the kitchen table with an ashtray full of cigarette butts and a glass of whiskey in her hand. Her older sister, Marlene, washing dishes at the sink. Her stepfather, Ralph, red-faced with sweat under his armpits, standing in the corner, cussing about something at work.

One good thing about being dead, the memories would finally go away. She chuckled at the irony. Wasn't that what she had always wanted? Freedom from those awful memories?

She rolled into Atlanta, amazed at the tall buildings sprouting up everywhere. The city was like a Monopoly board full of new hotels and houses. Cars tooted at her snail-like pace. She had grown up in this city. One would think she would know how to get around. But after nearly twenty years, things change. She stopped at a gas station to fill up. Afterward, she pulled out her iPhone to search hotels downtown. She wanted to stay near two places, the old C&S Bank and Lawton and Brady, Limited.

She paid for the gas and ventured back out onto those streets with bumper-to-bumper cars filled with people wanting to be someplace else.

She relaxed her white-knuckle grip on the steering wheel. *I'm more afraid of driving in Atlanta than of dying.*

Finally, she pulled into the parking deck of the Edgewood Hotel, a small facility within the shadows of the massive Bank of America building, formerly C & S Bank, and a few blocks from Lawton and Brady.

Her watch read 5:15 p.m. She imagined Sue Anne, unaware of her absence, making her weekly run to Kroger to stock up on groceries. Of course, this would include a bag of Milkbones for Charlie, their ninety-two pound yellow lab who was celebrating his fifth birthday tomorrow.

She unloaded her small suitcase and checked in.

While unpacking, she caught a glimpse of herself in the mirror. Her father's eyes stared back at her, bringing back a memory she'd long ago repressed.

"Daddy, when I get my kitty, can I name him Davy?" she had asked, yanking Marlene's Davy Crockett mug full of M&M's from her grasp. The colorful candy spilled all over the backseat of the car.

"Mama, tell Janie to—"

"Janie, behave," Daddy said, admonishing her for an instant with his eyes from the rearview mirror.

"Malcolm, look out—!" Mom screamed.

Janie slammed into Marlene. Pain. The world tumbled topsy-turvy. The mug flew across the interior of the car, colors of the rainbow falling all around her. Then, everything went black.

When she opened her eyes, Mom's blood-streaked face rose in front of her out of the darkness.

"Wrap your arms around my neck, honey." Mom lifted her from the wreckage.

Janie clutched her doll by the dress while the rain beat her curly hair flat. Marlene stood on the side of the road.

"Try to walk," Mom said, toppling her from her arms.

Her head pounded and blood trickled down her leg. She leaned on her good leg and limped in the direction of her sister.

"Mama, where's Daddy?" Marlene asked between sobs.

Mom took Marlene's hand and yanked her forward with Janie in tow.

Marlene lurched back toward the smashed Oldsmobile with smoke billowing from its hood and a big tree lying across the roof. The Davy Crockett mug lay shattered by the back tire.

"Daddy! We can't leave Daddy!" Marlene yelled, picking up pieces of the broken glass.

They had left Daddy that day and piled into an old Chevy pick-up truck with a bashed in headlamp, belonging to a man with carrot-red hair. Mom pushed them inside the truck and ordered the man to get help. But by then it was too late for Daddy.

It was too late for all of them.

Janie sorted clothes to hang in the closet. Her head throbbed. A sunbeam caught the golden edge of the music box sitting on the vanity. She rose from the bed, drawn to the one memento she had taken from her family home on Briardale Lane. She lifted the lid. Her mother's favorite song, Beethoven's *Ode de Joy*, hummed from the little box. If only someone other than the man with the carrot-red hair had stopped that night—a soccer mom or an elderly couple.

After the funeral, the man with the carrot-red hair, whom she later learned was called Ralph Cooper, had stayed. In a dark corner of the church, she and Marlene ducked down in the pew to get a good view of him talking to Mom. When the man bent his head toward Mom and touched her arm as if by accident, Janie gasped, and Marlene hushed her with a finger to her lips. Then the man kissed Mom's hair. Chills had run up Janie's arm, not from the cold but from some deep dread gnawing inside her like when Lewis Watring had punched her in the stomach on the playground.

When Aunt Sarah returned from the bathroom, the man with carrot-red hair had vanished.

Perhaps if they had told Aunt Sarah then, things would have worked out differently. As it was, she and Marlene had both kept quiet, and Ralph Cooper had wormed his way into their lives and had turned their worlds upside down.

Janie rubbed her temples. She lifted a pile of clothes and placed them in the small bureau under the hotel mirror. Marlene would be shocked to see her after all this time. After their daddy died, she and her sister had clung to one another—each becoming the other's lifeline, but all that had changed.

Now she wondered whether Marlene would hate her for leaving.

She stepped to the window and watched the sun travel lower in the sky. Tomorrow she would find her sister and explain everything to her. *I must have Marlene's help. I can't do this alone, especially with the clock ticking away.* Marlene and *only* Marlene could get what she needed from Ralph. She'd tried to do it once without her and failed. She didn't have time to fail again.

Moving from the window, she telephoned Sue Anne.

"I'm in Atlanta," she told her.

"What are you talking about, love? I thought you were going to the doctor. What are you doing in Atlanta?" The worry in her voice nearly broke Janie's heart.

"The doctor sent me here for a second opinion," she lied. "I should be home in a few days after the tests."

"But, what did he say? Are you okay? Did he say what was causing the pain?"

Janie cleared her throat to calm her voice. Lying to Sue Anne wasn't easy. "He's not sure what's going on yet. That's why he sent me here. I'll be at Emory all day tomorrow. Don't worry. I'm sure they'll figure out what's wrong, if anything."

Silence.

"Janie, what aren't you telling me? How could you go there alone?"

"Look, I had no choice. And, I thought it best to come here by myself. It'll give me a chance to see Marlene. She's going to freak out when she sees me. Imagine what she'd do if you came too."

Sue Anne laughed. "That's the Lord's own truth. Do you want me to call Steven?"

"That'd be great. I can call him from here, but it would save me a bit of time, and I don't know how much free time I'll have. Ask him to take care of the shops until I get back and not to let Lucinda drive him nuts."

"I miss you already," Sue Anne said before hanging up.

Janie went into the bathroom to shower. Her trained fingers massaged her head with shampoo fortified with lavender soymilk, opting against the standard hotel brand. How many heads had she massaged? Hundreds of women told her they had nearly fallen asleep while she gently rubbed their scalps. She moved her hands along the inside of her cranium and down her lower neck and rolled her head from side to side. The comforting fingers, the warm water, and the smell of lavender did nothing to reduce the knots that held her body in bondage.

Later, she studied the skyline from her hotel window and waited for the hamburger and sweet tea she'd ordered from a nearby restaurant to arrive. Being in Atlanta made her stomach queasy. She had abandoned this city the week after a jury had convicted Ralph Cooper of killing her mother. She had left with all her worldly possessions in a single duffle bag, hopped on a bus to Savannah, and resolved never to return.

She turned from the scenic view and took a deep breath to steady the wild beating of her heart. Everything inside her screamed go, run, escape.

I must finish this. I owe it to Marlene.

Chapter Two

Marlene lifted her head from the dining room table. The candles had burned down to cold wicks. Darkness had sneaked in and with it a heavy cloud of silence. The light on the CD player flashed. Outside a dog barked and a motor roared in the distance.

She wrapped her arms around her chest and rose with an aching stiffness in her legs. Her head pounded. The odor from the uneaten dinner —spaghetti and sausage—filled her nostrils. Her watch read 2:30 a.m. Fumbling for the light switch, she squinted when the glare hit her eyes.

"Oh, God," she murmured, her mind abruptly traveling to the day she and her husband, Peter, had bought this house.

"It's perfect," he had told her, beaming like a little boy on Christmas morning. He saw it and bought it without consulting her.

The dark mahogany plank floors, scratched and scraped from post-Civil War days, had begged for a good buffing. More recent owners had covered the walls with light green-striped wallpaper she instantly detested. Peter had guided her into the kitchen where he raved about the bay window and the spacious countertops. The flowery wallpaper had dulled to an ancient shade of yellow. She appreciated his enthusiasm but would have liked participating in the selection. *Typical. Pull on my chain and I'll follow you anywhere.*

"One of the things I like best," Peter had continued with an eager lift to his voice, "is the way the stairs curl to the top like in *Gone with the Wind*. They're not as steep as they look. Can't you imagine Scarlett O'Hara standing on the landing?" He had raced up the stairs and held out his arms to her, mimicking Rhett.

Tonight the steps felt steeper than the tallest mountain in the Rockies. She mounted one after the other while clutching the handrail like an old woman. Her stomach fluttered and her legs throbbed from the strain. Halfway up, she paused to catch her breath.

She had lived in houses with steps all her life. There had been steps in the house on Briardale Lane. Memories of those creaky stairs created a new wave of nausea. She swallowed hard to choke down the bile and continued her climb.

By the time she reached the top, her heart pounded as if she had sprinted a mile. The hallway was gloomy and silent. She switched on the lamp and inched to the bedroom where the drawers stood partially open, and clothes spilled across every surface. Peter had packed hurriedly and hadn't taken everything. *A good sign?* The note, written on his personalized stationery and probably with the gold pen she had given him on his last birthday, was propped on the pillow of the king-sized bed. Her hand trembled as she read:

I'll be back tomorrow to collect the rest of my things. P

A single sentence after almost nineteen years of marriage. She crumpled the note into a wad. The pink and green curtains and the matching comforter looked too cheerful in this large, lonely room. Her tabby cat, asleep in the middle of a pile of clothes, raised her head when Marlene walked in but didn't utter a sound. She scratched the cat behind the ears and crawled in bed.

"It's just you and me now, Nellie."

Nellie butted her face against Marlene's hand and purred.

Daylight woke her later that morning. She eased off the edge of the bed and rubbed her temples. Nellie meowed at the door. Marlene let the animal loose and peeked out the window at the bright sunshine piercing through dark, threatening clouds.

Gloomy days like this reminded her of Mama, who once said, "I love the crash of thunder and the blaze of lightning. It's so thrilling."

Marlene craved sameness, routine and calm sunny days.

The telephone jarred her back to reality. She reached for it, but didn't lift it. *Probably Peter, perhaps to arrange a time to get his clothes*. She had no idea what she would say to him and right now couldn't face him, even on the phone. But after the fifth ring, her resolve weakened, and she lifted the receiver.

"Hello, Marly."

She sucked in her breath, immediately recognizing the voice, but not knowing how to respond.

"Are you there?"

"I'm here," she finally said. "I'm just shocked to hear your voice."

"That's understandable." Janie paused. "I'm in Atlanta, and I'd like to see you."

Marlene answered with a rueful chuckle. She stood up, ran her fingers through her hair, and paced the floor. Of all days for Janie to reappear. She couldn't believe it.

"So you say you're in Atlanta, as if you were here for a weekend visit and just wanted to drop in for a howdy-do? You've got some nerve calling like this." She couldn't control her bitterness. And, why should she after all this time and not a peep from her sister? Her head thundered like a sledgehammer. She stumbled into the bathroom and downed two aspirin.

When Janie didn't answer, and when the silence on the other end of the receiver became oppressive, Marlene added, "Where are you?"

"The Yellow Star Café next to Lucille's shop. I came looking for her." Janie paused. "I guess her shop's gone."

"Lucille died in a car wreck," Marlene blurted out without any pretense of concern for her sister's feelings.

Janie gasped. "When?"

"God knows. Not long after you left. What difference does that make now? What difference does anything make? You abandoned her…you abandoned me…you abandoned all of us."

Janie didn't answer.

"I'll be there in thirty minutes," she said, and hung up.

Memories of the past shot in front of her eyes like gnats blurring her vision. A gun, a letter, blood. The memories kept coming back, usually at night when she closed her eyes.

She reached for the vodka bottle hidden under the bathroom sink and poured the last of the contents into a glass, swallowing slowly and savoring the warm liquid as it tingled through her body like a familiar, welcoming hug. Then she rose and dressed.

The Yellow Star Café sat on the corner of a back street not far from the Emory University campus. She caught a glimpse of herself in the window as she neared the café. Her hair hung loosely around her face. She couldn't remember the last time she had added highlights. She tucked the droopy strands behind her ears and pushed through the door.

Inside, several college-age boys in jeans and T-shirts lolled around the counter, drinking coffee and munching donuts. They didn't even look up when Marlene sauntered by. Instead, they elbowed each other and snickered when an attractive girl in skinny jeans passed by the window.

She spotted Janie in a corner booth. From this distance her sister hadn't changed much. She easily recognized the curly blond head glistening in the beam of sunlight from the window. Janie wore a gray suit with a white blouse buttoned high at the neck, very un-Janie-like.

She neared the table, wobbling on her three-inch heels but managing to keep her balance. When Janie rose to embrace her, she quickly slid into the booth, avoiding her sister's attempt at a hug.

"Want some coffee?" Janie asked, settling back in her seat.

"Yeah," she answered, and caught the waitress's eye with a motion for a cup.

Marlene clenched her jaw, not sure how to begin. She studied the waitress who poured from a steaming pot. The woman's tired face was marred with wrinkles running across her forehead. She wore an apron, splashed with coffee and mustard. The waitress haphazardly poured fresh coffee into both cups without saying a word. Janie mopped up the spilled coffee with a napkin.

"Looks like you could use a nice breakfast," Janie said.

"What's that supposed to mean?"

Janie blinked. "You look tired. Your eyes are all red and puffy. Are you okay?"

"Fine and dandy."

Janie recoiled as if struck by a rattlesnake.

"What's the matter with you?" Marlene asked.

Janie sipped the coffee. "You just look different. I'm trying to adjust. That's all." Her sister's hand shook when she replaced the cup on the saucer.

Marlene let out a loud, ugly laugh. One of the boys from the counter glanced in her direction. "You don't look so hot yourself."

Janie didn't answer.

"Well?" she said, after tasting the coffee.

"Well, what?"

"Come off it. You disappeared, vanished without a trace, and you pop in this morning as though you never left after almost twenty years of silence. How can you just sit there? Talk, tell me what happened. Why didn't you write? Why didn't you send me something, anything, to let me know you were still alive?" She turned away and studied the flecks of gold on the Formica table.

Janie didn't respond.

Marlene took a deep breath. "So what did you do? Where did you go? Are you married? Do I have nieces and nephews that I don't know about?"

"That doesn't matter now," Janie said, waving away Marlene's questions. "I'm not married, and you don't have to worry about any nieces and nephews. Mostly I wandered around. I got jobs doing hair. I have my own shops now. I hoped I might see Lucille while I was here. She'd taught me so much, and I never really thanked her." She looked toward Lucille's former salon, her eyes luminous with emotion.

"I told you. Lucille died." Marlene's voice was harsh, as if she were talking to a forgetful old woman.

Silence.

"I needed you at my wedding. After everything—for God's sakes." She choked back a sob. "When people ask me if I have any brothers and sisters, I tell them they're all dead."

Janie continued to watch her with a maddening scowl, like her fifth grade teacher when she gave the wrong answer.

Marlene lifted the coffee cup to her lips with trembling hands. More brown liquid splattered across the Formica tabletop.

"My disappearing act happened a long time ago. It has little relevance to today, to now," Janie finally said.

"Maybe to you."

Janie took a deep breath. "I'm sorry I missed your wedding. But I couldn't come back. I wasn't able to breathe until I got out of this town. I felt as if a big giant hand was holding me down, keeping me away. You've no idea."

"No, I wouldn't know, would I? How do you think I felt?" Marlene's voice rose again.

The boys at the bar turned and stared in their direction. This was probably the most exciting thing that had happened in this café since Ted Turner bought the Braves.

"I know Mama wasn't what she should have been," she continued, "but she loved us. I know she did. What the papers said about her wasn't fair. She didn't have it so easy, married to someone like Ralph. No wonder she drank." Her voice shook while she spoke. "You left me to face this community alone." She paused, licked her lips, and tasted the coffee mixed with her raspberry flavored lipstick.

"You had Aunt Sarah and Peter," Janie corrected her.

"Naturally you don't understand. You'll never understand what it was like. I wanted to believe you weren't selfish, but when you left like that, leaving me to bear the burden alone—"

"I can't explain it. I felt suffocated in the same town as Ralph."

"He was in prison."

"It didn't matter. I had to leave." Janie stopped and then said, "Or die."

Marlene stared at her. "Then why come back now?"

Janie drank her coffee and wrinkled her brow. "I've got things I need to do. Seeing you for one."

"So, you've seen me. You can check that off."

Silence.

Finally Janie asked, "Where's Ralph now?"

"Where do you think? After he was released, he hightailed it to Briardale Lane. Living in our house, if you can believe the nerve. He calls me every day, wanting to know if I've heard from you. He's possessed with you. Why won't he leave it all alone?"

"All I can say now, Marly, is I'm sorry. I'm here to make it right. I can't do anything else."

"It's too late. All you'll do now is cause trouble. Ralph paid his price. Mama's dead. It's over."

"I wish it were that simple."

"What do you mean?"

Janie ran her hand over her forehead. "I don't think he's paid his price —not for what he did to our family."

Marlene's stomach clenched. "What are you talking about? Talk to me, Janie!" She slammed her fist onto the table, rattling the cups and spilling more coffee.

A pain stabbed Marlene's head. Flashes shot across her mind—her mother lying in a pool of blood, face turned sideways, eyes vacant, the smell of gunpowder.

"Ralph claims he's innocent," Marlene said.

Janie's face drained of what little color it had. "What do you mean he claims he's innocent?"

"He says he never killed Mama. I've had to bear the brunt of it—the letters and telephone calls begging me to help him. Maybe he really is innocent. With all the new stuff they're doing with DNA, he could prove he didn't do it, couldn't he?"

Janie blinked. "You're crazy. DNA won't help him."

Marlene shook her head.

Janie sat up. "What? Tell me what you're talking about?"

"The jury convicted him without the gun—mainly on your testimony. Would they have done so had they found the gun?"

"Of course they would have, and they might have sentenced him to life instead of twenty years. He killed Mom."

"I wish I could remember. I keep seeing images."

"What images?"

Tears filled Marlene's eyes. "I've tried to bring it back, but all I see are pieces and I'm not sure what's real and what's a dream. Ralph thinks I know something. He thinks I have the answer."

Janie leaned toward her. "He's up to something. Why would he pressure you now that he's out?"

Marlene shook her head and sniffed into a tissue. "I've no idea."

Janie reached for her hand. "You can find out. He'd tell you. He trusts you."

She stared at her sister. "Don't open all this up again. I can't take it. Promise you won't."

"Please, Marly. Help me do this. I want to make this right before—"

"I can't. Don't make me." More tears. "If you want to make things right, then go away."

Janie pulled away and took a deep breath.

After a few minutes, Marlene wiped her nose and reached inside her purse, and drew out a cigarette.

"When did you start smoking?" Janie asked.

"Who cares? Peter hates it. I think I do it to drive him crazy." She laughed a bitter laugh. "I'm not going to light up so don't panic."

Janie shifted in her seat.

Marlene twirled the cigarette.

"Marly, I don't like the way you look. You're so thin. Don't you ever eat?"

"You've got some nerve. Showing up here like this after not having shown the slightest bit of interest in me in twenty years and then telling me I need to eat. If this situation weren't so pathetic, it would be hilarious."

Janie narrowed her eyes. "Somebody needs to say it—you look like hell. Your eyes are all bloodshot, and your skin looks pasty. But your hair, good God, Marly, you had such amazing hair."

A burning heat rose to her cheeks.

"Talk to me. I'm scared for you."

"Oh, cut the crap." Marlene jerked away from her and snapped the cigarette in two. "You're a stranger to me. You don't know me from, from say that kid over there." She pointed to a young student who sat alone at the counter. The others had left.

"We're connected. Like it or not, and I don't like what I see."

"Sounds like you see a washed up old hag to me," Marlene retorted. She finished the last of the bitter coffee and smacked her lips.

"Not exactly. I see a very angry woman who is irritable, tired, and a little drunk. I see a woman who frightens me because she reminds me of my mother."

Marlene swallowed hard, steadied her voice, and then said, "You don't care about me anymore than you cared about Mama. Go back to wherever you came from. You can do nothing here but cause more trouble, and believe me, I have enough of that without you."

She got up from the booth and staggered from the café.

Chapter Three

Downtown Atlanta may have been one big puzzle to Janie, but Decatur —the small town on the outskirts of Atlanta, clinging to its quaint Southern charm—remained unchanged. She found the house on Briardale Lane, nestled among the old Decatur streets, as if she had been there yesterday.

As she drove, she thought over the scene with Marlene in the Yellow Star Café. One thing her sister made clear, she would not help Janie with her plan. She must carry it out by herself. That meant trying to find out what Ralph was up to without him knowing she was in Atlanta. Although frustrated by her sister's response, she understood her anger. At age seventeen, she had not been thinking about Marlene. She could only think one thought—get out of town and as far away from Ralph as possible.

She steered along the narrow streets. Thick grass covered hilly lawns. Huge magnolias and oak trees spilled out onto Briardale Lane. It was a bit narrower and the houses smaller from her adult point of view, but the atmosphere stayed the same. Moms rolled kids in strollers down the sidewalk and neighbors talked across their yards. Squirrels ran up and down the oaks. Nature went on year after year. Little mattered to the squirrels and chipmunks of the world.

The Johnson's house across the street had been painted a strange shade of pink, and she didn't see the terrier that used to greet her whenever she came home. Mrs. Dover's house next door looked exactly the same, including a big yellow cat sitting on the fence, preening itself. She doubted the old woman was still alive. Maybe her daughter lived there with her own yellow cat.

She stopped the Honda three houses down from number 409, the family home, and strolled along a path she had trod hundreds of times either on foot or on her bicycle. A cool breeze caressed her face. She reached a place on the sidewalk where she and Jake had etched their initials, *JP + JK Forever*. The letters remained but were now faded and dark from many passing footsteps.

Memories flooded back like hail in a torrential rain. On a rainy summer afternoon, when she had been thirteen and Marlene fifteen, not long after she had carved those initials in the newly paved sidewalk, she had stood in the shadows of the hallway outside Mom's room—a place she hated to enter.

On that day, Mom had announced she was going to sell the house. She had joined the family for dinner for the first time in weeks. After having teased her hair into a high nest and freshening her pale face with red rouge, she replaced her tattered, light blue robe with the blue and white short-sleeved dress Marlene had picked out. She wore black patent-leather three-inch heels with pointy toes. A cloud of jasmine and baby powder rose from her skin each time she moved. No one spoke of her sudden appearance. The tension in the room weighed heavier than humidity right before a summer storm.

They ate leftover roasted chicken, green beans and potato salad. The late afternoon sunlight filtered through the window blinds and threw a beam of light across the table. Janie concentrated on the way that light beam bounced around. She aimed for it when she reached for the jug of iced tea and spilt some onto the tablecloth.

"Janie, dear," Mom said, "you shouldn't reach across your sister. It's bad manners."

Janie mopped up the tea. "Yes, ma'am." The meal went on in endless progression like a stream of ants marching across a desert.

While Janie and Marlene cleared away the dishes, Mom announced, "I've decided to sell this house."

A knife crashed to the floor.

Ralph wiped his lips with a napkin, pushed his chair from the table with a loud scrape, walked into the den, and powered up the television. He stared at *People's Court* as though it was the most interesting show in the world.

Mom marched after him, her heels clicking across the linoleum, and switched off the TV. She stood in front of the set with one hand on her narrow hip. "Did you hear what I said, Ralph Cooper?" Her voice shook, but her huge eyes were as steady as steel.

"I heard you. Now turn the television back on. I was watching it."

"Don't you have anything to say?"

Janie stood next to Marlene at the threshold to the kitchen, clutching a pile of wet dishes with trembling hands. *She couldn't sell this house. This was Granny Jennings' house. Where will we live?*

"It's your house. Do as you please, but the girls and me won't help you none. What do you think will become of us? The girls are settled in school. Do you plan to yank them out? You're just talking gibberish like you always do after one of your spells. Now get the hell out of my way."

He shoved her away from the television. She stumbled, grabbed his arm, and dug her fingernails into his flesh.

He yelped.

"I know about you," she said, her upper lip curled. "I nearly confided in Sarah today, but I didn't 'cause I was too embarrassed. Besides, I know what she'd say. She'd tell me to throw you out and lock the doors. That's what she'd say all right. And that's what got me out of my sick bed. You're a no account bastard. I got up to protect my girls from the likes of you. If I sell this house, I can afford to find somewhere else to live without depending on you for nothing—'specially that piddling salary you make cleaning shit from the hospital floors.

"Betsy Jane told me about you and that little girl at the hospital. She told me how you scared that child. And only nine years old, for God's sakes."

Ralph stepped back and collapsed into his chair. At first he stared at her, but then his face crumpled into laughter. "So, what'd you say to your fat-lipped, gossipy friend? Did you tell her that you're too filthy, withered, and drunk to attract your man to your bed? Did you tell her that the sight of you makes me puke? Ha, ha, I bet she found that funny. She's such a high and mighty lady. I bet she loved hearing that the town's beauty queen can't even attract a cockroach to her bed!"

Black mascara streaked down Mom's cheeks.

"Shut up, Ralph," Janie said, looking from him to her mother.

Mom slapped Ralph across the face leaving a red patch on his cheek. "I should have never married a sorry man like you."

He continued to laugh. "Don't think you had them lined up, did ya now? Nope, surenuf not. If my memory serves me rightly, you didn't have much choice. Nope, not a one."

Janie turned to Marlene for help. But her sister had torn off her apron and raced out the backdoor. Janie didn't see her until later that night when she pleaded with her to run away to Aunt Sarah's.

At the time, Janie didn't understand why Marlene wanted to run away, and she had no idea what her mother had meant when she accused Ralph of scaring a little girl, but she had gone with her sister anyway. Later, when it was too late, she had understood.

A cat mewed and rubbed against Janie's leg, breaking up her memories like balls on a billiard table and reminding her she didn't have time to stand and gawk. She blinked and reached down to stroke the animal's long, yellow fur, but the cat dashed across the street.

She faced the family home, studying the changes. The grass was overgrown and the shrubs looked as if they had not been pruned in years. Aunt Sarah was supposed to keep everything maintained, but apparently that didn't include the yard. The sidewalk leading to the house was cracked and covered in moss with ugly yellow weeds growing out from the cracks. Marlene had said that Ralph had moved back in, but she saw no sign of him or anyone else. If she was lucky, she could slip in the backdoor and take a look around to see if there were any clues as to Ralph's plans and get out before he returned.

She suspected he had found new evidence, something that would enable him to reopen the case. From what Marlene had said, he had tried to elicit her help while he was in prison and was still trying to get information from her. Eventually Marlene would remember what happened that day and then all would be lost. *One step at a time, Janie.*

She stepped over the cracked sidewalk and surveyed the surroundings like a sightseer. Once she had rescued a baby bird at the foot of the big pine tree growing next to the front entrance. She had nursed that bird for several days before it died. She touched the base of the pear tree her mother had planted not long after her dad had died. Eloise had held both daughter's hands in hers and announced, "This tree will mark the years. It will grow taller as your father's death grows older. One day when his memory fades in your minds, this tree will remind you of what a good man he was." The majestic green limbs stretched toward the sky. There was nothing to remind Janie of her mother. They had planted no tree in her memory.

She pulled her scarf closer around her neck and edged along the side of the house toward the back, close to her childhood bedroom. She tried to lift the window where she had snuck out every night for her rendezvous with Thelma, one of her wilder high school friends, but it was bolted. No surprise.

When she walked up the back stairs to the porch, she stubbed her toe on a loose board. The screen door screeched open as if it had not been used in years. Put a little WD-40 on it, Sue Anne would say. The porch furniture was black with mildew and spider webs. An ashtray her mother had used sat on the picnic table but empty of cigarette butts. She tiptoed over to the backdoor leading to the kitchen. If Ralph were here, he would probably have the television going and never hear the door open. But the house appeared deserted, at least for the moment.

She turned the knob, but it was fastened. When they lived in this house, they had never locked the doors. She wiped the surface of the window with a tissue and peered into the kitchen, spotting its yellowing wall paper and battered kitchen table. Nothing obvious had changed.

She sighed and moved away from the window, wondering what would have happened had they managed to stay with Aunt Sarah on that fateful day. How different everything might have turned out. Marlene had changed after that incident. Although still the one responsible for their mother, Marlene had drifted into her own world, excluding everyone, including her sister.

Mom never sold this house, and she probably never meant to, just wanted to antagonize Ralph or scare him away. Ralph's red laughing face shot in her head. His veins bulged at his neck. His yellow teeth and rancid breath mocked them all.

She pushed against the backdoor in a futile attempt to bash it down. She held back a scream threatening to escape from her lips when a white SUV pulled up in the driveway and stopped.

A big black man with a red bandana on his head stepped out of the driver's side. Ralph descended from the other. Her heart jumped into her throat. She froze at the sight of the carrot-red hair.

The black man stopped by the car and lit a cigarette. If he turned slightly to his left, he'd spot her on the porch. She crouched down low. A dog approached him. The man bent down to jostle the animal, but the dog pulled away and growled.

Ralph walked toward the garage at the back of the house and unhitched the garage door.

"Come on. Leave the beast alone. I'm gonna get started." The sound of his scratchy voice caused her heartbeat to race. Her hatred had not died with the years. She clinched her fists deep in her pockets.

The black guy stomped out the cigarette and followed Ralph inside without closing the garage door.

She watched them to make sure they didn't come back out and tried to figure out what they were doing. She had not been in that old dusty place in years. Undoubtedly her mother's '69 Chevy—a gift from Grandpa Jennings when she turned sixteen—still sat in there, untouched. If Ralph was hiding something there, she could find it later. Now it was more important for her to get out.

Still crouched low and with her hands down in front of her as if she were walking on her knees, she exited the back porch, closing the screen door slowly and as quietly as possible. She eased herself across the edge of the house. Fortunately, they were throwing things around inside the garage making enough noise to cover her steps. Once far from their view, she broke into a run.

Halfway to the Honda, she stopped to catch her breath and regain her composure. She rested on the back of a bent tree where she and Marlene used to play "horsey" as children. A vision of her sister as she bounced up and down on that tree while her silken hair blew in the wind brought an ache to her chest. So many dreams vanished, unrealized.

She rose from the bent tree and headed for the street.

Although her scheme to learn more about Ralph's plans came to a halt, she did discover one thing—he was not alone.

Time was running out and her plans had become increasingly complicated.

Chapter Four

Marlene arrived home sometime after 1:00 p.m. She called the cat, hoping to arouse a little company, but even Nellie had disappeared. She threw her purse onto the table in the foyer and walked toward the den where she collapsed in a chair. How dare Janie show up like that and then accuse her of being like Mama! Marlene cursed her sister's arrogance.

The ringing telephone forced Marlene to get up.

"Janie," she said, assuming her sister was calling to apologize.

"Well, well, well, you're in touch with Janie are you now?" the voice answered.

"What do you want?"

"Is she back in Atlanta? If she is, I'll find her."

Marlene put her hand to her head. "Why don't you just leave us alone? Haven't you done enough?"

"What's that supposed to mean?" He barked into the phone. "I ain't bothering nobody. All I want is to prove I ain't done nothing and get paid for what the state done to me. Now tell me where the hell Janie is."

"I'm finished with you, Ralph. I have my own life with my own problems. You're not a part of it anymore. If you want to talk to Janie, find her yourself." She banged the phone down.

Thunder rumbled outside. The morning storm she had anticipated was on its way. She took a deep breath and walked back to the living room where she opened the liquor cabinet and stared at the bottles—Jack Daniels, Dewar's, Smirnoff, Tanqueray—nothing but the best. Much as she wanted to be different from her mother, she couldn't stop herself from picking up a bottle, opening it, and pouring some into a glass. Nothing else helped erase the panicky feeling that surged through her body. The lights flickered, and clouds darkened the sky outside. No wonder Nellie was hiding.

Once fortified, she walked up the stairs to the guest room where she kept old papers. She reached for a hatbox on the back shelf, opened it, and dumped the contents onto the floor. Pitter-patter sounded on the roof in heavy dollops. Janie's visit sparked some questions in her mind. She sifted through the papers until she found the clipping she was looking for.

A superior court in DeKalb County found Ralph James Cooper guilty in the death of his wife, Eloise Jennings Cooper. Although the jury took seventeen hours to deliberate, they finally reached a verdict of voluntary manslaughter and put an end to one of Atlanta's most vicious cases.

She licked her dry, chapped lips. The last thing she wanted was for Janie to open everything back up or perhaps do something that would spark a new trial. But things kept nagging at the back of her mind.

The chief prosecutor, Robert Massey said, "We never located the murder weapon. But, I have no doubt that Cooper committed the crime. All the evidence pointed to him. With the strong testimony from Janie Knox, his stepdaughter, to corroborate his violent behavior, the jury had no doubt. Justice was done today."

The gun kept intruding on Marlene's consciousness. Ralph swore he didn't kill Mama, and he said he never had the gun. But when she closed her eyes, the scene flashed before her. The room dark, her mother's head turned toward the window away from her view. One hand resting at her side and the other flopped over the edge of the bed. The gun lying on the floor. Maybe Janie hid it someplace in the house, counting on Marlene not to remember. Perhaps Janie buried it in the yard or tucked it faraway in the recesses of the attic or basement. She had many theories about where it could be. And only one theory about why she had hidden it. *Could Janie have killed our mother?* Why else would she hide the gun and then run away right after the conviction? Marlene took a deep breath to steady the shaky feeling inside. The outside rain pelted the roof now in a steady force.

She read through the series of articles that described the murder. "I got home late that afternoon," Janie Knox testified. "I found Mom dead when I arrived." *Late that afternoon?* She closed her eyes again to recall that day. What time had she arrived? *I think it was before lunch.* Yes, she'd arrived around 11:30 a.m. Janie was already there. She had found Janie in Mama's room, not late in the afternoon as she had testified. If Janie had killed Mama, why had she come back here now? Perhaps she feared Ralph might reopen the case and prove his innocence and her guilt. *Impossible!*

She stared at the photo of her mother that had appeared in the *Atlanta Journal* throughout that awful time. A young, smiling Eloise Jennings Cooper beamed from the yellowing frayed clipping. It had been her wedding photo, the day she had married Ralph Cooper. She had worn her hair up in a French twist. The dress had been stark white. Marlene could still smell the whiff of mothballs as Mama came down the aisle. The young Marlene had noticed the deep red nail polish on Mama's fingers. Ralph walked next to her in scuffed brown shoes with a big, toothy grin on his face. So much mystery remained behind her mother, both in life and in death. A sharp pain surged across Marlene's head. She wanted it all to go away.

Later, she went to the bedroom to straighten out Peter's things. She anticipated he would contact her today, and she wanted to prepare everything and hopefully avoid seeing him.

She pulled out two big suitcases and began folding his shirts and sweaters across one another in a nice crisscross pattern, trying to banish thoughts of him. Their life together had been doomed from the start. They had married shortly after the trial, which Marlene had never gotten over. Actually, she had never recovered from her mother's death. It was all too much. *Why couldn't Peter see that?* He expected more from her than was possible.

She had packed these suitcases once before when they had travelled to Hawaii for a belated honeymoon. Peter had draped the tickets with red ribbons and put them in her Christmas stocking that year. She was thrilled with the gift. They both danced around the Christmas tree like a couple of teenagers. When she had packed the suitcases for that trip, her heart thundered with joy. She and Peter had been married two years, and she thought this trip would help her relax, make loving him easier. But that didn't happen. She had depended too much on the flask of gin she had sneaked in her bag. He had smelled it on her, and he flew off the handle. She had never seen him so angry. They had a huge row. The trip ended early.

She placed the two large suitcases by the door with a note for Peter. *I love you and I'm sorry.*

The missing gun, the discrepancy of time, too many things didn't add up. She finished the last of the vodka in the glass and straightened her shoulders. She would do what Janie wanted. She would find out what Ralph was up to. She gathered her purse, rain jacket, and car keys, and exited. The rain had ended, leaving everything looking moist, clean and refreshed as if just washed. She filled her lungs with the damp air and stumbled over the pooled puddles on the sidewalk next to the driveway.

The trek to Briardale Lane took longer than usual because traffic clogged the back roads leading to the small Decatur neighborhood where more and more of Atlanta's commuters preferred to live. Rain in Atlanta always snarled traffic and caused accidents. Today was no exception. A car sat by the side of the road flanked by blue flashing police lights. She joined the long line of crawling commuters.

As she inched along, she reached into her glove compartment and withdrew a small flask, held it in her hand, and debated. Drinking and driving, not such a good idea, but to get through the next couple of hours, she needed all the help she could get. She took a long, slow swallow. The warm liquid soothed her from her lips to her toes. Gripping the steering wheel, she peered ahead as the car rolled forward, still at a snail's pace.

Marlene had not been to Briardale Lane since the day her mother died. Aunt Sarah took care of everything and now Ralph lived there.

Ahead the red light turned green. A car tooted behind her. *What a jerk.* She pulled forward with a screech. Then she braked. The car behind her skidded to a stop on the wet pavement and then sat on the horn. She smiled and took another drink. *That'll show him.*

The streets blurred before her eyes. She weaved around Clifton Road and Scott Boulevard. She was sure she went by the big church on Scott Boulevard twice. Her tire hit a curb, and she jerked back onto the road. Another car honked. She pulled out of the line of traffic and into a small shopping center, stopping to catch her breath. *Maybe if I wait here a few minutes, I'll calm down.* The last thing she remembered was reaching for the flask one more time.

Marlene opened her eyes. Everything was dark except for the harsh glow of the streetlight in the distance. She touched her forehead and winced. The moon floated in front of her as if underwater. Frowning, she rubbed her temple. *Oh my God, where am I?* The clock read 6:00 p.m. Her tongue ran across her parched lips. She reached for the flask, but it was empty.

Blinking to clear her fuzzy vision, she peered at the signs. *Scott Boulevard and North Decatur Road*. Emory campus was to the right a few miles down. Briardale Lane, a short distance from there. Oh, yes, now she remembered why she had come, but not how she had ended up in this spot. *Maybe I stopped here after I went to Briardale Lane.* Nothing. Her mind registered nothing.

She took a deep breath to steady her nerves and started the car. Seconds later, she was back on the highway, and ten minutes later turning onto Briardale Lane. She slowed her speed. The house loomed in the distance, a large Victorian with green shutters on all the windows. A dog barked from next door. A dim light glowed from the front window. She parked at the curb.

Having come this far…she could go the rest of the way. Surely if she had been here already, her mind wouldn't be a total blank. Passing out at the shopping center and having no inkling about how she had gotten there sent a spasm of fear up her back.

He would be surprised to see her. She had never gone to see him in prison even though he had begged her to come. She had no idea how many letters she had from him. She had burned most of them, except some of the more recent ones. But she had read them all. He begged her to find Janie. He said she had the key to her mother's death. *Trust me, Marly. She knows what happened. She's got the proof that I didn't kill your ma.* He pleaded with her to help him. He described what it was like in prison. How people taunted him, beat him, tortured him. *You wouldn't leave a rat in this place. Have some mercy on your step daddy. For ol'times sake. Please, I'm begging you. They kicked me almost dead last night.* Later he'd written about another con who believed he didn't kill Mama and told him so. This guy beat people up if they messed with him. His letters came less frequently after that, but they never stopped, and she could always count on a card on her birthday, usually simply signed *Love, Ralph*.

The streetlight near the front lawn was burned out. A dim light glowed from the corner at the bus stop, but otherwise everything looked dark. The wind whistled through the car windows, and clouds moved across the moon making it darker still. She gripped the steering wheel with both hands, dreading getting out.

Images flashed before her. She blinked twice, staring at the front entrance, a door she had only used once before, always entering and exiting through the back. She pushed memories of that day aside, but they came back like flashes from a recurrent nightmare.

It had been high school graduation day. Aunt Sarah was coming to take her to live and work with her on what they all called a trial basis. Marlene would attend Georgia State and study finance. For Marlene it was a dream come true. But, Ralph had fought her departure like a bull. In the end, thank God, her mother had won.

That day, Marlene had lugged two oversized suitcases from her bedroom, not unlike those she packed for Peter today. The house had been as quiet as a tomb. Even her mother had turned off her stereo. Marlene tiptoed through the silent house, cringing each time the old floorboards groaned under her feet. Rain fell intermittently outside.

She placed the suitcases in the front room and sat by the window, chewing on her thumbnail. Granny Jennings's grandfather clock ticked away each minute with an agonizing pace. She couldn't believe she was finally leaving. When she heard a car drive up, she threw back the curtain. Ralph leaned on the hood while trying to open an umbrella. After a struggle, he tossed it on the ground and staggered up the walk. Rain pelted his head.

The mat under the living room rug had worn away years earlier, and no one had bothered to replace it. Ralph's foot hit the carpet and slid out from under him. He tumbled face down. When she ran to help him, he grabbed her wrist.

"Got you now!" He lifted himself as far as his elbow because his left foot was caught in the tangle.

"Let go so I can help you." Marlene twisted her arm to loosen his hold. "Come on. Let me go."

"No!" He screamed so loud she jerked back, freeing her wrist. Seconds later he had her by the hair. He yanked her head down close to his.

"You'd better not tell that snooty aunt of yours about you and me. Not ever, do you hear me?" He stared straight into her face. The red lines around the green of his eyes looked thicker and bloodier than ever. His hot breath smelled like rotten eggs. Water dripped from his wet head.

She didn't answer.

He grunted and pulled her hair harder. "Do you think you'll get away from me? Have you forgotten the last time?"

"Ralph," she said as calmly as she could even though heat surged through her scalp, "I'll be close by and—"

"Shut up. Quit lying to me, you little bitch." He yanked her hair tighter. She winced and groaned.

When he sat up on his knees, she sank to the ground, twisting as he pulled her head close to the floor. "You'll do as I say. Do ya hear me, missy?"

She struggled to get away, but he held onto her like he might a rope. The hairs close to her scalp felt as though they were being wrenched out of her head. Her mind raced. He might lock her away somewhere, hold her prisoner. Fear gave her strength to lift her knee and ram it into his jaw. He screamed and let loose. She dashed from the house.

The big pine tree, where she had hidden until Aunt Sarah drove up, still stood, guarding the house. The ugly memories parked next to it.

Marlene never told anyone about the day she left Briardale Lane. Aunt Sarah, who clearly knew something had happened, had never asked. Had she told the police, Ralph's conviction would have been assured. But she couldn't bring herself to say anything. As it turned out, she never had to because Janie was the one who drove the nail in Ralph's coffin.

When she opened the car door, a gust of wind tore at her skirt, sending chills up her body. She stepped over the broken sidewalk and around the sticks and twigs that blocked the path. She lifted the doorknocker and rapped.

Chapter Five

Janie pushed through the doors of the high-rise office building that housed Lawton, Brady and now Tetford, Ltd. Marlene's husband had really come up in the world. Of course marrying Mark Brady's niece hadn't hurt.

People milled around the lobby with coffee cups or cans of Coke. A mirror faced an arrangement of red tulips and jonquils in a hand-blown glass vase.

She glanced at her reflection, puffed her hair, and bit her lower lip to add a touch of pink. Her suit jacket fell to her hips and covered her bulging stomach. To an unpracticed eye, she looked young and healthy.

She entered the elevator joined by a group of men, carrying briefcases or laptops under their arms and women in pointy shoes, grasping leather bound satchels. No one spoke. Most fiddled with their smart phones. She punched the button for the top floor. Carrying a handbag and a coat, she looked neither like a working woman nor a housewife.

Perhaps they think I'm a law student. She smiled at the thought as the elevator climbed quietly from floor to floor.

When she pushed through the doors with Lawton, Brady and Tetford stenciled on the glass, she took a deep breath to steady her jumpy nerves.

The receptionist looked up as soon as the doors breezed shut. Her smile put deep creases near her luminous green eyes. "May I help you?"

Her auburn hair needs touching up. She probably does it herself. I would add a smidgen of blonde to make it appear more natural.

"I'm here to see Peter Tetford."

"Do you have an appointment?"

She squared her shoulders, wishing she were three inches taller. "No."

"And your name?"

"Tell him it's an old friend."

The woman frowned. "It helps if I tell him who is here. He remembers all his clients, of course, but—"

"Listen, it's personal. Trust me on this. He'll know who I am."

The woman rose. "Have a seat. I'll tell him you're here." She marched from the room, her heels clicking on the glistening marble floor of the lobby.

Before Janie had a chance to sit down, Miss Auburn Hair returned. "Mr. Tetford will see you now. It's the third door on the left."

She rustled up a grateful smile for the receptionist, who didn't return the favor. Maybe she should have given her name, but she wanted to see the look on Peter's face when she waltzed in. She savored drama, and this was definitely a dramatic moment. Furthermore, surprise would give her the slight edge she needed. After all, she was on his turf.

Peter sat at a huge mahogany desk, outlined with stacks of folders and papers. Lush chocolate brown upholstered chairs encircled a glass-top coffee table. Two straight back leather chairs faced his desk. A floor to ceiling bookcase lined the sidewall complete with panoply of books, all looking legal and impressive. She spotted a golf trophy in a far corner of the bookcase but no sign of family photos neither on his desk nor on the bookcase. Maybe lawyers didn't want their clients to see their wives and children. Not that Peter had any children—at least as far as she knew.

Peter hunched over a thick file.

She tiptoed in, hoping to study him a moment before he spotted her. He had a shorter, crisper and probably more expensive haircut than he once had, and his cheek-long sideburns were gone. He wore a dark blue suit and a red tie with yellow polka dots. One of his thin, elegant hands held a gold pen.

No sign of the scuffed briefcase she had seen him carrying so many years before when a soft breeze had blown his long maple hair off his face. Memories of a different Peter flashed before her. They had sat in a club in a steamy part of town with two mugs of beer in front of them. She didn't know his name then. He wore a long-sleeved shirt and jeans. Thelma had set it all up. Later in his apartment, he touched her in a way no man had ever done or would ever do again. So much had happened since that fateful day. Nonetheless, he had changed little. But, she didn't really expect to find a bald man with a potbelly. *Never!*

"Good afternoon," she said.

Peter lifted his still beautiful eyes toward her and gasped. All pretense of professional façade fell from him like a useless cloak.

"No need to look so alarmed," she said, amused and delighted by his shock and discomfort. *Miss Auburn Hair eat your heart out!* "And, you don't need to call security. I come unarmed and defenseless." She raised her hands, palms out, balancing her purse and coat in the crook of her elbow.

Peter edged around his desk, his hand trembling when he pulled out the chair for her. "I was never good at hiding my emotions, I'm afraid."

She settled herself in the slippery leather chair, smoothed out the wrinkles in her skirt like a prim schoolgirl, and crossed her legs.

He sat next to her, opting not to return behind his desk. *A good sign?* Dark circles and tiny lines encased his eyes, which looked slightly bloodshot. Too much late-night work.

"So what prompts this surprise visit?"

"You were never one to fill time with small talk," she said and paused. The last thing she wanted was for him to call the shots. She pushed a blond curl behind her ear and studied a broken fingernail. *I should have touched it up. Oh, well, life's little annoyances.*

"Give me a break, Janie. You waltz in my office out of the blue after years of total silence—not so much as a phone call—and expect the world to stop for you. You've got to want something. So, what is it?"

The harshness of his tone surprised her. "So that's the greeting I get after all this time. No 'hello, Janie, how are you. It's been a long time. We've all missed you' and all that good stuff?"

Peter looked away. "I suppose you've called Marlene?"

"I saw her this morning," she said, glancing out the huge window behind his desk. Gray clouds and a steely looking sky filled the panoramic view of tall buildings with Stone Mountain in the distance. "She looked tired," Janie added, unable to think of how to describe her sister's appearance.

Peter shifted in his seat. "She's missed you."

Janie still gazed out the window. "As kids we used to be so close. People thought we read one another's minds. After our dad died and Mom married Ralph, we were drawn to each other, until…" She paused before continuing, "That was a long time ago. God, I don't even remember when we drifted apart." She turned back toward him. "I doubt she's missed me much. She's had her life. Things haven't been easy."

Peter nodded. "I can see that."

"What's that supposed to mean?" Fear bubbled inside her.

"Nothing," he said with a shrug. "You just look a bit…worn. Your face has lost its adolescent plumpness, I suppose."

She sniffed. "Adolescent plumpness. You didn't seem to mind my adolescent plumpness at one time, if I remember correctly." She twirled a button on her jacket and hated what she had just said. Peter brought out the worst in her. God only knew why.

"Is that what this surprise visit is all about then? I wondered when you'd try to blackmail me."

"Blackmail you? Blackmail you about what?" Then it dawned on her what he meant and what he feared, perhaps what he had feared for a long time.

She had been mortified by what had happened on that fateful night so long ago. Particularly after she had gone back to see him, hoping for something more, and he had tossed her out in the rain, letting her know he wasn't interested in seeing her ever again. She would have stayed out of his life forever if he hadn't met Marlene. Another of life's little ironic twists.

She chuckled. "Don't be a fool. I didn't come here for that. What good would it do my sister to learn of your little escapades before marriage? The last thing I want to do is hurt Marlene."

Peter uncrossed his long legs and shifted away from her. "I've always regretted what I did to you. You were so terribly young. I suppose we both were. I was terrified, that's for sure. I couldn't believe what I'd done. Of course, there was no excuse, but I was high on weed and later I learned that my ol' pal, Jack, had laced it with LSD. I never meant to hurt you."

"Forget that. My God, that's totally ancient history." *Please don't remind me of my adolescent humiliation.*

"Okay, then, what is it you want? Something to do with Marlene?" The soft cadence of his voice had changed. It was as if he was talking underwater, not as clear as it once was.

Janie faced him. "No, it's not about Marlene. I came to see you."

"I can't imagine why. This couldn't exactly be a friendly visit, even though you're my sister-in-law."

That comment triggered a throaty laugh and, judging from Peter's frown, brought back flashes of their past. "Indeed," she said with another chuckle. "Actually," she added, "I came here on business. I need a lawyer."

Peter leaned back in his chair and let out a sigh. "I am probably not the best lawyer for you. There's too much history between us. Besides, I don't have time for any new clients. My practice is full." He pulled on the cuffs of his shirt and glanced at his watch, signaling this meeting was over.

But Janie wasn't finished.

"I need a will," she said in a clipped tone.

Peter drew in a breath. "Don't you have lawyers wherever you live now? Can't one of them draw up a will for you?"

"Sure, I know lawyers, but I want you. There are things that I trust you to handle for me that another lawyer couldn't. You understand what I mean, don't you?"

"No, I don't understand. My clients do not hide things from me." He paused. "If I do this for you, I expect honesty. Why don't you come out and say whatever it is you want to say without all these games?"

She stared at him, determined not to blink. Peter looked away.

"I told you," she said. "I want a will. It's as simple as that."

Silence.

A stabbing pain cut through her body. She bit her tongue to mask it. In a slow, steady voice, she said, "Peter, let's put the past behind us. A lot has happened since that night when we were kids. We've both come a long way. All I want you to do is help me go through my things and draw up a will. Is that too much to ask?" *Please, Peter. I don't have a lot of time here.*

"Perhaps it is." He paused. "First, you must tell me where you've been and why you haven't written to your sister or your aunt. Marlene's needed you. Sarah has worried herself to death over you."

The pain worsened. She shifted in her seat. "Where I've been doesn't matter now, does it? How could it pertain to my need for a will? Besides, I doubt Marlene needed me much. She never has before." Her voice cracked. She looked away, wanting to double over until the pain subsided. Instead, she gripped the arms of the chair and clenched her jaw.

Peter leaned forward. "You have no idea what you're talking about. Take my word for it. Your sister needed you, and you deserted her."

Her heart quickened. She wasn't going to let him get to her. Guilt over her mother's death was enough for one person to live with. "Are you going to help me or not?"

He expelled a deep moan and looked up at the ceiling as if the answer were written there. "Okay," he finally said. "What exactly do you need done?"

She reached into her purse and pulled out a manila folder. "This document contains a summary of my assets and liabilities. You'll see I have no debts at the moment. I'm about to sell off one final bit of property." She handed him a thick envelope. "I also have a codicil that I want sealed until my death."

"Why all the mystery?" Peter asked. "You haven't done anything illegal or left any children abandoned by the road, have you?"

"Just precautions, that's all."

"Like I said, I'm not sure I can help you unless you're honest with me."

"Everything is right there for you to see with the exception of the codicil. You don't need to know what's in that, do you?"

"Not the specific contents. But I must know if there are instructions pertaining to your will that might be awkward for me to carry out on your behalf, considering my relationship to your sister."

"The codicil is merely an explanation. It has nothing to do with the will itself. There's a letter to Aunt Sarah, and I'm still writing one to Marly. There'll be other items that I don't have yet, but I'll get everything to you before I leave town. I don't think you'll find anything awkward to carry out on my behalf—as you would say in your lawyer-lingo." *And, if I do what I plan to do, I'll need your help big time.*

"An explanation of what? Forget it. I don't need to know that and hopefully I never will. You'll probably outlive all of us."

She smiled, put her purse back on the ground and re-crossed her legs, hoping he wouldn't notice her grimace.

"Janie, why me? Surely you must know another attorney."

She leaned back in the hard chair. "You've shown how much you care for my sister. You never left her side during those wretched weeks after Mom died. I was jealous of the way you stood by her. I wanted someone like that for me." She paused, blinked, and looked away. "I guess I've always had a soft spot for you." Then she quickly added, "The bottom line is you love Marlene."

Peter cleared his throat, his face a mask but Janie sensed she had hit a nerve. "But what about Mark? He loves Marlene like a father. Besides, he's your uncle. That's got to weigh in heavier than a brother-in-law with whom you have a rather sordid history."

"That's just it, Peter. You and I go way back. I hardly know Mark. It's you I need. I want you for my lawyer." She touched his knee.

He slithered away from her touch and gathered the papers. "You're up to something, and I sure as hell don't want to be part of it."

She sighed. "You'll never completely trust me, will you? I suppose I get that. But I trust you because of our past and your love for my sister." *When everything is over, she'll need you, Peter. Please do this for her if not for me!*

He shook his head, picked up the folder, and pulled out his cell phone. "Where can I reach you?"

"You can't."

"What do you mean by that?"

"What I mean is I'll call you in a couple of days. Then we can set up a time for me to sign on the dotted line so to speak."

She lifted her purse and got up. "By the way, Peter, don't tell Marly about any of this, okay? You know, client privilege and all that good stuff."

She turned and walked out the door before he had a chance to respond.

Once back on the street, she filled her lungs with the blistery February air. It had rained while she was with Peter and the streets glistened and smelled fresh. Although the pain had softened, she still felt jittery inside, probably from her meeting with Peter. His presence stirred feelings she had long ago forgotten. She sucked in more fresh air and turned in the direction of the hotel.

As she walked a chill ran up her spin, causing her to shiver, not from the cold but from a distinct feeling of being watched. She glanced back at the stream of people behind her and studied the faces in the crowd. One man across the road turned in the opposite direction as if to cross the street. She moved under the shadow of a nearby building to keep an eye on him. He stood on the curb but didn't cross when the lanes cleared. Instead, he looked down at his shoes and slithered away, disappearing from sight.

She peered skyward at the offices of Lawton, Brady and Tetford. Impossible to see her from that height.

She shrugged. *I'm being paranoid.* She turned around and headed for the warmth of the Edgewood hotel and her meds.

Chapter Six

Marlene stood outside the door on Briardale Lane. She lifted the knocker again and banged harder this time.

Rustling, murmurs, movement, footsteps, but no answer.

She pounded again, sensing someone on the other side, breathing, waiting. She shifted from foot to foot, uncertain what she should do.

The door cracked, and Ralph peeked around the edge. His eyes widened. "Marly?" he said, flinging the door wide open.

She stepped inside the house, holding her purse in front of her like a shield. Ghosts from the past threatened to shatter her confidence. Nothing had changed.

Aunt Sarah had left all the furniture intact during Ralph's incarceration. She and her aunt had talked about renting the place, but that had never happened. Marlene always hoped Janie would come back and want to live here. Instead it was Ralph who returned.

"No one ever comes 'round," he said. "I guess I never thought you would neither," he said while switching on lights. "Especially after that phone call. You did hang up on me." He grinned. His teeth were yellower than ever.

She stepped farther into the room—the living room. She and Janie had huddled in this room the night Mama had died. They sat on the couch facing the window while Mama lay dead in the bedroom. Aunt

Sarah handled everything for them, even packing Janie's clothes so they could leave that house forever. People had walked in and out all night.

She rubbed her arms and shivered. "Haven't you turned on the heat?"

Ralph shrugged. "I mostly stay in the back or upstairs."

A noise came from the rear of the house. The television, perhaps. Ralph always switched on the TV or the radio as soon as he walked inside, claiming he couldn't abide quiet.

She drew in a breath, wishing she had something to drink, but she would never ask Ralph.

"Do you want to come to the kitchen?" he asked.

She shook her head, shuddering at the thought of the kitchen where too many memories of her mother resided.

"Well, then, sit here, okay?" He perched on the edge of the couch, looking smaller than she remembered. His carrot-red hair had dulled to a darker shade of auburn. His face was covered in lines, but still rough like the skin of an alligator. She had no idea how old Ralph was, but he looked older than Grandpa Jennings had when he lay dead in his coffin.

The memory of Ralph holding her down in this very room floated back. He seemed gigantic then. Huge. She stared at him, shocked that he had shrunk into this nothing of a man. Amazing. She had a hard time putting the two together. Her head pounded. She zipped up her jacket and edged over to the other end of the couch—as far from Ralph as she could.

"You look a lot like Lacy," he said with a smile, referring to her mother with the pet name only he ever used. "More'en ever."

She froze inside. "Don't you dare tell me that."

"I meant it nice. She was so pretty. I loved her hair. It was yellow like the sun. I bought her them yellow flowers when we first courted. Remember 'em? She sat 'em right over yonder." He nodded to the table under the front window. "I got them flowers every day till she agreed to marry me."

"Ralph, stop! I didn't come here to talk about my mother."

"Why did you come, then?"

Her ears buzzed so loud she thought her head might explode. She took a deep breath. "It's about Janie."

"Yeah, I know Janie is here," he said. "You didn't have to come to tell me that."

"Stay away from her."

"She's staying downtown," he continued, ignoring her comment. "Did you know she went to see your husband today?"

"You've got to stay away from her. You've got to leave here now."

He stared at her. "What are you talking about?"

She moved over to the end table and picked up her grandmother's hand-blown aqua vase, leaving her prints in the thick layer of dust. "Just what I said. You've got to go. Leave Atlanta."

"I don't have nowhere to go. Atlanta is my home. 'Sides, what would I do? Don't be talking foolishness. Is that what you come all this way to say to me? And here I thought you wanted to pay respects to your ol' stepdad."

She faced him. "You've got to leave tonight or tomorrow. You can't stay here. Get ready. I'll drive you out of town, myself."

He laughed. She froze at the haunting sound. Then, he lifted his lip in the ugly way he used to when he threatened her. "You will not 'cause I ain't going nowhere. I got things to do here."

She stared at him. "What kind of things?"

He didn't answer.

"Look, Ralph, I'll give you money if you leave. I have some of my own money that I saved after Mama died, and I'll give you all of it. It's over five thousand dollars. But I won't give you a dime if you stay here. You have to leave this house, go as far away from Janie as possible. If you leave, you can start over. Don't you want to do that?" Her heart boomed like a bomb exploding. She had never confronted him like this. He had made the demands, not her.

He shook his head. "I aim to prove I ain't kilt nobody. I got me a lawyer. He said he'd help me prove it. Thataway the state'll have to pay me for my time in prison. They'll give me more money than you ever could. My lawyer said there weren't enough evidence to convict me proper back then. Not with no gun found and it being all circumstantial and all. He said if I could get more evidence, he could help. I'm gonna get your sister to tell the truth. Maybe some no-good junkie broke in the house and kilt your ma. Janie knows but won't say nuthin'. Me and Jinx will get her to talk. We've got a plan, and there ain't nobody that'll stop us. Not you with your fine house and big car or your fancy-pants husband for that matter. You can't run us off. Count on it. This is 'tween me and Janie."

"No!"

He stood. "You'd better go now."

She turned toward him. Such a little man. She couldn't believe she had been afraid of him all those many years. She could probably punch him, and he would keel over in a heap. But she didn't have the energy. If she had a drink, maybe. But, not now. "Who is Jinx?"

"I wrote you about him. He's my buddy from the joint. The only good thing that come out of that rotten place. Jinx done saved my life a time or two. He's big and black and 'cause of him, the others finally let me be. Me being small and all they was picking on me all the time. Jinx shot a convenience store owner in an attempted robbery but didn't kill him so he got released before me. He told me he'd come get them that put me in the joint and we'd get revenge. So I ain't afraid of you or Janie."

She shuddered. "There's no need to be afraid of us," she began, trying to calm her voice. "I'm only saying you have to leave. It'd be best for everyone. Don't you see?" She paused. "How about I come get you in the morning? I'll take you to Tennessee. You have family there, don't you?" *Please, Ralph, do this!*

"I told ya, I ain't going nowhere. I reckon my lawyer's gonna call you. You and Janie, both. That's what they told him to do. Them at the Georgia Innocence Project. They's the ones who help people like me. It's gonna start over, but this time I aim to win. Get out now."

She looked away from his angry face. She had trouble sucking in air. The cold room suddenly closed in on her. Sweat broke out on her forehead. "Ralph, wouldn't it be better for you to go away and start your life over? Why dig all this up again and risk more trouble? You'll never get those years back even if you win. Why keep pushing like this?"

"'Cause I didn't kill 'er. I'm innocent, that's why."

"I don't believe that. I believe you killed Mama. I saw you rape her, remember? I'll tell the police you raped her if you push me. But, if you go, I'll keep quiet—"

"You ain't seen nuthin'." The look he shot her made a chill run up her back. His red face glowed and the veins in his neck pulsated.

Flashes from the past blinded her—Ralph hunched over Mama, straddling her and pounding his body into hers with merciless force, Mama screaming, "Marly, run," Ralph belting Mama across the face.

She finally said in a quiet voice, "You want to hurt us, me and Janie. You're a vindictive old man. I don't know why you hate us so much. What did we ever do to you except what you wanted—"

"I said get the hell out!"

"If you do this, Ralph, I'll hurt you. I'll tell the world what you did to Mama and what you did to me as a child. Janie will, too—"

"I ain't done nuthin'. I never laid a finger on Janie. Now get out, I say. You can't possibly hurt me more than you already done."

She walked to the door. "I'll be back. Don't forget this house isn't yours. It belongs to me and Janie. We'll force you out."

Once in the car she couldn't stop trembling. She didn't turn and look at him, knowing he was watching her from the window. She vowed to get him out of this town and away from Janie. *He can't reopen the case. I'll stop him if it kills me.*

Images from that awful day filled her head—Mama screaming for her to run, but instead she had lunged toward Ralph like a wildcat and dug her claws into his arm. He had knocked her across the room. Her head crashed against the door. Pain riveted her body, and she fell unconscious.

When she'd awakened and tried to help Mama, her mother had slapped her away and said, "This is all your doing. God cursed me the day you were born. Go away and never come back."

Shaking away the memories, she fished out her cell from her purse and punched in Aunt Sarah's number.

"Can I come over? I hate to ask at the last minute—"

"Absolutely. Come on. Mark isn't home yet. He's got a late client meeting this evening. I'd love to see you."

Fifteen minutes later, she drove up the long wooded driveway leading to Sarah and Mark Brady's house. The Tudor cottage sat back from the road and was framed by huge hemlocks, oaks and sycamores. Even in the dark, it looked elegant and inviting.

Her aunt had married Mark three months before she and Peter had married. Mark had been one of Aunt Sarah's clients. It was a late-in-life marriage for Aunt Sarah, her first. Mark, on the other hand, had suffered through a bitter divorce before he married Sarah.

After she rang the doorbell, Aunt Sarah pulled the door open and embraced her. "Marly! We shouldn't wait so long between visits."

"It's my fault," Marlene said.

"No, I take responsibility. I always seem to let my work consume me."

"That's not news to me." Marlene laughed.

After high school, she had worked in her aunt's financial consulting business. Lawton and Brady had been the first client Aunt Sarah had allowed her to handle on her own. That's how she met Peter. His youthful face the first time she saw him flashed in her mind and nearly weakened her knees. His deep ocean blue eyes and maple hair had taken her breath away. *Don't think about that now!*

"Come in, my dear." Aunt Sarah moved away from the door. The house smelled of Lemon-Pledge and wood. They walked past the living room and to the back into the den.

"I was about to prepare dinner, but that can wait. I do hope you'll eat with us."

A fire blazed in the gas fireplace.

She put her purse on the inlaid coffee table and collapsed in a soft chair close to the fire. "I really can't. I came by because I need you to help me with something."

"Anything. But first would you like a glass of iced tea?"

Marlene didn't hesitate when she said, "I need something stronger."

Aunt Sarah scowled. "I really don't think that's a good idea. With you driving and all. I have a nice lemonade. How about that?"

She grabbed her aunt's hand. "Please, Aunt Sarah, I really need something. Just one glass. Do you have any vodka?"

After a brief pause, Aunt Sarah rose and walked toward the dining room. "Let me see what we have on hand. I'll be right back."

While she waited, she thought of Peter and how his departure would shatter both Aunt Sarah and Mark. They adored Peter. Mark had taken him under his wing at the firm and now Peter was a partner. God, they might even side with him. No way! She and Aunt Sarah had a special bond. Her aunt would never abandon her.

Aunt Sarah returned with two glasses. Marlene's contained a clear liquid with a slice of fresh lemon.

Once she sipped the cool drink, the tension inside her dissolved. Courage. She needed a lot of courage. "Thanks," she said with a sigh.

Aunt Sarah touched her knee. "You look so tired, dear. Is everything okay?"

"No, everything's not okay. Ralph is causing trouble. We need to toss him out of the house. I can't believe he had the nerve to move in like it was his house."

"Yes, it's shameful, but—"

"He won't listen to me. I tried to get him to leave. He won't. I want Mark to force him out."

"How can he? I suppose we could call the police, but that would cause a ruckus. I'm not sure we want that, do we?"

Marlene rose and began pacing the floor.

"I really don't care how it's done. We've got to get rid of him. Surely we can do something."

"Just relax, dear. Of course, we'll do what we can. I'm sure there's a way."

She faced her aunt. "He has to go now, like tomorrow. We can't wait."

"But why? I know it's an inconvenience and—"

"Inconvenience," Marlene shrieked. "Inconvenience to have the man who murdered your mother living in the family home? For God's sake!"

Aunt Sarah shook her head. "You're right, of course. It's unthinkable. I guess I have so many mixed emotions connected to Briardale Lane, especially remembering that ghastly night when Eloise died. But, you are right."

"I don't want Ralph there."

Sarah took a sip from her glass and then checked her watch. "Mark should be home in an hour. I'll talk to him as soon as he gets here."

Marlene sat back down. "Thanks, Aunt Sarah. You're the best. I'm sorry to be so edgy about all this, but I don't have the strength to deal with Ralph alone."

"Of course, you don't."

"It's just too much." A tear trickled down her cheek. She brushed it away. She needed courage, not tears.

They sat silently for a few minutes. The sound of the mantel clock ticked.

"Marlene, if you don't mind my asking. Ralph has been living there since his release—over two weeks now, I believe. What brought on this sudden urgent need to get rid of him?"

"He's been calling me and trying to make trouble. He wants to reopen the case. Apparently he has some kind of shyster lawyer. I can't listen to him talk like this. It's driving me crazy. I simply can't let him reopen all the wounds. Not again. I won't. I'd die first."

"Settle down, dear. He has no grounds to do anything. He's only trying to test your patience."

They both fell silent.

She finished her drink and rose. "I'd better get home."

Aunt Sarah rose with her. "Why don't you stay here? You could talk to Mark yourself at dinner and together we can devise a plan. You can stay overnight. Call Peter and tell him. I'm sure he won't mind. The guestroom is all ready, and I'll loan you a toothbrush and a nightie."

"That's so sweet, but no. I'm fine." She walked toward the front door.

"Let me drive you, Marly. I don't like the way you look."

"Really, Aunt Sarah, I'm okay." She leaned over and kissed her aunt on the cheek.

"At least call when you get home."

She smiled. "Of course. And—don't worry."

On the way to her car, she sucked in the cool night air and savored the delicious odor of pine. Her body relaxed. They'd join forces to take care of Ralph. Once she got him out of town, everything would be fine. Janie couldn't cause trouble without Ralph here. Soon she would have all this behind her, and it would finally be over. Then, maybe she could concentrate on Peter.

She started the engine and headed home.

Chapter Seven

Janie collapsed on the bed. Her visit with Marlene and then Peter zapped her diminished energy. She counted off the tasks she still needed to do—get the contents of the safety deposit box, finish Marly's letter, connect with Aunt Sarah, destroy Ralph, but her body wouldn't comply. She closed her eyes.

Her mind drifted to when she had first arrived in Savannah. She had found a job in a homespun beauty salon downtown near Lafayette Square. The owner, Lonnie Jessup, who reminded Janie of Lucille, was a large-boned woman with bleached blond hair and a raspy voice. Lonnie taught her new techniques for doing hair as well as tips for running a shop. Janie learned quickly. Six months later, she moved to a larger salon where faster customer turnover quadrupled her pay. She saved for the day when she could launch her own business. In those days all she cared about was doing hair and forgetting everything about Atlanta.

She opened her eyes and stared at the ceiling covered in a pattern of sheet rock. The pain had turned into a dull ache. She lifted up on one elbow and gazed at the clock—8:00 p.m., time to call Sue Anne. She grabbed her cell and made the call.

After she hung up, she gazed at the people milling around the streets of Atlanta. A Japanese couple carried cameras and walked arm in arm. A group of men wearing nametags, probably attending one of the big conferences this city now attracted, strolled into a bar. Perhaps she had been like a tourist when she lived here, living on the outskirts of something she couldn't quite identify.

She didn't feel as if she belonged anywhere until she laid eyes on that run-down storefront on Tybee Island where she had opened her first salon. Everything about the place seemed right, from its squeaky screen door to the sand imbedded in the floor's wooden planks. The clientele on Tybee varied from local people to tourists. She developed instant rapport with her customers who told her secrets they would never tell anyone else. She listened to stories about extramarital affairs, divorces, the escapades of children, and every tidbit of gossip while she snipped off split ends and applied color. But she never once let slip one word about herself. No one would have believed she had been a drug-using teen who had prowled the local bars.

She walked into the bathroom, ran cold water over a washcloth, and dabbed her face. The pain meds had begun their magic. She stood upright, grabbed her purse and exited the cramped hotel room. Once downstairs, she strolled up to the desk to extend her stay for another week.

"You're in room 411, aren't you, honey?" the desk clerk asked after confirming Janie for seven more days.

"Yes."

"A man came in a little while ago, asking for you. He was a rude sort of person. Demanded to know your room number. We don't give out room numbers even when people ask nice. We like to protect our guests. I told him he could call you on the lobby phone. He changed his tune and tried to sweet-talk me, but I was having none of it."

Janie blinked. No one knew she was here. Her stomach flipped. She couldn't imagine who in the world could be asking about her. Maybe Peter had followed her after she saw him this afternoon. She couldn't imagine him demanding to know her room number in a rude manner. She cleared her throat.

"Did he give you a name?" she asked.

"Sorry, honey. He asked for you 'specially. Had your name and all. Just between you and me, he wadn't your type." She winked at Janie. *God knew what that meant.*

"How might you describe him?"

The woman thought a minute. "Well, rough around the edges, bad breath, garlicky. Not the usual sort we see—you know, businessmen."

That ruled out Peter.

"If he comes back, will you let me know? And please do not give him my room number."

"'Course not. Have a nice evening," she said before turning back to the computer in front of her.

Janie walked out the door and onto the street. She pulled her coat tighter around herself and shivered inwardly. The temperature had dropped considerably. Her mind raced. She couldn't imagine who might have asked for her specifically and gotten belligerent when the desk clerk wouldn't give him her number. Why hadn't he simply called her room?

Perhaps she had not imagined someone watching her this afternoon. But who in the world could it be and why? Surely not Ralph. Even if he knew she was in town, he couldn't know which hotel she was in. The only people she had seen since she arrived were Marlene and Peter.

A neon sign flashed on the corner, "Jack's Diner." She headed in that direction with her head down against the wind and her teeth chattering. It baffled her how people could live in this freezing town. Images of Sue Anne sipping wine on their patio made her shoulders sag. Life just wasn't fair!

Inside she found a table in the back. The place buzzed with lively conversation. A frizzy-haired waitress with a tired expression tossed a menu at her and said she would be with her in a minute.

Janie removed her coat. The restaurant heater worked overtime, fogging up the outside windows. As she studied the menu, her mind travelled back to the man who had asked about her. If it wasn't Peter, who could it have been? *Think!*

She knew very few people in Atlanta. She had told Sue Anne the name of her hotel but no one else. Maybe Sue Anne told someone and that person was looking for her. Perhaps it had nothing to do with why she was here. It could be someone wanting to talk to her about one of her shops. Perhaps someone wanting to franchise in Atlanta.

People had approached her with those kinds of propositions, but it's been a couple of years. She'd even considered doing it once, but she decided to wait, mainly because she didn't want to come back to Atlanta, ever. If someone had asked for her, why hadn't Sue Anne mentioned this when she'd talked to her? The sensation she felt when she left Peter's office returned. She shifted in her seat. Something definitely strange was going on.

The waitress returned and took Janie's order of a salad and a beer, looking around as if distracted or annoyed to be taking orders. She could use some customer relations training.

Janie had taught all her stylists how to respond to clients. Lucille had been a great believer in more than simply doing hair. She used to say, "People come here to relax. If you make them feel good, they'll come back. You may be the best stylist on the planet, but if the lady doesn't like you, she'll go someplace else. It's our own version of bedside manner. Remember that."

She had. Once she'd fired a very competent stylist who alienated customers. The woman couldn't believe it when Janie fired her.

"I'm the best in town," she had said in a huff.

"Then you shouldn't have trouble finding another job," Janie had responded.

A foursome sat directly in front of her, consulting tourist books. The woman closest to her view held a brochure about the Georgia Aquarium. Janie had never been to the Aquarium, which opened after she had left the city. Mary Lynn Pierce, one of her more travelled clients and a regular Friday morning customer had informed her that it was the biggest marine exhibit in the world, housing over eight million gallons of water. Apparently they had three beluga whales, but she had read that one had died.

Once, nearly ten years ago, she and Sue Anne had gone to Marineland in St. Augustine. Seeing the dolphins that close had been an amazing experience. *Maybe I'll go see the Aquarium while here.* As soon as the thought entered her head, she stopped herself. She would be lucky to finish what she set out to do before her time ran out. The Aquarium would have to wait for another life. So many things left undone, unseen.

The waitress placed the beer in front of her and walked off without a word.

Janie shrugged. *Maybe she just doesn't like me.*

The beer went down slowly and tasted cool and fruity. Sue Anne preferred the fancy wines to beer. Janie liked a crisp malt, even in the winter. But she hadn't always enjoyed beer. The first time she tasted one she was with Thelma, who was older by a couple of years. Thelma enjoyed introducing her to the Atlanta's seediest clubs, and she had a knack for getting them into places they didn't belong. Thelma handed out fake ID's as if they fell from the sky, and then she ushered her younger cohorts, including Janie, from bar to bar. That was where Janie had met Peter and where she had tasted her first beer. She had very nearly spat it out, but didn't want to appear uncool to Thelma and her friends. Back then they didn't ask the customers what kind of beer they wanted. You got what they had, often served in an ice-cold mug with more foam spilling over the edge than a bubble bath. After that initial tentative sip, though, it got easier. By the end of the evening, she was guzzling beer like a pro. Of course, the healthy supply of grass helped disguise the taste.

She hadn't thought of Thelma in years even though she had kept in touch with her, most every year sending Christmas cards. Thelma still lived in Atlanta and had a couple of children. Somewhere in the recesses of her mind, she dredged up her last name—*Shor*. If she scanned in the phone book, she would probably recognize her address, but she doubted she would have time to reconnect with her old friend.

And Jack, Peter's friend. Jack Saunders had been another club buddy. He, too, was older than Janie. They had become friends after the Peter episode. Jack never asked her out or made any moves on her, but she always liked him. Attracted, she guessed, by his aloofness. In one of Thelma's Christmas greetings she told her that Jack had joined the Army and had fought in the Gulf War. She had no idea what happened to him after that. Maybe Jack got wind of her arrival in Atlanta and had found her hotel and wanted to see her. *Absurd!* Even if that unlikely series of events had happened, surely he would have called her room.

Janie drank more beer. In her mind's eye she could see Jack stretched out with a frosty mug in one hand and a cigarette in another, wearing his signature floppy fedora. She had glimpsed under that hat once and caught sight of thin, straggly wisps of hair. He probably had none now. The desk clerk described her mystery visitor as somewhat seedy. The Jack she remembered might qualify in that regard.

Janie's food arrived at the same moment a man plopped down across from her, as if invited.

"I believe you have the wrong—"

"Shut up," he said, looking around. "You're Janie Knox, right?"

Her heart nearly stopped. She glared at the man. He wore a dingy white shirt, frayed at the collar and dark glasses. He had a receding hairline and a large wart on the side of his nose, making his face look lopsided. He smelled of mothballs, stale tobacco and garlic.

"I'll take that as a yes," he said.

"Get lost," she said, flagging the waitress who chose to ignore her.

"We've got some business to take care of first. Then I'll get lost."

She studied his grimy face. "Was that you who came looking for me at my hotel today?"

"Maybe yes, maybe no."

"I said get lost."

She picked up her salad and fork and started to move, but the man grabbed her wrist with surprising strength.

"Listen, if you're gonna play hardball, I've got the goods. But my guess is when you hear my proposition, you'll change your tune but fast."

"Who the hell are you?" she said, settling back down. He released his hold.

"Name's Samuel D. Whitaker, attorney at law." He held out a card. "I represent Mr. Ralph Cooper, your step daddy."

When she ignored the card, he dropped it on the table beside her dish.

"Well, Mr. Samuel D. Whitaker, attorney at Law, whoever you are, you didn't represent him too well. He spent lots of time in the joint where he belongs. Can't imagine why he needs a lawyer now, unless he's killed someone else."

Mr. Whitaker scanned the room again as if he expected Elliot Ness would jump out from a nearby booth. "That's between me and my client." He pulled a yellow sheet of legal paper from his shirt pocket. "Take a look at this. All's you gotta do is sign on the bottom line. Right here. Then, I'll be on my merry way and you can finish your dinner in peace."

She peered at the piece of paper but didn't touch it. "You've got some nerve showing up and accosting me like this. I have a mind to call the police."

He smiled, displaying lopsided teeth the color of mustard. "I'm just doing my job. Come on, now, honey. Take a quick look and be done with it. Your step daddy says he ain't done nothing wrong. He says you lied about him during the trial. We can get you for perjury and get a new trial or you can just sign and be done with all of us."

She started to munch on the lettuce. She wiped her mouth with a napkin and then said, "Hell will freeze over before I do anything of the kind. I never lied about Ralph. I told the God's truth about him and what he did to me and my family. You can give him a message for me. Tell him I'm gonna finish him off if it's the last thing I do before I die." She picked up the piece of paper and without unfolding it, ripped it in half. "I'll have nothing to do with you or with Ralph Cooper. Now get lost before I tell the management to throw you out."

"So, that's how it's going to be. Remember, sweetie, we found you once, we'll find you again. Next time we won't be so friendly like."

He rose and slipped out of the diner, disappearing into the night crowd.

When she looked at her partially eaten salad, her stomach tightened. With a trembling hand she placed a twenty-dollar-bill on the table and left.

Chapter Eight

The next morning Marlene woke up drenched in sweat. She crept downstairs to the kitchen and gulped down a glass of water. Afterward, she refilled her glass and stared out the window while the dream replayed in her mind.

She ran through a thick forest. "Rosie!" she called, pushing monster-looking tree limbs out of her way. A cold wind burned her cheeks.

She stumbled on a tree trunk, brought herself up, and called again, "Rosie!"

A shadowy figure stood next to a tall evergreen. A chill ran down her back.

"Marly, I've got Rosie. I'm making her better." The voice belonged to her father.

She inched closer to the figure and squinted at the man's face, but she couldn't make out his features. "What's wrong with Rosie?" she asked.

"She's sick," he replied. "I took her to the doctor. Come here, Marly." He motioned for her to sit on his knee. "Let me show you."

Although she trusted her father, a tiny suspicion held her rooted in place.

"It's all right. I won't hurt you."

The sound of his voice caused the tension to slide from her body, and she approached him, straining to see his face through the shadows. He bent behind the tree where he retrieved Rosie, cradling her in his arms and stroking her hair. When she reached for the doll, the man grabbed her wrist, and she saw Ralph's deformed fingers. Her eyes popped open, ending the dream.

Rosie had been Marlene's favorite doll. Time had twisted and deformed her rubber legs. Her eyebrows, lashes, pink cheeks, and lips had faded after years of a child's rough love. On her fifth birthday Daddy presented her with a box wrapped in glittering gold paper and a big red bow. She dove into the package with a child's innocence, unaware of what lay inside. She uncovered her favorite doll but with the face of a stranger. Daddy had asked a friend to paint new features on Rosie, thinking it a perfect gift for his darling daughter. She had let out a blood-curdling scream, had thrown the doll aside, and had fled from the house.

Over thirty years later sitting in the gray-dark kitchen and watching a new day unfold, she struggled to recall Rosie's original face. But all she could see was her own pained reflection mirrored in the kitchen window.

She removed the chocolate chip cookie mix from the pantry, dumped the contents into a bowel with the required egg and milk, and began stirring.

Her thoughts traveled back to the day when she was fifteen and Ralph had told her about his deformed fingers. She had been in the backyard reading, minding her own business. A shadow fell across her book. She continued to read. Ralph stood over her, reached into his shirt pocket, withdrew a cigarette, lit it, and plopped down beside her.

He moved his hand close to her leg. His finger on her skin made her stiffen as if touched by a cockroach. She shifted away from him. A cloud moved in front of the sun. He rubbed his dry, chaffed hands over the grass. Gnats swarmed around his skin. "Did I ever tell you about how I lost my fingers?" he asked.

They both knew he hadn't. Early on she had wondered about his two missing middle fingers on his left hand and then later she forgot or lost interest or just didn't care.

Sweat ran down Marlene's back dampening her thin cotton dress. Her mind wandered to what other people might be doing at this exact moment on this bright summer afternoon—eating a bowl of ice cream or finishing a tennis match, maybe even splashing in a backyard pool.

Her book lay open on her lap. She returned her gaze to the heroine's words, *How do you take your tea? With lemon or with milk?*

"When I was eight years old," Ralph began. "My daddy'd come home drunk. He did that a lot so I never gave it no thought. But that night I heard my ma yelling. He barged into my room with the biggest kitchen knife you ever did see. His eyes looked black like you might imagine the devil's eyes looking. I just stared at that knife, scared out of my wits. I remember thinking he was gonna kill me, surenuf. I couldn't hear my ma screaming no more, but I did hear a pitiful sounding moan from somewheres way off. Later I found out he'd done near slapped the screams right out of her.

"He grabbed my arm and stuck my hand flat on the floor. He rammed that knife clean through my fingers. I think I screamed, but I ain't for sure. I must've passed out 'cause all I remember is waking up with bandages on my hand and my ma crying. Not long after, I heard her telling a lady friend that he cut off my fingers as a wager in a poker game. He won fifty bucks." Marlene swallowed hard. She couldn't force a word from her lips. Her stomach tightened. She pushed the hair off her face and studied the starlings flouncing from tree to tree before returning to her book. *Lemon*, the man in the book responded. *The woman studied the man's handsome face. She wanted to reach up and smooth his brow, but she knew he would be shocked at her boldness. Instead, she passed him a small slice of lemon.*

Ralph stomped out his cigarette and grunted. "Ain't never told nobody that story. Not even your ma."

Marlene had felt sorry for him that afternoon. She despised him, but she couldn't help the pity that had welled up inside her for the scared little boy he had once been.

She dropped the cookie dough onto the sheets in tablespoons, one by one. If Ralph had not killed Mama, who had? She wouldn't let herself believe Janie had done it, but clearly Janie knew something she wasn't saying. Thoughts buzzed around in her head like swarms of bees. Little mattered now except to stop Ralph from reopening the case. If they couldn't chase him away, she'd have to find another way.

Afterward, with the smell of fresh cookies wafting throughout the house, she went upstairs to dress. This afternoon she was hosting a baby shower for her friend, Nikki. Many of her friends, including Nikki, had never heard of Ralph Cooper, and she aimed to keep it that way.

Her eye caught sight of a business card next to the telephone. Detective Harlan Daniels had been the investigator after her mother's death. A week before Ralph walked out of the Atlanta Penitentiary a free man, Officer Daniels came by to see her. They shared a cup of coffee in the kitchen and talked about nothing.

"Call me anytime," he'd told her before departing.

She picked up the card and dialed the number.

Her voice shook when she said, "Office Harlan Daniels please."

"He has retired," the girl on the phone said. "But I could ask him to call you."

Marlene gave the girl her name and number even though she had no idea what she would say to the detective when and if he called.

Just as she stepped out of the shower, the phone rang. It was Detective Daniels.

"I heard you called. Is everything okay?"

She towel dried her hair while sitting on a bench in her bathroom. "I'm sorry to have bothered you. But I've been thinking a lot about the day Mama died and I remembered something. It's probably not important—"

"Why don't we meet for coffee? I'm living not far from you. There's a Starbucks on the corner near Clifton Road."

"Yes, I know that place. I could be there in twenty minutes."

She spotted the detective in his rumpled brown suit, sitting in a soft chair in the corner, a cup of coffee in front of him. She joined him there after ordering a latte for herself.

"Has your stepfather been in touch?" the detective asked before Marlene sat down.

"Every day. He's living in our house on Briardale Lane. I tried to get him to leave, but he won't." She looked away and added, "But that's not why I wanted to talk to you. Janie is back."

"Ah," he said, and sipped his coffee.

"You don't seem surprised."

His mouth twitched as if stopping himself from smiling. "I suspected she might turn up after he was released."

"I'm afraid I wasn't terribly gracious when I saw her. I couldn't help myself. Between Ralph calling me all the time and her showing up, well —"

"Yes, I can imagine." He paused. "You said you remembered something?" He drew out a small pad and pen.

"I thought you had retired."

He smiled again. "In my line of work no one really retires and besides, you know what they say about old habits. Go on."

She glanced around the café. People milled about at the counter. A dark-haired woman pecked away on a laptop nearby. Two businessmen talked head to head across from her.

"I'm not sure I want you to report what I'm about to tell you."

"What are you afraid of?"

I'm afraid my sister killed my mother, but that's the last thing I'm going to tell you. She didn't answer him, instead she said, "Tell me what you remember Janie said about how she found Mama?"

He sipped from his cup. "Your sister said she arrived home late in the day, around six p.m. if I remember correctly, and found your mother already dead. She testified that Ralph was not there when she arrived, and she hadn't seen him since that morning. According to Janie, she didn't think anything was wrong when she walked in and found the house dark and quiet. In fact, she had not realized that your mother was dead until after she had raided the refrigerator and then went to check on your mother in her room. It wasn't until she pulled the drapes to let in the late afternoon light that she noticed she was dead. Apparently, she didn't see the blood until then. I think that about covers it."

Marlene nodded. "I think Janie got there earlier."

Silence.

She swallowed hard. "Janie came home sooner than she said. I'm sure of it. My guess is she arrived home around eleven."

"How do you know that?"

"Because I came home about eleven-thirty, and I saw Janie in Mama's room."

"You didn't tell us you were there. You said you were with your aunt."

Her heart thundered in her chest. She wanted something a lot stronger than this latte. "I know. I didn't remember. It must've been the shock of seeing Mama. Janie ushered me out of the house. I don't remember why I left or what I did, but it's like everything went blank, and I couldn't remember any of it. I didn't even remember seeing Mama dead. But it has come back to me little by little over the years, usually at night. I see Mama's face. Yesterday when I looked through the old newspaper accounts and read Janie's statement about getting home late, I saw it all again as if it had just happened." She stopped. "Why would Janie lie?"

He shrugged. "I can't answer that. I do know I always suspected she was holding something back. But I never doubted that your stepfather killed your mother. Maybe she wanted to put a cover over your mother. A lot of kids try to do that when they find a dead parent, especially one as needy as your mother. All I know is we just couldn't get all the proof we needed. Your sister's testimony was crucial."

"Ralph wants to reopen the case. He wants the state to pay him restitution. Is that possible?"

"Anything is possible these days, but in this jurisdiction, I'd really doubt it. The cases that they are opening are usually related to new DNA evidence. When there's DNA that proves someone might have been innocent, the judge is likely to agree to a new trial. But in this case there is no DNA, just questionable testimony coming to light."

"So I can relax and not worry about a new trial."

"Now I wouldn't quote me on that. I'd say the chances are slim. If Janie actually recounted her testimony or admitted to killing your mother, then there would be a good chance. Your sister's testimony was the strongest piece of evidence we had with the exception of Ralph's behavior. He ran and that counted for something back then—at least with the jury. It sure would have helped had we found the murder weapon."

That's something else I won't ever tell a soul.

"I just don't think I could go through it all again." Her voice trembled. She closed her eyes. She didn't want this sharp policeman to see the panic raging inside her.

"Do you think your sister will recount?"

"My sister hates Ralph. I don't see her doing that."

"Humm."

"What?"

"I can't help but wonder why she came back."

Marlene shook her head. "I don't know. She wanted me to find out what Ralph was doing—see if he'd confide in me. I did go see him, but to make him leave. That's when he told me he aimed to get a new trial." She paused and then added, "I really don't know what Janie is up to, but it makes me nervous."

"What are you so nervous about?"

She took a long drink from her now tepid latte to pull herself together.

"I really don't want all this to come up again. I've made a new life for myself with friends who don't remember what happened to Mama." She took a breath. "Look, you've made me feel better."

"I will need to report what you've told me to Detective Melani who replaced me. But I wouldn't worry. I doubt he'll be interested in reopening a twenty-year-old closed case on your remembering something that slightly changes the timeline. Your stepfather will have to have a lot to go on in this county to get a judge to reopen the case."

Marlene sighed, her jumpy heart finally relaxing. "Thanks for meeting with me," she said, and promised to call again if she needed him.

* * * *

The doorbell began ringing at 2:00 p.m. Marlene had placed vases of fresh jonquils and daisies in the living room and all the guest bathrooms. Her kitchen still held the odor of freshly baked cookies. She had put little silver dishes of roasted cashews throughout the den, living room, and parlor. To the untrained eye, her home looked warm, relaxing and happy. No one would guess that her husband had left her and her mother's killer was threatening to turn her life into a circus.

Soon fifteen women filled her living room. Their voices elevated with happy giggles of surprise and congratulations for Nikki who was expecting her second baby.

Marlene's mind wandered throughout the shower. Peter hadn't called since he left. The suitcases were still in the hall when she came back last night. *Maybe he's changed his mind and will come home.* Hope sprang inside her as she drained her wine glass.

"Knock, knock, Marlene, are you there?" Nancy Morgan asked.

Marlene shook her head. "Sorry, did you say something? I guess I was off in another world."

"You were that," Nancy said, laughing. "I wanted to know how you made this shrimp spread. It's divine." She was standing at the kitchen island, stuffing herself with crackers and dip.

"Uh-well, I actually got it at Trader Joe's."

"You're kidding. Remind me to stay away from there."

Her phone rang and her heart jumped—*Peter*, but when she recognized Janie's voice, she didn't answer it. She let it go to voicemail. She would call her back after the ladies left.

Her best friend and neighbor, Amanda, edged up close to her. "It was really nice of you to do this for Nikki."

Marlene and Nikki were not that close. She and Peter had gone out with Nikki and Robert a few times, but they didn't have much in common. Couples with children talked about their children, particularly the wife, and Nikki was no exception—Jamie's first day of kindergarten, Jamie's skinned knee. Marlene had little to say to Nikki. But when Nikki told her about her second pregnancy and that no one had thrown her a baby shower when Jamie was born, she volunteered her house. Something about Nikki reminded her of Janie. Maybe it was her big, dark sad eyes.

"How about I stay to help you clean up?" Amanda offered.

"You don't have to. I'll be fine."

Amanda gave her shoulder a squeeze. "I want to."

Later, after she hugged the last guest good-bye and while Amanda helped Nikki carry her loot to the car, she gathered an armload of the dishes and glasses to take to the kitchen. Amanda joined her with more dishes.

"Really, you don't need to stay," Marlene said.

Amanda piled a bunch of dishes into the sink and put on Marlene's chef apron. "Probably don't need to, but we can knock this out in no time. Do you think Nancy's put on more weight?"

Marlene wiped her brow and filled the sink with sudsy water. "I couldn't tell. She's always dieting, but never seems to lose an ounce. Of course, I think she ate every bite of the shrimp dip."

"She's not been to Pilates in months. I don't think she's motivated," Amanda said, while putting more dishes in the sink.

"Listen, it's almost six. You've got to get home to prepare Jack's supper. Please, go." She slid on her rubber gloves and turned and faced Amanda. "Don't make me chase you out."

Amanda sighed and took off the apron. "Okay. But this doesn't make me happy. It's the least I could do."

"You were a great help all through the shower—my right-hand. Washing dishes is mindless. I actually enjoy it. So, get on out of here!" *Besides, I need a real drink!*

Amanda hugged her. "I'll see you Thursday. Don't forget we've got a date with our boys."

"Oh, yeah, I'll call you about that. We may have a conflict."

"Don't you even think about it. And tell Peter I said so, ya hear?"

As soon as the front door closed, she took off her gloves and went to the liquor cabinet, pouring herself a tall glass of Smirnoff and drinking it down with a deep sigh. After refilling her glass, she returned to the sink.

She needed to call Janie back but had no idea what she would say to her sister. She scrubbed lipstick off a wine glass and wished everything wasn't so hard with Janie. If Ralph would leave town then everything would be okay. But with Ralph here and out of jail, it was too dangerous.

She didn't doubt for a minute Janie had returned to cause trouble. Her stomach tightened. She drank more vodka.

A sound came from the front of the house.

"Amanda, is that you?"

No answer. She continued stacking the dishes.

Another sound, like a footstep landing behind her.

She turned and gasped. The wine glass slipped out of her hand and shattered across the floor.

Chapter Nine

Janie packed her belongings and departed the hotel room at 9:00 a.m. Another desk clerk stood behind the front counter, absorbed in the television news. *The Dow took another blow today when word came out about the Euro. And more protesters flooded the streets of Cairo in opposition to the interim government.*

Janie cleared her throat and said, "I'm sorry. But, my plans have changed. I must check out this morning." She placed her key on the counter.

The clerk moved to the computer. "You paid up until the fifteenth." She clicked a few more times on the computer. "We can refund your money except for tonight."

"That's fine, and again, I apologize."

When the girl smiled, her cheeks dimpled. "These things happen. Don't worry. I hope you had a nice stay." She counted out Janie's money and handed her a receipt. Janie returned the girl's smile. "Very nice, thank you." She gave the girl an A-plus on customer relations. If events had been different in her life, she would have asked this girl if she would like to move to Savannah to work in one of her shops—great climate, wonderful boss. That's how she found her best employees. Sometimes in restaurants, sometimes in boutiques, once in a supermarket.

Back on the street, she looked around to make sure no one was watching her. A man in a long coat and scarf stood across from the hotel, thumbing through a newspaper. A couple in business attire and carrying laptops marched down the street, looking set on a certain destination. She glanced at the man again. He'd put the paper under his arm and turned in the opposite direction.

Satisfied, Janie hurried to her car to stash her stuff in the trunk. Although she had no idea where she might stay, she couldn't remain at the Edgewood hotel. Not after what happened last night. She never wanted to see that sleazebag attorney again.

Thelma's face popped in her head. If she could stay there, no one would find her. She slammed the trunk closed. She had one more important task to do downtown before she took off. With that accomplished, she could think more clearly.

Ten minutes later, she waltzed into the lobby of the Bank of America building. At the information desk she asked a fifty-something woman with bright blue eye shadow, too much blush, and thin gray hair where she might locate the safety deposit boxes. The woman directed her to the opposite side of the bank. There, she gave a stern-looking woman—who could use more blush—her key.

"This key looks quite old," the stern woman said with a sniff. She eyed Janie as if she'd dropped out of the sky from Mars. "Please wait here a minute." She clicked across the marble floor to an office on the other side of the lobby.

Whatever happened to Southern charm? She'd been spoiled living in Savannah where the charisma of the old South lived on.

Janie shifted her weight from foot to foot, trying not to look as impatient as she felt. She had paid the fee each and every year. Although she repressed thoughts of returning to Atlanta, she had kept this safety deposit box and its contents under her thumb, just in case. Surely her numbered, designated box had to be here somewhere. She sighed, trying to slow the thumping of her heart, and waited.

The woman returned with a man in a navy suit and a red polka dot tie. He shook her hand and introduced himself as James Ferber.

"I take it you haven't visited your box in quite some time, Miss Knox," he said, with a big toothy grin that worried Janie.

I need what's in that box, and I need it now, not tomorrow, not the next day, now!

Janie nodded. "I live out of town."

"Of course, let me explain. When C & S merged with Nation's Bank in the early nineties, all the safety deposit boxes were cleared out by their respective patrons. Contents not claimed were later re-assigned to new boxes with new keys. Some of those people had no known addresses or had disappeared—"

"You have my address. I sent the fee every year."

"And, I suspect you got the notices about these changes along with the other patrons." He cleared his throat and adjusted his polka-dot tie.

Yeah, she probably had and had ignored them along with everything else about this part of her life. She frowned as images of envelopes from the bank flashed in her head. Had she even opened them?

"Let's continue this discussion in my office. He escorted her across the lobby to a cubical and motioned for her to sit across from him in a straight-back chair.

She adjusted herself in the chair and folded her hands in her lap, trying to steady her nerves.

"Bank of America took over some time after the first merger," he explained. "When that happened, we found a number of unclaimed boxes that had been dormant for over ten years. Yours, undoubtedly being one of them. The items in those boxes were placed in a secure spot at our headquarters building in Charlotte."

"Are you saying I have to go to Charlotte to get my documents?"

He shook his head and pulled out a Montblanc pen from his whiter than white shirt pocket. "We can have your documents sent here or to a particular address you might wish to authorize if you plan to leave town. Or, we can scan them and have them sent to you electronically, if you prefer."

"Electronically won't work. I need originals, and anyway, not everything can be scanned." She paused. "How long might all this take?"

"Not long, depending on when we find your contents."

She leaned in on his desk and stared into his nutmeg colored eyes. "I've paid the fee every year. I never let it lapse. Your bank prides itself on serving its customers. Right now I'm not a very happy customer."

"There's no need to worry," he said, blinking fast and pushing his chair back. "I'm sure your materials are safe. One thing about banks—we never throw anything away." He smiled. "It just may take a few days to locate the items and get them to you. We can't keep everything here because we don't have the space."

"I really need for you to expedite this matter, Mr. Ferber. I'm not planning on being in Atlanta long, and I must get those items sorted out before I leave." *Tick, tock. My time is running out.*

He smiled that same toothy, fake grin and held his pen poised over a small pad. "I understand. Let's begin by getting some information from you. How can we reach you?"

Janie gave him her cell number and signed all the papers he placed in front of her.

When she exited, a chill ran up her back. Her plans were not working out. First her less than successful reunion with Marlene, then that surprise visit last night, now this snafu with the bank. She gripped her handbag tighter and put her head down against the wind.

The voice in her head kept nagging, *What will you do if they lost your documents?* A safety deposit box was the securest place in the world—a place no one could touch. There's no way her important papers were gone. Ferber said she might have to wait. *Wait!* What if she had to wait days, months? She took another deep breath to calm herself. Banks don't lose things. But could they find them in time?

She stopped in a café for a cup of coffee, hoping caffeine would ease the panic inside her. She stood in line, ordered a latte, selected a small table far from the door, and plotted her next move.

Her watch read 10:15 a.m. It wasn't too early to call someone, was it? When the line at the counter diminished, she asked the young barista who sported a pierced lip and a tattooed bracelet, "Might I borrow a phone book?"

"Sure thing." The woman disappeared and came back with a newlooking yellow book.

Janie scanned the names until she found the one she wanted and jotted the phone number on her napkin. Then she drank more of the warm, milky coffee. Her jittery heart had slowed to an even thud. She would get through this. *Take one step at a time and don't panic.*

"Excuse me, are you related to Mary Ann Downs?" a bearded man, who wore a scarf around his neck and an expensive looking topcoat, asked.

Janie shook her head. "You've got me confused with someone else."

He chuckled. "I'm sorry. But you really look like her. She's one of my daughter's best friends. I haven't seen her in a while, but I knew she lived here in Atlanta, and I just thought, gosh, it's amazing the likeness."

The man's coat brushed against the table when he turned to depart, knocking the napkin with the phone number and her cell to the floor. He stopped, bent over and picked them up before she had a chance to move. In the confusion, he held onto to her phone for several seconds and glanced at the napkin.

She pocketed the napkin and her cell and accepted the man's apologies. When he'd turned to leave, she realized where she'd seen him. He was the man reading the newspaper across from her hotel this morning.

* * * *

An hour later, Janie stood in Thelma's driveway, her friend's mouth hanging open in shock.

"I can't believe you're in Atlanta," Thelma kept saying in her raspy, smokers voice. Her t-shirt and jeans stretched over a thick waist and lumpy hips. "And you want to stay here. We don't have a lot of room, but we do have a comfortable couch. I know Jerry won't mind. He's rarely home, anyway. Gosh, I can't believe you're here!"

That miserable lawyer and his bearded friend would never connect her to Thelma. Even Marlene hadn't known of Thelma. As a teen, Janie kept her doping friends at a distance—actually she'd kept all her friends at a distance. The Cooper house didn't lend itself to family-style dinners around the kitchen table. Oh, there were dinners around the table, but they were strained, tense, awkward. Neither she nor Marlene invited friends over. Not a soul knew of her friendship with Thelma, except perhaps Peter who had forgotten everything about the night they had met, undoubtedly Thelma included.

Janie had trusted her GPS to lead her to Thelma's house located south of Atlanta in a small town called Digby not far from Hartsfield-Jackson airport. Thank God for modern technology. Twice she had made wrong turns and had to back up and regroup. As soon as she pulled off the interstate, she navigated through small one-stop-light towns and narrow streets, constantly scanning her rearview mirror for men with beards until she drew up to Thelma's door.

"I'd know you anywhere," Thelma said as she continued to look her up and down. "That curly mop hasn't changed a bit."

They embraced. Janie couldn't say the same thing for Thelma. When they were young, Thelma had been weed thin, and her long, stringy red hair always dangled in her eyes. This woman was plump and had short brownish hair cropped off as if by a barber's razor. Her face had the worn look of a woman twice her age. But, her eyes were Thelma's. Small green slits that never seemed to stop moving.

"Thank you for this. I didn't know what else to do."

"No worries. You can tell me everything when we get inside. It's too cold out here." Thelma turned to a skinny boy about age ten. "Jimbo, get our guest's bag out of the car for her."

"I can do it," Janie protested.

"No, he needs to learn."

The boy went to the car and lifted Janie's bag, which although not large, consumed all his strength. Red-faced, he held it with both hands and pushed it with his knee.

They all moved inside the small house.

The front room overflowed with baseballs, gloves, Lego's, puzzle pieces and well-loved dolls. A baby sat in a high-chair next to the couch. Children's sippy cups filled every tabletop. An open box of Triscuits lay on the floor. The room had a slight rancid smell mixed with cigarettes.

Thelma plopped down on the couch. A little girl crawled into her lap. "This is Sherri," Thelma said.

"Hi there. Your mama and me were friends a long time ago."

The child put two fingers in her mouth and stared. Janie judged her to be about five. Jimbo placed her bag next to the Triscuits box and switched on the television.

"Turn that off," Thelma said. "You can watch it later."

Jimbo did as told and then left through a backdoor.

Janie removed a few Lego pieces and a box of half-eaten raisins before settling in a chair across from Thelma. "Why aren't they in school?" she asked.

"I'm home schooling Jimbo, and Sherri won't start till next year. I'm planning on keeping her here, too. It's easier that way."

"How many children do you have?" Thelma a mother. Never in her wildest imagination could she have predicted this scene.

"Just these three. Rocky there is the youngest, fifteen months. I still haven't gotten the weight off." Thelma shifted Sherri in order to pat her tummy. "It gets harder with each one. You got any?"

Janie shook her head.

Thelma reached for a pack of cigarettes next to the couch and tipped it toward Janie, her eyebrows raised.

"I don't smoke anymore. But thanks."

Thelma lit up. She blew smoke away from the little girl. How considerate.

"So, tell me what brings you to my door after all this time?"

"Big surprise, I suppose."

"No kidding."

"Something happened, and I decided I needed to get back here to finish up stuff."

"This got anything to do with that lowlife step daddy of yours, the one supposed to have kilt your mama? Just saw he got himself released."

A cloud of smoke filled the room.

"Yes, actually. I have some business I need to finish with him."

"I bet you have."

Thelma might not look the same, but she sounded exactly like the old Thelma.

"I was staying at a small hotel downtown. Last night Ralph's attorney —if you could call him that, more like a sorry scoundrel—barged into the diner where I was minding my own business and interrupted my dinner. It freaked me out that he knew where I was staying. He started harassing me, threatening me, you know the drill."

"How'd he find you?"

"God only knows. But it spooked me. That's why I called. I don't think he'd ever find me here."

"You got that right." She moved Sherri off her lap with a grunt. "How 'bout a beer?"

"No thanks, I'm fine."

"Too early, eh?"

Janie's stomach tightened. "I'm not drinking as much as I used to. Maybe later, though. I still enjoy a good beer."

"Suit yourself." Her friend rose and walked into the kitchen, trailed by Sherri.

Janie looked around the room. Envelopes spilled off the rickety end table by the door. Old issues of *Field and Stream* stood in a big pile nearby. Who was the man of the house? From the looks of the Lazy-boy next to the couch and the overflowing ashtray nearby, he watched lots of television. Thelma had said he was rarely home. Working out of town? Prowling?

Thelma returned with a beer. She lifted Rocky out of the high chair and carried him to the couch.

"So, Janie, tell me what's really going on."

Chapter Ten

When Janie finished her story, Thelma lifted her shirt to nurse Rocky. Sherri sat at her feet, playing with a deck of cards on the floor.

"Jerry might have some friends who could help you."

"What kind of friends?"

"People willing to do things for the right price. People who could put a scare into this lawyer guy or worse if you want."

Janie gnawed at her lower lip, staring at Thelma. Back in high school Thelma had bought and sold pot, never wavering from risk. In fact, they'd all gotten arrested once. Thelma and her unsavory friends had convinced Janie to run away in a car they'd stolen from one of their parents. They didn't tell her that they had also broken into a house and snatched some money from an elderly couple. Fortunately, Janie got off with a reprimand because she was a first offender juvenile. Mark Brady, Aunt Sarah's husband—although they weren't married then—had come to her rescue. She didn't see much of Thelma after that incident. Now with kids, a baby even, how could she or her husband, Jerry, take such risks?

"I don't want to get y'all involved in my mess. You're doing enough just putting me up. I can't tell you how much I appreciate that. Hopefully it won't be for too long."

"I can see you've done good. You're wearing nice clothes and I bet those shoes cost more than Jerry brings home in a month."

Janie glanced at her Cole Haan slides. "There's an outlet near where I live," she said, a little embarrassed. "But, I have done well, actually. I own fifteen salons and a hundred people work for me. I've done all right, considering…" She paused. "That doesn't mean y'all should get involved in all this. I'll pay for staying here, if that's what you mean."

Thelma shook her head. "Nah, what I mean is you could pay to make all this flat-out disappear, if you wanted. Jerry knows people." She wiped the baby's mouth with a towel.

Janie considered what Thelma suggested. She could pay someone to get her stuff, mail it at the right time, maybe even take care of Ralph. Then she could go back to Sue Anne and spend the last of her days on their back patio, watching the sunset. *So tempting*.

"How does Jerry know these people and how could I trust them?"

"He spent some time in the slammer. Got caught doing drugs and some other things. It was a few years back, but he's kept up with people."

"You're not still doing drugs, are you?" She studied the little girl at Thelma's feet and the baby in her arms. What kind of life would they have with a father in prison and a junkie mom?

"Nope, not often," she said with a slight smile, bringing back memories of the old Thelma. Rocky burped, and Thelma put him back in his chair.

"And what about Jerry? Is he dealing?"

Thelma tossed her head back and laughed. "Would we be living like this?"

Possibly. If they were both still using, they could go through a wad of cash quickly. With Thelma it was hard to tell.

"I could use a private detective if Jerry knows somebody. I'd like to dig up some information and maybe keep an eye on Ralph. I need to get a feel for his movements."

"I don't know why you're so worried about him. He can't hurt you anymore. He's done his time. Why bother?"

"I'm afraid he'll try to prove he didn't kill my mother and get restitution. I've read about people claiming their innocence and using DNA and other things to get off. Then they convince the state to pay them for their jail time, and they spend the rest of their lives living happily ever after."

"But he did kill your mom. He can't get off."

Janie shook her head. "You don't know Ralph. He'll sleaze his way around all this, make up stuff, who knows? There's an organization here in Atlanta called the Georgia Innocence Project. They've already gotten several people off. I want to watch Ralph, see what he's up to, and make sure that doesn't happen. I can't trust him or that lawyer he hired. Why else would he have a lawyer, anyway? I want him suffering, and I'm the only one who can do it." She paused to calm the pounding in her chest. "I have to do this myself." *Especially the last part. That's mine to do.*

Thelma shrugged and emptied her beer. "Whatever. Like I say, Jerry can help. I'll ask him if he knows any private dicks."

Jimbo returned from outside. "I'm hungry," he said.

"How 'bout some lunch?"

The clock read 2:00 p.m. "I need to run some errands first. But, if I can leave my stuff here, I'll get out of your way."

"Sure, whatever. And, think about what I said." She rose and rummaged through a drawer under the television. "Here's a spare key. Come and go as you please."

Thelma and her kids disappeared into the kitchen. Janie exited out the front door. In the car, she pulled out her cell to call Marlene, but the phone went to voicemail. She would try again later.

She dialed Dr. Mill's number in Savannah and requested his nurse. "I'd like a referral to Emory. I'm in Atlanta and thought I'd get a second opinion while here."

She wanted to make sure she had no options left before she set her plans in motion. Since the bank didn't have the contents of her box, she would have to wait it out anyway. Besides, if she went to Emory, she'd feel better about what she'd told Sue Anne.

The nurse told her they would arrange an appointment for the following Monday and she would call back with the details. Janie thanked her and hung up. Her phone rang before she put it in her purse. She didn't recognize the number but answered anyway, thinking it could be the bank.

"I see you left the hotel," the voice said.

"How did you get my cell number?"

"We'll find you." He hung up.

Janie's hand shook. She looked in her rearview mirror. Nothing. *Don't be a fool. They can't find me here.* When a kid on a scooter raced around the corner, she nearly ducked beneath the dash. She took a long, slow breath. *This is what he wants. He's trying to scare me—throw me off. I won't let him.*

She started the engine. She would find out the name of a private investigator and put some pressure on Ralph. He wasn't the only one who could play these games.

Twenty minutes later, Janie stood in Aunt Sarah's office, clutching her close to her and breathing in her rich lavender smell. Aunt Sarah had been there during her father's funeral, her mother's marriage to Ralph Cooper, and her mother's funeral. She'd sat between Janie and Marlene at United Methodist Church in Decatur for each event. She'd listened to the white-haired woman wearing a pea green dress with perspiration stains under her arms bang out "Amazing Grace" and "The Wedding March." Aunt Sarah had been there for everything. She'd done all she could for both of them. But it wasn't enough. With Ralph for a stepfather, nothing would have been enough.

"You've done well," Janie remarked, looking out the oversized window at the downtown Atlanta skyline.

Purple leather chairs flanked a glass top coffee table. The walls held colorful watercolors and an oil painting depicting a European scene. On her aunt's desk sat a slim Apple computer and a glass vase stuffed with purple hydrangea and baby's breath.

When her aunt smiled, small creases formed around her eyes. She was thinner than Janie remembered, and her hair a duller blond. Otherwise, not much had changed.

"I suppose I have," Aunt Sarah said with a dismissive wave.

They both settled in the purple chairs.

"Mark said you kept in touch with him," her aunt said. "I didn't worry so much after that. I guess I wondered why you didn't contact Marlene and never told us where you were, but—"

"It's okay. I appreciate everything Mark did. I felt I could trust him because he'd helped me out of that jam when I was seventeen. All I wanted was for y'all to know I was fine, and besides, I didn't want to lose all ties with the family. Coming back wasn't an option for me then. I can't explain it. Even with Ralph in prison, I just couldn't."

"It was hard for all of us." Aunt Sarah looked away as if she stopped herself from saying more.

Janie admired her for the self-made woman she was. Her aunt would never have run away from anything. *Never shrink from responsibility* was her mantra. Aunt Sarah had put herself through college and had begun working twenty years before women did that sort of thing. Janie's grandfather objected, but she'd ignored him. Janie's mother called her bull-headed and un-ladylike. Janie saw it differently. Her aunt was independent. Maybe that's where Janie got her entrepreneurial streak.

Today, though, she needed information from Aunt Sarah. She had to know what Marlene remembered about the day Mom died. If Marly confided in anyone, it would be Aunt Sarah.

"Hey, let's go get a bite to eat. Have you had lunch?" Aunt Sarah asked, glancing at the gold Rolex on her wrist.

She shook her head, not hungry even though she knew she should eat. She'd need all her energy.

They walked across the street to a bar/restaurant under the nose of the gold-domed State Capitol. The restaurant's dark décor and gentle lighting along with the hum of Neil Diamond music suggested privacy. The place was nearly empty at this hour. Most people had finished lunch and were back at work, except for one group of men in business suits, sitting in a far corner with folders and laptops. No men with beards or sleazy attorneys.

They found a table near the window.

After they ordered, Janie got right to the point. "What do you know about Ralph's plans? I know he's at Briardale Lane, but I'm not sure how long he'll be there."

"Don't you think you should leave well enough alone, dear?"

The waitress put glasses of sweet tea in front of them.

"I can't." Janie searched her aunt's face for any clue. Aunt Sarah squeezed lemon into her tea. "I don't know anything about his plans, but I do know he's not going anywhere. Mark went over there yesterday to toss him out. Marlene was desperate to get him out of the house."

"Why?"

"She said she didn't want him there. She wanted him gone. She came to see us late yesterday evening. She was adamant about it. I had a hard time calming her down."

The waitress placed a plate of chicken salad in front of Janie. Her aunt had ordered shrimp bisque and a roast beef sandwich.

Janie picked at the salad. "Is he harassing her in some way?"

Aunt Sarah shook her head. "She didn't say so. She didn't like the idea of him coming back to that house, y'all's house, that is."

"What did Ralph say when Mark tried to get him to leave?"

Aunt Sarah finished chewing a bite of her sandwich. "Just that he wasn't going anywhere. He had things to do and this was as much his home as anywhere. He told Mark he'd been married to Eloise for over ten years and they'd shared a life in that house—some life," Aunt Sarah said with a huff. "Anyway, Mark reminded him that he killed Eloise. But, he denied doing so. From what I gather, Mark got nowhere."

"Have you told Marlene?"

She took a deep breath. "Not yet. We're going to see them this evening for dinner. Maybe Peter can work his magic on Marlene, and she'll calm down about this."

Janie nibbled on the salad. She tasted coriander and basil. "Is everything okay with Marlene and Peter?" she asked.

"What do you mean?"

"I don't know for sure, but I got the impression there might be issues."

"Don't be ridiculous. They're fine."

Typical Aunt Sarah denial. She had known bad things were happening in the Cooper household, and she had looked the other way. Well, she didn't exactly look away, but she didn't push it as hard as she could have. *In my humble opinion.* Of course, she didn't know everything, but she did know Mom was drinking herself into oblivion and very depressed. She also knew Ralph was a worthless lowlife. That should have been enough to get the children out of the house. Aunt Sarah checked on them all the time, but she never filed a complaint or took any real action. Of course, Mom would have fought her like a lioness if she had tried to take them away from her.

After several minutes of silence, Aunt Sarah said, "How long will you be here?"

"I'm not sure. Probably about a week. I had hoped to leave sooner, but there's been a delay." Too many delays.

"Do you want to stay with us? We have a nice big guest room."

So typical of Aunt Sarah not to ask too many questions.

Janie shook her head. "It's best for me to be on my own." *Where no one can find me.*

"If you change your mind, we'd love to have you." Her aunt paused. "How have you been, my dear. You look so thin and you're not eating your lunch."

"Sorry, I'm not real hungry. Actually my life has been good. I love my work. I have fifteen shops now."

"My goodness!"

"Yes, it's amazing. I'm pretty well known in Chatham County. And, I have someone whom I love. So, I have a life companion."

"But, you're not married and no children?"

She smiled. "You're a good one to ask about that. You sound like my mom."

Aunt Sarah laughed. "I guess it's hard not to be traditional sometimes. If I'd had to do it over, I would have married sooner and had kids. But, of course, I didn't meet Mark until late in life."

"I love my work. I'm happy and fulfilled." She paused. "I just have a few more things to do and then, I'll feel complete."

Her aunt raised an eyebrow. "A few more things?"

She shrugged. "Oh, you know, reconnecting with my family. Trying to rebuild what I destroyed, particularly with Marlene." She studied her aunt's expression.

"Yes, that's good."

Janie ate more chicken salad and the grapes garnishing the plate. Aunt Sarah sipped her soup. Both remained quiet.

"Aunt Sarah, did Marlene ever talk to you about the day Mom died?"

Her aunt's eyes widened. "Why do ask?"

Janie shrugged, trying to act as though it really didn't matter. "She's so clamed up about everything, I simply wondered if she'd ever opened up to you."

"She never talks about that day. It's a taboo subject as far as she's concerned. After you disappeared, I tried to get through to her and so did Peter, but neither of us were successful. We were grateful Ralph was in jail where he couldn't torment her. But I think she had her own demons to deal with. I know there were nightmares. I heard her crying during the night and pacing the house in the wee hours. I've always suspected more happened that day than either of you let on."

Janie looked away and choked down a few more bites. "I'm worried about Marlene, about her sanity."

Her aunt put down her fork. "Marlene is perfectly fine. Except, well, she does have a little too much wine sometimes. But, she's perfectly sane."

"Not like Mom?"

"Janie, your mother had some serious problems. I'm afraid no one knew what to do with her. When things didn't go as she wanted, she went into a shell. Marlene is nothing like her."

She studied the frown across Aunt Sarah's brow. "I do hope you're right." What she didn't say was—*You never really knew Mom. You never understood her, and I'm not sure you understand Marlene.*

She left the restaurant ten minutes later, knowing what she needed to know—Aunt Sarah knew nothing about the day Mom died. Marlene, on the other hand, couldn't be trusted. At some point she would explode.

Janie prayed it wouldn't happen until after she had completed what she set out to do. She tried calling Marlene again and once again the phone went to voicemail. After leaving another message, she tossed the phone in the passenger's seat.

Why won't she call me back?

Chapter Eleven

"You scared the life out of me," Marlene said, catching her breath.

"Sorry," Peter said. He moved toward the broken glass and started to pick it up.

"You don't have to do that. I was cleaning up after Nikki's shower." She removed her rubber gloves. "I can get that later. Let's go to the living room and talk."

Peter put several pieces in the trash and followed her to the living room.

The house still smelled of cookies and perfume, but Peter's presence loomed like an all-consuming haze. She perched on the edge of the couch with her hands in her lap. How much had she had to drink? She'd left the glass of vodka in the kitchen. Hopefully Peter hadn't noticed.

He plopped down and groaned like an old man. "I haven't been sleeping well," he said, shifting on the chair. "The office couch doesn't lend itself to stretching out, and I'm sore all over."

"You could come back here."

He lifted his gaze to hers. Her stomach fluttered at the sight of those amazing eyes the color of the ocean in the morning. Today, though, they looked tired and bloodshot.

"I'm finished, Marlene. I can't go on the way we're going."

"I'm trying. I really am," she said, fiddling with the string on the couch. "But, first Ralph was released and then all the bad memories. I'm stretched emotionally."

"You're always stretched. If it's not Ralph being in prison and writing you all the time, it's Ralph out of prison. There's always an excuse. I can't take watching you destroy yourself like this. It's killing me."

She closed her eyes. It was too hard to look at him.

"Janie came to see me yesterday," he said.

She perked up. "What did she want?"

He shrugged. "I'm not certain. She acted as though being there was a natural as going to the movies. I, on the other hand, was shocked to see her. What made her come back?"

"I don't know. We had a rather bad confrontation, I'm afraid. I wasn't very nice. Her indifference drives me nuts."

"Yeah. She's changed, though."

She snickered. "Who hasn't, my God? That's what I couldn't believe. She acted as if we should all be the same."

"Did you tell her about us?"

"Did you?"

He shook his head. "I'm not sure what I'd say."

They sat in silence. What could Janie want with Peter? And how had Ralph known she'd been there? Maybe Janie had already been in touch with Ralph. She opened her mouth about to tell him about seeing Officer Daniels and what he'd said, but she stopped herself. He'd made it clear he didn't want to hear more about any of this.

At least Peter was here talking. Hope rose inside her. If she could convince him to give her one more chance, just one, she was sure she would be able to do whatever he wanted. She noticed a napkin that Amanda had missed next to the lamp and made a mental note to get it later.

"You need to get some help," he finally said. "I can't deal with this any longer by myself. You've never recovered from your mother's death. It couldn't have been easy, but it's been a long time. You need to get over it."

Anger boiled up inside her. "So, I should just say to myself, get over it. Then, everything'll be okay? Is that what you're saying? Don't you think I've tried to get over it? Every day I struggle to do what you want, pretending that everything is okay. I've tried to be a good wife." Her voice broke. She choked back tears and gripped the edge of the couch.

He shook his head. "You don't get it."

The cat slithered into the room, nervous from the smell of all the previous intruders. She immediately edged close to Peter, rubbing against his leg. He reached down to pet her.

"I love you, Marlene. You're what I live for. Being away from you is the hardest thing I've ever had to do. But, I can't keep living a lie. You say you'll stop drinking, and then I find half bottles of gin under the bathroom sink or stashed in the closet. You promise never to do it again, and when I come home, you're teetering around, barely able to stand up. Your face is red and your eyes bloodshot. Your once beautiful skin looks faded. You're slowly killing yourself right in front of my eyes."

"Please, Peter. Give me another chance. I know I can do it, please." Her chest tightened.

He picked up the cat and scratched her behind the ears. Her purring filled the room. God, why couldn't her life be as simple as Nellie's—eat, sleep, purr?

"People like me are called 'enablers.' Do you know what that means?" he asked.

She sighed and looked away. She didn't want to talk about this. She only wanted him back. It took everything in her not to run into his arms and melt against his strong chest. She couldn't live if he left her.

"Enablers ignore the signs of alcoholism," he continued. "They actually make it easy for the alcoholic to drink—"

"I'm not an alcoholic. My mother was, but I'm not. I can stop any time."

Nellie jumped off Peter's lap and moved under the window to sit in a beam of sunlight. She lifted her paw and began washing her face.

"That's the problem. Don't you see? If I come back, I'm just as guilty as you are. It's my tacit agreement that you aren't an alcoholic. By coming back and pretending everything is okay, I'm enabling you to keep doing what you're doing. After a day or two, I'll find stashes under the sink again. I'll call you in the middle of the day, and your voice will slur. It'll start all over. I can't do that again. It's too much. I'm tired of enabling you."

She rose from the couch to get an ashtray. "So, you're blaming me for all this. It's my fault our marriage is in trouble. Just say it. That's what you think." With a trembling hand she lit the cigarette even though Peter hated it. She had to do something before she exploded.

"No. I'm blaming both of us. We both have to work at it. I admit that when I left here the other night, I was furious. You could barely hold your head up at dinner. But, I was as angry with myself as I was with you."

"What do you want?"

He pushed an unruly curl of maple-colored hair off his face. Creases lined his forehead and a worried frown marred the bridge of his nose. His usually pressed shirt looked wrinkled and dull. "I'm going to get some clothes and stuff together and move out for a while. I found a small apartment across town. I signed a lease for ninety days. Maybe we can use that time to decide what to do."

Her heart fluttered and her hand shook when she tried to stomp out the cigarette. Ninety days without Peter. Ninety days alone in the house. Separation. "Can't we try once more? I'm begging you."

He shook his head. "You aren't ready." He got up. "I'd better go."

"What will we tell Aunt Sarah and Mark? They want us to come to dinner tonight. What will we tell our friends? I can't stand this, please, Peter."

A leaf blower blasted from next door—life as usual.

He stood near her and took her hand. "You have to see how serious this is. Tell your friends what you wish. I'll join you for dinner with Mark and Sarah tonight. We'll try and get through this one step at a time. I'm not saying it's over." He paused and choked back a tear. "I have to go." He dropped her hand.

She squeezed her eyes shut and clenched her fists. She felt as if someone had punched her in the stomach. After a moment, she rose. "I packed your things. They're in the hall closet."

She returned to the kitchen, slid her gloves over her shaking hands and continued washing the dishes. Her ears rang so loudly she barely heard the door close when he left.

* * * *

At 7:10 p.m. Marlene pressed the doorbell at the Brady's house, clutching a bottle of wine and a vase of flowers.

"Oh my goodness, look at you," Aunt Sarah said, relieving her of the flowers. "You didn't need to bring all this."

"I hosted a shower today and thought you'd like some of the flowers," she answered, shrugging out of her coat and leaving it on the chair by the door.

Aunt Sarah took the flowers to the kitchen. "Look at those jonquils. They're beautiful. Are they from your garden?" She added water and fluffed up the greenery. "Where's Peter?" she asked, stretching to look behind her.

"No, they're not from the garden. Mine aren't up yet, and Peter's coming from the office. Apparently he had something late going on."

Mark entered the kitchen with a booming, "Hello, beauty!" He scooped her up in his arms, lifting her off the floor. "How's my favorite niece?"

"Your only niece," she said and added, "Oops, I forgot about Janie."

Mark released her and settled on a barstool. "She hardly counts."

"She's in Atlanta," Marlene said.

"So I've heard."

"I saw her today," Aunt Sarah said from the stove. She was stirring something that smelled of curry. She tasted a bit of it on a wooden spoon and then added some more seasonings from a small bowl. "It was a wonderful surprise."

"What is that delicious smelling thing you're cooking?" Mark asked with a raised eyebrow. He had put on a few pounds since they had married, and he wasn't slender to start with.

"I'm trying a Red Lentil Curry. I thought it would warm our souls on this chilly night."

"Not too spicy, I hope," Mark said.

Sarah shrugged. "I omitted the chilli powder." She tasted another bit. "It tastes fine to me. I've had it simmering all afternoon in the slow cooker. Wanna try some?" She held the spoon to Mark.

He bent down. "Yum. It's delicious." He turned to Marlene. "Your aunt is the best cook in Atlanta."

Aunt Sarah's culinary skills still surprised Marlene. Her mother had been the cook in the family. She had made homemade applesauce using Granny's famous recipe, and she never served anything from a can— everything had to be fresh. When she lived with Aunt Sarah, her aunt had been too busy to cook. They often ate out or consumed frozen dinners. Canned vegetables were a staple in Aunt Sarah's kitchen. The first time Marlene tasted powdered mashed potatoes, it took all her strength not to spit them out. She had grown up eating freshly mashed spuds mixed with cream and butter.

Aunt Sarah wiped her hands on her apron. "That's a big exaggeration. Marly knows all about my cooking."

"It's different now," Mark said. "Look at me." He patted his belly. "I'm a walking poster child for your meals." He gave Aunt Sarah a huge bear hug.

They all laughed. Marlene still marveled at the change in her aunt. Before she married Mark she had been so serious. In Marlene's teenage mind, she was a perfect old maid. She wore her hair in a tight bun and donned gray, navy or black clothes. She enjoyed a good mystery and a movie now and then, but mostly she worked. Married to Mark she became a changed woman—wearing a loose French braid and flowing, flowery dresses, and becoming a skilled cook and entertainer. Her aunt had learned the art of having fun.

"Remember the time we made your granny's applesauce together?" Aunt Sarah asked.

"I had to wrestle Granny Jennings's pots and strainer from Mama. She didn't think you could do it." She didn't add that at that time in her mother's life, she no longer cooked. Marlene prepared all the meals.

"I wasn't sure I could do it either. But with your help, we managed to make several jars. Once we peeled the apples, cooked and strained them, it wasn't hard. The straining part was quite an ordeal, though."

"We got applesauce all over your white kitchen."

They laughed. "I can still taste that applesauce, though. It was the best in the world," Aunt Sarah said.

"Why not make it again?" Mark asked, practically licking his chops.

Aunt Sarah and Marlene exchanged a look. "Easy for you to say!" Sarah said in a teasing voice. She lowered the heat on the stove. "We're all set. Let's settle in the den until Peter arrives."

"How 'bout a glass of wine?" Mark asked Marlene.

Although she had consumed several glasses of vodka—God only knew how many—before she left home, she accepted.

Mark returned to the den with two tumblers of red wine and a glass of something else for himself. Marlene sat down on the Louis XVI chair, her favorite from Aunt Sarah's house before they married. Covered in pink and green striped silk, it sat like a throne. Mark preferred the Lazy-boy that didn't seem to fit the room's décor. Her aunt perched on the couch.

After a few sips of the wine, an Italian grape, probably Mark's favorite, a Brunello, she asked him, "Is Ralph gone?"

He glanced quickly at Aunt Sarah as if seeking permission. "I wasn't too successful," he began.

Marlene's stomach sank. She put down the wine on the coffee table to keep from spilling it. "What?"

He shifted in the chair. "Ralph is a devious little devil. I went over there to tell him to get out, and he flat-out refused."

"But he can't refuse. It's not his house."

"I know that. I told him I was acting on your behalf as your uncle and your attorney. I demanded that he leave immediately. He stared me down with his hands on his hips and said we'd have to evict him."

"How long would that take?"

Mark shook his head. "That depends. The sheriff will come and notify him to leave by a certain date. This is an unusual case because it's not your typical landlord tenant situation. In those cases the tenant has sixty days to clear out."

"Sixty days!" Marlene stood and began pacing the floor. "That's ridiculous." She paused and faced Mark. "He's living in our house without our permission. He's not a tenant."

"Yes, yes, I know. He says he has permission to live there because he lived there with his wife. He's got a lawyer—"

"Yeah, some sort of shyster dial-a-lawyer he probably found online."

Mark sipped his drink. "We can get him out of the house, but it won't happen as fast as you'd like."

Her heart thundered. She lifted the wine glass to her lips to stop the trembling inside. Janie had probably already seen Ralph. Events were moving too fast.

"Look, honey," Aunt Sarah said, "Mark will get Ralph sorted out. You must not worry about any of this. Leave it with us."

"I don't get it. The man who was convicted of murdering my mother is living in our house, mine and Janie's. Don't we, as the victims, have any rights?"

"It's a very complicated situation," Mark said. "I've got a buddy who might be able to help us. He works in the Attorney General's office and has been active with crafting Georgia's victim rights laws. I'll give him a call tomorrow to see what he suggests. Trust me, Marly, I'll take care of it, okay?"

The doorbell sounded.

"That must be Peter," Aunt Sarah said, rising.

* * * *

Somehow they made it through dinner. Marlene couldn't look at Peter, who fortunately sat next to her and was therefore out of her direct line of sight. But, she did notice the way Aunt Sarah scowled at him with a worried expression. After the last glass of wine, Marlene realized she had guzzled one too many. Her head twirled in circles and she had to lean on the table to stand up. People talked as if in a tunnel.

"Peter," Aunt Sarah said, "why don't you leave Marlene's car here. Mark and I can run it by your house tomorrow."

Peter answered something, but she couldn't quite make out what he said.

The next thing she knew she was in the car next to Peter, heading home. He remained silent. She was sure he was angry with her for drinking too much wine, but Mark kept refilling her glass. What was she supposed to do? She leaned her head against the window and closed her eyes. Everything began spinning. She opened her eyes to stop the wooziness. If she vomited all over Peter's car, he would never forgive her.

Peter pulled the car up close to the house. Before getting out, he said something to her—asking if she'd be okay or maybe if she wanted him to walk her in.

Marlene navigated over the stone walkway, trying hard not to stumble as Peter walked her to the front entrance of their house. The cold night air hit her hard and jarred her out of her tipsy state like a splash of icy water.

"Don't you want to spend the night here instead of going back to wherever you're living now?"

He shook his head. "No, Marlene, I've already explained. I have to be away from you when you're like this."

"That sounds so drastic." She suppressed a nervous giggle. When he didn't answer, she added, "Please come in, and I'll make us both some coffee. It wouldn't kill you to stay a few minutes, would it?"

His touch on her elbow tightened. "Thanks, but I'd better go."

She fumbled around in her purse for her key and unlocked the door. By the time she opened it, he had returned to his car. A sob burbled up from her throat while she watched him disappear out of her line of site.

He was gone.

Chapter Twelve

Two hours after having had lunch with Aunt Sarah, Janie returned to Thelma's. She entered a quiet house with no one apparently at home. Although tired, she vowed to make a few more phone calls before the day ended. She searched through the phone book and after two rings, a woman answered.

"May I speak with Jack Saunders?" Janie asked.

"He's not here, honey. How 'bout I have him call you?" The woman spoke in a deep, rich Southern voice, reminding her of Sue Anne.

"Please. My name's Janie Knox. We used—"

"My land sakes alive! You're Marlene's sister!" she cut in.

"You know Marlene?"

"Lord knows I do! We're across-the-street neighbors. But beyond that, I'd say Marlene and I are best friends. I was her maid of honor when—"

"When I disappeared," Janie filled in for her and laughed to ease the embarrassing moment.

"I'm Jack's wife, Amanda. I've heard a ton of stuff about you, honey child. I'll be glad to ask Jack to give you a jingle when he gets his sorry self home, probably around six-thirty. I know he'll be tickled to death to hear you called."

Jack's wife sounded bubbly and full of life and as different from the Jack she knew as anyone could be.

On a sudden impulse, Janie said, "I wonder if you'd mind terribly if I dropped by. I'd love to meet the woman who finally snared Jack, and also, I'm concerned about my sister."

Silence.

"Well, let me think. I'm pooped tonight. And Jack's an absolute bear when he gets home from work."

"How about tomorrow morning?"

"Jack goes to work early."

"I know this sounds odd, but I'd like to talk to you if you don't mind. Is nine o'clock too early?"

"I'm an early bird, dear child," Amanda responded and gave her directions.

A loud muffler choked outside the house. She peeked through the curtain. Thelma was getting out of a dark green sedan with two men in tow. Jimbo and Sherri tumbled out from the backseat.

Once inside, Thelma introduced Janie to her husband, Jerry, and his friend, Nelson. Then she ducked into the kitchen with the children who were demanding something to drink. Janie had no idea what Thelma had done with the baby, and she didn't ask.

As soon as Jerry appeared, she recognized him. Actually she didn't so much remember him as the tattoo on his forearm—a woman wrapped in the embrace of a serpent.

"You've changed," Jerry said, lighting a cigarette and plopping down in the Lazy-boy.

"It's been a while," she countered.

Jerry had been one of the boys she at age seventeen and Thelma at twenty had run away with when they'd been arrested. She didn't like him back then, and on first impression, time had not changed him for the better.

Screams came from the kitchen. Apparently Jimbo grabbed something Sherri was eating. More howls and protests.

"Shut them kids up," Jerry yelled without moving.

"Nelson here is a private dick," he said, turning to Janie. "Thelm said you wanted someone to spy on your step daddy. Me and Nelson are your men." He shot her a toothy grin full protruding gums.

She studied Nelson, who stood about six-two with cropped hair and sharp eyes the color of mahogany. What kind of private detectives hung out with ex-cons?

"Nice to meet ya," he said, holding out his hand.

She shook it and sat down in the chair opposite Jerry. Nelson remained standing by the absent baby's high-chair.

"Bring us some beers," Jerry called to Thelma.

"Get your own damn beers. I'm busy in here."

That's my friend, Thelma!

With a groan, he rose. "We can talk about what you need and how Nelson and me can help in a minute. Right now I gotta have me a cold one." He disappeared through the kitchen door.

Nelson stepped farther into the room. He moved the pieces of a Lego set off a straight back chair standing by the desk and sat down.

"Thelma says you're from Savannah," he said.

She nodded. He looked to be about thirty-five and strong. His t-shirt stretched over gym-rat pecs designed to impress the likes of Sue Anne who never ceased to pump iron.

"I got me an uncle that lives down there. He likes it a lot. But says it gets mighty hot in the summer."

"Savannah's more humid than it is here."

Jerry bounded through the door, gripping two beers by the neck and guzzling another. He passed a beer to her, but she declined it.

"Suit yourself." He handed a longneck to Nelson.

Jerry's small dark eyes never stopped moving. Does he have some sort of eye problem or is he simply hyper?

"Y'all getting acquainted?" he asked with a sneer.

Nelson smiled and rubbed his arms as if cold, but the room was stifling.

"Miss Janie," Jerry began. "Nelson here is the best private dick you can get for the money. He done finds things most people give up on. He uses his powerful self to get what he wants. That might come in handy with that step daddy of yours. Don't ya think?"

"That depends," she said.

At seventeen she'd sized up Jerry as a kid with no brains. So far her opinion of him had not wavered. She kicked herself for telling Thelma so much and now getting tangled up with these troublemakers.

"Tell her, Nelson."

Nelson rubbed the beer bottle between his hands. "I ain't sure what you want, but Thelma says this lawyer dude threatened you. I could put a stop to that real easy like. Or, if you wanna know more about what Cooper is up to, I could get information for you. You just gotta tell me what you need."

"How would you put a stop to the threats?" she asked.

Jerry snickered. She didn't like his laugh. How could Thelma stand this guy?

"I bet that ol' shyster ain't very big. Well, all Nelson's gotta do is talk friendly while he breaks his arm."

"Nah, Jer, I won't do nothing like that. I'll just talk to him. That's usually all it takes. You see, Miss Knox, they think you're all alone, and they can scare you. Once they meet me, they realize the stakes are higher. They can't just come around and poke at you."

She liked that he called her Miss Knox. "So, you'd go tell him to stay away from me."

He nodded. "If that's what you want."

"What about finding out what Ralph is up to?"

Nelson's eyes shot to Jerry. "That's a bit more complicated. I'd need to stake out where he's living and do some digging around. It's possible, but it'll take more time."

"In other words," she said. "It'll cost more."

"She's a smart one, this," Jerry said, reaching over and elbowing Nelson in the ribs.

"How much for each job?"

"I could do the whole thing for a grand," Nelson said.

"And what about you, Jerry? What's your part in all this?"

Jerry darted a quick look at Nelson. "Me and Nelson are partners like. He cuts me in for finding you, and I can help him put the fear of God in these cons. Never know what you might uncover when you lift an ugly rock. Don't hurt none to have a bit of backup, right man?" He laughed again.

Nelson didn't respond.

She reached for her coat and purse.

"I'll think about it. Meantime, I'm going out. Tell Thelma I'll be back later tonight."

"Don't wait too long," Jerry hollered as she exited out the door. "Me and Nelson are busy fellows."

Back in the Honda she sucked in the fresh night air, glad to be away from the stale smells in Thelma's house. Stars peered out of the sky, promising another clear day tomorrow.

She started the engine and headed back toward town.

Nelson's offer wasn't so bad. If it weren't for Jerry, she would have agreed right on the spot. She had plenty of money and no time left to spend it. A thousand bucks to find out what Ralph was up to sounded like a good deal, and it would save her precious time. But Jerry worried her. He was a loose cannon. She would have to figure out a way to negotiate with Nelson and not include Jerry.

She drove into the parking lot of a Cracker Barrel restaurant and pulled out her cell.

On the fourth ring before the line went to voicemail, Sue Anne answered.

"Sorry, I was out back, and I couldn't get a hold of my phone," she said, catching her breath.

"I thought you might be at kick-boxing class."

"I didn't go tonight. Marcia isn't teaching so I decided to play hooky. Anyway, why look beautiful when you're so far away?"

"You're not brooding, are you?"

"Well, a little, maybe. We've never been separated for this long."

"It's not even been a week."

Water was running in the background.

"I know. I just hate every minute. Please tell me you're coming home soon."

She couldn't promise that. Everything seemed to be more complicated than she'd thought.

"Does your silence mean no?"

The water stopped running.

"Are you washing dishes?"

"I'm cleaning out the kitchen cabinets. It gives me something to do. So, you're not coming home soon."

"I promise I will come as soon as I can."

Sue Anne sighed. "Steven said he talked to the guy at the bank. He said you could sell that property anytime you want. He also said to tell you to call him. He's having some trouble with one of the stylists."

Probably Lucinda. "I'll call him first thing tomorrow morning."

"Oh, yeah, you got some sort of notice about a package."

"Who's it from?"

Rummaging.

"Wait a sec." More rummaging. "Okay, well, that's weird."

"What's weird?"

"It's from the bank. Why is the bank sending you a package?"

Her heart leapt. "Could you FedEx it to me as soon as it arrives?"

"Sure thing."

"Oh, one more thing. I've moved. I'm staying with a friend now." She gave her Thelma's address.

"Why did you move?"

"I wanted to see Thelma while here, and she insisted I stay with her." *God, another lie!* "She's an old high school buddy. That's all."

"You've never mentioned her." Jealousy rose in Sue Anne's voice.

"Don't worry. She's married with three kids. Besides, she's not my type. I promise, just a friend."

"Did I say I was worried?"

"You didn't have to."

Sue Anne laughed. "You're such a bad girl. Now you get yourself home really fast or you'll see a really bad side of me!"

She ended the call with her heart racing. The bank had located her stuff and it would arrive soon. She would have everything by Monday at the latest.

She opened the car door and went into Cracker Barrel where she hoped to enjoy a quiet dinner alone without any surprise visits.

* * * *

Back at Thelma's house, she found Jerry asleep in front of the television and Nelson gone. Beer bottles lined the floor around the Lazy-Boy.

She gathered the bottles and slipped into the kitchen for a glass of water.

When she returned to the living room, Jerry was gone, the TV off, and presumably Thelma had placed sheets and a pillow on the couch.

Crawling in the make-shift bed to sleep, she tossed and turned, trying to find a comfortable spot on the narrow sofa pillows. She threw off the covers. Voices, not too quiet, rose from other parts of the house. Footsteps —long slow strides and fast little feet—pounded constantly.

She rose on her elbow and switched on the lamp.

Her mind wouldn't relax. Tomorrow after her visit with Amanda, she would find somewhere else to stay. Thelma's house, although remote, didn't lend itself to sleep, and she didn't want to be around Jerry.

She scrolled through the emails on her smart phone. Dogs barked, doors slammed, and tires squealed outside. Who said living in the country was quiet? She spotted an email from Dr. Mill's office letting her know her appointment at Emory had been arranged for 10:00 a.m. Monday with a Dr. Sams. They advised reporting to the oncology section of the hospital thirty minutes ahead of time. She deleted everything else in her inbox. What else mattered at this point in her life?

Sometime after midnight, the house quieted, and she closed her eyes, hoping to block out the noises from outside. Exhaustion overpowered her. Sleep almost came when a siren blared. She turned over and pulled the sheet over her head. The siren neared closer and closer, then it faded away. The last thing she heard was the sound of the heater switching on.

A bright beam of sunlight shone on her face when she opened her eyes the next morning.

Sherri stood right in front of her, staring.

Janie blinked. "Good morning," she said, rising on her elbows.

Sherri ran behind the couch.

Janie peaked over the edge. "Want to play hide-and-seek?"

The little girl grinned.

"You hide," Janie said, closing her eyes and counting to ten.

When she opened her eyes, Sherri was gone, but she glimpsed little pink Crocs behind the chair.

"Wonder where Sherri is?" She rose from the couch and pretended to be searching underneath. "She's too big to get under here. Unless she can get real flat."

A soft giggle came from the other side of the chair, and the little girl peaked around the edge.

"Maybe she's hiding under the desk?"

Sherri jumped out from the chair. "I'm here!"

Thelma entered with Rocky on her hip. "Sherri, what are you doing disturbing our guest?"

Janie stretched. "It's no problem. I was getting up anyway." The clock read 7:15 a.m.

"I've got coffee made. Want some?"

"Sure," she said, sliding into her jeans.

Janie followed Thelma into the kitchen. Sherri trailed after them, grabbing onto the end of Thelma's shirt.

Jimbo was seated at the table with a bowl of Cheerio's.

Thelma poured coffee into two cups. "Want anything else? I've got toast, cereal, and a couple of bagels."

"Coffee is fine. Thanks."

Janie pulled up a chair next to Jimbo.

"Do you have a dog?" he asked, studying her out of the corner of his eye.

"I do. How did you know?"

He shrugged and shoveled a spoonful of cereal into his mouth. "What's his name?" he asked, munching on a mouthful.

"Charlie, and he's bigger than you are."

Jimbo's eyes widened. "Is he a Great Dane?"

Thelma placed a coffee cup on the table and plopped down with Rocky on her knee. The baby gurgled slobber, and Thelma wiped his mouth with a napkin.

"He's got a friend with a Great Dane, and he's been nagging me to get him a dog. I told him I've got enough to do without adding another hungry mouth."

"My dog's a yellow lab mix," Janie told Jimbo. "And, I miss him a lot."

"Who feeds him when you're gone?"

"I have a good friend who takes care of him for me."

Jimbo nodded, seemingly satisfied and continued to munch on his cereal.

They sat in silence for several minutes.

Thelma lit a cigarette and exhaled smoke toward the ceiling.

"What do you know about this Nelson guy?" Janie asked.

"I don't know him as well as Jerry does. But Jerry says he'll do what you need."

"A thousand dollars is a lot of money."

Her friend shifted in her seat, causing Rocky to fuss. "Yeah, that's what I said to Jerry. Bet you could get him to come down if you wanted."

"If I pay him, do you think he'll do what he says?"

She shrugged and blew another large cloud of smoke over her head. "That's a risk you'll have to take. I've no idea."

Janie sipped the vile-tasting coffee and added a few grains of sugar. How could she tell her friend she didn't trust her husband?

"I was surprised to see you married Jerry."

Thelma looked away. "Jerry talks worse than he is. Besides, I didn't have many choices now, did I?"

Images of Thelma in torn jeans with unwashed, straggly hair and acne marring her face and neck flashed in Janie's head.

Probably not, Janie thought but said, "Sure you did."

Thelma shrugged. "Well, maybe I did."

Later, Janie called Nelson and arranged to meet him at the Yellow Star Café that afternoon at 2:00 p.m.

"Don't bring Jerry," she told him before she hung up.

Chapter Thirteen

The house echoed like an empty tomb. Marlene turned on the lamp next to the door. Nellie greeted her with her tail high. She picked up the cat and scratched her behind the ears. Nellie scrambled to get down with a meow of protest. *Even my cat wants to be away from me.*

The telephone answering machine light flashed. She pushed the button and listened to two messages from Janie, "Please call when you get a chance. We need to talk."; one from Nikki, "Thanks so much for the shower. You're the greatest. Jamey loved the big tiger,"; and one from Ralph, "You can tell that lawyer uncle of yours to stop bothering me. I ain't leaving here, Marly. That's the end of it." She sighed and walked into the kitchen where she uncorked a fresh bottle of Pinot Bianco. *Just one glass. I promise.*

Before she knew it, the bottle was empty. Her head ached. She rummaged around in the medicine cabinet for some pain killers. She found some Peter had taken a few years back when he'd had minor foot surgery. The label read, *Take as needed for the pain.* The date had expired, but she downed two of them anyway and put the rest in her pocket, just in case.

Returning to the living room, she switched on the CD player. Her mother had always listened to records to cheer herself up, but of course, they never actually did that. Instead they distracted her from the silence engulfing her—exactly as Marlene felt. Silence. Emptiness. Fill it up with music.

Her mother scoffed CD players, preferring records and record jackets lying scattered all over her room, her favorites being the classics. Tonight, Marlene selected something booming, *Pictures at an Exhibition* by Mussorgsky. She poured herself a glass of Tanqueray and plopped down on the couch to soak in the majestic sound. Someone once told her that this piece had been written for the piano, but she'd only heard it played by orchestras. How could a piano alone give this music the vibrancy and depth that an orchestra did? The London Symphony performed on this CD. It had been a gift from Aunt Sarah when Marlene moved into the apartment with Janie, not long after Mama died. The music filled her head like a sweet dream. She drank more gin and stretched out on the couch.

Her imagination took her to a beautiful field of red poppies where she frolicked with Peter, laughing and tickling him. The day they'd made love for the first time flashed in her mind. Peter had joined her, Aunt Sarah and Mark on a picnic at Lake Rabun during a beautiful October Sunday afternoon. She and Peter had sneaked off from her aunt and Mark, who both stayed back on the pier to fish. They walked along the lake, kicking stones and looking into each other's eyes. Her heart flew faster than the motorboats dashing on the water. When he kissed her for the first time, a spasm ran through her body, and she hungrily kissed him back. He pulled away—always the perfect gentleman.

"Please," she had said. "I need someone like you, someone who will handle me gently."

That was all it took. They'd made love deep in the woods under the tall Georgia pines. Even all these years later, the smell of pine reminded her of that afternoon.

After finishing that bottle of gin, she staggered up the stairs toward the bedroom, carrying a glass and a fresh bottle of Beefeaters with her. Perhaps she would conduct a private gin taste testing tonight. The Beefeaters brings out more of the juniper flavor than the Tanqueray. She giggled. The clock read 11:00 p.m. It was too late to call Janie. She would wait until tomorrow.

She turned up the music full throttle, and it blasted up the stairs as if signaling some sort of triumph but frightening Nellie, who dashed under her foot, nearly knocking her over.

"My God, Nellie—"

The cat disappeared under the bed, her way of putting her paws over her ears.

She switched on the television. After surfing around for several minutes, she lit on an old Audrey Hepburn movie, *Wait until Dark*. Hepburn had been one of Aunt Sarah's favorite stars. As a teenager, she had accompanied her aunt to see several of her films, her favorite being *Breakfast at Tiffany's* which they watched together on Aunt Sarah's TV. Marlene loved the music almost as much as the story. In *Wait until Dark* Hepburn played a blind woman. Marlene squinted at the screen, having trouble focusing. The images blurred together into a large blob. The gin began to work its magic. Her mind zoned out. Before she realized it, the credits scrolled down the screen.

After the movie, the throbbing in her head started up again. She swallowed two more pills, then fell on the bed and began fading back in darkness while the murmur of commercials—moms hugging little girls after they took the prescribed antidepressants—carried her away.

A memory of her mother floated in front of her, sitting at the kitchen table, shucking corn in a red-checked, sleeveless dress. She'd combed her hair into a shiny ponytail, covered her lips with bright red lipstick, and topped her eyelids with a thin uneven line, looking a bit like a blond Audrey Hepburn, slender and youthful. That day Mama had acted as though her appearance in the kitchen was as natural as the plop of the evening paper on the front step even though she had not been out of bed in weeks.

Marlene had stumbled on her when she'd come racing through the backdoor after school.

"Mama?" she said, trying to keep the surprise out of her voice, "Can I help you?"

"Sure, but watch out for worms. I've found quite a few."

She sat down across from her mother and lifted a large ear from those spread on newspaper in the middle of the table. "Where did the corn come from?"

"This morning I went to the market on the east side. I got some strawberries and some cooking apples, too. Tomorrow I'm gonna make applesauce. Wanna help?"

She stared at her mother's pale face, her jaw gnawing back and forth on a piece of gum. Mama's smile looked as though it had been painted on, her eyes empty like exposed sockets without the bulbs. Mama hadn't been shopping in so long, Marlene couldn't recall the last time.

"That'd be great," she said.

"While I was out, I saw Suzanne Deets," Mama continued. "She told me about the church bazaar next week. You should have told me about that, Marly. Maybe I'll take some fresh pound cake. Everyone raves over my pound cakes. We'll need to stock up on eggs and butter. I couldn't believe how gray Suzanne's hair is. It's a wonder she doesn't color it. I suppose being married to that no good, pot-bellied car salesman, she probably doesn't think it matters how she looks." Mama laughed. "But I can remember when she was belle of the ball."

"I thought you were the belle of the ball, Mama." She peeled a tough husk off an ear of corn and flicked a worm onto the newspaper before reaching for another.

"Indeed I was, but Suzanne was my arch rival. She and that fat Rhonda Sue." Mama sighed and pressed her lips into a smile. "Boys lined up at the door to take me out. Poor Sarah. Nobody paid her one wink. When I was a sophomore in high school, three boys asked me to the senior prom. I came galloping into the house like the lucky winner of a blue ribbon. I can still see Mama sitting in the kitchen, shucking corn, just like us today, Marly. 'Mama,' I cried, 'Jerry *and* Bobby asked me to the prom. But Bill asked me first. What am I to do?'" Mama paused in her story for dramatic effect and put her hand on her hip, mimicking her mother.

Marlene leaned forward as if she'd never heard this story. It was one of her mother's favorites.

Mama flicked another worm onto the paper and continued. "'Eloise,' my mama said, 'You know this is Sarah's senior year. She hasn't been asked to the prom ever, not by one boy. This year she must go. She'll never have another chance. Do you understand that, honey?'

"Well sure enough I felt sorry for Sarah, but what could I do about it? Then she told me, 'You must tell those boys you can't go at all unless your sister gets to go. You gotta help her get a chance to go to her senior prom. It's your duty.'

"I sat there shocked out of my wits. She could've hit me with a sledgehammer, and it've felt better.

"When I didn't say anything, she continued, 'Tell them that you'll go with the first boy who gets Sarah a date.'

"I flew to my room where I cried for hours. How could she make me do such a thing? Instead of being proud of me for getting three invitations to the prom, she was punishing me. Finally, when I realized that crying wasn't gonna change Mama's mind, I stopped. I told each boy what Mama said. Even though they were as shocked as me, they started searching for a date for Sarah. It was like some sort of competition and got to be almost fun." She smiled radiantly, looking as beautiful as she must have looked then. She pushed her hair off her face with her arm.

"It was Bill that won out. I sorta hoped Jerry would coz he was my favorite, but Bill found Sarah a date so I accepted his invitation. But guess what happened?" Mama's face crinkled in laughter as sweet memories poured from her lips.

"What?" Marlene asked while she peeled the last ear of corn, careful to remove all the silks.

"Sarah flat out turned the boy down. Leave it to Sarah." Her mother patted her thighs and laughed. "She told the boy she wouldn't go to the dance just to please her parents. 'I've got better things to do with my time,' she said. The poor boy begged but, of course, it was useless. Sarah always had a will about her."

"Did you get to go to the prom?" Marlene knew the rest of the story, but she wanted to keep her mother talking.

"I went with Bill. And it was one of the best nights of my life." Mama stopped talking and her hands quit working the corn. She walked toward the window. A blank stare settled over her face as if someone had taken an eraser and removed the previous glimpse of happiness. "The best night of my life," she'd finally muttered again, "and I didn't even know it."

Marlene opened her eyes and poured more gin in the glass, emptying the bottle. Rising, she stumbled to the bathroom, holding on to the walls for support. She splashed cold water on her face and glimpsed her own tired reflection in the bathroom mirror. With a start she recognized that same empty look she had seen in her mother eyes that day in the kitchen.

She gripped the edge of the sink, her head pounding. If Peter left her and never came back, she would end up exactly like her mother, a tired angry drunk with nothing left but memories and old photos. She slammed her fist onto the counter. Pills and jars fell to the floor with a bang. Nellie scurried out the door.

"I'm not like you, Mama. I'll die first!" she screamed.

She returned to the bedroom and groped in the back of the closet for her stash of liquor. When her hand landed on a bottle of Jack Daniels, she popped it open and drank directly from the bottle, not wasting time with a glass. Her head reeled. What did it matter if she passed out drunk? No one was here to see her. No one cared. Tomorrow she would stop cold turkey. She could, too. She'd done it before. Unlike Mama, she was not an alcoholic and could stop anytime she wanted. She swallowed more, collapsed on the bed and fell sound asleep.

She awoke to the sound of the phone ringing and light streaming on her face. Her head felt as if two giant forceps pressed on both temples. The voicemail answered the annoying phone. She reached for the bottle next to her bed, drank more and swallowed the rest of the pills in her pocket. Everything got fuzzy in her head. Her arms moved, but they felt heavy, as if they were under water and she was trying to swim against a strong undertow.

The pain in her head pierced her vision. *Why is everything so complicated? Ralph won't leave. Peter hates me.*

The next time the telephone rang, Marlene barely heard it and then everything went silent.

Chapter Fourteen

The next morning, Janie drove along the downtown streets toward Buckhead—one of the nicest areas of Atlanta—on her way to the Saunders's house. On route, she passed The Governor's Mansion, a multi-story brick dwelling with handsome white columns, looking slightly false like a picture from *Southern Living Magazine*.

Maneuvering through traffic and pausing at stoplights, she fought off thoughts of her sister's angry words—*you don't care for me anymore than you cared for Mama*. Janie couldn't deny her own blame. She had indeed abandoned Marlene, left her to pick up the pieces alone.

She tightened her grip on the steering wheel. She had called Marlene twice yesterday and left messages. Nothing, not even a voicemail response. All she wanted was to apologize and try to start over.

When she fled Atlanta as a teen, she wasn't thinking about what her departure would do to her sister. All she could think about was getting away. And now, even though everyone made it clear Marlene needed her more than ever, her first impulse was to run away again, to escape from this quicksand of a city, and return to the bosom of her friends. The urge to flee filled her like a balloon about to burst. All she had to do was turn left onto the interstate and head south. She sucked in her tummy and straightened her shoulders as her gaze followed the I75 turnoff, south toward Savannah. *Soon, soon, I'll be on my way home, but not yet.*

She steered the Honda around the corner and up the Saunders's steep driveway. The gray slate two-story structure looked luxurious and elegant, like an English manor, perhaps belonging to a duke. Ancient magnolias and large well-pruned boxwoods filled the yard. Dozens of dogwoods lined the front entrance.

Janie stood at a magnificent door at least ten feet tall, made of some kind of heavy, dark wood. Ivy crawled up the sides, encasing it like a winter coat. She lifted the iron knocker.

A small woman, no taller than Janie, with baby doll features framed in a mop of reddish blond hair, greeted her wearing a purple warm up suit, tennis shoes, and a wide smile.

"Hi! I'm Amanda. Please come in. Hope you don't mind my casual appearance. I've got a tennis match later today. It promises to be a rough one, too, with a group of women from Braselton. Lord knows those ladies are hard to beat! I play tennis three times a week, or more sometimes, just to maintain my weight. It's a constant battle for me. Tennis, Pilates, you name it, I do it. You obviously don't have a problem. Gosh, honey, you look nothing like Marlene. It's amazing."

Amanda rattled on as they traveled across the marble-floored foyer into a glorious living room full of antiques and crystal vases of fresh purple and yellow mums. Heavy plaid drapes—purple, pink and yellow—stood open at the windows. Bright sunlight penetrated the room.

Janie sat down on a pink and gold silk striped Chippendale chair, too stiff to give with her weight. Amanda settled across from her on a matching couch.

"My sister and I are different," Janie agreed.

Amanda giggled. "You don't mean it? Can I get you something? A Diet Coke or a cup of coffee?"

"Oh, no, thanks. I just wanted to talk to you. What a beautiful home you have."

Amanda smiled, showing off dimples. Her face reminded Janie of the Miss Alexander dolls she collected as a child and were probably still stashed in the attic at Briardale Lane. "Most of the furniture belonged to Jack's parents. They moved to a condo in Florida five years ago, thank our lucky stars! The house, oh yes, we love it. We got such a deal, you wouldn't believe. After Jack and I married, we lived in his tiny apartment for six months."

Janie recalled being in Jack's apartment once. He had invited her there when they both were in a marijuana stupor. He'd stuffed his small quarters with beautiful chairs, tables and special doodads reminding Janie of Aunt Sarah's house. He told her his mom went to estate sales and collected antiques.

"I remember that apartment. I can't imagine how you both managed to live there."

Amanda's pencil-thin eyebrows shot up. "So you knew my husband really well, then?"

Janie laughed. "Oh, no, not what you think. I knew Jack before he fought in the Gulf War. We were more like brother and sister." She paused, not wanting to tell Jack's wife about their visits to the Atlanta clubs, their use of drugs or their friendship with questionable people like Thelma, whom she could never imagine sitting in this house. "It was a difficult time for both of us. Me because Marly and I had a tough adolescence and him because of life in general, I suppose. I must say I was shocked when I learned he had enlisted."

"Jack told me about his ambivalence toward the war. Actually, that's what drew us to each other."

Amanda was a talker. Janie just needed to say the right thing, sit back, and listen. Before long, Amanda told her how she had met Jack.

"He came to talk to our class at Agnes Scott about his military experience. He had such a passion. He hated war and politics, and that attracted me lickity-split, with no holding back."

"If I remember correctly," Janie said. "He wasn't one to share much about himself."

Amanda let loose a deep, trickle of a laugh bringing a smile to Janie's lips. "You got that right! It took months for him to ask me out and then it was to dinner with his parents. Yikes, can you imagine?" She rolled her eyes upward. "What an experience that was. My gracious! Their house was bigger than most hotels in Pascagoula. That's where I'm from.

Pascagoula, Mississippi. Most Atlantans don't consider themselves Southerners, you know. It's us folks from Mississippi and Alabama who are the *real* Southerners." She laughed again. "At first I'd get mad when they'd tease me about my accent. Then I realized they saw themselves somewhat removed from the South like butterflies from a cocoon." She paused and looked at Janie sideways. "Oops, now I've stepped in it, you being from here and all."

"No, not one bit. I know exactly what you're talking about. But how did you meet Marlene?"

"At the dinner with Jack's parents. Peter and Marlene came. Marlene and I hit it off like bees to honey. She's much quieter than me, but we talked about clothes and music and realized we liked a lot of the same things. Peter was the most gorgeous man I'd ever seen. I believe I envied Marlene her Miss America beauty and her handsome boyfriend. But by then I was totally snookered with Jack and didn't give a rats you-know-what about anyone else. Your sister and I became tight. During that ghastly trial about your mama, Marlene needed a shoulder. We cried, cursed, and prayed together during those awful weeks. I saw you there, too, but you've changed a lot."

"Hopefully for the better," Janie said, adding, "That was a difficult time for all of us. Marlene was lucky to find a friend like you." Truth was she didn't remember seeing Amanda at the trial, but at that time she was too preoccupied to notice the multitude of spectators packing the courtroom every day.

"Anyway, Marlene and Peter married two weeks before we did. I was her maid of honor and she was mine. I have a sister, too, but she lives in California and couldn't come for my wedding, being pregnant and all then. The four of us celebrate joint anniversaries. That's what's happening tonight by the way…"—she glanced at her watch without pausing—"as a matter of fact. It's our nineteenth—whoa, I can't believe it. This year is my turn. I'm catering dinner here. Marlene likes to cook. She can whip up the best meals. I wish I had her touch in the kitchen. We take turns."

Who would have thought that the most unconventional man Janie had ever known would marry a Southern belle and live like a king in the middle of Buckhead?

"Since you know my sister so well, perhaps you know what's going on with her."

Amanda leaned forward. "What do you mean, honey?"

Janie shifted in her seat, not sure how to begin. "Have you seen Marlene lately?"

Frowning, Amanda said, "I saw her yesterday. She hosted a little shower for a mutual friend who is going to have a baby soon. She's not even a friend we know all that well. I flat-out couldn't believe it when Marlene told me she was going to do it, but she entertains so easily. Me, I'm a basket case when I have to feed anyone, except Jack, of course. But, now that I think about it, she did seem distracted." She paused. "I have to admit, I was kinda preoccupied with helping and all, but-but that's about all I noticed."

"I had coffee with Marlene Tuesday morning," she explained, "and I was shocked by her appearance."

Amanda shook her head. "She's changed that much, huh?"

"Granted I haven't seen her in a long time, but it doesn't take a genius to see something is terribly wrong."

"Yeah, well, I guess I've seen it coming. I've tried to talk to her, but she won't say a word about anything. She denies anything is wrong, but she's always been a sad person, full of pain. She'll only let me go so far, I'm afraid. She's got all these walls around her precious self that nobody can penetrate. It makes me cry sometimes I can hardly stand it. Jack and I have talked about her, but he tells me to mind my own business."

Janie sighed and studied the floral prints hanging behind the couch. "It's partly my fault for leaving when I did. I had no idea she was in such bad shape. Being rather messed up myself, I couldn't see it. But now I want to help if I can. She's clearly in trouble."

Amanda jumped up and headed toward the kitchen. "Let's go over there right this very minute and talk some sense into her. Between the two of us, we can convince her to get some help."

Janie followed. "I don't know. She's awfully mad at me. I told her she reminded me of our mother, and she's not returned any of my phone calls."

Amanda lifted the telephone and leaned out the window, oblivious to what Janie had said. "Her car is there. I'll just give her a little jingle to tell her I'm coming over to borrow something. She'll think nothing of it, tonight being the party and all."

What an amazing woman. If anyone could get Marlene to face her drinking problem, Amanda could. After a moment, Amanda hung up.

"That's odd," Amanda said. "There's no answer."

"Maybe she's in the shower or out in the yard."

"Nope, she wouldn't be in the yard—not that I've ever known." She paused. "Let just go have us a look-see."

Five minutes later, Amanda and Janie knocked on the Tetford's door. No one responded. Amanda banged away on the brass knocker. Janie peered in a window, but it was too dark to see anything. An ominous feeling gripped her like a gnarled hand from the past.

Amanda expelled a long sigh and said, "I don't know what to make of it. Maybe someone picked her up and took her off somewhere. Let me think. Today is Thursday. No, I don't think she's got anything regular that I know of, but come on. Let's call Peter."

As they walked back toward the Saunders's house, Janie's mind filled with worry.

Back in Amanda's kitchen, Marlene's friend telephoned Peter. "Is Marlene doing okay, honey? Her car is in the driveway, but she doesn't answer the door or her cell. I thought you might know where she is. Today isn't Pilates day, and I can't imagine where else she could be without her car. Y'all are coming tonight, aren't ya?" Amanda's frown deepened.

"Good gracious, you didn't forget. I've got plans up the wahzooie for this evening and the best Dom Perignon to celebrate. You better have gotten her a nice little trinket, too. It's not the biggie yet, but us girls expect something."

Amanda clicked her long fingernails along the countertop. The kitchen held rich smells—coffee, bread. "Our anniversary celebration, you dodo head," she said with a laugh. "You aren't kidding me, you sorry husband you? You did forget. You'd better high-tail it out of that fancy office this instant and head on over to Kay Jewelers to get your wife a gift. Otherwise you can say hello to the dog-house."

Amanda paused, gasped, and grabbed her throat. "Lord. I don't know what to say. I'm so sorry."

Janie's stomach tightened.

After Amanda hung up the receiver, she said to Janie, "They're not coming. They've separated. How could she not tell me? I just saw her yesterday, and she didn't say a word." Tears sprang to her eyes. "If she's in that big house all by her lonesome, we've got to go to her and fast."

The tightness in Janie's belly grew. "Why didn't she answer the door? Where is she now? Her car is there. Did Peter have any idea about where she might be?"

"He said he brought her home last night about ten thirty. Beyond that he didn't have a clue." Amanda turned suddenly. "I believe I've got a key." She wiped her face with a Kleenex. "Now where is it?"

She flew toward the pantry and searched through drawers and cabinets, tossing utensils helter-skelter but with no success. Just as they both neared total frustration, her cell phone buzzed.

"Hello?" she said and rolled her eyes at Janie.

"Oh, right, the caterer," she said. "Mr. Nance, I'm sorry to do this, at the last minute, but we'll not be needing the dinner tonight. We've had a slight change of plans. I hope you understand." She paused and sighed. "I'll pay for whatever expense you've gone to. Just send me a bill." She clicked off and said to Janie, "Come on. Let's keep looking."

Moments later, after Amanda found an envelope marked *Tetford*, she and Janie tiptoed into Marlene's dark house. A large gray tabby cat greeted them with a loud meow and a tail lifted upward.

Janie stroked the soft fur while she looked around. The house smelled like wilted flowers. She and Amanda wandered through cavernous rooms where they found dirty glasses and empty liquor bottles everywhere. It looked as if Marlene and Peter had hosted a big shindig the night before and had been too tired to clean up, but Janie knew that hadn't happened. It was as if she'd opened the backdoor to her home on Briardale Lane and had entered the past.

Amanda collected the glasses and put them in the kitchen like a nervous housewife.

"Hey, those can wait. Let's go upstairs," Janie said.

"I don't get this," Amanda said. "Yesterday she was standing right there washing the dishes from Nikki's shower. She was a little tipsy, but maybe I was, too. We had lots of wine. How could there be this many glasses and bottles so soon?" She held a Smirnoff bottle by the neck. "What happened here?"

Janie knew what had happened. She took the glasses and bottles out of Amanda's hands. "Come on."

As she climbed the stairs, her stomach somersaulted. *I'm not up to this. Please, God, let Marlene be all right.*

"Marly," she called in a shaky voice.

No one answered. Suddenly, the telephone broke through the silence, ringing and ringing.

Amanda couldn't resist. "Who is this?" she demanded. "She's not here, and we don't know when she'll be back." Then she slammed down the receiver.

"Who was that?" Janie asked, standing by the phone on the landing.

"Just some rude man, said he was some sort of lawyer who needed to talk to her. Come on." She took Janie's hand.

"Was it Samuel D. Whitaker?"

"Yeah, that sounds about right. He said he was tired of leaving messages, and she'd better call him or else. What a nerve."

Before Janie moved on, she spotted a letter by the phone. She dropped Amanda's hand and lifted the letter. *If you don't tell me what happened, I'll send my friend, Jinx, to talk to you. He has a knack for getting people to talk.* She held her breath, praying this Jinx person wasn't that big black man she'd seen with Ralph.

"What's the matter?" Amanda asked with wide frightened eyes.

She tucked the letter in her purse.

"Nothing. Come on."

They opened the door to the master bedroom where they found Marlene reeking of alcohol and in a place where threatening letters, telephone calls, doorknockers, and anniversaries lost all meaning.

PART TWO

Chapter Fifteen

Eloise Jennings spied her reflection in the shop window when she strode by. Her new short and sassy haircut bounced as she walked and the sun glistened on the yellow strands like golden wheat. She straightened her shoulders and sucked in her flat belly. Once again she'd been elected homecoming queen, this time for her senior year. That meant she would live on forever in the Dexter High School yearbook as the most beautiful girl in the class of 1969. Suzanne Deets could eat her heart out. Her rival had tried to launch a campaign against her, but it had failed. Suzanne will always be the also ran, the bridesmaid, and in this case second place to Eloise.

She pushed through the revolving door to JP Allen Department store —one of Atlanta's finest clothing establishments for women—where Mrs. Peters greeted her as soon as she entered.

"Are you here to pick out your prom dress?" the woman asked with a grin. She had red lipstick on her teeth.

"Yes, ma'am. Mama said for me to try on a couple. She's coming shortly and will help me make a decision." Eloise put her books on a chair opposite the dressing room. This had to be the best day of her life.

She drifted over to the wrack of new spring clothes and pulled out several Villager blouses—a green one, a pink one and one with tiny stripes—measuring them against herself in front of the full-length mirror.

Mrs. Peter's returned with an armload. "I've been expecting you. What about one of these three?" She held up the dresses—a yellow taffeta, a maroon lace, and a celery green chiffon.

Although Mrs. Peters wore ugly drab clothes, either black or gray, and clumpy old lady shoes, she had an eye for exactly what would look good on Eloise, what would emphasize her long shapely legs and make her sapphire eyes shine.

Her heart exploded with excitement. "I like them all!" she declared, tossing the blouses aside.

"Let's just see how they fit. Once you get one on, come on out, and we'll have a look in the big mirror for all of us to see."

Eloise shut the curtain to the dressing room where she threw off her clothes and stepped into the green silk dress whose diaphanous material seemed to melt on her skin. She struggled to get it over her shoulders and then had to tug on the zipper. She called to Mrs. Peters for help. The sales woman entered and yanked at the zipper, pulling the dress roughly this way and that with many frustrated grunts. Once zipped, it hugged over Eloise's hips and breasts like the skin of a lizard, desperate to be shed.

"You haven't put on a little weight, have you, honey child?"

Eloise froze. *Is she saying I'm fat?* The thought nearly paralyzed her. "No, ma'am, I don't think so." Her voice shook, and her mind raced.

"Well, these dresses sometimes run a bit small. Don't you worry your pretty little head. Let me get the 6 and 8 to see how those might work."

Size 8! Impossible!

As it turned out, size 8 in all the dresses glided over Eloise's form without the slightest tug. While she glared at her reflection in each gown, her heart fluttered with worry. She'd had these cravings recently and, not being one to deprive herself, she had indulged in a couple of scoops ice cream and a few too many Oreos—her favorite cookie. Yesterday, she emptied the entire box and then tore it up in tiny bits so Mama wouldn't find it. Dear God, maybe she had gained a few pounds. She would start a starvation diet immediately. She didn't want to look like Twiggy, but to get fat, like Rhonda Sue Hawkins, no way! That would be the end. She vowed to start her diet that moment. She could live without food. It was possible.

An hour later, she and her mother selected the green silk dress, and they purchased a pair of matching pumps. Mrs. Peters packaged everything in a beautiful crimson bag, tying it all up with a gold ribbon.

"Let's stop in to see Sarah before we go home. I'm sure she'd love to see your new dress," Mama said as they walked out of the store.

Eloise moaned. "Why must we always go to Sarah's when we come downtown? I need to get home." Her boyfriend was supposed to call and anyway, she wanted to get on the scales, like, immediately.

Her mother unlocked the car door, got in, and turned to face her. "Sometimes you can be a very thoughtless young girl. Your sister is working her way through school and never had a chance to go to the prom, unlike you—"

"That's 'cause nobody asked her," Eloise butted in.

Her mother sighed. "Boys are not as important to Sarah as they are to you. She has other interests."

"Are you saying she doesn't like boys?"

Mama's eyes widened. "I'm saying no such thing. I'm just saying she's busy with other things—things that—let's not bring all that up again." She paused. "The least we can do is pay her a visit now and again. So don't give me a long face."

When Daddy started having financial problems, Sarah left home in a huff. She landed a job in an accounting office as a file clerk to earn enough money to pay for classes at Georgia State where she insisted on going no matter what anyone said to her.

Daddy had a hissy-fit, yelling, "No girl in my family ever worked."

Of course, no girl in the Jennings family had ever gone to college either. Sarah fought back, saying she wanted to go to college even if it meant paying every dime of it on her own. The fights ended in a standoff with Mama trying to make peace.

Eloise crossed her arms across her chest and expelled a long sigh. "Okay, but promise we won't stay long. I've got things to do." She shifted herself to face the outside window and watched the cars whiz by. Her stomach growled. Lord, no way she was hungry again.

Sarah lived in a tiny one-bedroom apartment within walking distance of Georgia State College. Mama pulled the car into a parking place nearby. Sarah's yellow Camaro sat under a tree farther down the street. How could her sister abide this hole? The only redeeming feature was a huge sycamore spreading a wide swath of shade over the building, and on this spring day it burst with bright green leaves. A few sad jonquils peeked out from the base of the tree.

Sarah greeted them in baggy shorts and a long-sleeved oversized blue shirt that brought out the soft color of her eyes. She had looped her hair back in a ponytail and wore not a smidgen of makeup. Eloise wouldn't be caught dead looking like that.

"Hope we're not interrupting," Mama said after hugging her.

"Not a bit. I'm snowed under with studying and could use a break. Exams start Monday. Come on in." Sarah moved from the door. "I just made up some iced tea, and the lady next door baked some brownies for me. She seems to think I need taking care of." She laughed, but her eyes darted, as if she'd said something wrong.

"We brought you a few fresh apples that I picked up at the market today, and Eloise wanted to show you the pretty dress she got at JP Allen's for the prom."

Sarah smiled, taking the apples. "Thanks." She turned to Eloise. "So, who's the lucky guy this time?"

"Jerry asked me at the first of the year. I don't like any of the boys in school. They're such babies. But Jerry is polite and cute enough. It'll be fun 'cause I'm homecoming queen this year." She spread out the dress on Sarah's small couch.

"Oh, my, the material is amazing—so soft. Whoa, and low-cut." Sarah grinned at her. "I bet you look like a million bucks in this."

"She does," Mama said. "Now tell us about school and how you're doing. Your father is very worried about you living out here all by yourself."

Sarah poured iced tea into three unmatching glasses—one tall and thin, another short and fat and a third tall and fat. "I'm working for a financial firm on the weekends. If I stay there, they promised to hire me when I'm finished with school."

"That's marvelous. Which firm?" Mama asked, acting really interested. Eloise couldn't care less about all this, but she was trying hard to concentrate on what they were saying instead of the plate of brownies wafting with a divinely sweet smell.

She sipped the tea and focused on the poster hanging behind Sarah's couch. It depicted Audrey Hepburn—Sarah's favorite actress—and Cary Grant riding in a convertible along the Amalfi Coast. *Someday that'll be me.*

"It's called Financial Advisors, Inc. and they're owned by one of my teachers at Georgia State. When I spread the word that I was looking for an internship, he got the job for me."

Mama shook her head, "I hate that—"

"Don't say it, Mama," Sarah cut in. "You know I have to do this. In times like this, we can't be proud. We have to do what we have to do. Daddy's friend, the one I helped with his investments—remember? Mr. Carmichael, from the law firm downtown, promised to be my first client. It's all gonna be fine, you'll see. You and Daddy don't have to worry about me, especially if Daddy sends more of his friends to me." She laughed again, but it came out as a nervous trickle.

"Who is this teacher of yours?" Eloise asked, forcing herself back into the conversation. "Is he someone special?"

Sarah shook her head. "I really don't have time for someone special. My teacher simply thinks I work hard and would be an asset to his firm. He's about twenty years older than me and married, if that helps clarify things for you, El."

Eloise frowned. How could Sarah stand not having a guy around, living alone like she did in this tiny place with just one window? It wasn't natural.

She glanced toward the kitchen and wondered how her sister could cook in that nothing of a kitchen barely bigger than her closet on

Briardale Lane. Of course, Sarah never cared anything about food, either cooking or eating. And, look at her—ridiculous clothes and no makeup. No wonder the boys don't give her a second look.

She crossed her legs, admiring her slender ankle but wishing her calves weren't quite so skinny. She'd seen big fat girls who still had toothpick legs as if all the fat stopped at the knees—Humpty Dumpty girls. *Why can't my weight gain go to my calves instead of my hips?*

"We simply want you to be happy, Sarah," Mama said, patting Sarah's knee. "You know your father saved enough for us to manage until you girls get married."

"I don't have to get married to manage," Sarah said. "That's the point. Don't you see? Here you are depending on Daddy, and now he's lost the business. I can't afford to depend on someone like that."

"Your father has always provided for us," Mama said without looking at either of them.

Sarah drank tea and turned back to Eloise's dress. "I love this color. What is it called, emerald?"

"Mrs. Peter's said they call it moss green. She said I'll be the only one there wearing this shade because it's the newest thing, right out of New York."

"She tried on a pale yellow, too, that looked wonderful with her hair, but this one fit the best," Mama said, rubbing Eloise's shoulder. Mama's eyes told her she approved of her. Unlike Sarah, she wasn't running around town telling everyone they were poor.

"I'm sure you looked amazing in all of them. Be sure to take lots of photos," Sarah said.

Eloise knew her sister couldn't care less.

With the conversation now on Eloise and the prom and no longer on Sarah and her work, the tension in the room lifted.

They left fifteen minutes later after she had finally succumbed to the temptation of the brownies, wolfing down two.

As they approached Briardale Lane, canopied by large oaks, her shoulders sagged with relief. Being around her older sister caused her heart to race and her stomach to tighten. Sarah always looked at her as if she were an idiot with nothing better to do than sit in front of her vanity mirror and pick at her pimples. No matter how well she performed in school, Sarah shrugged it off as if it were a trifle. She was the head of the cheerleading squad and even though Sarah had never even made the tryouts, being head cheerleader rated nothing to her sister. What's more, Sarah kept reminding the family they were in financial ruin. This was something Eloise preferred to forget, and she certainly didn't want it broadcast to her friends.

Last week Suzanne asked her in front of everyone, "So, what's your daddy doing now that he's unemployed?"

The heat rose to her face both from embarrassment and from anger. She held back the urge to punch Suzanne in her pretty little mouth and watch her perfect teeth—which she knew were perfect because she wore braces in the third grade—pop out, one by one. Instead, she muttered something about retiring early—something she'd heard Daddy say to Mama, and then she had swished away with her entourage close on her heels.

What did Suzanne's or Sarah's opinion matter anyway? *I've got things neither of them have—a beautiful prom dress and I'm the homecoming queen. Suzanne won't ride at the top of the float in the queen's seat. I will. Sarah, on the other hand, will be working for a bunch of stuffy accountants. Ha!*

She bounded from the car and raced to her room upstairs. She tore off every stitch of her clothes and ran into the bathroom to get on the scale, naked. She preferred to weigh first thing in the morning, but she hadn't done that in a while. The scale registered ten extra pounds. *Oh, my Lord, ten pounds!*

Her head throbbed. She had weighed two weeks ago after her date with Jonathan, who had fondled her breasts and moved his hand to her tummy which felt more rounded when she tried to pull it in. She remembered because she had run upstairs and jumped on the scale and seen she'd gained three pounds, but that had not alarmed her. Ten pounds, on the other hand, and in two weeks. Now that was serious.

Slowly, she stepped off the scale and back on again. If she did it bit by bit, holding onto the wall until the last second, sometimes it registered less. The needle bounced from 118 to 120 and finally stopped on 119. Nine pounds. She couldn't deny it.

Fear gripped her heart. Why was she having cravings? Why was she hungry all the time? She knew the answer to these questions but couldn't believe it. This kind of thing happened to the slimy girls, the ones who lived in South Dekalb or to someone like Judy Clarke, whom everyone knew slept with anything in pants. Not to someone like Eloise Jennings, the most likely to succeed and the most popular girl in the school. She clawed at her tummy leaving deep scratch marks.

"No!" she screamed.

"Eloise," her mother called from the bottom of the stairs. "You all right, sweetie? I thought I heard you call."

"I'm fine, Mama." She put on a loosely-fitting dress and her favorite record, Beethoven's *Ode to Joy*.

Her friends listened to the Beatles and the Beach Boys ...but she preferred the relaxing melodies of the classics.

She flopped onto the bed and allowed the music to seep into her soul. She tried to remember when she'd had her last period. Two months ago. Normally, she wasn't very good at keeping track. She remembered though because she wanted to go to the movies with Valerie Lewis, but she had been doubled up with cramps that day and decided to stay home. Last month she didn't have a period. But that wasn't too unusual. Skipping two months in a row, however, was serious. Maybe her period would start soon. She would wait, and in the meantime, not tell a soul.

When the phone rang, she grabbed it.

Chapter Sixteen

Eloise bent over the commode and vomited her guts out. This had been going on for the last two weeks during which her period had not come. Last night, she dreamed she had retched up the creature inside her, spat it out, and flushed it away. She held onto the edge of the toilet seat and vomited some more. Nothing came out except some grey slimy bile smelling like rotten eggs. She reached for the washcloth on the sink and wiped her face. Bloodshot eyes stared back at her, deep creases marred her forehead, and her cheeks looked sunken. She could no longer deny her predicament.

Later that afternoon during cheerleading practice she cornered Molly.

"I need to talk to you alone. Can you meet right after practice?"

Molly's big brown eyes widened with curiosity. "Me?" she said with almost breathless enthusiasm.

Eloise wiped a stream of sweat from her forehead, overheated from the practice. At this time of year they worked with new recruits, trying to teach them the moves. No one seemed able to do a decent back jump. She demonstrated how to do it over and over until she thought she would scream. Her back ached and her feet burned.

"Yes, you. Can you?"

Molly tossed her head in a move Eloise recognized as one of her own, particularly now that the silly girl had copied Eloise's new haircut. She, too, had blond hair, but it was thin and wispy, not thick and luxurious like her own. Lately, though, she had noticed handfuls of hair coming out.

Is losing my hair another thing that's going to happen to my body? Dear God, no!

"I'm supposed to meet Robert at the Varsity after we're done here, but I didn't tell him when," Molly said.

"Great."

An hour later, they strolled along the school track. It wasn't a hot day, but after that taxing drill, rays from the sun pressed heavily against Eloise's head, causing sweat to seep down her blouse.

"I have a secret that you must not tell a soul."

"Oh my God, you can trust me. You know you can. I promise I won't tell anyone."

"I need more than promises. Let me put it this way. If you do tell, I'll show Robert that gushy letter you wrote Jerry at the first of the year, remember?"

"You wouldn't! Robert would break up with me for sure. He thinks I've never loved anyone but him. You have to promise you won't do that, El."

"I said if you tell my secret, I'll show him. If you don't, you have nothing to worry about."

Molly expelled a sigh. "Good, 'cause I'd never tell your secret. Never. I cross my heart." And, she did so.

The poor girl mimicked her like a pet monkey. She took the same classes, wore the same clothes, and never disagreed with anything she said. No question. Molly would hold her secret till death.

A car honked around the corner and kid's voices sounded in the distance near the front of the school.

"This isn't about me. It's about my sister." Eloise lied easily, never having had trouble lying and not understanding why some people found it difficult. All she did was pretend she was acting. She dreamed of becoming an actress someday, maybe like Sandra Dee, who most people told her she resembled. "She's gotten herself in a bit of a jam."

"What kind of jam?" Molly's big eyes couldn't get much bigger.

She lowered her voice even though there wasn't a single soul within fifty feet of them. "She thinks she's pregnant."

Molly stopped walking. "Sarah! Holy Cow! Who would have thought? She's so, you know—"

"Yeah, I know. Apparently there's some teacher at her school. She goes to Georgia State now. I think he's married or whatever. Anyway, she needs to—" She lowered her voice even more.

Molly moved in close enough for her to smell her sweat. "She wants to get rid of it."

"An abortion?" Molly whispered. She pressed her books close to her chest.

"That's right. And, I'm telling you because I promised Sarah I'd ask you as long as you kept your mouth shut. We thought your daddy might know what to do, him being an ob doctor and all."

"But, it's illegal," Molly said as if Eloise didn't know that.

"People do it all the time, Molly. Don't be such a baby. Your daddy will know who I—uh, I mean Sarah can contact. He just needs to give us a name."

"How will I ask him? He might think—"

"I've thought about that. Tell him you're writing a paper for Miss Welch's class in English on the pros and cons of legalizing abortion. Then, you can ask him if there's someone you can interview for the paper, you know, someone who might be performing abortions. Beg him as I'm sure you know how to do. Tell him if you talked to a real abortionist, you'd surely get an A and impress the teacher. If that doesn't work, let me know. We'll think of something else."

Molly bit her lower lip and shook her head. "Couldn't I just say a friend wants to know?"

"No, you couldn't. He'd think it was you, or worse still, he might make you tell him who, and you can't do that, remember? You promised on pain of that letter to Jerry."

"Yeah, sure, and you're probably right."

"You need to ask him soon. Sarah thinks she might be two months pregnant, and she wants this taken care of like yesterday. She's already got symptoms—you know, throwing up and stuff like that."

"Really? Gosh, how horrible." After a pause, Molly asked, "Do your parents know?"

"My God! Of course they don't know. She hasn't told a soul, just me. And now I'm telling you."

Molly lifted her shoulders high, preening like a peacock, upon hearing the lofty company she was in. "I'll ask him tonight."

At 9:30 p.m. Molly called Eloise.

"It was so easy. He said he thinks abortions should be legalized. In fact, he thinks that would save the lives of a number of innocent girls. I've never seen him so worked up. Anyway, he gave me a strict lecture on how innocent babies shouldn't suffer because young people can't control themselves. He turned all red when he said that. Then he told me he had a colleague that agreed with him but did quiet abortions. You know, just for certain people, and all. He's a real doctor, not some fly-by-night butcher. Those were Daddy's words. Anyway, tell Sarah his name is Dr. Willard North, and he's in the phone book. But, El, we have one problem."

Eloise lifted the phone book and began searching for the name. "What's that?"

"He wants to read my paper."

She laughed. "Guess you'll have to write it."

When she hung up the phone, she wrote down Dr. North's address and telephone number.

* * * *

The next night, she and Jonathan went to see *Butch Cassidy and the Sundance Kid.* She adored Paul Newman and couldn't wait to see this film. Jonathan agreed to take her even though he would have preferred going to the new 007 movie. She had seen about as much of James Bond as she cared to—all those girls in skimpy bikinis. No wonder Jonathan couldn't keep his hands off her, and she was in this fix.

Not that this film didn't have its moments. Her gaze followed the silhouette of Paul Newman in bed with a young, beautiful woman. Flashes of the girl's naked back and leg, accented with warm, sensuous music, titillated the imagination.

Jonathan wrapped his rough, clammy fingers around her hand. Newman gazed into the eyes of the beautiful brunette with pointy breasts while Jonathan started to rub her arm. His fingers moved around her wrist and up to her elbow. A chill traveled up her back as his hand crept higher along her arm. She stiffened, released his hand, and folded her arms across her chest.

"What's wrong?" Jonathan asked.

She shifted away. "Nothing. I'm freezing."

He wrapped his arm around her and tugged her closer while Newman lured the brunette back to his bed and planted kisses on her lips and neck. The muscles across the actor's back flexed, and the music blared louder.

After the movie, they went to the Varsity—a hamburger joint within walking distance of the Georgia Institute of Technology and a student hangout—for a Coke and some fries. Jonathan slid in the booth next to her and studied her as if she were a painting on exhibit.

"I'm really gonna miss you," he said.

"Let's not talk about that tonight."

Jonathan had been drafted and was leaving for active duty in a week. He would probably be on his way to Vietnam before the end of the year.

"You'll look mighty good in a uniform," she'd said to him when he'd told her he'd been drafted.

That was the night they'd gone all the way for the first time. She held on to him as if she would never see him again. They had done it several times since then and each time had been better than the last. She didn't try to stop Jonathan when he touched her because it felt too darn good. Not that she loved him or anything like that. She liked him and enjoyed her friend's envious stares.

Jonathan was twenty one, went to Georgia Tech, and had the nicest body she had ever seen—all muscles. His blond hair hung over large, round blue eyes with a haze of thick lashes. He wore glasses but that only made him seem mysterious, like Clark Kent. Remove the glasses and poof, Superman appeared.

He told her he wanted to be an industrial engineer. With the war looming in his future, he would be lucky to finish college. She couldn't tell him about her predicament not with him worrying about fighting the Viet Cong in a swamp full of mosquitoes. She had not actually planned to tell him or anything, but the thought had occurred to her now and then.

A band of sweat glistened his upper lip. A few whiskers jutted out from his neckline. He reached up and moved the hair off her face. "I want to remember this moment." His breath held the slight odor of tobacco.

"My gosh! Don't be so gloomy. You'll be back before we know it, and probably after having had several slanty-eyed girls along the way." She paused and looked around. "I'd give anything for a beer."

She hated losing him but knew once he went away, he would never be back. They would both move on.

He laughed. "Not here, my sweet. I've got a few in my car, though." His eyes ran to her chest and lingered there.

The noise in the diner buzzed in her ears, and the smell of burnt grease turned her stomach. She wiggled away from him.

"What's with you tonight?" he asked. "You're acting all weird on me."

She poked around at the fries swimming in a pool of red Ketchup. "It's just, well—" She took a deep breath.

"What?"

She shook her head. "Nothing."

He touched her hand. "I want you." The heat from his words nearly fogged his glasses. Her body tingled in response. *If I'm pregnant, could I get pregnant again if I did it again? Maybe I'd have twins.* She laughed inside at the silly thought. Jonathan pulled her close again, reacting to her unspoken response.

David Irving, a friend of Jonathan's, approached their table. David was one of the few Jewish boys at school. He had thick, dark, wavy hair and tanned skin. His rugged handsomeness drove the girls crazy. But he didn't hold a candle to Jonathan. Tonight, he clutched Diane Smother's hand while she rubbed her body all over his like a cat in heat. "Did y'all just come from the Butch Cassidy movie?" David asked, wrapping Diane's arm around his back and pulling her closer to him all the while staring at Eloise.

"Yeah," Jonathan said, grabbing Eloise's knee under the table and squeezing.

Diane eyed Jonathan as if she could eat him alive. She had graduated last year and was now on the prowl for a husband. "Us, too," she said. "I think Paul Newman is the handsomest man alive." She giggled in a way that made Eloise wonder if she were high on something.

"Where are y'all going from here?" David asked. His gaze penetrated Eloise's blouse.

Eat your heart out. You'll never touch my precious puppies.

Diane reached around him and pulled his head close to hers as if nuzzling a pillow and planted a kiss on his cheek.

"Don't know yet," Jonathan said, shifting in his seat.

"We're going to a party at Jeff Farley's house. Why don't y'all come, too? Everybody'll be there. His parents are out of town."

Jonathan shrugged. "Maybe." He shot David some sort of male message.

David nodded and winked at Eloise. "See ya," he said.

The couple walked out the door so closely entwined they looked like a four-legged monster.

Eloise shifted on the hot plastic seat. The harsh light in the restaurant pierced right through her. She eased closer to Jonathan, wanting to feel the heat of his skin against hers.

"Let's get out of here," he said, reading her thoughts.

They walked the few blocks to Jonathan's red convertible Mustang. The spring sky was black, sprinkled with a few bright stars. The trace of moonlight from the slice of moon was overshadowed by the glare of streetlights. Bugs flew around the lights like happy partygoers. Sounds of car horns tooting and tires screeching filled their ears.

As soon as they settled in his car, he groped for her, pulling her close to him and planting kisses on her lips with as much passion as Newman had done with that brunette in the movie. A faint taste of Ketchup lingered on his tongue. When she parted her lips, he took that as an invitation and pressed against her harder. The windshield clouded with fog. He slowly pulled at her blouse, one small portion at a time. Finally, cool fingers touched her skin, sending a shiver down her spine.

"You're driving me nuts," he panted, and firmly pressed against her, grappling under her blouse.

"Wait," she said. "Take me somewhere dark. The streetlights here are too bright."

As they rode in silence, she relaxed under the crook of his arm, listening to his breath and watching his muscles flex when he maneuvered the steering wheel. The radio hummed with Motown music —The Swinging Medallions singing, *Double Shot*. People milled around on the streets. A group of tourists passed, looking around at everything as if they had never seen a skyline.

He drove until he found a quiet, residential neighborhood where outside lights illuminated large porches and walkways. The traffic sounds faded to a quiet buzz, replaced by the howls of dogs and the occasional scream of a catfight. Jonathan stopped the car at the end of a small, wooded cul-de-sac, facing one dark house. When he switched off the head beams, everything turned black except for the whisper moonlight.

They fell on one another like starving wolves on raw meat, oblivious to the cramped conditions in the car.

Afterward, they both lit up cigarettes. She caressed his broad chest, wondering if she would ever find a man this good again. Maybe she did love him after all.

Jonathan popped open a beer and gave it to her. Although lukewarm, it tasted wonderful.

"You're in a strange mood tonight," he said, his thumb making circles around her nipple and arousing her once again.

"Am I?" She pushed away his hand and swallowed more beer. Then, she began to slip into her clothes.

He sat up. "It's like we were making love for the last time. I don't leave for another two weeks. There's plenty of time between now and then." His grin looked ravenous.

"I don't think so."

"What's that supposed to mean?"

She finished buttoning her blouse. "Just what I said. We ought to quit while we're ahead. I'm not the kind of girl who likes good-byes. And, I'm really not the kind of girl who'll sit home, knitting sweaters while waiting for you to return."

He'd pulled on his clothes without looking at her. "So, this is it, then?"

She puffed on the cigarette, tossed the beer can out the window, and fluffed her hair. "It's been great, but yeah, this is it."

Twenty minutes later, she was back in her bedroom.

Jonathan didn't seem heartbroken. Perhaps he'd been relieved. Two people as beautiful as they were couldn't possibly live together. She would fight him for attention and vice versa. It would have been hopeless. Tears sprang to her eyes.

She would never see him in uniform.

Chapter Seventeen

The bus ride downtown took Eloise along the same road where Sarah lived, but she didn't stop for a visit. When they passed Sarah's apartment, she looked the other way and glared out the window, the more important immediate task pressing on her mind. She had one more week before the prom, and her dress already fit too snugly. She couldn't believe she was getting so fat. Even though she tried not to eat anything, her body craved food all the time. The creature inside her was like a ravenous parasite.

Sometimes she wished she had told Jonathan. She longed to talk to someone about all this. She feared, however, that he would get all sappy on her and want to get married or something horrid like that. One thing she knew for sure was she didn't want to marry anyone right now and Jonathan in particular, especially after the cavalier way he let her disappear from his life. What a jerk.

Her reflection in the window caught her eye. Her widely set eyes and even features stared back at her with a new kind of determination. She sat up straighter. She could do this. She would take care of this problem, and no one need ever find out.

Imagining talking to this doctor about getting rid of the creature made her stomach flutter. What would he think of her? *He'll think I'm Sally Smith. You dodo bird you!*

Right after Molly had given her Dr. North's name, she'd made an appointment under a fictitious name. She'd withdrawn all the money out of her savings account. If all went according to plan, she could do this without anyone ever finding out.

The bus drew to a stop and she descended, winking at the two young men she passed on the way out. She may be fat, but she hadn't totally lost it.

The sky had turned dark and the wind kicked up, blowing dust and debris in her face. She wished she had thought to bring an umbrella. Spring storms popped up nearly every afternoon. *Maybe I'll get lucky and the rain will hold off until I get home.*

She peered at the numbers on the buildings until she reached a tall, brick structure sitting back from the street and matching the number she had written down. The outdoor marquis listed several doctors' names including Dr. Willard North.

What kind of a name was Willard? She imagined a short, balding man with thick glasses, wearing a long white coat dragging the floor. He had probably never had a passionate day in his life. She smiled, trusting her ability to cajole Dr. Willard North to do whatever she wanted.

The elevator swished her up to the top floor along with two other women, both rather advanced in their pregnancy. She stopped in the lady's room to reapply lipstick and comb her windblown hair before entering through glass doors to find a waiting area choked with people. She walked up to the desk and signed in. A gray-haired receptionist with a kind smile handed her a form to complete.

Eloise took the form and sat down between a woman with two toddlers—both marking up coloring books—and one lone man. On the form, she created a fictitious address to go with her false name, but she put her actual telephone number in case the doctor needed to get in touch with her. She figured if Mama or Daddy answered the phone, they would think the caller had the wrong number. After all, they would ask to speak with Sally Smith.

Twenty minutes later, Sally Smith sat in the examining room with nothing on but a sheet and another fresh coat of pink lipstick, awaiting the doctor.

Her eyes widened in shock when in walked Dr. Kildare, or a very close resemblance to the handsome TV doctor. She stifled a gasp. The palms of her hands oozed sweat. Her hormones kicked in with such force, she nearly swooned.

"Good afternoon, Miss Smith," he said with a clipboard in his hand and a voice to match his looks.

A nurse stood behind him and from the half-smile on her face she was equally enthralled with the handsome Dr. North.

"My name is Will North."

Will, of course. So much better than Willard!

He reached for her hand and gave it a light shake as his eyes raked over her.

Dear God! She couldn't possibly drop the sheet in front of this man, not without several passionate kisses and a few beers.

He glanced down at the form she had completed. "It says here you're eighteen and in need of a routine pelvic exam?"

"Um, I'm not sure." She cleared her throat and crossed her legs under the protective sheet. "I thought we might talk a bit first."

He raised his brows. "Talk?"

Eloise took a deep breath to gather herself. Sitting naked across from such a man was a new and not altogether pleasant experience. "You see. I'm pregnant, and I'm not sure I want to be or am ready to be, you know, a mom."

He sat down on a little stool in front of her, his eyes meeting hers. "Perhaps you should have thought about that before you engaged in sexual intercourse." His deep soothing voice seemed to roll over the word *sexual.*

"Yes, I'm sure that's true. But, you see, I didn't and now I have this problem." She shifted under his intense gaze. Sweat ran down her knee.

"I take it you're not married?"

She shook her head.

"Does the father of this baby know you do not wish to carry it to term?"

I wish he wouldn't call the creature a baby.

"He knows nothing about my condition. He's about to leave for Vietnam."

"Miss Smith, abortions are illegal in this state and in all the states in this country as far as I know." He moved over to the sink and began to wash his hands. "Let's just have a look to see how far along you are and what's going on."

The nurse moved behind him to gather the instruments for the exam.

She gripped the sheet. "No! I want to talk first. See what options I have."

He turned his perfect profile away from her. "Options? I'm not sure what you expected when you came here, but perhaps talking is a good idea." He paused and sat down again in front of her.

The nurse remained standing behind his chair.

"When did you have your last period?"

Talking about periods to this man was like talking about sex to a priest. She bit her lip and looked away from his face. "I think I've missed two months."

"And that's unusual for you?"

She nodded. "I've had other symptoms—I'm sick every morning and well, I've gained some weight." Instinctively she sucked in her tummy.

"Okay, so you're probably about two months pregnant. As far as abortions go, you're in the early stages, and that's good. If you wait too long, it's not only harder, but less likely you'll find someone willing to perform it—"

"Can you do it for me?" She jumped in.

He shook his head. "I do not make it a practice to perform abortions. I've done them on very rare occasions when a young woman has been raped, for example. I don't see you in a situation like that, correct?" He raised one eyebrow.

"I wasn't exactly completely willing," she began. "If that's what you mean, but to say I was raped might be stretching the truth."

"What do you mean you weren't completely willing?"

She smiled shyly at him. "The boy is older than me and he was rather pushy, anxious actually. It was my first time in that kind of situation." She swallowed. "And I wasn't sure how to handle it. I don't think you could say he raped me. But, I was totally shocked by it all and inexperienced." Her voice cracked on the last word. She glanced down at her hands, which still clutched the sheet.

"I see."

But she suspected he didn't and wasn't sure she would have believed herself.

She sniffled and forced a tear to trickle down her cheek. "I don't know what to do now."

"Have you talked with your parents?"

"God, no!"

He smiled as if he pitied her. She hated the smug look on his handsome face.

"I'm sure your parents would not kill you if they learned of your predicament, particularly if you explain what happened—being inexperienced as you say. They may be less forgiving if something happened to their grandchild."

Grandchild!

"But, you don't understand. It's not my parent's decision. It's mine. I don't want to do this. I'm not ready for such a life-changing event. I'm hardly out of high school."

He smiled again that awful smirk-like smile. "Miss Smith, I know it's hard for you to think about, but you are carrying a new life, a little baby. Ending it because you're not ready to be a mother hardly justifies the action." He shook his head. "I wish I could help you, but I don't think I can. What I could do is perform an exam to make sure everything is going well. Young women like yourself are high risks for miscarriage. Furthermore, for all you know, you might not be pregnant. Without an exam, we can't say for sure."

She didn't answer, her mind a jumble of thoughts.

"My suggestion," he continued, "is that you talk to your parents. There may be another solution. Perhaps someone would like to adopt your baby—"

"But I'd have to get big and actually have it," she nearly shrieked. *Fat! Ugly, swollen, hair loss!*

"That's how it works. Now, if you don't want me to examine you— and I'd be glad to do so—I must get on with my other patients."

Eloise lifted her eyes to him. Why couldn't she make him see? She practically whispered, "Is there someone else you might recommend— someone who does this sort of thing in less disparate circumstances?"

His frown deepened. "I'm sorry. I really can't help you. I wish you the best of luck." And with that he swished out the door with the nurse close behind.

She put on her clothes with trembling hands. Anger boiled inside her, anger at herself, at Jonathan and at Dr. Willard North.

On her way home, she stopped at the Varsity to gather her thoughts. Naturally, she was starving.

As she nibbled on a sandwich, a dark-haired boy blatantly ogled her from a stool at the counter. When she gave him the onceover, he grinned, a nice smile with beautiful even teeth and dimples. He wore a tie and short-sleeved shirt revealing healthy biceps.

The next time she looked his way, he moved over to her booth.

"What's a girl like you doing here all alone?"

She studied him from under her long lashes. "Just having a late lunch, that's all."

"Can I sit with you a minute?"

She shrugged.

He eased into the booth across from her.

"My name's Malcolm Knox," he told her. "I'm an engineer with the city. And you're much too beautiful to be having lunch all alone on a glorious spring afternoon like this."

She grinned and sipped Coke through a straw. "That's an awfully nice thing to say, Mr. Knox," she said, not offering her name.

"Please, call me Malcolm." He waited. When she didn't answer he continued. "I like to come here for ol'times sake."

"Ol'times?"

"Yeah. I graduated from Tech in '66. And you?"

She caved in to his charm, told him her name, and added she was a senior at Dexter.

"Just a baby," he said with a grin.

Great smile. A warm tingle traveled through her body.

Eloise raised an eyebrow at him, enjoying his musky smell. "Not as much of a baby as you might think."

"Any plans for college?" he asked her.

She nibbled on potato chip. "I want to be an actress or a model. Maybe I'll head out to California when I graduate."

Yeah, right. Not unless I can do something about that creature growing in my belly.

"That would be a great loss for Atlanta, but you sure have the looks to do whatever you want."

"Flattery will get you everywhere," she said with a lift to her voice, settling in to learn more about him. This young man was pulling her out of the gloomy mood she'd been in.

Malcolm grew up in Atlanta, but spent most of his life in town and knew little about Decatur where Eloise lived. He had enlisted in the National Guard to avoid being sent to Vietnam and went through basic training after he finished college. Last year he had an opportunity to spend two weeks in Germany. "That's about as far from Atlanta as I've been," he told her. "But, I must say it was a great experience. I definitely want to go back someday when I'm not in the military."

"I've never been anywhere," she said.

"Sounds as if you have big dreams, though—California and all."

"Yeah, well, maybe dreams are what I have, nothing more." She took a giant bite into the sandwich to avoid more talk about California.

Malcolm winked at her. "Dreams are the beginning. Give it some time."

Before long the last potato chip was gone, and it was time for her to head home.

"Can I call you?" he asked, while she gathered her purse and he paid her check.

"Sure thing. I'm in the phone book. The only Jennings on Briardale Lane."

"I'll find it."

That evening, Malcolm called and invited her to dinner for the next night. She was supposed to go to a party with Rhonda Sue and the crowd, but decided a dose of Malcolm was exactly what she needed right now.

* * * *

The next morning, she was doubled up over the commode again. When she lifted her head, her mother stood in the doorway, hands firmly on hips.

"What's going on, Eloise?"

She clutched her tummy. "I've got some sort of stomach ache. I think I ate something bad last night."

Mama walked in and shut the bathroom door. "I've heard you in here for several weeks now. Every morning. At first I thought you might be a little sick, but it kept up. I don't want to believe what I'm thinking. Tell me I'm wrong."

Eloise rinsed out her mouth with Listerine and spit it in the sink. Then she faced her mother. "I have no idea what you're talking about, Mama. I guess I've had this virus for a while and—"

"Don't lie to me, Eloise. I'm no fool. Even though sometimes I act like an idiot when it comes to you. Sarah was so easy. I trusted you to be careful."

"But Sarah didn't have any opportunities—"

"She's more sensible about everything, opportunities or not." Mama paused and watched her with eyes that seemed to penetrate her skin.

"Okay, you may as well know. I think I'm pregnant. I don't know for sure, but I've missed two periods."

Her mother put her hand to her throat and let out a small groan. "As I feared. What are we going to say to your father?"

"Is that all you can think about? Don't you care about what it will do to me? I'm already twelve pounds overweight. I hate this thing inside me and want to get rid of it."

A deep frown creased Mama's brow. "I can't believe what I'm hearing. This thing, as you call it, is a baby. It's your baby. You may not be ready to be a mother, but as I see it, you have no choice. Of course, we'll help you. Don't we always? Meantime, I don't want to hear another word about getting rid of anything." She took a deep breath. "Now clean yourself up because you are going to be the one to tell your father."

Eloise stomped to her bedroom and slammed the door. If she could roll down an embankment or tumble out of an airplane and kill everything inside her, she would do it.

"Young girls like yourself are high risk for miscarriages," Dr. Kildare had said.

Please God, why not?

She put on a short skirt and a blouse, combed her hair out of her eyes, and marched down the stairs to face her father.

Chapter Eighteen

Daddy sat in the den with the *Atlanta Constitution* open in front of him. He glanced up when Eloise entered and smiled. "How's my precious daughter today?"

She plunked down across from him in the wingback chair next to the window where Granny used to knit. *This isn't going to be easy.*

"I need to tell you something," she began, looking at her hands and wishing she were any place else.

"What is it, honey?" He folded the paper and laid it beside his chair. "Boyfriend troubles?"

She shook her head. "Not exactly."

"Well, you know you can count on your ol' Dad for whatever you need."

She sucked in a deep breath. She'd endured that embarrassing visit to the doctor and now this face-to-face with her father. How much more could she stand? If only Dr. North had agreed to the abortion, she wouldn't have to confront her father like this.

"I'm in trouble."

He blinked and waited.

Mama walked into the room, collected some old newspapers, and then turned and walked out.

Eloise looked at her father's concerned face and whispered. "I think I might be pregnant."

"What, honey? I didn't quite hear what you said." He leaned closer to her, his eyes wide, the smell of tobacco on his breath.

"I'm pregnant, Daddy. That's what I said," she uttered in a loud voice. "Mama knows, but she made me tell you. I want to get rid of it, but Mama won't let me." Her voice cracked.

He stared at her without blinking. At first, she wasn't sure he understood what she had said. Then she saw the way his eyes dilated and his lip twitched. "Who's the boy?"

"What's that matter?" she said, shrugging. "We need to figure out what to do." She sat up straighter as if a weight had been lifted from her shoulders.

He got up, paced the floor, and then loomed to his full height over her chair. "Who is the boy?" he asked again, a whiff of his aftershave trailing in his wake.

She shrank down. She'd never been afraid of her father, who had never once in her life spanked her or even disciplined her—it'd always been Mama. But a spasm of fear ran down her spine as he stood over her with pinched features and fists clenching. "Daddy, it doesn't matter because he doesn't know anything about this. It's my problem, my mistake, not his." She leaned as far away from him as she could.

"I'll kill him. You're too young. I'll kill him."

She reached up to touch his arm, but he jerked away. Tears filled her eyes and started to flow down her cheeks.

"Please, Daddy. I'm so sorry. I didn't mean for this to happen." She sniffed and wiped her face on her arm.

"Of course you didn't. You're just a child. Who is he? I want to know his name right this minute. Tell me, Eloise."

What could she do? If she told him, he'd be on the telephone to Jonathan and God knows what would happen next. She hung her head. The ceiling fan squeaked.

"I really don't know."

"What?" he yelled.

Mama came into the room and stood beside Eloise. "Carl, there's no need to raise your voice like that. It's done. We have to accept it for what it is and move on."

"Did you hear what your daughter just told me?" he demanded in a voice she had never heard him use. "She said she doesn't even know who the father is. Our daughter has slept with so many boys she can't identify the father of her child, and she's only eighteen. Imagine her at twenty-five! What kind of world is this where young people can go off and do whatever they want without a care? Where are the rules you and I had to obey? Hippies in California live on the streets. No wonder our children are getting themselves in trouble." The veins in his neck throbbed.

Mama approached him to coax him back to the couch. "You're getting all worked up. Part of Eloise's punishment was to tell you. She needs to take responsibility for what she's done. But, I feel I had a part in this mess as well. I'm her mother, after all. I should have put more restrictions on her. We've been too lenient with her. We've let her run wild. We never did that with Sarah."

He yanked his arm from her grasp. "Sarah was different. She'd never have done this to us. You can blame yourself all you want, but the truth is Eloise did this to herself. She and some boy, whoever the bastard may be. She's no better than a whore."

Mama gasped. "Carl!" Then she took a deep breath and turned to Eloise. "You'd better leave this to me. You see how you've upset your father. All that crying won't make any of this go away. Go to your room, and I'll let you know what we plan to do next. Now go!"

"But, Mama, what about school. We're supposed to—"

"Forget about school. You're not going anywhere today."

She escaped up the stairs and threw herself on her bed. She cried and cried until her chest ached.

When the phone rang later that evening, her father barked into the mouthpiece, "Are you the one? You know perfectly well what I mean. My daughter won't be going out with anyone, not for a long time. And don't call back." He slammed down the receiver. New tears ran down Eloise's cheeks.

Her father hollered up the stairs, "And don't you even think about going to the prom. Your mother's going to take your dress back tomorrow."

"But, Daddy! You can't do that!" she shrieked. "I'll kill myself and this creature inside me! I will!"

That night she remained in her room. Her stomach growled, reminding her she had not eaten since the night before. But there was no way she was going downstairs where she would have to face her parents. *Maybe I can starve this creature out of me.*

She leaned outside her window where the sky blinked with stars. If she jumped off the roof, she might break a leg, but it would surely kill the creature. *Open the window. Do it now before you get scared.* Terror bubbled inside her.

She turned away and walked back to her desk where she found an old love letter from Jonathan. *You're the best. I want to be with you forever.* It sure didn't take long for forever to come and go. New tears tumbled down her cheeks. She hiccupped.

How could her life have crashed so fast? Less than a month earlier she had picked out her prom dress and the whole world loomed in front of her, full of promises. She tore Jonathan's letter into tiny pieces and tossed them over her head like confetti. One piece landed at her foot. She reached down. On it was one word—*love*. She ripped it in half twice.

From inside her desk drawer she withdrew a sterling dagger in a gilded sheath. Uncle Willis, her mother's youngest brother, who traveled the world, had found this knife in North Africa and sent it as a gift. Eloise snatched and hid it here years ago, not knowing what she would do with it but wanting it.

She pulled the dagger out of the sheath. It glistened in the sunlight. She lifted her shirt, placed the dagger point on her bare tummy, closed her eyes, and pushed on the knife. A sting ran through her body. *Do it! Cut the creature out, bit by bloody bit.* She held her breath and pushed harder. Blood spurted from her skin, sending a shiver up her back. She tossed the knife across the room. With her heart thundering and her palms sweating, she bandaged the wound.

The next day after school, she spotted Malcolm standing on the sidewalk near the elm trees. He leaned on a sleek red Thunderbird, looking like a movie star.

When she approached, he smiled and opened the door.

"What makes you think I'll go with you?" she said in a playful voice. Two of her friends flanked her like sentries.

"Just a hunch."

"Who's that?" Molly asked. "He's really cute, El."

"A friend I met the other day. Nobody special."

"What about Jonathan?" her friend said with wide eyes.

Eloise flipped her hair off her face. "I'm done with Jonathan."

Molly sucked in a breath. "Oh," she murmured.

"Are you gonna go with that boy or not?" Rhonda Sue asked. "Because if you're not, I just might." She elbowed Eloise in the ribs.

The car's interior was creamy leather. A wooden gearshift knob sat between the bucket seats. "Is this your car or your big brother's?" she asked, her hand caressing the back fender while her friends hung back and watched.

"I don't have a big brother."

Of course not. You're the big brother.

Rhonda Sue let out a long breath full of moans. Eloise shot her a get-lost look, and she hopped in the car.

Malcolm sauntered around to the driver's side and slid in next to her.

From the side mirror she glimpsed her friends standing on the street and looking as amazed as the Road Runner's Wile E. Coyote. Her heart fluttered. By this time tomorrow everyone in school would know that she had a new boyfriend who drove a car like the one on *Route 66* and looked like George Maharis. Malcolm had a knack for showing up at just the perfect moment.

"So, what's with your dad?" Malcolm asked.

She flinched at the reminder of yesterday's disaster. "Don't know what you mean."

"I called and he chewed me out."

She eased closer to him and rested her head on his shoulder. "He does that with all my new boyfriends."

* * * *

Three weeks later, Eloise ditched Jerry at the prom and snuck out the backdoor to meet Malcolm. She padded up to him in stocking feet with shoes in hand, wearing the beautiful, although snug, moss green dress. From the way Malcolm's eyes raked her body, the dress still showed off her every curve. She guessed this was going to be a memorable night.

Her daddy had calmed down after a few days. He wouldn't look at Eloise, and she couldn't engage him in conversation. Whenever she walked into a room, he got up and left.

"We may as well let Eloise enjoy the last few months of school before she graduates," Mama said, convincing him to let her go to the prom. "After that, we'll see."

He relented without too much of a fight, saying, "You decide about the prom. I'm done with her." All the fight seemed to have drained right out of him after that first day and the initial shock.

Mama had insisted on dragging her to Dr. Brigman, their family doctor, who looked everywhere except at Eloise when he confirmed she was pregnant. Even though he had cured her of everything from measles to poison ivy, he now treated her as if she were some sort of criminal. He gave Mama the name of an obstetrician. No one mentioned getting rid of the creature, not Mama, not Dr. Brigman, not Daddy.

Once she and Malcolm pulled out of the school parking lot, she reached for a cigarette and lit it.

"Where are we going?" she asked between puffs.

"I know a place under the stars that will make your hair shine like the moon."

She peered over at him. His long sideburns curled around his cheek and a few dark hairs escaped from the top of his shirt. They had kissed a few times, and she had hoped he might do more. The heat of his passion nearly burned through her clothes. After a bit, however, he had pushed her away. She wondered if he would maintain such restraint tonight.

The car meandered through the dark streets, heading south. They arrived at Piedmont Park where the city staged some of its largest outdoor concerts. This park hosted the World's Fair in the late 19th Century and later underwent improvements by the architects who had designed New York City's Central Park. Eloise had seen the Allman Brothers perform here last summer. On this evening the entrance to the park was lit up brighter than a birthday cake, and the beat of music traveled over the tall pines.

She removed her shoes, shimmied out of her pantyhose, and exited the car, walking barefoot alongside him.

Inside they joined a mob of people who were dancing to the music, kissing in the dark, and drinking from beer bottles.

Malcolm carried an armload of blankets and spread one down in a relatively isolated spot where they could hear the music but were hidden by darkness and the trees.

"I'll get us a couple of beers," he said.

She sprawled out on the blanket, arranging herself in a comfortable position and allowing the music to seep inside her. A gravelly singer crooned tunes that mimicked Bob Dylan. Normally she didn't care much for Dylan but tonight the words fit her mood. She lit another cigarette and stared at the bright stars peeking through the tree limbs.

Malcolm returned with two beers and stretched out next to her, pulling her close. "Are you cold?"

Her heart beat against his chest.

"No," she whispered. "I'm burning up."

His beer-flavored lips met hers and everything inside her exploded. Maybe this was love. She had never felt this much desire with Jonathan —lust maybe, but nothing like this. She groped for Malcolm's head, running her fingers through his thick curls and moaning. He pulled away and stared into her face.

"What do you want, little girl?" he said in a soft caressing voice.

"I think you know what I want," she said with a smile. "Take me, here, now, tonight."

He pulled the other blanket over them in a manner that made Eloise wonder if he had done this before and formed a makeshift private tent. His lovemaking to the sound of Dylan aroused her beyond what she imagined possible. She had never experienced such tenderness mixed with passion. Her heart swelled and her body opened up to this man.

Afterward, while Malcolm held her under the crook of his arm, she matched her breathing to his. Then she sat up, allowing the blanket to drop from her naked shoulder, and reached for a cigarette. Malcolm didn't smoke, but he never criticized her for doing so. While she lit up, she kept her eyes on his face, still full of hunger for her.

"What are you thinking?" he asked.

"I'm thinking about you. You're so good to me."

He took her hand in his and rubbed her palm with his thumb. "I've never felt about anyone the way I do about you, El. I didn't mean for us to do this so soon, but I'm not apologizing."

She tossed her hair back. He was such a gentleman. She couldn't believe it. "It was incredible. You're really great."

"No, I'm not. But, I'm in love. I want you with me all the time. I think about you constantly." He paused and took a breath. "I know we haven't known each other that long, but I know what I feel. I believe I felt it the first moment I saw you sitting all by yourself in that booth at the Varsity. So beautiful and so sad."

She studied his solemn features—large dark eyes, lush with lashes and overflowing with emotion. Then a flutter ran across her tummy, reminding her of the creature. She frowned.

"What's wrong?" he asked. "Are you okay?"

She blew smoke into the darkness and squeezed his hand tighter. "I'm just about as fine as any girl could be."

He pulled her close, crushed out her cigarette, and kissed her. A soft breeze stroked her bare skin. They made love again, this time more slowly. As he moved inside her, she smiled to herself as a new plan started to uncurl in her mind.

* * * *

Two months later, Eloise stood next to Malcolm before the minister at Glenwood Presbyterian Church. They spoke their vows before her parents and his father—his mother had refused to come, saying she was sick, but Eloise suspected otherwise. A quick marriage like this sparked all kinds of gossip. Sarah stood behind her, holding a small bouquet of lilies.

Her mother's sniffles and hiccups probably could be heard three streets away. Did they signal Mama's relief or sadness? Eloise couldn't say for sure, nor did she care.

Chapter Nineteen

Eloise woke up five months later after a grueling night of labor. Her mother sat in a chair opposite her. Click, click, click went the knitting needles. She had been knitting ever since she'd learned of Eloise's pregnancy. She must have created enough cute little things to keep the baby clothed in sweaters and toboggans for the rest of its life. One would think they lived in Alaska instead of Atlanta.

She took in the gloomy, gray room. Sun beamed through the industrial blinds. A radiator in the corner under the window rattled and gave off too much heat.

She tugged at the hospital gown that stuck to her sweaty skin and shifted her weight, shooting achy pains across her tender abdomen, as if an army had conducted a fierce battle inside. She slid her hand along the top of her tummy. Although no longer swollen like a watermelon, it continued to bulge. She would never regain the beautiful flat belly she once had. The creature had destroyed her beauty, wiped it away in one swift motion. She let out a long, tired moan.

Mama looked up. "You're awake," she said, moving to the bed. "You have a beautiful baby girl." When she smiled, her eyes disappeared and a smudge of foundation clumped on her right cheek. Eloise wanted to wipe it away, but her tired arm remained motionless by her side.

"I know."

"Do you want to see her?"

She shook her head. "Not now. Can I have something to drink?"

Mama put a straw to her lips. She sucked the icy cold water. Her throat scratched with dryness and her head throbbed. Never had she felt so awful not even when she had that bad case of the Hong Kong flu two years ago, forcing her to miss a week of school. She swallowed more water. Her one desire was to crawl into a cave somewhere and never come out. Memories of screams and excruciating pain surfaced in her mind.

"Malcolm said you had not decided on a girl's name yet. He said he wanted you to name her." Her mother paused. "And, I think that's best." Mama didn't look her in the eye.

What was that supposed to mean? He could name her as easily as she could.

She pushed away the straw. A dribble of water ran down her chin and onto her neck. "I don't care. Tell him to name her whatever he wants." She turned her head from her mother and curled her legs up close.

"Really, Eloise, you could show a little more motherly love."

Mama expelled a long sigh. A moment later the sound of the knitting needles started again, lulling her back into a deep sleep.

When she awoke the next time, Malcolm and her father stood at the end of the bed, talking in low voices. She couldn't make out what they were saying. Panic rose inside her. She listened closely, fearing Daddy would say something to lead Malcolm to realize this creature wasn't his. She'd led him to believe otherwise, and she would go to her grave to keep him from knowing the truth.

After they had dated a month, she'd told him she might be pregnant. With a gleam in his eyes he'd said, "Let's get married, then." By then they had made love five times—glorious times, she might add. He called her his princess and touched her with an irresistibly gentle passion. He had no reason to believe anything but that the baby was his. He never questioned or doubted her.

When her parents met Malcolm, both had accepted him as the baby's father. And why not? They'd only met a few of her boyfriends—never having set eyes on Jonathan. Daddy had been antagonistic at first but later he acquiesced. She guessed he figured Malcolm couldn't be all bad since he had agreed to marry his wayward daughter.

Right or wrong, it didn't matter to her. Her body had grown bigger and uglier with each passing day. Her legs swelled and her heart hardened to the invader inside her. She simply wanted it out. As far as she was concerned the creature had stolen her beauty along with everything else that mattered to her.

A few months before she was due, she had shown Malcolm an article she had unearthed in the *Journal of British Medicine*. Actually, she'd spent hours in the Emory University library, scouring the dusty archives for just such an article. She told Malcolm her doctor had given it to her to explain the fast progress of her pregnancy. It said that first babies are often premature, particularly when born to young mothers. Malcolm believed he was the father. Her plan had worked.

Malcolm and Daddy exited when a nurse breezed into the room with a bundle in her arms.

"Here she is, looking for her mama," the woman said. "Are you planning to nurse her?"

"Absolutely not!" *How horrifying!* Her breasts had swelled full of milk and throbbed with agonizing discomfort, but she'd die before she would allow that creature's lips to suck life from her bosom.

"Okay, honey. We'll have to pump you. You'll feel better when you get all that milk out of you."

No kidding. I want everything related to that creature out of me.

The nurse placed the bundle in Eloise's arms. "She's a gorgeous little girl, just like her mama." She grinned and stood back as if taking a photo of the happy mother and child.

Eloise stared at the baby who looked at her with wide-eyed wonder. Could this really be the creature who had caused her life to turn upside down? She was no bigger than her arm. She caressed the baby's warm head covered in yellow fuzz.

"I'll tell your husband to come in," the nurse said.

Malcolm peered around the door. "What an amazing sight," he said entering with a huge smile on his face. "The baby looks just like you, thank God! What a little angel."

Fear gripped her. What if the baby looked like Jonathan? She searched the little scrunched-up face. Nothing looked familiar to her. Tiny nose, little bud of a mouth, nothing anyone could recognize. Maybe she would stay like that, in descript, looking like no one in particular. *Please God!*

"Have you thought about a name yet?" he asked.

"Here, take her." She handed the baby to Malcolm without answering his question.

He balanced the tiny package in his arms like a pro, as if he'd handled babies all his life. He cooed at her. "How about Elizabeth? That was my grandmother's name as well as your mama's. Elizabeth Knox. Sounds kinda good, don't you think?"

She lifted herself on her elbows and grabbed the mirror next to the bed. Her reflection revealed tired, bloodshot eyes. Her hair was plastered to her head as if it hadn't been washed in months. She noted swelling under her eyes and pencil-thin lines around her mouth. She had aged ten years in just nine months.

"God, I look like hell," she said, falling back against the pillow.

He turned to her. "You look more beautiful than ever. Come on, El. What about Elizabeth?"

"I really don't care what you name her. You decide."

The nurse returned with blood pressure equipment. She strapped the band around Eloise's arm and began pumping it up. "She's a precious one, that," she said.

"No name yet, though," Malcolm said. "I can't get my wife to decide."

"That's always a hard decision," the nurse agreed while recording Eloise's blood pressure on the clipboard. "It stumps the best of us. Just thinking the child will have that name for the rest of its life is enough to scare the blazes out of most new parents. Then you worry that she'll hate her name when she grows up."

"What's your name?" Eloise asked.

"Marlene," the nurse said with a smile. "I'm not sure—"

"That's it then. We'll name her Marlene," she cut in.

Malcolm and the nurse exchanged a startled look.

Marlene, the nurse, shrugged. "Give it some more thought, deary. I'm sure you'll think of something that suits her." She floated out before either could answer.

"You're not serious," Malcolm said, returning the baby to the little bed next to Eloise. "What if the nurse's name had been Gertrude or Matilda? You're going to pick a name out of the sky and that's it. Naming her after some stranger. Don't you care about how it fits with the child or our family?"

She chuckled. "Fits? What's that mean? It's a baby, hardly old enough to breathe on its own. What's wrong with Marlene?"

He shrugged. "Nothing. If that's what you want, I'll take care of the paperwork." He walked out without kissing her or calling her princess.

She glanced at the sleeping bundle. It gurgled and saliva ran out of its mouth.

"Well, Marlene, you've already caused the first disagreement I've ever had with your father."

* * * *

Eloise arrived home with the baby and immediately turned childcare over to Malcolm and her mother. The new couple had moved into her childhood room upstairs on Briardale Lane. Malcolm had purchased a double bed and a crib. He and his friends moved it all in right after the wedding.

During the evenings Malcolm fed the baby while Eloise slept like a brick. Her mother cared for her during the day while Eloise drank coffee, smoked cigarettes, and thumbed through *Glamour Magazine* at the kitchen table.

Eloise tried to see something redeeming in the miniature face, but all she saw was a creature that had destroyed her life. Her stomach tightened each time she looked at the giant-size needy eyes, blue with a fringe of yellow lashes, Jonathan's eyes. She shuddered. Those eyes mocked her.

Ha! Look at you, an aging old lady with a screaming baby and look at me, young and gallivanting as always.

She grimaced, moaned, and turned away from the baby who slept in a bassinet in the kitchen. A rancid odor infused the room. She rose with a long sigh. Gagging and struggling not to vomit, she changed the diaper. Then the creature yowled for food. What a nuisance. Always hungry. But the doctor said she wasn't gaining enough weight. Eloise hated feeding her. Milk gurgled out of her mouth, leaving stains on the bib and her clothes. *Yuck!* She couldn't stand another minute.

As soon as she could, she abandoned the baby to her mother and escaped to her room where she sat alone, filing her fingernails.

Last year at this time her major concerns had been beating Suzanne Deets for head of the cheerleading squad and getting Jonathan to ask her out. Nothing else mattered. That was the extent of her world. Little did she know her life was about to implode.

Later, even though her friends remained envious of Malcolm whose charm wooed everyone, rumors about her condition spread like a hot coal in a bale of hay. It didn't take long for Molly to put the pieces together and realize that it wasn't Sarah who had been in trouble but Eloise. Once she and Malcolm married, she stayed close to home and ignored her friend's calls to go out, unable to bear the stares and the whispers behind cupped hands.

Mama's voice floated up the stairs. She was talking to the baby as she ironed. Why waste her breath? The creature couldn't understand doodle.

Eloise lifted the hairbrush and ran it through her long tresses now hanging to her shoulders. She'd not colored it in months, ever since she'd grown elephant size. She pinched her cheek. Her skin looked dry and sallow, the color of an old potato. *Fine homecoming queen you are.*

Before Marlene was born, Malcolm worshipped her. His eyes had seemed to eat her alive. She tingled from head to foot whenever he was near. They shared a passion she'd never experienced with anyone. His touch electrified her body. Her only desire was to be close to him.

Now Malcolm looked at her with a narrow gaze that seemed to criticize rather than devour. He no longer cajoled and teased. Instead, as soon as he came home, he went to Marlene. Eloise had vanished from his life and been replaced by this tiny unwanted creature. She longed for Malcolm the way he had been, but she couldn't force herself to act the good little mother. It sickened her.

Tears darkened her eyes. She slapped her face, cringing at the sting and leaving a red patch on her cheek. She yearned for her old life.

She withdrew the sterling dagger in a gilded sheath and caressed the blade of the knife as she would a close friend. She put the point next to her inside thigh and made a tiny cut. The sting sent a shiver through her body, but the pain deadened her inner torment. She made another tiny cut and then another. As the blood tricked down her leg, she breathed a deep sigh. Then she placed the knife back in the sheaf, closing it away in the drawer, glad to know it was there when she needed it.

While Mama continued to make baby noises at Marlene in the kitchen, Eloise sneaked into the living room and opened the cabinet where her parents stashed the liquor. Inside she found a bottle of Smirnoff vodka that had never been opened. Looking around as if someone might jump out from behind the couch, she hid the bottle under her sweater and slipped back up the stairs to her room.

In the privacy of the upstairs bathroom, she poured the liquid into a paper cup and sipped. *Yuck!* She spit it out and glared at herself in the mirror. Even though the inside of her mouth burned, she pressed her lips to the cup and tried another sip, swallowing this time. The liquid scorched from the tip of her tongue till it hit her stomach. Several drinks later, the taste no longer burned but soothed like a soft white glove. The jitteriness inside her relaxed to a quiet purr.

Back in her room, she placed Mussorghy's *Night on Bald Mountain* on the phonograph, music that soothed her like nothing else. The strong beat and fanciful sounds took her to another place, another world, far away from that creature who was now crying downstairs. She turned up the volume so loud her head throbbed with the notes. In the distance, her mother shouted something, but she collapsed on the bed with a pillow across her stomach.

* * * *

"Eloise, come down here this minute. Dinner is on the table."

The record had stopped playing. She rose on her elbows and returned to the bathroom where she drank more from the stolen bottle. She rolled her head around to regain energy but her eyes felt heavy.

Malcolm knocked on the door. "Are you okay?"

"Tell Mama I'm not coming down. I don't want anything."

"You need to eat," he said with a voice that sounded angry, not concerned.

"Just tell her. I don't feel like eating anything." When was the last time she'd been hungry? The creature had made her hungry all the time but no more. Her body felt wasted, empty and worst of all, fat. She shunned all thoughts of food.

He left without answering.

She ran a bath to cover the racket from downstairs and nearly fell asleep in the tub.

Later in the bedroom, she dialed Jonathan's number. Martha Sue, her last remaining friend, had told her he was back from Vietnam but planning to return for another tour. Her heart boiled with anger whenever she imagined his cocky face. All this was his doing. And yet he went on with his life just like before, dating new girls, drinking beer. The phone began ringing.

"Hello," he answered, breathless as if he'd had to run to catch it.

Silence.

"Who's there?"

She breathed into the phone, wanting him to sense her presence but not letting on. Her heart thundered in her chest.

After a moment, he hung up with a thud.

She returned to the bathroom and retrieved the Smirnoff, finishing what was left.

Chapter Twenty

Eloise had been stalking Jonathan for nearly a week and tonight she stood outside Jason's bar in downtown Atlanta, smoking a cigarette and watching the door. Lights flashed from another bar across the road, and cars whizzed by, blurring the faces of people going and coming.

She wore a loose-fitting dress that whipped across her legs in the cool breeze. Her clothes still didn't fit her new ugly body, and she couldn't stand the snug feel of her skirt waistbands around her middle.

After waiting over an hour, she spotted Jonathan coming out of the bar with his arm wrapped around a dark-haired girl wearing a skin-tight miniskirt and high-heeled boots. She accented her wasp waist with a black patent leather belt, the way Eloise used to do when she had a waistline.

Jonathan laughed at something the girl said.

Eloise smashed her cigarette onto the pavement and moved out of the shadows, trailing them down the street to Jonathan's convertible parked near a streetlight.

He opened the girl's car door and jaunted around to the driver's side as if anxious to get away so he could ravish this lovely new conquest.

Eloise pursued them to a seedy part of South Dekalb County where they slowed on a deserted street in front of the Shady Rest Motel with a neon sign announcing vacancies.

Jonathan had never taken her to a motel. They had always done it in his car, often sitting up. He used to grope for her about to pop out of his pants. No way he could have made it to such a faraway love nest as this. She sniffed at the thought, shifting in her seat, desire burning inside despite herself. Perhaps he'd become more adept in his seduction techniques and more controlled.

Once Jonathan pulled to a stop, she found a parking place nearby in order to watch. He hopped out of the car, leaving his date inside. Eloise spied the silhouette of the girl as she pulled down the visor mirror and adjusted her hair and make-up. Could she really be planning to sleep with Jonathan after having just met him in a bar? Surely they had known each other before tonight, unless, of course, she was a prostitute. How delicious if he'd sunk that low!

All week she had followed him from bar to bar, usually with a gaggle of boys. He would drink himself into a stupor and go home. This was the second time he had picked up a girl. Eloise's heart quickened.

The night was cool, humid, and full of the rancid smell of car fumes. Eloise wrapped her bare arms with a shawl, one her mother had knitted in between all the little woolies for Marlene, and slid out of the car, careful not to close the door with a bang. Under the shawl, she gripped the cool handle of the long, silver dagger. Its cool point lay against her arm. She knocked on the girl's window.

With a startled jump, the girl lowered the window. "Can I help you?" she asked, her heavily made up dark brown eyes wide with curiosity and innocence. She wasn't even pretty. A large wart sat on the right side of a slightly crooked nose. But, even in the dim light Eloise saw a mountain of cleavage. So typical of the girls Jonathan seemed drawn to these days.

She dug her fingers in the girl's upper arm and put the knife to her cheek. "Get out of the car."

Innocence quickly turned to fear. The girl gasped and tried to jerk away from Eloise's grasp.

"I said get out of the car." She dug her nails deeper into her skin and placed the knife at the girl's neck. "Now!"

"Please don't hurt me." Trembling and hyperventilating, the girl released the door handle and practically fell out of the car. Her purse tumbled to the ground, spilling lipstick, brush, wallet, a condom, gum and other odds and ends onto the pavement.

Eloise kept the knife so close to the girl's neck that she may have even pricked her because the girl tensed and moaned. "If you move, I'll cut you. If you scream, it will be the last thing you'll ever hear."

"What do you want?" asked a shaky voice, full of terror.

"I want you to disappear." She loosened her hold on the girl's arm. "Run as fast as you can and don't turn around."

It didn't take much for the girl to forget all about Jonathan. She leapt for her stuff and with amazing speed considering the high heeled boots took off into the darkness, disappearing in minutes.

Eloise wrapped the shawl tighter around her shoulders and returned to her car where she waited for Jonathan to reappear. She switched on the radio and rested her head back while soft jazzy sounds echoed in her ears.

Jonathan came bounding out of the lobby, gripping something shiny in his hand, probably a key. He didn't seem to notice the girl gone until he opened the car door. The streetlight shone on his beautiful face, a frown of confusion stretched the length of his brow. He shut the door and walked around the car, looking up and down the street.

"Mandy?" he called.

He returned to the motel reception area but came out a few minutes later, alone.

"Mandy!" he called again. His voice echoed off the empty glass-front buildings and sounded desperate.

He peered up one side of the street and then the next. She crouched low and imagined the speed of his heartbeat as fear and wonder swept over him. His stomach would sink when he realized the girl had gone and was not coming back. Had she been kidnapped? Did she simply duck out on him? His evening was destroyed. Just one evening, though. He would recover and move on to another girl tomorrow evening or the next. For him there would always be a tomorrow.

Not so for her. He had destroyed her entire life, every evening gone from now until the day she died.

She lit a cigarette and made smoke circles in the air. The bottle she had brought with her lay empty in the passenger's seat. She licked her lips, wanting more. But she waited until Jonathan gave up and pulled away.

* * * *

"Where have you been?" Malcolm asked when she walked into the house twenty minutes later. He held Marlene in the crook of his arm.

"Out." She pushed past him and started up the stairs with him padding on her heels.

"Eloise, I'm worried about you. What's going on?"

"Nothing," she said. "I just need some time to myself, that's all. The baby demands too much of me." She tossed her purse onto the bed.

"What can you possibly mean? Your mother takes care of her all day, and I take her at night. How can she demand too much from you?" He placed the sleeping infant in her crib by his side of the bed and gently covered her with one of the newly knitted blankets.

She turned away from the domestic scene. "You don't understand."

"You're right. I don't understand. You aren't making any sense. How could you walk out without telling anyone and leave the baby like you did."

"Mama was here."

"Look, we didn't plan to have a baby so soon. We hardly know each other. But, these things happen. I love you, Eloise. I want you to be happy."

"I can't be happy right now." She breathed in the smell of him mixed with the rancid odor of diapers.

His hair stood up at the back as if he'd been running his hands through it, and vomit spots dotted his shirt. She wanted to get away from him and the baby and close herself in a room, alone. But she couldn't.

"I think you need to see someone," he said, taking her hand in his.

She jerked away. "I don't need to see anyone. I'm fine. I just need some time to adjust. A lot has happened to me. My whole life—" She hiccupped and choked back the words that almost tumbled out. "Can't you see?"

"What I see scares me. You're not eating and you hardly come out of our room. Now, you're suddenly disappearing at all hours. I don't know what to make of it." He ran his hand over his head. "You need to see someone who can help you adjust. I've read that this sometimes happens to new mothers, and—"

"Did Mama ask you to talk to me?"

"What does that matter?" he said, looking away from her. "Someone has to talk to you. I'm your husband. Won't you let me help you?"

The baby cried as if sensing the tension between her parents. Malcolm rose and lifted her from the crib. "It's all right, sweet one," he cooed. The baby quieted as soon as he touched her. Turning back to Eloise, he said, "I'm going to take her downstairs and rock her until she falls asleep. Then we'll talk some more."

"I don't need to talk anymore. I'm tired."

He walked out of the room without responding.

As soon as he left, she snuck into the bathroom and dug around under the sink for the bottle she had placed there. She unscrewed the cap and poured some of the fiery contents into her toothpaste glass. The liquid no longer singed her throat as it had that first day. She savored the taste now and longed for the tingly feeling it produced. After a few minutes her heart stopped pounding so fast and her body relaxed.

She returned to the bedroom where she lifted the telephone receiver and dialed Jonathan's number. He answered on the first ring.

"Mandy? What the hell—"

Silence. She breathed into the phone, suppressing a giggle. So, precious Mandy had not called him. Maybe he'll never see her again.

"Mandy? Is that you?"

She breathed again, louder this time.

"Who the hell is this? Stop calling like this." He slammed down the phone.

The next day she rose at 10:00 a.m., later than usual. The baby was not in the crib. She stretched and savored the absence of people.

Downstairs she found her mother sitting at the kitchen table thumbing through coupons. The baby gurgled from the high-chair by the table. Mama looked up when she entered.

"Eloise, we have to talk."

"Whatever happened to 'good morning'?" she asked. "Don't you think my hair is almost as pretty as it was?" She tossed the long strands over her shoulder.

"Yes, dear. You've always had beautiful hair. But that's not what I want to discuss with you." Her mother put the lid on the coupon box and faced her the way she used to do when she had done something terribly wrong. A deep frown cut across her brow. "I'm worried about you."

"Good grief. Why is everyone so worried about me? I'm fine." She laughed but the sound came out like a bitter croak.

"Look, I don't know what's going on with you, but we're all worried. You've been home a month now, and you hardly touch your own baby. Marlene needs to feel her mother not her grandmother. You've always been a self-centered person, but I can't believe you'd abandon your own daughter like this." She paused and walked over to the desk and lifted the notepad. "We've made an appointment for you to see Dr. Cannon." She tore off a page and handed it to her.

"I don't need to see any doctors," Eloise said, crumpling the note in her palm.

"Yes, you do. I got Dr. Cannon's name from Dr. Brigman. He's one of the best psychiatrists in Atlanta. Dr. Brigman thinks you're suffering from postpartum depression. He says it's very common and not something to be ashamed of or embarrassed about. He also said it can be treated, and you shouldn't just let it go and hope it'll go away."

She shuffled over to the coffee pot and poured herself a cup. "I don't know what any of that means. Why can't you just leave me alone? You know I didn't want this baby. I wanted to get rid of it." She sat down on the chair opposite her mother and far away from the creature. Already her diaper reeked.

"Don't ever say such things in front of Marlene," her mother said.

"Good God, she doesn't understand."

"Maybe not now but someday she will. Eloise, wake up. You don't have time to wallow around, getting up at mid-morning when your husband and your mother have been up half the night with your baby. You have no right to act like this. I'm ashamed of you. Embarrassed for Malcolm." She turned away but Eloise saw the tears. "I can't believe I brought up a daughter who is behaving like this."

Eloise got up. "That child stinks," she said, and she left the room.

"Eloise, get back down here this instant," her mother called from below the stairs.

She went to her room and closed the door. Inside, she placed Bach's Brandenburg Concerto, No.5 on the record player and turned up the volume full tilt. She drank more from her hidden stash before passing out on the bed.

The next thing she knew, Malcolm stood over her with the empty vodka bottle in his hand. She squinted at him.

"What's this doing here?" he asked.

She turned over and faced the wall in a fetal position.

"I knew you were drinking. I could smell it on you. What's going on? You never drank like this before we were married—maybe an occasional beer—but nothing like this. Please, talk to me."

The bed moved when he sat down next to her. His hand touched her arm, and he rubbed it gently. After a few minutes, he sighed deeply and left her alone.

Her time was running out. She would have to make her move tonight before Malcolm and her mother took her to see some shrink.

She edged her way down the stairs on tiptoe. Voices came from the kitchen. The baby yowled. Pots and pans banged around.

If all went well, she could finish the job tonight.

Chapter Twenty-One

Eloise had never before bought liquor in a liquor store. She had seen the stores all over town, but had never been in one. While sitting in the parking lot at Jackson's Package Store on Ponce de Leon, she watched people, all men, enter and exit with brown paper bags tucked under their arms. It would take all her courage to walk in that shady establishment and get what she needed to accomplish her deed tonight. Drizzle trickled over her windshield. Car horns sounded all around her. Tree frogs croaked from a nearby pine.

She sucked in a deep breath before grabbing her purse and meandering into the store. The lights inside glared like spotlights on a stage. Whatever happened to her dream to become an actress? Tonight she would act, pretend she was Barbarella, able to defeat the world's meanest villains. Actors often needed drink or drugs to get over stage fright. She headed toward the back aisles.

More brands of vodka than she ever imagined occupied a wide display of shelves row after row. She scanned the labels until a man approached.

"Can I help you, young lady?"

She shot him her best Barbarella smile. He wore a white shirt and a narrow dark tie. He'd combed a few strands of hair over the bald spot in the middle of his head.

"I'm having a party and need some vodka. But, I'm totally lost in here. My husband usually does this, but he's having to work late. So, here I am, trying to make heads or tails out of all these different kinds. What might you suggest?"

"That depends on how much you want to spend." He moved over to the shelves. "We've got a nice Absolut that's on special. Are you going to mix it or drink it on the rocks?"

"Oh, my, I wouldn't know, never having gone near the stuff myself, of course. We'll probably mix it with something or other. Orange juice? Isn't that what people usually mix with vodka? My husband takes care of all that."

"Naturally." He paused and looked at the shelves of bottles. "I'd suggest this one." He pulled out one of the Absolut's. "Or if you prefer a more unusual taste, this Smirnoff is another brand, but very smooth. Great to drink alone or mixed with orange juice." He showed her that bottle.

She took it and balanced it in her hand as she might a precious vase. "Let's try one of each," she said with a big grin, handing him her ID and a twenty-dollar bill snatched earlier that day from Malcolm's wallet.

She left the store with two brown-bag clad bottles of vodka under each arm. That should be more than enough to get her through this night.

Ten minutes later, she sat in her car under the weeping willow tree at the curb near Jonathan's parent's house.

The two-story wood frame Victorian with green shutters on every window sat on the outskirts of Buckhead where the richest Atlantans lived. The yards in this subdivision spanned more property than the houses on Briardale Lane, probably three to five acres each. Most sat up on a hill with the exception of Jonathan's house situated flat on the lot. She had been here before, once when she dated Jonathan and several times in the last week.

He usually came out around 8:00 p.m. Her watch read 7:15 p.m., but the car clock read 7:20 p.m. Either way she wouldn't wait long. The drizzle had turned to a steady rain splashing on her windshield and fogging her windows. If things went as usual, he would exit, get into his car, and she would follow him to one of his favorite haunts where he would meet up with his friends.

She lit a cigarette and opened the Absolut vodka. The taste warmed her all the way down to her stomach. Her tummy had flattened again, and she liked tucking it in without feeling as though she were pulling against gravity. Even though her waistline had not returned, she had begun to hope her body would recover some of its shapely form. She had lost fifteen pounds in the last month. As long as she continued to stay away from food, she could lose another ten pounds without too much trouble. Drinking satisfied her desire to eat.

What did you have for dinner?

Just a splash of vodka. She giggled and drank some more.

She pulled down the visor mirror on the passenger side and added a touch of pink lipstick to her full lips.

Under the glare of the streetlight, her hair looked dull in the mirror. After she finished with Jonathan, she vowed to add some color. A box of Clariol sat unopened under her sink in the bathroom. She and Molly used to do each other's hair every so often. They would spend all Saturday morning in one or the other's house, washing, massaging, mixing color, drying, and combing. Those blissful days seemed like an eternity ago.

A light flickered from inside the house. Someone had looked out the window and moved the curtain. Could they spot her car sitting here? The big tree blocked some of the view, but she suspected the hood of the car was visible from the front bay window. She had not noticed other cars parked on this street. Briardale Lane hosted cars on the street all the time. There, no one cared or noticed. She flipped up the visor, turned on the motor, and quietly rolled the car back a few feet. Afterward, she puffed on the cigarette and waited, hoping her presence had remained undetected.

A dark pick-up truck pulled up in front of Jonathan's driveway and drew to a stop. Two guys got out and walked to the door.

Darn! He was going out with friends tonight. She needed to corner him alone.

Moments later, the guys returned with Jonathan, and the truck scooted down the road at a fast clip. She slipped out of hiding and followed them, keeping a safe distance and hoping they would end up at one of Jonathan's favorite haunts where they might disperse. The rain had stopped, but the streets were still wet.

Finally, the truck drew to a stop outside of Underground Atlanta where there was a bar or a nightclub in every cranny. When she had dated Jonathan, they had never gone to bars. Clearly this was a pastime he had acquired since his return from Vietnam.

She found a parking place a couple of rows behind the boys and hung back as they piled out of the truck. They carried beer bottles and stood around, drinking the beer and cutting up with each other, one nudging the other after some comment. People milled about on the street outside Front Page, another popular bar, and up and down the sidewalk leading into Underground. She recognized one of the boys with Jonathan as someone who had gone to Dexter, but she didn't know his name.

The empty beer bottles went flying into the street with a crash, and the boys sauntered toward Underground, supposedly on the prowl for girls, at least, that was Jonathan's usual game. He sometimes got lucky—as he had last night—and he sometimes did not.

She slumped down in the car seat with her vodka and waited. The temperature outside had dropped, but the car remained warm so long as she turned on the heat every so often.

By the time the boys came out, she had nearly finished the Absolut and considered opening the other bottle. But her head buzzed, and she didn't want to pass out like last night. Two shadows appeared under the streetlight near the boy's truck. Eloise peered through the windshield but didn't see Jonathan. The other two drove off.

This is my chance.

She got out of the car and headed inside. She had been sitting in the car too long. One foot had gone numb and tingled as it came back to life. She stopped to lean on a lamppost to shake out her numb foot. The street was slippery but she managed not to fall down. Clumps of people laughed and milled about along the entrance to Underground.

She followed the narrow path to Mulenbrinks Saloon where Jonathan had gone two times this week. She'd start there. Once inside, it took her a moment to adjust to the dim lighting. She scanned the place for him.

A large strobe light circled above her head, giving the room an eerie, bouncy feel, flashing on faces as it made its way around the room. A haze of marijuana perfumed the air. The Rolling Stones blared from the jukebox, singing their latest hit, "Satisfaction." A few dark figures bumped around on the dance floor.

Her ears buzzed, and when she closed her eyes everything swayed. She clutched the knife under her coat to give her courage to move forward. She ventured farther into the room, squinting at the dancers.

Someone grabbed her hand and twirled her onto the dance floor. She tripped and almost dropped the knife.

"Whoa! Get away from me!"

The guy was bumping up close to her. "Can't let a pretty thing like you get this close to the dance floor without dancing." He seized her elbow.

"Leave me alone." She jerked away from him and stomped off the slick floor toward the bar. Once there, she ordered a double vodka on the rocks.

"You never used to drink vodka."

She spun around to face Jonathan who sported a big grin as if he had just found a million bucks.

She sucked in a deep breath. His beauty nearly choked her.

"Surprised to see me?" He pulled up the stool next to her.

She drank from her glass to compose herself. "A little," she lied. "When'd you get back?"

He motioned for the bartender to refill his glass. "About a month ago. But, I'm heading out again in a few weeks."

She nodded but didn't say anything.

"I've missed you. I almost called before I left, but you seemed determined that we break up. Then I heard you'd married some guy. I couldn't believe it." He touched her hand with his little finger and a spasm ran up her arm.

She peered at him from under her lashes without moving her hand. "Why shouldn't I marry?"

"Oh, I don't know. I guess I didn't see you as the settling down type of girl. And, I suppose, I thought we had a good thing going there for a while. Maybe even..." His hot breath touched her ear. "L-O-V-E."

It took all her courage not to spit in his face. Instead, she simply kept the slight smile on her lips, hoping he wouldn't notice the heat rising up inside her and burning through her eyes. Jonathan had never been too sensitive. He wouldn't notice anything but her cleavage. She touched the collar of her dress and unbuttoned the top button. Her breasts still swelled some from the pregnancy—not as much, but enough to catch Jonathan's eye.

"Hey, are you gonna be here a while?" he asked with his gaze on her chest.

"Yeah."

"I need to ditch somebody. I'll be right back." Stepping back, he sauntered across the bar to a table full of girls. He leaned down and whispered something in one of the girl's ears. Eloise could guess what he said, something about a friend needing him but let's get together tomorrow night—a quick Jonathan-type brush-off. Moments later, he was beside her again with his hot body sidled up next to her.

She finished off the drink and ordered a second. Combining the strobe lights with Jonathan's presence made everything inside her tumble around. She tossed her head back and laughed along with Jonathan all the while pressing the cool knife inside her sweater sleeve and hidden by her coat firmly against her arm.

He reached over and touched the top of her dress. His finger traced her cleavage and ran up her neck to her lips. She let him trace her lips and touch her tongue.

"You're still the sexiest girl I've ever seen. It's like you light a fire under me every time I see you."

She kissed his finger and moved his hand back to his glass. "I'm married, remember?"

"Is your husband here with you?" He craned his neck to look around.

She laughed, louder than she meant to, but the music drowned out the sound. "No way."

"Then I'd say you came here looking for something you can't find at home." His white teeth gleamed at her.

She turned away from him and swallowed more vodka. He drank from his glass as well, but she had consumed two drinks to his one.

He moved his hand close to hers again. "Wanna get out of here and find a quiet spot? Like ol' times? I know some good places we could go."

Night after night she'd dreamed of hearing that question. Her heart raced. "I've got a car parked nearby," she told him.

"What are we waiting for?" he asked. "Just like ol' times," he repeated, his gaze devouring her from head to toe.

When she stood, everything turned sideways. She reeled backward on her heels.

"Whoa, you okay?" he asked.

She grinned at him and held his elbow as he led her out to her car. It took all her strength to concentrate on standing upright and to clutch the knife.

You can do this!

Once outside, she couldn't remember exactly where she'd parked. She looked from side to side and stumbled on the sidewalk, nearly falling on her face. He managed to catch her, but the knife fell to the pavement.

"What is this?" he said with a frown, bending down to get it. He stared at the long silver blade.

She grabbed it from him and tucked it inside her coat.

Someone laughed in the distance. A few people milled nearby. The streetlight shone on his puzzled face.

She nudged him along. "I think my car is over here." She pointed behind him.

"That knife," he said without moving. "It looks like the one…" His eyes darted. "Something strange happened last night. And, the girl I was with told me about a long silver knife and a pretty blonde." He grabbed her arm. "Eloise, what's going on?"

She gripped the knife harder, the hatred in her rose to her throat. Her heart raced and a flush penetrated her cheeks. She talked slowly so as not to slur her words. "You ruined my life."

He backed away from her, but she lunged at him with the knife pointed at his muscular chest and aimed straight for his heart. He jumped sideways, grabbed her wrist, and twisted the knife out of her hand as if she were a small child. Then he seized her by the arm.

"I don't know what you're talking about. But I think you need to go home, and you're in no condition to drive. Come on."

He dragged her down the street. "Where's your car?"

She pointed down the row of vehicles to hers.

He opened her purse and removed her keys while still holding her by the arm.

"I can't believe you did that to Mandy. Are you crazy? What in the hell has gotten into you?"

"Look at me!" she screamed at him and tried to jerk loose. "Look what you've done to me?"

"You're drunk. You did that all on your own, sweetheart. Other than that, you look great. At least as far as I can see." He pushed her into the car and slid into the driver's seat, tossing the empty liquor bottle in the back. "Holy shit," he muttered.

She held onto the armrest as he swished around the corners.

"Briardale Lane? You still live there?"

She nodded. Her head pounded as if an army were marching inside. Tears fell down her cheeks, but all she wanted to do was scream and keep screaming. She bit her tongue and tasted blood.

Once he pulled up to the house, he got out and dragged her to the front entrance. Malcolm answered immediately.

"Eloise?" he said, the shock registering on his face.

"Look," Jonathan began. "I take it this is your wife."

"She is. What—"

"As you can see, she's pretty much out of it, but she threatened my girlfriend and tried to kill me tonight." Jonathan paused. "I don't know what's going on with her, but you'd better get her some help."

"My God," Malcolm said, taking Eloise by the arm and leading her inside. "I'm so sorry. I don't know what to say."

Mama approached with Marlene in her arms.

Jonathan sent an incredulous glance at Eloise.

A scream erupted from Eloise's mouth. Malcolm buried her head in his chest, but she kept screaming, louder and louder, unable to stop the panic inside.

Jonathan yelled above Eloise's screams. "Just keep her the hell away from me. If I see her near me or any of my friends, I'll call the police."

The next day, Malcolm committed her to Fulton County Psychiatric Hospital under the care of Dr. Cannon.

PART THREE

"What's her prognosis?" Mark cut in.

The doctor looked around as if buying time. "I can't say for sure at this moment. I will say, she's in critical condition." He paused again. "We found these in the pocket of her dress." He pulled out an empty pill container. "It's a prescription for you, I believe." He handed the container to Peter.

"Good God! I never took these. About three years ago I had a bone spur removed from my foot. They gave me Loratab for the pain. But, these have expired." He looked to the doctor, his face full of hope.

"Unfortunately, most medications do not actually expire on the label date. Most are still good. But, it helps us to know how many she took. Given you didn't take any, she must've taken fifteen pills, and that mixed with the alcohol in her system caused the reaction." He bit his lower lip and added in a low voice. "I'm not a psychiatrist, but it looks as if your wife tried to take her own life."

"No!" Janie shrieked.

Aunt Sarah moved over to her and put her arm around her. Janie started shaking so hard she couldn't say another word. The pain in her belly intensified. Her aunt rubbed her arms and held her tight.

Aunt Sarah asked the doctor. "Could there be any other explanation for what happened?"

"It's doubtful, but as I said, I'm not a psychiatrist."

"What are her chances?" Mark asked.

The doctor swayed from foot to foot. "That's hard to say at this moment. We don't know how long she was unconscious. We plan to put her on dialysis to purge the blood of toxins. Then it's just a question of wait-and-see. But, I'm going to transfer her to our Intensive Unit. That's on the third floor. We'll do that after the dialysis team gets here." He spoke in a monotone and didn't give any of them eye contact.

When he left, no one spoke.

Aunt Sarah pulled Janie closer. "Don't worry," she whispered. "Marlene is a strong girl. She'll get through this. I just know it."

An hour later, a nurse told them that Marlene was on dialysis, but she would be moved to room 301 within the next couple of hours. They could remain there or go to the waiting area on that floor. When the nurse turned to leave, she nearly collided with Jack.

Janie would have known Jack anywhere. With the exception of no hair, he had not changed in appearance since the last time she'd seen him when he was twenty years old and smoking pot in the Starlite Lounge. He went over to shake Peter's hand. Amanda rushed up to him with a bear hug and lots of tears. She tried to say what was going on, but it came out as a garble of sobs.

Jack turned and saw Janie. The surprise on his face told her she had changed much more than he had. He went over and patted her shoulder. "I'm so sorry about all this."

"When I called you, I only wanted to catch up some—" her voice broke. "If we hadn't agreed to meet this morning—Amanda and me. Something told me Marlene was in trouble. I just didn't know how much trouble."

"It's okay. I only wish we might have met over a beer like in the ol' days. But, it's good to see you anyway, kiddo."

Not even Jack, who knew a side of Janie no one else knew, could fathom the real reason she'd returned.

Chapter Twenty-Three

The doctor entered again with a deep frown on his face and sweat pooling on his brow.

"She's still in critical condition," he began. "But we've got her stable. I've called in a neurologist. She's showing some signs of consciousness and is out of immediate danger."

Relief flooded Janie. Even though Marlene was still very sick, her sister was alive.

Janie left the hospital to call Nelson to arrange for a later meeting. His text indicated that he could meet her in thirty minutes at the Yellow Star Café. Then, she called Sue Anne.

"What's happening?" Sue Anne asked. "Are you on your way home, I hope?"

"I'm afraid I've had another complication." She told her about Marlene. "She's just regained consciousness so we're hopeful. But things are touch and go."

"My God! Can I do anything for you?"

"Just pray for all of us." Janie choked up. Hearing Sue Anne's concerned voice was the last straw.

"Oh, honey, I'm gonna come there, right this minute. I need to hold you."

Sniffling, Janie said, "No, don't. I'd be useless and there are so many things to do here." She blew her nose. "It's just so good to hear your voice."

"Really, Janie, I can come. I can cancel my appointments. Tomorrow I've only got this one client that wanted to meet me at the Decorator's Market. We need to pick out some lamps for her new office. She won't mind one bit. I could be there by noon."

"I'm fine. I've got Aunt Sarah here, and Marlene's friend, Amanda, is great. I've got lots of people around me."

Silence.

Finally Sue Anne said, "If you insist, but I could be there in a flash, honey. All you've gotta do is say the word, okay?"

"You're so good for me," Janie said. "Love you."

"I love you, too, and I expect you to keep me posted."

"Promise."

A light freezing rain splashed on the car windshield on her way to the Yellow Star Café. Late February in Atlanta. *Burr.* Her winter coat, left haphazardly at Amanda's house, sure would help. She tightened the scarf around her neck, but cold chills ran from her numb feet to her back.

Students filled the Yellow Star Café, drinking steaming mugs of coffee and studying alone and in clumps. Nelson raised a hand from a back booth. She headed toward him, unwrapping her scarf as she walked. The radiator pumped with a mighty force, fogging the windows.

"How'd you find this place?" Nelson asked.

She tossed her scarf and purse onto the booth. "It's not far from where I used to live. And, actually I worked in a beauty shop next door when I was in high school." She shivered. "God, it's either freezing or burning up in this town."

"You adjust."

"You maybe. Fortunately, I don't have to."

When a waitress came up, she ordered a latte. From the looks of his coffee cup he had been there a while. "Sorry about having to change our meeting."

"I hope your sister is doing better." He paused and peered over her shoulder.

"Thanks. They think she's over the worst."

"Like you asked," he said, still peering around. "I didn't tell Jerry about our meeting. But I'm not too cool about that 'cause Jerry and I go way back. He likes being in the loop. If he hears I'm doing business without him, he might freak. Jerry isn't the best enemy to have."

"He won't hear unless you tell him. I just have a couple of small jobs, nothing that should concern Jerry and, besides, I don't trust him."

He narrowed his eyes at her. "What makes you trust me?"

"I've got good instincts about people. I've known Jerry and Thelma for a long time. They're too—what's the word—unpredictable. You seem steadier to me. I hope I'm right." *I don't have too many choices right now.*

"I'm guessing this has something to do with that stepdad of yours."

The waitress placed Janie's latte in front of her and refilled Nelson's coffee cup.

She tasted the milky drink while Nelson added several tubs of cream to his coffee.

"You said you could find out what Ralph Cooper is up to," Janie said, picking up where they had left off. "He's got someone with him, looks like an ex-con to me. I need to figure out what they're doing. I don't have much time so I wanted to see if you could start right away."

He nodded. "I should have some information for you in a couple of days. What's his address?"

She handed him the address to Briardale Lane. "Also, that lawyer I mentioned. He's been calling my sister. I don't know if that's what drove her over the edge, but I think he might be partly responsible for her breakdown. I heard a pretty nasty message from him at her house. I'd like for you to put a scare into him like you said you could do, without hurting him. I especially don't want him bothering Marlene while she's in the hospital, and I can't guard her every minute."

"Sure, no prob."

She gave him Samuel D. Whitaker's name, and added, "I'm sure he's in the phone book."

"Is that it?" Nelson asked.

"For now. How 'bout I give you half now and half when you're finished?"

"Sure."

She pulled out her checkbook and wrote Nelson a check for five hundred dollars. "That should cover it. You can reach me on my cell when you have something."

Once back in her car, Janie drove to the Holiday Inn in Decatur and checked in. Her plan was to move around until Nelson told her he had taken care of Samuel D. Whitaker. She didn't want to find that creep on her doorstep ever again.

After a long steamy shower, she put on layers upon layers of clothes and returned to the hospital where she found Amanda and Aunt Sarah in the waiting area for critical care patients.

"What's happening?" Janie asked.

"Not much has changed," Aunt Sarah answered, her face pale and drawn. "The doctors said they're getting a reading on her EEG, which means she's dreaming. But she hasn't opened her eyes again. She woke up and then drifted off almost immediately. The nurses told us that's common. Peter is in there now. Her kidneys are working fine, though. That's good news. Mark went down to the restaurant to get a bite to eat. I couldn't eat a thing, but I hope you ate something, dear."

Janie shook her head. She had not even thought about food.

"I couldn't either," Amanda said. "They've sent a psychiatrist in to talk to Peter. A Dr. Averett, I think. Apparently he specializes in addiction cases."

"So, I guess we wait." Janie collapsed in a chair opposite Amanda. She had taken her meds while she was out. Although they made her drowsy, they dulled the pain. Her eyes drooped but for the first time since that morning, the tension drained from her body. Marlene just might live.

"Aunt Sarah," Janie said. "I've been thinking a lot about Mom, particularly after finding Marlene the way we did. As you can imagine, that brought back memories." She paused. "I know she spent some time in a mental hospital—"

"Your mother had issues. I'm afraid she wasn't a very happy person. Although she had every reason to be happy. She was beautiful and sought after by everyone who knew her. My parents doted on her from day one. I thought she would perk up after she married your daddy—who, by the way, was great to her—a little older and a lot more stable. But things seemed to get worse after Marlene was born. I don't know what happened, but she never got over the funk she fell into after her pregnancy. They diagnosed her with postpartum depression."

"So was that why she was hospitalized?"

"Maybe I should leave," Amanda said, standing.

"Oh, no, my dear," Aunt Sarah said. "You're almost like family to us. I'm sure Marlene wouldn't mind your hearing this. There's really nothing to hide anymore anyway. Most of the people we're talking about are dead."

"But y'all might want a bit of privacy, and I may as well mosey on home, rustle up some dinner for Jack, and get some sleep, if I can. There's nothing I can do tonight."

She gathered her purse and hugged Janie. "Thank God for you," she whispered in Janie's ear and gave her shoulder a squeeze. "Y'all call me if things change, doesn't matter what time."

They watched her disappear around the corner.

"So postpartum depression was why Mom was in the hospital. I always thought it was something more."

Aunt Sarah's eyes darted. She rubbed her temple before answering. "There's so much that even I don't know." She paused. "You're right, though. There was more to it." She licked her lips. "Your mother hurt herself."

"She tried to kill herself?"

"Not exactly."

"Well what then?"

"She cut herself."

Janie scowled. "Stabbed herself?"

Aunt Sarah shook her head. "No, apparently she cut herself, like with small cuts, particularly on her stomach and inner thighs. Nothing life threatening, but it scared Mama who caught her doing it a couple of times. Thinking back, I suppose cutting herself like that was an indication of her unhappiness. It was certainly self-destructive. Your mother was drinking a lot then, too."

Janie nodded. Her main memory of her mother was seeing her dead drunk in the back bedroom surrounded by old photographs and the soft sounds of classical music.

"What's more, I do know she became a danger to others," Aunt Sarah continued.

"Was she a danger to me and Marly?"

"Oh no! Never. She loved you both. But unfortunately, she became a mother when she was much too young—only eighteen when Marlene was born, as I'm sure you know. It was hard for her to give up her teenage life to take on the responsibilities of motherhood. I'm sure the drinking had a lot to do with that. We didn't notice it at first. And then, it was too late. She got herself hooked on alcohol and nothing any of us could do ever changed that, even poor Malcolm." She stopped talking and studied her hands as if the memories danced on her palms. "I lived away from home then. So, I didn't know a lot about what was going on. I heard second-hand, mostly from Mama."

"So who was she a danger to?" Janie had never felt threatened by her mother.

"From what I understand, she threatened some people, some friends from her high school years, kids like her. It was all very innocent, I'm sure. But Malcolm and my parents forced her to get help, which must have been a good thing. Malcolm supported everything my parents wanted to do. He loved your mother to distraction and would do anything for her. When she was hospitalized the first time—"

"First time? I guess I missed something here. I thought she was hospitalized after I was born."

"Well, yes, she was. But the first time was right after Marlene was born. That was the worst. She stayed in the hospital over a month, maybe six weeks, I don't remember exactly. It was traumatic for everyone, particularly my father. He couldn't understand any of it. He blamed Eloise for her drinking and refused to allow her back in his house. He could be very stubborn." She sighed. "All this put a great strain on my parents because Mama always protected Eloise. She and Daddy fought a lot. Malcolm wanted to move out of the house on Briardale Lane with Marlene, but my mother insisted they stay."

Janie shook her head. "That must've been horrible for Daddy—living in the same house with his wife's parents and her in the hospital. I had no idea."

Aunt Sarah stroked Janie's hand. "Your mother meant well. Things calmed down for a long time after this episode. Once Eloise got out of the hospital that time, she stopped drinking and started acting like a mother to Marlene. I don't remember too much about that period because I was finishing school and starting my first job. But, from what I understood everything calmed down, until—"

"Until I was born."

"Unfortunately, yes. She spiraled down and began drinking again, more heavily this time. She neglected Marlene who by then was a toddler. I helped out with babysitting because Mama wasn't well then, and Daddy had recently died. Your father did his best but with you an infant and Marlene a toddler, he couldn't manage without help. Marlene spent many nights with me. What an angel she was. I loved having her." Aunt Sarah stopped talking. A tear trickled down her cheek.

"I'm sorry. I didn't mean to bring all this up. It's just with Marlene in there fighting for her life, I couldn't help but think about Mom."

Aunt Sarah sniffed and blew her nose. "I'm just so tired. Today has been a nightmare."

"I know."

They remained silent for several minutes. Janie stared at the poster on the wall behind Aunt Sarah's head, depicting a vacation spot in the mountains. Happy people in winter gear skied down a snow-covered peak. The clock above the window ticked away each minute.

"One thing I've never understood," Janie said as if to herself, "is why Mom married Ralph?"

Aunt Sarah took a deep breath. "That's truly a mystery. I did everything I could to talk her out of it and so did your granny. But, she was hell bent. Afterward, she seemed unhappier than ever. I know for a fact she was embarrassed by Ralph. She refused to go anywhere with him. But whenever I said anything, she tore into me like a bull. We had some pretty fierce arguments back then."

"She didn't need his income, did she?"

"After Mama died, there was enough for Eloise to live on, particularly if she remained in the house. I didn't need my inheritance so I signed it over to her for you girls. And she had your father's social security as well as proceeds from his life insurance policy. She could have done fine without Ralph."

"Then why? I think she hated him."

Aunt Sarah shook her head. "I don't think she hated him. I think—" She paused and looked away. "I have nothing to base this on except my gut feeling, but, I think she was afraid of him, not physically afraid, but something else. Obviously as things turned out, she had every reason to fear him. Sometimes I blame myself for not insisting she leave him."

"It was hopeless. She never would've," Janie said.

"I should have gotten closer to her, but I was too wrapped up in my business. If I'd tried harder, maybe she would have confided in me. We always seemed to disagree, I'm afraid."

Janie didn't say anything.

"There was one time actually," Aunt Sarah continued, "when she did let something slip. We were in the middle of one of our arguments and I said, 'Why don't you just throw him out?' She said, 'I can't,' and immediately stopped herself. I had the impression he had something on her, but she never said another word about it."

"Like he was blackmailing her?"

"I don't know. It was just a feeling, but I remember thinking that her marriage made more sense if he was holding something over her."

"But what?"

"That, my dear, is something we may never know."

Peter walked in, looking as if he had been run over. His hair was messed and his shirttail was partially pulled out of his pants.

Aunt Sarah jumped up. "How is she?"

"Still not awake. I spoke with her new doctor. Patel is his name. He'll be taking care of her from now on. He suggested we all go home. He'll call if anything changes." Peter looked as if he was about to melt into the floor.

"That's a good idea. I'll go down and get Mark. Janie, do you want to come home with us?"

"I'm staying with friends," she lied. Aunt Sarah's was the last place she could go.

* * * *

Janie spent the next two days at the hospital. She had heard nothing from Nelson and her package had not arrived at Thelma's. She cancelled her appointment at Emory, not wanting the distraction and not feeling up to what they would probably tell her.

At the hospital, she watched Marlene's eyes move in her sleep and wondered what she was dreaming about. She had awakened again but didn't seem to know anyone and fell immediately back to sleep. Perhaps her dreams were better than real life. Janie rubbed her sister's hand, thinking about all the times Marlene had comforted her.

As a child, Janie felt uncomfortable around Ralph. She never liked him, and she sensed Marlene didn't either.

That first night after Mom married Ralph, he sat down to dinner in the kitchen at Briardale Lane, taking the seat that had once belonged to Daddy. Mom stood facing the stove with her back to them, chattering about whatever she was cooking for supper. When she turned and saw Ralph sitting there, she flushed a deep shade of pink and stopped talking.

Why would Mom marry a man who even a six-year-old sensed was trouble? What did he hold over her that would make her do it?

Janie's cell phone beeped bringing her back to reality. She pulled it out of her purse and found a text from Thelma.

Your package just arrived.

Now she could move forward with her plan.

Chapter Twenty-Four

Marlene squinted at the daylight coming in from a nearby window and licked her parched lips. She lifted her head and frowned at the unfamiliar surroundings, a bed in a small room that looked like a hospital. A tiny vase of white carnations sat on the table next to the bed. The room smelled of disinfectant. Her head pounded as if it were being pressed between two boulders.

After a few minutes, a pencil-thin nurse with ruddy skin and a large mole on her lip entered.

"Good afternoon," she said, with a smile that stretched the mole flat. "Would you like some water?"

Marlene nodded and swallowed from the cup the nurse offered. Then she fell back on the pillows. "Where am I?" Her voice sounded raspy.

"You're in Piedmont Hospital. Your husband and some friends brought you here Thursday evening."

My husband? Peter? "What's wrong with me?"

Without responding, the nurse lifted her wrist and took her pulse. Then she wrapped a blood pressure band around her arm. Marlene watched the woman's detached, unseeing eyes.

"You've been pretty sick," the nurse said, "I'll page your doctor. He'll answer your questions." Once done, she hurried out.

Marlene propped herself on her elbows in an effort to rise, but every bone in her body ached. She let out a quiet moan and slid back onto the pillows. Maybe she'd been in some sort of car accident. Snippets from the last day she remembered floated in her mind. She had lunch, no, coffee with Janie. Maybe it wasn't Janie. Maybe she dreamed it was Janie. Her dreams had been wild. Running away from something or someone. She rubbed her temple. She couldn't remember beyond being in that café with Janie.

A forty-something, dark-haired man entered. "I heard you were rousing," he said. "My name is Tim Averett. I'm a psychiatrist."

"A psychiatrist? Why on earth do I need a psychiatrist?"

The doctor sat his clipboard on the table next to her bed and studied her behind black-rimmed glasses. "It seems you tried to take your own life." His tone was bland as if he had just told her what was on the lunch menu.

"What?" *Kill myself!*

What a ridiculous idea! This man clearly had mixed her up with someone else. She had to correct his impression and fast.

"Your sister and your neighbor—" He lifted the clipboard."—a Mrs. Saunders found you and called your husband."

"Janie and Amanda? But that's impossible. They don't even know each other. It couldn't have been them. You must have the wrong patient, doctor."

Once again he glanced at the clipboard. "That's the information we have. Your sister, a Miss Knox, and Mrs. Jack Saunders came to the hospital with you in the ambulance. You had ingested quite a few Loratab on top of a bit too much bourbon for your system. Had they not walked in when they did, you might not have survived." He smiled, but his amber eyes, hidden behind dark lashes, shot her a look that was deadly serious.

A few hazy things started coming back to her. Peter had left her, and she had begun drinking. *Who wouldn't?* The last thing she remembered was taking a few Loratab—or something she had found in the medicine cabinet, just a few, so she could sleep. Oh, yes, those awful telephone

198 | JOAN C. CURTIS

calls from that sleazy sounding lawyer of Ralph's. That's right. She had tried to block out the sound of the telephone. That's what she had done, blocked out the awful ring of the phone and that horrid voice. She had not tried to kill herself, no way! She had gone to see Ralph to make him leave. But he wouldn't go. Everything was starting to come back to her. Nothing in her memory bank suggested a desire to die.

"Don't excite yourself too much now. We'll have plenty of time to talk when you get your strength back. We've emptied your stomach and are pumping more fluids into you. You're dehydrated and very weak, but your vital signs are good. You're strong and healthy. You'll be up and about very soon. Try to rest for now. You'll need all your strength during the next couple of days."

"But, Doctor, I didn't try to kill myself. It was an accident, a mistake. You've got to believe me."

He smiled. "Of course."

Marlene turned away. He didn't believe her. He didn't realize she would never kill herself. Not after all the stories she had heard about Mama. She spent most of her childhood worrying she would come home and find her mother dangling from a chandelier.

Three days later, she awoke to the sight of Amanda peeking around the corner of her hospital room with a box of candy under her arm and a plastic grocery bag overflowing with paperback books, dangling from her wrist.

Amanda's large green eyes took in the surroundings with a worried frown. "Oh, my God, sweetie, how are you?"

"Much better," Marlene said.

They had put her through what Dr. Averett called detoxification. Basically, that meant they got all the drugs and alcohol out of her system so she could start afresh. At first, she felt jittery and anxious and wanted a drink to calm her nerves but all the begging in the world wouldn't get her one. She constantly licked her lips. Sores popped out like boils inside her mouth. Her tongue felt thick and heavy. She couldn't keep her head still, making it difficult to talk to anyone. And each night she slept with the restlessness of a prisoner before execution.

Finally, yesterday she came out of the fog. The shakiness settled down, and she slept until the skinny nurse with the mole on her lip came to her room with the morning juice. She drank the cool liquid like a thirsty athlete and decided she might live through this experience after all.

Seeing Amanda brought tears to her eyes. When they embraced, she caught a whiff of Pasha, Amanda's favorite scent.

"They wouldn't let me come until today. In fact, they only let Peter in to see you," Amanda explained and set the candy down on the table. "I smuggled these in past Nurse Ratched at the desk." She giggled. "Also, I've brought enough trashy reading to keep you occupied for months. You'll love the new Alexander McCall Smith I put in here for you."

"Geez, I hope I won't be here months."

"'Course not, darling, but you still gotta read."

Amanda wore a bright floral dress, full of yellow, red, and green, selected no doubt to contrast with the bland hospital room.

"You didn't have to get all gussied up on my account. I must look a sight," she said.

"You'd look gorgeous in a concentration camp. It's people like you that make the rest of us paint our faces with makeup. Besides, I didn't put on my Sunday best for you. Have you seen your doctor? Talk about hot."

Marlene giggled. "God, you're good for the soul. How's Jack?"

Amanda eased herself up on the corner of the bed. "Fine. Worried about you like all of us."

"By the way, what's this I hear about you and Janie finding me?"

"Oh, you won't believe it. Janie came to my house all in a tizzy about you."

"But why'd she come to your house?"

Amanda crossed her legs as if ready to tell a bedtime story. "She called because of Jack. Apparently, she knew him a long time ago, when she was in high school."

Marlene shook her head. She knew so little about her vagrant sister. "Where's Janie now?"

Amanda blinked several times. "She'll probably be in to see you today. I haven't seen her since that morning when you were waking up.

We were all here, your Aunt Sarah and Mark, everybody. Dr. Patel told us you were conscious but in a great deal of distress. He ordered us out—everyone except Peter, of course."

"I'm sure Janie has other things on her mind besides me," Marlene said with a shrug.

"But, Marlene, don't be that way. If it hadn't been for her…" She paused and drew in a breath. "My God! You could've died!" She put her perfectly manicured hand to her mouth. Tears tumbled from her eyes.

"Yes, that's what Dr. Averett told me. I've got you to thank for being alive."

"And Janie," Amanda said, wiping her eyes. "I suppose you're mad at us for rescuing you."

"Don't be silly. Although I might not have said that yesterday. Boy, was I sick. Really, though, I'm grateful. The two of you saved my life."

"Seriously, Marlene, did you want us to?" Amanda's eyes looked red, and deep dark circles surrounded them. She sat with her hands laced in her lap and her head bowed.

"Of course I did. The doctor thinks I tried to kill myself. But I didn't. It was a mistake. I was depressed, and that drove me to drinking too much. When I couldn't block out the world with enough sweet-tasting Jack Daniels, I decided to take a few pills. That's all there was to it. I never intended to take my life, and I'm grateful to you and to Janie for saving me."

Amanda threw herself across Marlene. Tears poured down her cheeks. She hiccupped and sniffed while sobbing. Mascara streaked her cheeks. "I don't know what I would have done—"

"Don't even think about it."

They released each other.

"You're like a sister to me," Amanda said. "Better than my sorry sister, actually." She laughed and then faced Marlene with a frown. "Why didn't you tell me about you and Peter?"

"I couldn't quite, I guess. I'm sorry."

Amanda put her hand on Marlene's heart. "Next time you swear you'll talk to me. Scouts honor?" She made a cross over her heart.

Marlene smiled through her own tears. "Okay, I swear. My gosh. You look a mess. Better hope that handsome doctor doesn't decide to pay me a visit now."

Amanda giggled, blotted her face with a rumpled tissue, and said, "Who cares? I just love you so much. The thought of losing you…" She caught her breath again. "I just couldn't handle it. When we found you like that, we thought you were already dead. I'll never forget that empty look on your face as long as I live."

"Don't be haunted by such a horrible memory. Even though I'm sure I don't look a lot better now, I'm alive. I feel more alive than I have in years."

Amanda grinned. "You look wonderful. Later I'll braid your hair so you won't have to worry about it."

A feeling of loss passed over her. Janie used to braid her hair.

"Only if you want me to," Amanda quickly added.

"I'd love that. I was just thinking about Janie again. It must've been horrible for her, finding me that way. I can't imagine. Janie found our mother, and I've always felt guilty for not getting to her sooner." *God, poor Janie.*

"Everything happened so fast. We called the ambulance. I made all the calls. Janie stood next to you, holding your hand. She looked white as a sheet, that's for sure."

"Did she tell you we had coffee?"

Amanda nodded. "She said y'all had a bit of a set-to and she was real worried 'cause you hadn't returned her calls."

"Seeing her probably depressed me more than I realized. I suppose it brought back memories. And then, with everything else." She stopped before mentioning the calls from Ralph's lawyer. "I was so angry with her. I couldn't help it. I asked her why she left, but in a typical Janie style, she shrugged off her disappearance as she would clothes destined for the Salvation Army. Then she had the nerve to lecture me about drinking. Of course, considering my present situation, what can I say?"

"She's a strange one, that little sister of yours."

"I wonder what brought her back to Atlanta," Marlene said.

Amanda's eyes widened. "You mean you don't know?"

"She never said."

"Your sister drops out of the sky after twenty years, and you don't know why. There must've been a reason."

Marlene frowned. She should have found out what brought Janie back, but she didn't. Or if she did, she couldn't remember.

"I'll say this much," Amanda went on. "Janie's nothing like you. Had I not known you were sisters, I wouldn't have believed it. How come she got all those curls? And those dark eyes. Wow. She's pretty, don't get me wrong. But, in a different way."

"Janie's always been intense."

Before Amanda could respond, Dr. Averett entered and strolled up to the edge of the bed. "How's the patient today?"

Amanda kissed Marlene on the cheek. "I'll come back later," she said before exiting.

"I'm feeling much better thank you, Doctor."

"I can tell. Your eyes look brighter this morning. Perhaps your attractive friend helped cheer you up."

"She's got a knack for bringing in the sunshine. I'm fortunate to have such a friend."

He picked up the clipboard at the end of the bed and made a few notes on it. "Was she the one who discovered you?"

"Yes, you were right. She and my sister. I believe finding me nearly dead really traumatized poor Amanda. I suppose it would anyone."

"Un-huh," he mumbled.

Marlene remained quiet for several minutes. Dr. Averett glanced in her direction and then looked away before saying, "I've talked with your husband."

"I haven't seen him."

"Oh, he's been here every day, on and off. You probably don't remember. He didn't come any farther than the door threshold. But, he kept an eye on you from the window."

Marlene trembled at the image of Peter staring at her as she tossed in the bed and begged for a drink.

"What we've decided," the doctor continued, in what Marlene speculated was his all-business voice, "is to transfer you to Ridgeview Psychiatric Hospital later this afternoon or tomorrow, depending on when they can get a bed."

"But why?"

"Even though you didn't intend to kill yourself, you came mighty close to succeeding." He raised his brows slightly. "Perhaps you subconsciously wanted to end your life."

"But I didn't. I told you it was an *accident*." Her heart pounded faster.

"Ridgeview is a very pleasant place and one of the finest psychiatric facilities in the country. I'll continue to follow you. We'll talk. You'll have a chance to explore your past, understand yourself a little better. Peter agreed to join us in therapy. He told me he wants to help you recover and to work on saving your marriage, that is if you're willing."

Those words stung Marlene. If she didn't agree to go to this psychiatric hospital, would Peter divorce her? Obviously, she had little choice. Through a clenched jaw, she asked, "If I decide I don't want to go, do I have to?"

"I could commit you," the doctor said, no longer smiling.

She let out a loud sigh. "In that case, what choice do I have?"

"I'm recommending this transfer in your best interests. We want to help you, but you must want to help yourself. If you aren't willing to share the burden of your treatment, we're wasting everyone's time."

Marlene turned away from the doctor. Of course he was right. Her heart thundered at her chest. She balled up her fists. This doctor with kind eyes and a soothing voice along with Peter and his noble interests charted her course of treatment without consulting her. Just like when Peter picked out their house without her consent.

A few minutes later, Dr. Averett closed the door behind him.

"Damn," she muttered aloud.

Chapter Twenty-Five

By the time Janie found a hotel in midtown it was noon. She checked in to the Marriott, unloaded her stuff, and collapsed on the bed for a thirty-minute rest. Moving around like this was taking its toll. She had an appointment with Nelson at 2:00 p.m. If he had some good news, maybe this would be the last time she'd have to move.

Just as she settled down, her cell rang. It was Aunt Sarah. "The doctors are finally allowing visitors. Mark and I are on our way to the hospital now. Do you want to come?"

"I can't right now, but thanks for calling. I'll try to get there later this afternoon."

Silence. Aunt Sarah probably wondered what Janie had to do that was more important than visiting Marlene, but she simply said, "Okay, dear. Maybe we'll see you later."

Janie shut her eyes. How had her days gotten so full? She hardly had time to get up and gobble down a banana and a bite of yogurt before she was running through her to-do list, and poof, the day was over. She felt as if she were at home and in the midst of opening a new shop—always the busiest of times.

Because she planned to drop off the envelope with the rest of her documents at Peter's office on her way to meet Nelson, she dialed Peter's number.

The auburn-haired receptionist, who didn't much like her, said in clipped professional tone, "He's not coming in today. Care to leave a message?"

Of course he won't be in! He is attending to his wife, a.k.a., my sister in the hospital, she nearly yelled into the phone but instead said, "Thanks. I don't need to see him. I simply have something to drop off."

After hanging up, she went over to the closet where she had stashed the box from the bank. Thelma had left it in the living room by the door on Sunday morning. Janie had arrived fully expecting to see the family in the midst of another chaotic breakfast but found no one home. She placed Thelma's key on a side table with a note thanking her for everything. She did not intend to see her or Jerry ever again.

The next morning, she called James Ferber at Bank of America to inform him that the contents from her safety deposit box had been received.

"Thanks for your help," she told him.

One crisis averted.

Inside the box she rifled through the papers until she caught sight of the flimsy blue stationery with yellow flowers around the border. It had gotten itself lodged at the bottom. Janie caressed the crinkly blue paper— yellowed with age—amazing for blue paper. The ink had smeared. Perhaps she had cried the first time she had read it. She unfolded the letter and was about to re-read it, but quickly changed her mind. Instead, she retrieved the fresh envelope she had purchased that morning and tucked it inside, licking the flap.

On the outside she wrote: *For Marlene* and placed that note and one she had written last night to her sister in a larger manila envelope along with a letter to Aunt Sarah. She sealed the whole thing with tape. On the outside she wrote—*For Peter Tetford.* Then she put her typewritten codicil instructions on a separate sheet with Peter's name on the outside. She took a deep breath. Done.

And, that was supposed to be the easy part.

Before resealing the box from the bank, she lifted another object she had safely tucked in there nearly twenty years earlier. It felt heavier than she remembered and cold to her touch. She removed the red bandana she had wrapped it in and opened the bullet chamber—not having ever checked—to see if the gun was loaded. Five bullets gleamed from the chamber. Her hand trembled from touching the icy metal.

Memories of her last days in Atlanta flooded back—blood, the look on her mother's face, Ralph's screams, the smell of death, Marlene's fear.

Pistols baffled her, and she found this one, a .38 Smith and Wesson, particularly ominous with its ugly black trigger. She turned it in her hand, wishing she could figure out how to put the safety on, but she had no idea how to do that. As a child she had seen this gun in Mom's bedside table drawer, but strict warnings from Marlene had kept her curious fingers away—until the day when she had hidden it under her mattress. She had made plans then, too. If only she'd had the courage to execute them. Maybe now with the clock ticking away everything would be different.

She rewrapped the .38 in the bandana and placed it gently in her handbag. Then she grabbed the papers and headed for Peter's office.

After she dropped everything with Peter's secretary, a blonde by the name of Mrs. Quinn and much nicer than Miss Auburn-hair, she took off to meet Nelson. She had ten minutes to get to the Yellow Star Café, but downtown traffic clogged the roads. She crawled from stoplight to stoplight as cars whizzed past her as if she were not moving.

In the week that Janie had been in Atlanta, she had grown accustomed to Atlanta drivers, if not pleased. People in Savannah drove like tourists, even residents who had lived there their entire lives. No one was in a hurry to get anywhere. Life in Savannah moved in slow motion while life in Atlanta moved in fast-forward. That was one of the many things Janie loved about the beautiful, historic town she had adopted as her own.

Even though she would be late for her appointment with Nelson, she had no desire to rush. When she stopped at a caution light, the car behind her tooted its horn in angry frustration as if she'd broken the law.

A woman pushing a baby in a stroller crossed in front of Janie's Honda. The man behind her pounded on his steering wheel and shook his head. Perhaps he would have preferred crashing into this young mother and child than stopping at a red light. Whatever happened to pedestrians having the right of way?

When Janie lived in this town, she walked everywhere or hopped on a bus. Even though she knew how to drive, she never had a car. Her mother's '67 green Chevy, a gift from Grandpa Jennings, sat on flat tires in the garage at Briardale Lane where it gathered dust. Mom drove it when they were young, but hadn't touched it in her later years. At age sixteen Marlene had asked her mother if she could drive that car.

"Don't you dare!" Mom had responded. "Do you want to end up like your father?"

Janie turned up the volume of her radio when Fresh Air started. She loved Terry Gross's interviews. Today she was talking to one of her favorite actors—Tom Hanks, about his new film. As she listened, she wondered if she had stayed in Atlanta would she feel more akin to it and less impatient.

"I doubt it," she said aloud.

Atlanta had lost some of its charm by allowing so many cars to clog the beautiful old streets. Although she had read that more young couples had moved to midtown—buying up and restoring the old houses—they preferred to hop in a car rather than use public transportation. Even more mystifying was that these same people jogged miles and miles but never considered walking four or five blocks to the grocery store.

Oh, well, I must be getting old. I simple don't get it.

The car behind whizzed by her as soon as he could. She watched him shoot through a yellow light, wondering where he was going in such a hurry. Then she turned left into the Yellow Star Café parking lot. Her clock read 2:10 p.m.

Just like before, the place overflowed with young people tapping on computers and sipping tall cups of coffee. Most people quietly studied or surfed around on their computers or smart phones. With the exception of the sound of the coffee machine and the clanking of dishes, the place was as silent as a library. Again, she spotted Nelson in a back booth, alone.

He held his iPhone and was scrolling through his messages, looking like one of the crowd except he had at least ten years on most of them.

"Sorry I'm late," she said when she reached him, sliding out of her coat. "Traffic was horrible."

"Where are you staying?"

She smiled, not about to reveal that to him or anyone else. "I'm moving around. But, I had errands downtown."

He nodded. "Traffic downtown is the worst," he said as if that explained it all.

She signaled the waitress for a small coffee and waited for Nelson to begin.

"I watched the house near on twenty-four hours," he said in a low voice. "Came back and stayed another twelve. There wasn't much coming and going, but they were very busy."

He stopped when the waitress put Janie's coffee in front of her and refilled his cup. He added cream and scrolled through his electronic notes. "I checked out the black guy living there with him. He's an ex-con just like you thought by the name of Jinx Lewis. He was in the joint for armed robbery at the same time as Cooper. They're clearly up to some kind of no good."

"Any clues as to what?" She sipped the coffee while he spoke.

He shook his head. "But, they were looking for something. They took each room apart, even ripping up some of the floorboards. I watched them through the windows. They were so preoccupied, I could have gone in and stood in front of them and they wouldn't have noticed. Any idea what they're hunting for?"

Janie had an idea, but she wasn't going to share it. "What else?" she asked, ignoring his question.

He tapped, tapped, tapped on his phone. "That lawyer came a couple of times. At least, I'm guessing it was him from your description. This him?" He showed her a photo on the phone.

Janie studied the blurry image. There was no question it was Samuel D. Whitaker. "That's the creep," she said, taking a deep breath.

The photo gave her a better look at the black man as well. He towered over Ralph by at least a foot. His head was shaved and tattoos covered his chest. He had biceps that could crush Janie in seconds.

"Tell me what Whitaker did," she said.

"He didn't stay long. They had this little powwow in the living room. I peered in from the window. Whitaker had some papers with him that he gave to Cooper and later he and Cooper took off. I followed them to town. My guess is they went to the lawyer's office. Lewis never left the house. Well, not exactly. He goes out every morning around six-thirty to jog, usually for an hour."

"Does Cooper stay at home then?"

"Yeah."

"Was there any time when both left the house?"

"Only once Cooper went out while Lewis was jogging. I followed him to a donut shop on the corner of Ponce. He sat near the front window, drank coffee and read the paper. He was there for about forty minutes. He returned with coffee and a newspaper, I guess for Lewis."

"Okay. There's a possibility the house is unattended from six-thirty to seven-thirty in the morning, right?"

"Not every morning, but, yeah. Want me to keep watching and see if they find what they're hunting?"

"I don't think so. Anyone else come to the house to see them?"

He shook his head. "Not while I was there."

Janie ran her thumb around the edge of her cup. Finally she said, "Fine. That's all I need."

"You sure you don't you want me to keep watching 'em?"

"No, you've done enough. I don't have time to wait forever. They'll probably finish with their inside search soon. I want them preoccupied with that, possibly even digging up the yard. You've given me enough to gauge their movements."

"I'm going to see Mr. Whitaker this evening. I should have that finished for you by the end of today."

"Thanks, Nelson, I really appreciate this." She reached for her coat.

"That's it. You don't need nothing else?"

She studied him in surprise. "You did what I asked. I can't think of anything else."

"But what are you gonna do? You don't want to tangle with those goons by your lonesome, not with that big ex-con hanging around."

"I don't need any help." She paused and reconsidered. "I have your number. If I need you, I'll contact you. Send me a text once you've taken care of Whitaker, and I'll get the rest of your money to you."

She left a five-dollar bill on the table to cover both tabs. Then she drove to the hospital to see Marlene.

The door squeaked when she pushed it and Marlene opened her eyes. A smile crept across her sister's face when she walked in.

"Didn't think you'd come back," her sister said in a weak voice. "Figured you'd go off on the lamb again after what I put you through."

Janie sat on the edge of the bed. "Yeah, you did scare the life out of us. How are you feeling?"

"I'm pretty wiped out." Marlene's blue eyes were cloudy like faded denim jeans, but her cheeks had a spark of pink.

"You look a lot better than the last time I saw you."

"When was that?"

"I was here on Sunday morning. You were sleeping but apparently you had been through a rough night. The nurse tried to stop me from seeing you, but you know me." Janie grinned.

"Yeah, that's like telling you to come right on in."

They both laughed. Janie couldn't remember the last time she had laughed with her sister. It sure felt good.

"I didn't stay long," she said. "They wouldn't let me. You were dreaming and looking awfully peaceful."

"It was horrible. I wouldn't wish detox on my worst enemy. That experience was enough to discourage me from ever touching a drop of alcohol for the rest of my life. God!"

"Do you think Mom ever went through detox?"

"My guess is she did. Maybe it wasn't as bad back then. Who knows? But, I can't believe anyone would start drinking again after that." Marly sighed and looked away. "Did they tell you they're moving me?"

"Aunt Sarah told me. She said you're going to Ridgeview." *Where Mom had been twice,* she didn't say.

Marlene set up on her elbows. "They think I tried to kill myself. I can't convince them that I didn't. Even Aunt Sarah doesn't believe me."

Janie didn't answer. She took her sister's hand in hers.

"Remember how we tiptoed around Mama and worried each time we walked into her pitch dark room," Marlene said. "Once I checked to make sure she was breathing. All those rumors we heard about her being crazy scared me. There's no way I'd stoop that low. I was depressed, sure, but I never even thought about killing myself. Have you?"

She had, actually. In fact, she had thought a lot about taking her own life in the last few days. But, she had too much to do. Later, maybe if things got worse...

Her hesitation caused Marlene to grip her hand tighter.

"You haven't have you, Janie?"

Janie smiled and shook her head. "Of course not. Just like Mom, I like myself too much." What she didn't say was she loved Sue Anne too much to ever take her own life even with the prospect of death looming over her, holding a giant ticking stopwatch.

"Please tell that doctor I didn't try and kill myself."

"I'll tell him, but no one will believe me unless you can explain how you got so many pills in you. That's what made everyone suspicious."

Marlene relaxed her hold on Janie and fell back on the pillows. "I took the pills so I could sleep. I was so tired. Then I got that call from that sleazy lawyer of Ralph's. What's he think I can do? I can't help him, and I wouldn't anyway. Why won't Ralph go away and leave us alone? I tried to get him to leave town, even offered to pay him, but he refused."

"Listen, Marly. Quit worrying about Ralph. It's my turn to deal with him. You've had him on your back for long enough. You just worry about getting better, okay?"

Marlene closed her eyes. After a moment she said, "So what's this I hear about you knowing Jack and hooking up with Amanda?"

Janie settled down next to her sister and told her the long overdue story of her wild adolescence.

Chapter Twenty-Six

Marlene pulled the draw cord to the heavy curtains in her room at Ridgeview Hospital and stared outside. The lawn simmered bright green under streaks of sunlight, and huge magnolias mingled with tall pine trees shaded the windows. Spring was sneaking up on her. Oversized leafy azaleas sprouted buds that promised to explode into white, red, and pink flowers.

Leaning out her window, she caught a glimpse of the gnarled dogwood tree at the front entrance. She'd been away from home for too long.

I sure hope Nellie isn't causing Peter too much trouble.

She returned to the chair next to her bed but still gazed out the window. When she first arrived at this hospital, she had insisted on a single room. She couldn't face the thought of dealing with a stranger. Dr. Averett made special arrangements, which she had never regretted.

She lifted the pad of paper in front of her and studied her words. Dr. Averett suggested she keep a journal. He asked her to recall the happy days of her past. She struggled to dig up good memories, but each time the bad ones invaded. She protested, telling him she couldn't think of any happy times. He insisted. Finally, she said, "Only when my daddy was alive."

"That's fine," he had replied.

Today, she recorded a memory that had come to her last night while sleeping.

"Girls, how about a trip up to Alpharetta to pick strawberries?" Mama had asked one bright Saturday morning in the dead of summer.

Marlene was eating a bowl of Cheerio's, trying hard not to spill the milk on the table. Janie watched her with little-sister admiration.

"Yeah!" they hollered at once.

"Finish your breakfast, and we'll head on up there. Mary Louise told me they have the biggest, juiciest berries ever this year. We can make strawberry shortcake for your daddy. Won't that be fun?"

They both leapt from their chairs to put the bowls in the sink. Because Janie couldn't reach high enough, she tilted hers and milk spilled all over the front of her shirt and on the floor.

"Yuck," Marlene said with a nasty scowl and stepped back.

"It's okay," Mama answered, reaching for a dishcloth. "I'll take care of it. Go help Janie put on a fresh shirt."

They skipped from the kitchen.

"Y'all better wear shorts. It'll be hot," Mama called after them.

When they came scooting back, Mama tucked in their shirts and smoothed their hair before they piled into the big green Chevy.

The trip to Alpharetta took about forty minutes. They drove away from the city and headed down a two-lane road northwest in the direction of Tennessee. After no more than five miles, all they could see were trees and green hills. A few roadside stands with fresh vegetables and jars of homemade jams popped up along the way. Marlene, who was five, loved raspberry jam and immediately begged for some.

"First the strawberries," her mother said. "When we come back, if there's time, we'll stop for jam. In the meantime, quiet down so I can drive."

Mama hummed a tune Marlene had heard before but didn't know the name of. In her mind, she called it Mama's Song.

Janie rode in a baby seat next to the passenger window. Marlene sat in the middle. On such a long trip it took all her willpower not to tickle

214 | JOAN C. CURTIS

Janie. She sat on her hands, but kept wiggling over toward her sister. Mama's hand constantly landed on her lap.

Just over the hill Mama pulled into an Exxon station.

"Where are we going?" Marlene asked.

"We're just stopping a minute at this filling station, honey," Mama answered as she rolled down the window of the Chevy.

A man with blue overalls, a denim cap and a big belly meandered to the car. "Can I help you, ma'am?"

"Fill it up, please, with high test."

The man grinned at Mama. His teeth were yellow, and his small eyes disappeared into a chubby red race.

"Want me to check under the hood, ma'am?"

"Please," her mother replied, without looking at him while fishing around in her purse.

Marlene watched the man while he cleaned the windshield. He moved a squeegee from one side to the next, but he left a large smudge in the center. He chewed something, and when he noticed her looking at him, he winked. She turned away, embarrassed. Her mother lit a cigarette and blew smoke out the window.

"That'll be five dollars and twenty-five cents, little lady," the man said, coming back around and wiping his hands on his overalls.

Mama dug out a ten-dollar bill.

The man wore a coin changer on his waist. He pressed the buttons to release the right change, and then he pulled a wad of bills from his back pocket. He peeled off four one-dollar bills and handed them and the change to Mama.

"Thank you, ma'am. Y'all come back now."

Mama waved to him as her tiny arms strained with each turn of the big green steering wheel. Finally, they returned to the highway.

Two-year-old Janie slept through the gas station experience but now woke up and began fussing.

"Hush, dear. We're here," Mama said, and pointed to an old piece of wood with red letters painted on it.

"What's it say?" Marlene asked.

"Strawberries. You Pick-em and Eat-em. Two dollars a basket."

Cars lined the edge of the road a short distance from the sign.

"Do you think there'll be any strawberries left?" Marlene asked.

"Strawberries left," Janie repeated and grasped Marlene's hand tighter than she would a rope on a mountain climb.

"Sure. There'll be plenty left, darlings."

Mama picked up Janie and grabbed hold of Marlene's hand. She wobbled on the soft ground in her high-heel shoes.

When they reached the entrance to the shack, a grizzled man greeted them. He had no teeth and his face was covered in gray stubble.

Marlene stared at him.

"Hi," Janie said, oblivious to the man's toothless, unshaven condition.

"Howdy, little 'un. You'uns here to pick strawberries?"

"Yessir," Mama answered, putting Janie down.

"Here are two baskets. The little 'un can help her sister."

"Now, girls," Mama said, leaning down so they could hear. "Don't you eat any berries before we get back. We have to pay for 'em first, y'all hear now? And for heaven's sake don't get strawberry juice all over you. Marly, you gotta help me keep an eye on your sister. I'm depending on you, honey."

"Okay, Mama," she said, while she tried to manage her basket and Janie's claw-like grip.

Together they marched into the strawberry field where the rows of bushes hung heavy with the fruit. Since Janie was the closest to the ground, it was easier for her to pick the berries, but not many landed in Marlene's basket. Most of Janie's harvest fell to the ground and got stepped on. Marlene knelt down with her basket between her legs and picked as many as she could. After a while her knees got sore, and they looked redder than blood.

Mama trailed along behind. "Y'all tired already?"

"No," Marlene answered, but her eyes drooped.

Mama unleashed Janie's hand from Marlene's. "Darling, come on with me a minute."

"No," Janie screamed.

Ignoring the outburst, Mama lifted her, and in no time she and Mama filled the baskets.

When they reached the shack with two full baskets, Mama laughed. "Y'all girls have done got strawberry juice all over your mouths and faces. You look like Indians preparing for a war dance."

Marlene laughed, too, when she looked at her sister's red mouth.

Mama turned to the toothless man. "I'll pay a little extra for the children."

"Ain't no matter, missy."

He charged them four dollars for two baskets of the biggest, reddest strawberries Marlene had ever seen.

That night, they served Daddy his favorite dessert—strawberry shortcake with fresh whipped cream they'd helped Mama make.

Marlene hadn't thought about that day in the strawberry patch in years, and the memory tasted as delicious as had the ripened fruit.

When she finished recording the strawberry memory, her eyes fell on an entry she'd made a few days earlier. She had titled it, *Poor Peter*.

It had been the first afternoon after she had arrived at Ridgeview. Peter had entered with a bouquet of white lilies. He reminded her of a sheepish adolescent trying to win approval from a girlfriend.

"Hi," he said. His eyes darted from the bed to the four walls.

Marlene was removing clothes from the suitcase.

"You sure thought of everything." She lifted a pair of shorts and a summer top. "I doubt I'll need these. I'm really hoping I won't be here till summer."

"I-I didn't know," he stammered. "I just wanted to make sure you had whatever you might need. Amanda helped. We thought it might get warm in your room."

He put the flowers on the table.

She didn't know what to say to him. He seemed like a stranger to her. She lifted the flowers to her nose and breathed in. They had no aroma.

"They're beautiful," she said. "I'll ask the nurse for a vase."

Peter sat in the chair across from her bed. "We've got to talk."

Marlene settled down on the edge of the bed, wishing she had put on some lipstick before he'd come. "So?"

"I've been sick with worry about you." He spoke fast and didn't look at her. "You can't imagine how shocked I was when Amanda called me that horrid day. Sarah said you're insisting you didn't try to take your own life. But—"

"I didn't."

He shot her a look of surprise. Deep creases cut across his forehead.

"Peter," she began in a softer voice. "You ought to know I'd never kill myself. I simply needed to drink to relieve the pain inside me. I haven't had a drink now, for what, going on four days? But the pain remains. Perhaps it will be good for me to stay here until I can get that under control." She paused before adding, "I can't believe you and Dr. Averett made the decision to send me here without consulting me. I'm not a child. I do have some say about what happens to me."

"I'm sorry. It's just that we weren't sure you would agree. And I couldn't stand it if something—"

"You could have asked me."

"Listen, Marlene, we haven't communicated too well lately."

His voice was clipped, angry, accusatory. "I had no idea how you might respond."

Marlene turned away. "I don't know what's going to happen to us. When you walked out on me, I thought my world had caved in. Everything good in my life was coming apart. Now, facing you here, I just don't know what I think or feel."

He ran his hand through his hair. "I left because I just didn't know what else to do. It wasn't that I stopped loving you. What I didn't love was watching you slowly kill yourself. I hope-I mean…" He paused. "You didn't do this because of me, because I left, did you?"

She took a deep breath. "Peter, I didn't do anything. It was an accident. How many times do I have to say that? I took too many of those pills without knowing what I was doing."

Dr. Averett's words rang in her head, *Denial, Marlene. It's not uncommon for people to deny they wanted to kill themselves. It's okay.*

That meant he still didn't believe it was an accident. Apparently, Peter didn't either.

"I really don't know what to think." He stopped again. "But, you shouldn't let that worry you now. It's too soon. I just wanted to tell you I love you, and I'm sorry if I had anything to do with this."

Marlene took his hand. "I'm not going to pretend it'll be easy. I've got battles raging inside me."

She glanced up, remembering those words. That first visit from her husband had been awkward and strained as if they were people from opposite sides of the world. But that was last week. Since then, their relationship hadn't improved. She lifted her pen and wrote in her journal: *I wonder if I still love him.*

Dr. Averett stuck his head around the door. "How are you feeling today?"

"I'm doing better." She lifted her journal. "I came up with a good memory."

He smiled. "Good, we'll talk about it this afternoon. Are the meds still giving you a headache?"

"I'm not sure if it's the meds. But my head feels better today. Maybe it's the spring air."

When she first came to the hospital, she felt as if she'd fallen into a deep empty well. All she could see was darkness. Now, a few days later, she had clawed her way closer to the top, but a long climb remained.

Dr. Averett gave her thumbs up. "I'll see you after lunch and we'll talk more."

She had shared much of the gruesome tales of her youth with the psychiatrist, specifically with regard to her mother's drinking, depression and neglect, but she had said nothing about Ralph. Of course he knew that Ralph had killed her mother and gone to prison, but he didn't know about Ralph's abuses. She wanted to tell him, but she couldn't muster the courage. How do you tell someone something so humiliating?

Several times he had asked about Ralph. She responded saying he was a weak little man who frightened her as a child. But she omitted how she felt about him. She couldn't put the right words together. Dr. Averett probed, but Marlene faltered. The demons inside her wouldn't go away until she told Dr. Averett all about Ralph and her mixed-up emotions. Still the words wouldn't come.

She got up from the chair and adjusted the temperature on her heater then she glanced back at her journal, reread her description of the strawberry patch, and savored the taste of those long ago days.

Ten minutes later, she joined a group therapy session with six other people whom she had met before, but she couldn't remember their names.

"Let's go around the circle and each of you share your feelings," Jennifer, the therapist said.

"I'm lonely," said one man.

"I'm angry," said another.

She shifted in her seat. When her time came, she said, "I'm hollow."

Later, people in the group started talking about wanting to drink. Each talked about the cravings that gnawed inside them—those little itches that seemed to never go away. Marlene listened with interest. She had not craved a drink. She wanted nothing to do with the poison that had ruined her mother's life and was threatening her own. Being in this place where drinking wasn't an option had freed her. But she feared what might happen once she got home and had to face living again.

After the group session, she went to the cafeteria for lunch. She settled by herself to avoid conversations with the other patients.

"Hello, the name's Nick Sims. I'm a successful businessman turned alcoholic. Do you mind?" The rather uninteresting man indicated the seat facing her.

She frowned and unwrapped a formless turkey sandwich.

He slid his tray opposite hers.

"So how long have you been in his beautiful resort?" he asked, ignoring her nonverbal rebuff. He brushed back a strand of jet-black hair that clung to his bald scalp.

"Four days." She drank from the dark liquid they called iced tea and didn't elaborate.

"Four miserable days, do I detect?"

She nodded.

"It'll get better," Nick said. "I've been here nearly two weeks. I've seen you sitting by yourself. It's not good to hibernate in this place."

She studied the way he unwrapped a dish of fruit. He had neatly manicured nails and slender fingers with a brush of dark hair on his knuckles.

"My name's Marlene Tetford," she said, with a trace of a smile.

"Let me give you a hint, Marlene. Don't ever try the chocolate cake they put up there to tempt us. People say alcoholics are chocolate freaks. That may or may not be true, but the cake they make tastes worse than frozen Sarah Lee."

She laughed. "I love Sarah Lee brownies."

"Oops."

They talked easily through the lunch period. His relaxed manner embraced Marlene like a comfortable terrycloth robe. She liked Nick Sims and the soft sparkle in his light hazel eyes. When she had to excuse herself to go to her session with Dr. Averett, a wave of regret passed over her.

She scolded herself. *I dare not get attached to anyone in this place.*

Chapter Twenty-Seven

Janie switched off her headlights when she pulled up to Briardale Lane and parked outside the house at 5:45 in the morning. A trace of sunlight appeared on the horizon. She would be able to watch the sunrise, something she had not done in years.

The sky had just turned a beautiful shade of magenta when she spotted a figure coming around from the back of the house. Although it was still nearly dark, she deciphered the form of a large black man. He was dressed in sweats and tennis shoes and wore a bandana tied around his head. He peered to the right before turning left and running up the street away from Janie's Honda. She glanced at her watch again. Fifteen minutes. If Ralph didn't exit in fifteen minutes, she would return the next day.

While she waited, she removed the gun from her purse and placed it in the pocket of her coat. Then she scrolled through her emails. She couldn't get Wi-Fi here, but she picked up several new messages from yesterday, including one from Steven letting her know he had sold the property in Garden City. He had attached the documents and told her she would need to return for the closing in two weeks.

She sighed. *I hope I'm back in Savannah by then, sipping a glass of wine on the back patio with Sue Anne.*

Who was she fooling? Carrying out her plan meant she might never return to Savannah. The gun, nestled in her coat pocket, sent a chill up her spine.

An engine cranked nearby. She spotted a car rolling down the driveway next to Briardale Lane. Just as Nelson had said, Ralph was leaving for breakfast while his friend jogged.

It was now or never. Her stomach tightened. She watched the taillights of Ralph's SUV disappear around the corner. The rest of the neighborhood remained clothed in darkness and sleep.

Like a cat she crept out of the car and around to the back of the house, slipping through the screened door and onto the back porch. The back lock hung loosely and had not been re-fastened as it had been when she had come here before. She had stashed a screwdriver in her pocket in case she would have to pry it open. Instead, she merely turned the handle and edged her way into the kitchen.

Once inside, she blinked several times to allow her eyes to adjust to the dim light. Then she switched on her flashlight. Aunt Sarah employed a woman to clean so the smell of Pine Sol and Lemon Pledge didn't surprise her. Nor did the other odor. She recognized that smell— perspiration mixed with stale cigarettes and cheap cologne, the scent reminding her of a dog left out in the rain for too long. A shiver ran through her body as a distant memory popped in her head—Ralph at the kitchen table, eating with his elbows propped on both sides and stuffing mashed potatoes into his mouth.

She moved to the staircase toward what had been Marlene's room. Willing her feet to lightness, she eased herself up the stairs one at a time like she had done many times before as a teenager. The staircase seemed narrower. Images of Ralph and Marlene in that bedroom flashed before Janie's eyes. Her body stiffened and her stomach turned. She gagged and stopped her assent. With clenched fists she regained her composure, climbing another step, cringing with each creak beneath her feet. She had vowed never to step foot in this house again. *Never!*

She peeked around the half-closed door. Country music blared from the radio. She recognized the sound of Brenda Lee, an Atlanta native, singing "Johnny One Time. " Ralph had left the radio on, always unable to function without noise.

Lee crooned in words that triggered memories of Peter. She had certainly felt shame that morning she had walked out of Peter's apartment in the rain. She had chased him down after their one-nighter and tried to seduce him again. God only knew why—adolescent pride perhaps. Instead, he sent her home like a toddler who had misbehaved.

From the looks of the room, Ralph was camping out in this space, the place where he had always felt the most at home. She suspected the black man was living downstairs either in her or Mom's room. She would check that out later. Right now she had other things to do.

She inched farther into the room, stumbling on an old pair of shoes lying in the middle of the floor and nearly knocking over a glass of half-drunk iced tea.

Ralph had strewn his clothes from one end of the room to the other. Drawers were half-open with shirts and pants spilling out.

She moved over to the desk and sifted through newspapers, old issues of *People* magazine, mail and a partially eaten Reece's bar. She rifled through the papers underneath the mess when the announcer on the radio said, "The time is six fifteen. Today's high will be fifty-two under sunny skies."

Six-fifteen. She knocked stuff onto the floor as she searched. By the time the radio returned to music, this time a Willie Nelson tune that she couldn't name, she found what she was looking for—a manila folder with a document inside from the Georgia Innocence Project. She tucked it under her arm.

The closet in this room was actually a small attic space under the eaves. She and Marlene had played in it as kids. She doubted Ralph used it, particularly given the chaotic state of things. She opened the door and just as she thought, she spotted nothing belonging to Ralph. The marionettes she and Marlene had used to conduct neighborhood puppet shows sat in one corner, looking eerie. This would be a perfect place to wait. But first, she needed to check out the downstairs.

She tiptoed along the hallway near her mother's room when she heard a noise. A car engine outside the window stopped and a car door slammed. Ralph was back, sooner than she expected.

Without thinking, she ducked into the closet underneath the staircase. Marlene used to accuse her of listening in on her telephone calls, having had no idea that Janie often hid in this closet where she learned everything that went on in the house. She shifted the vacuum cleaner and a box full of old blankets and crouched low, her knees creaking in protest. Even if someone opened the closet door, she could conceal herself behind the blankets. The same quilts and woolen Afghans remained in this closet untouched as if twenty years had not passed. Surely the vacuum cleaner no longer worked.

Footsteps passed through the den and climbed the stairs. They moved from side to side above her as if dancing to a tune. She used to listen to Marlene's feet when she had lurked here as a kid and wondered what Marlene was up to alone in her room, moving around so much. Today she reflected on Ralph. Had he forgotten to bring his wallet? She didn't notice a wallet upstairs, but it could have been lodged in a pair of pants thrown helter-skelter in that room.

The musty smell of the blankets mingled with the thick stale odor from the vacuum cleaner twitched at Janie's nose, threatening to make her sneeze. She breathed into the sleeve of her coat to deaden the odors. If she did sneeze, no one would hear her. Still, she didn't want to risk it. She sucked in her breath and held it. The urge to sneeze soon vanished.

Even before her teen years she had hidden in this closet because it gave her a perfect vantage point for hearing everything that happened from the kitchen to her mother's bedroom without anyone seeing her or knowing where she was. Voices from the past filled her ears: Ralph arguing with her mother, usually about Marlene.

"You can't let her go out with that group of near-do-wells. They're up to no good."

Her mother countering, "She can take care of herself. Just leave her be."

They would go back and forth like this until Ralph won. Mom called Ralph a terrier because he nibbled away and nibbled away until he won.

"He just plain won't ever quit," she used to say.

That thought gave Janie a jolt. Maybe that explained his persistence with proving his innocence. He would never give up no matter what she did. She reached inside her pocket and fingered the .38's cold metal. *I'm just gonna have to persuade him. Give him no choice.*

Another voice from the past joined those of her mother's and Ralph's. This time Aunt Sarah was hollering at her mother. "Marlene needs to get away from this house."

"She's my daughter and I'll say what she needs," Mom yelled back.

These arguments went on so long, she used to lose interest and fall asleep among the old blankets. It was Marlene they always discussed, never her.

Something fell to the ground upstairs making a loud clank above her head. Ralph must've knocked over a chair. He seemed to be looking for something, perhaps the document she held under her coat. She pulled it closer to her.

As she listened to the frantic movement above her, another memory intruded. Once, she'd hidden in this closet with a kitten she had found in the street. When her mother had refused to let her keep the tiny black and white creature, she escaped here—the perfect place for her and the kitten to live forever where no one would ever find them. She could sneak out for food whenever the house grew silent. She had stayed tucked away for a few hours and then decided to come out when the kitten mewed with restlessness. No one had missed her.

Ralph eventually let her keep the kitten. She had named him Bianco for his white fur. Unfortunately, Bianco had disappeared after a couple of years.

If Ralph didn't leave again and the black guy came back, what would she do? Unlike when she was eleven years old with the kitten, she didn't think she could stay here all day and into the night. Her plan had been to hang out in the upstairs closet where there was more room and where she'd have access to Ralph alone. She needed to get out of here and back up those stairs when no one was around.

Minutes later, elephant-like footsteps descended the stairs. Was he carrying a suitcase or furniture? Her heart pounded. Then the backdoor slammed shut. She clicked on her iPhone to check the time. 6:41. The big man would be back soon. She needed to get out of there before it was too late.

She eased herself up to a bent standing position and placed her ear against the door. She held her breath and listened hard.

Nothing.

She sighed.

Still nothing.

Minutes passed like hours. The dim light from under the door had lightened. Daylight had arrived. Visions of what Ralph would do to her if he found her flashed in her mind. He would definitely be surprised. She imagined his eyes popping out of his ugly red face. This was the last place he or his slimy lawyer would search for her.

Crash went the backdoor. Footsteps lumbered back up the staircase. She couldn't fathom what he was up to, going back and forth like this. Maybe they'd begun searching in the yard, digging up the garden. Janie let out a long breath. The boards above her head creaked again, threatening to lull her to sleep. Maybe she would make an attempt to escape while he messed around upstairs before he had a chance to come back down. She could sneak out the backdoor and return tomorrow.

She clicked on her iPhone again, 6:50. Her heart pounded with indecision. *Just go! Now!* But, it was too risky. Back and forth, back and forth. She waited. The air in the closet grew thin. She wrapped her arms around herself. Her legs tingled. She shifted her weight to relieve the numbness.

Silence. Janie continued to wait. Nothing. The silence grew louder. He had stopped moving. Maybe he had gone back to sleep or maybe she had dozed off, and he had left. She could only hear herself breathing. The sound of her exhales seemed to echo as if she were in a tunnel. She slowed her breathing, but it still sounded loud enough to set off an alarm.

Everything was so black she could barely tell if her eyes were open or closed.

If she concentrated real hard, eyes closed, she could hear the tick, tock of the grandfather clock in the living room. Tick, tock. Tick, tock. How many tick-tocks made a minute? An hour? Tick, tock.

Why hadn't the grandfather clock been sold or moved to Marlene's house? Aunt Sarah had left the old home intact. The only thing she carefully removed was the dust. It was like a mausoleum to her mother and her miserable life. They should have sold it all off. Every last item.

She touched the gun. It remained tucked in her coat pocket along with the screwdriver. She reached into the other pocket for the flashlight. It wasn't there. *Oh my God!* She fumbled around on the closet floor in search of it. All she felt was dust. Her heart sank. She must have left it on the dresser upstairs.

Footsteps raced down the stairs, faster this time. The backdoor slammed shut and a voice shouted, "Ralph, you in here?"

She froze. The big man was back.

"Jinx, c'm 'ere."

Ralph's voice felt as if it were next to the closet door, and the sound of it made the hair on her arms stand up.

She bit her lower lip. Her heart pounded. Both sets of feet lumbered up the stairs as if they were in no hurry.

Now was the time, while they were upstairs. *Go now!* She had to get out of there. She had delayed too long. *Go!*

Finally, she unfolded herself to release the cramps in her dead legs. She inched herself back into a standing position, still listening. Creak went the ceiling above. She considered opening the door and peeking out. Her hand moved to the doorknob and stopped. Her stomach clinched imagining him waiting for her, the sunlight catching the green glint in his eyes and the red in his hair. She could almost feel his breath on her neck and smell the rancid onion he always ate. She froze. Her heart blasted against her chest. Taking a deep breath, she squared her shoulders and cracked the door.

Another creak sounded maybe from the staircase. She edged from the closet as quietly as she could. With the lights off and no windows she had trouble seeing. The last thing she wanted to do was knock something over that might alert them to her presence. Moving one foot in front of the other with her arms outstretched, she inched along like a blind person. *Just get to the kitchen and out the door*, she coaxed herself.

Suddenly a big hand grabbed her arm and yanked her to the floor.

Chapter Twenty-Eight

After that chance lunch encounter, Marlene joined Nick every day at meals, and she looked forward to seeing him. He had been vice-president for a marketing firm called Nortex. He managed to hide his alcoholism until he showed up drunk for an important sales presentation. His staff closeted him in his office, poured coffee into him, and made excuses. The next day he was shipped off to the hospital.

"Of course my personal life didn't fare so well either," he explained. "My wife couldn't take all the booze. She walked out on me last year. I haven't seen my little girl in months. That's something I'm gonna change as soon as I get out of here."

Marlene told him about herself and her own drinking. She explained how she nearly killed herself but didn't mean to.

"Are you sure you didn't mean to?"

They talked alone in the game room. The other patients had gone on a special outing to the Fox Theatre to see *Fiddler on the Roof*. Marlene had begged off, having seen the play numerous times, and Nick opted to hang around with her. Old magazines covered the tables. A Scrabble game in progress sat in front of them.

"I'm sure," she answered, annoyed he would even ask.

Nick placed the word *vixen* on the Scrabble board. "I didn't mean that the way it sounded. What I mean is—" he paused "—sometimes we get so down on ourselves for drinking and for everything else that, you know, we take that extra handful of pills and think, what the hell? If it kills me fine, if it doesn't who gives a rat's ass, if you'll pardon my French."

Marlene frowned, considering what Nick suggested. No one described what happened to her in such a cavalier, haphazard manner. Others intimated she had planned her suicidal attempt, thought about it in some deliberate fashion. She kept calling it an accident—something she had never meant to do. Nick, on the other hand, made it sound as though it just happened, naturally, no plans, no motives. Maybe he was right. In truth, she couldn't consciously remember what happened on that day except she wanted to hide from those awful telephone calls and from painful thoughts about Peter.

Nick took hold of her hand. A tingle ran up her arm. She studied him like a child begging for approval and saw nothing but tenderness on his round, slightly tanned face.

After a few minutes, she looked away and added the word, *oxen,* to the board. "Have you ever done that?" she asked him.

"You mean accidentally taken too many pills?"

She nodded. He still held her hand in his, his long slender fingers pulsating. Finally he released his hold on her. He studied the words on the board.

"Is poltrice a word?"

"Never heard of it."

"Okay, how about..." He placed *pumice* on the board. "I must say I have thought about killing myself," he began. "When Sally left, taking Jenny with her, I had trouble facing each day. I felt like such a loser. I'd screwed up everything that mattered in my life. What was the point of continuing to live? Yep, I sure thought about it then. Probably even said so to anyone who was fool enough to listen. But, I never got the chance. And to be honest, I'm not sure I would have had the courage."

Nick won the Scrabble game a few moves later. Afterward and before everyone returned from the play, they took a stroll outside. Marlene wore a light jacket to block out the wind, but the sun penetrated the thin material and warmed her from head to toe. She liked being in Nick's company. Except for Dr. Averett, he was the only person she felt safe talking to. She had told him about her mother, not everything, of course, but how she drank and how she and Janie had found her dead. When she mentioned Ralph, he surprised her by saying,

"Your mom must not have liked you girls much," he said.

"What do you mean?"

"To marry a man like that. Why did she do it?"

Marlene shrugged. "As a kid I sometimes wondered because Mama was so pretty and Ralph was ordinary at best and not educated. Not that Mama had much education, but she did graduate from high school and had she not gotten pregnant with me, my guess is she would have gone to college like Aunt Sarah. Anyway, I think she married him because she needed someone. Mama couldn't be without a man, even one like Ralph."

He shook his head. "Nope. There had to be more to it than that. Think about it. Your dad was dead just a few months. Your grandmother was around to take care of y'all, and you said she didn't care much for Ralph. Why would she marry this man, against everyone else's better judgment?"

Marlene didn't answer because her mind was blank. Finally she said, "So what do you think? Why did she marry him?"

Nick laughed. His eyes disappeared when he laughed, reminding Marlene of her father.

"I could only hazard a guess, mind you. But I'd say she did it out of anger, maybe even spite. When someone dies, one of the stages of grief is anger. Maybe your mom was angry at your dad for dying. She knew how much he loved you kids. What better way to get back at him then to sic y'all with that jerk of a stepdad?"

Marlene shook her head. "That's pretty cruel. I never saw Mama as being cruel, thoughtless, maybe, but never cruel."

"I'm sure she didn't mean to be cruel. She probably was thinking about herself or maybe responding to the grief in the only way she knew how. Unfortunately, once the anger left and the earlier stages of grief moved through, she was stuck with this man and so were you."

What an amazing idea. Mama had married Ralph to spite Daddy for dying and then to get back at her and Janie. *Unlikely.* "As things turned out, though," Marlene said. "Mama was the big loser. After all, Ralph killed her in the end."

Nick stopped walking. "Yeah, life's little ironies. No one will ever know for sure, will they? All this is past history now. You need to let it go." He cocked his head at her. "Let's sit on the bench and soak up the sun before they call us in for dinner."

The next day, Marlene learned that Nick was leaving at the end of the week. Alone in her room, she closed her eyes and tried not to think about this place without Nick. A deep emptiness settled over her.

She had just opened a Ruth Rendell book when her door swooshed open, and Amanda stood in the threshold.

"Howdy," her friend said with a big grin. She had a smudge of lipstick outside her lip line as if she applied it too quickly, probably in the car.

"What a nice surprise." She closed the book, having only read the first page but already gripped by the story. "But you'd better get rid of that pink smudge on your face. You wouldn't want Dr. Averett to catch you like that!"

Amanda slapped her on the knee and pulled out her compact. She grinned at her reflection and wiped away the lipstick with a tissue. "My mama always said that's a sign of old age. We get so we can't see our lips any better than we can the phone book."

"Well, I'm already there."

Amanda laughed and opened the shopping bag she'd brought, full of gifts—perfumed soap, a silk pillowcase, a pink nightie, and a coffee mug. As she unloaded, she chattered away. "Nikki had a baby girl the size of Texas. Apparently it weighed eleven pounds and poor Nikki was bigger than the Governor's mansion. God knows how long it'll take for her to get her figure back."

"They did a C-section I take it?" Marlene breathed in the rose smelling soap.

"Oh, yes and she's already complaining about the scar." After a moment's silence, Amanda said, "Has Janie been by?"

Marlene shook her head. "I saw her on Monday but not since, why?"

"Nothing really. It's just that we invited her to dinner last night, and she said she would come but never showed up."

Marlene shook her head. "Here we go. She assured me she wasn't going to disappear this time, but Janie is Janie. She can't change that. She might be thinner and wearing conservative clothes, but underneath it all, she's still Janie."

"I disagree, kiddo. I'm a smidgen worried."

"Don't waste your time," Marlene said with a sniff. She put the silk pillowcase over her pillow, smoothing out the soft cover.

"Nobody knows where she's staying, even your Aunt Sarah. I called Janie's cell a bunch of times, but it just goes to voicemail."

"She gave you her number? Aren't you little Miss Special."

Amanda shrugged. "I insisted. Besides, I asked her at a vulnerable time, when you were at Piedmont and everything was touch and go. She didn't have a chance to think and handed it right over."

"Look, I wouldn't worry about Janie. She's a big girl who is perfectly capable of taking care of herself. When she wants to turn up again, she will, and trust me, it will be without warning."

Amanda scowled. "We'll see, won't we. Tell me when they're gonna let you out of here."

"Soon, I think. Dr. Averett said I could go home the first of the week maybe, but I don't feel ready." She fiddled with the button on her dress. She didn't know how to tell Amanda she feared walking into her own house, worried she might start drinking again. Peter had removed all the liquor, but that wouldn't prevent her from buying more.

"Look, sweet pea, you're about the strongest person I know. Just think what you've been through, first your daddy and then your mama, all so tragic. You can lick this. I know you can." Amanda reached over and gave Marlene a big hug.

The smell of her Chanel soap tickled her nose and sent a warm thrill through her.

A soft knock sounded on Marlene's door. Amanda looked up just as Nick walked in.

"Oops, I didn't know you had company. I'll come back later," he said.

"No, wait," Marlene said, rising. "I want you guys to meet. Amanda, this is Nick Sims. He's been my lifesaver in here. Nick, Amanda is my best friend."

Amanda shot him one of her big grins, making her entire face crinkle. "So pleased to meet you, Mr. Lifesaver. But, don't you go letting Marlene get too comfy here. We want her to come home."

Nick settled himself in the recliner near the window and stretched out his long legs. "Nobody gets too comfy in here. Trust me."

When Amanda got up to leave, she kissed Marlene on the cheek and whispered in her ear, "Don't you go getting yourself too attached to that big man."

On Sunday after Nick was discharged, he visited Marlene with armloads of lemon-colored roses. He placed the glorious yellow flowers in vases all around her room. "This place is entirely too drab."

Marlene laughed. "You didn't complain when you were here."

"Who would I complain to? I didn't see anyone begging to bring me flowers."

They shared a friendship and a growing intimacy—dangerous, though it was. Peter had noticed the flowers but had said nothing. Even though she saw the hurt on his face, she didn't have the strength to fight the powerful wave of Nick's personality. He gave her courage to face her illness. Through Nick's eyes she saw herself for what she really was without the perpetual denial, guilt, and fear.

Later that afternoon, she put on her shorts and a t-shirt and went to the gym for a workout. There, she spied only one woman on a stationary bike, reading; otherwise the place was empty. She and Peter used to jog together when they first married. He continued to run nearly every morning, but she had stopped, preferring Pilates or Yoga. Lately, though she had done nothing. She vowed that would change when she returned home. She reached down and increased the speed and the incline on the treadmill, and facing the television, she lost herself in a *Murder She Wrote* rerun. Sweat dripped down her cheeks and into her eyes.

At seven o'clock that evening Aunt Sarah and Mark peeked into her room.

"I hear the doctor says you're ready to come home," Mark said without preamble.

"Next week, probably," Marlene answered.

"How about I come and stay a few days with you," Aunt Sarah said. She was adding water to Nick's flowers and pinching off the dead leaves.

"That's not necessary. Peter will be there, and I'm sure I'll be fine." But, she wasn't sure Peter would be there. He had agreed to help her get settled, but he had made no commitment to move back in.

"Really, dear. It's no trouble. I need a few days off anyway."

"Aunt Sarah, tax season is approaching. You can't possibly need a few days off."

"She's got help," Mark interrupted.

"Laura can't do what you do, and you know it. Your clients count on you. Now is not the time for you to take off. I promise. I'll be fine."

Aunt Sarah sat down on the bed. She crossed her long legs and clasped her hands in her lap. "I sure wish Janie hadn't disappeared. She could have—"

"Janie can't be counted on. You should know that by now," Marlene said. Her voice sounded bitter even to her own ears.

Although she told Amanda she wasn't worried about Janie, a little voice in the back of her head kept asking what brought her back here after so long an absence and then what made her leave just as suddenly.

"I suppose I had hoped she'd changed," Aunt Sarah continued. "And, to not even say good-bye to any of us. I had no idea she was gone until Amanda told me."

Mark flipped on the television. "You get great reception on this flat screen. A lot better than what we get at home." He surfed around until he found a basketball game and muted the sound.

"Have y'all heard anything else from Ralph?" Marlene asked.

Mark shook his head. "Not a peep. But, he's still at the house. I'm working on a court order to get rid of him, but it's a bit awkward. We can order him out, but if he refuses, which I'm sure he will, we'll have to get the police to remove him."

"With Janie gone now, it really doesn't matter," Marlene said.

"But, dear. You were so desperate—" Aunt Sarah said.

"I was desperate about a lot of things. I'm calmer now. Let's just leave Ralph alone. As long as he's not bothering anyone, what difference does it make? If we're not going to sell the house, it's probably not a bad idea to have someone living there, right?"

Aunt Sarah shot Mark a look. "Honey," Aunt Sarah began. "We really think you should sell the house. It's pointless keeping it. Janie won't ever want to live there again, and I doubt you will either."

"Let's talk about that later," Marlene said, not wanting to make any major decisions until she and Peter figured out their future. "How are the Spanish lessons?" They had begun learning Spanish at the community center about three months ago.

"*No hablamos muy buen*," Mark said with a grin.

"Wow!"

"We know all the numbers and parts of the body," he added. "But I still don't know how to say, prune that bush or water the lawn."

Marlene laughed. After they left, while preparing for bed she thought about Janie again. She wished she had at least learned where her sister was living. They'd had a great visit the last time she saw her, but they had left so many things unresolved.

She brushed her teeth, rinsed out her mouth, and crawled into bed with her book.

If only I had known then that she wouldn't be back.

Chapter Twenty-Nine

Janie opened her eyes to total darkness. She blinked and looked overhead where a pencil-thin streak of light came through a small window way on the other side of the room. She smelled mildew and something rancid, possibly a dead animal. Twisting her hands, she fluttered her fingers to deaden the numbness. They'd tied her wrists with a rope behind her back. She slid her wrists around, but the rope was too tight to wiggle out of. Her ankles were also bound. She lay on a cold, dank floor. A shiver ran up her spine both from fear and from the icy air penetrating her clothes. She ached all over.

The last time she had been in this basement she had been no more than seven or eight. Mom never went down here, and she ordered them to stay out.

"It's full of diseases," she used to tell them. "Don't you girls ever set foot in that Godforsaken place."

Of course, she had disobeyed and sneaked down the creaky stairs when she and Marlene were hiding from one another, knowing Marly would never find her because she always did what she was told. She had come halfway down the stairs and stood close to the wall. Cobwebs tangled in her hair, blocking entrance to the lower level. She had imagined bats flying at her and rats running under her feet, maybe even a snake. It had smelled bad then, too. She had stayed on the stair ledge for as long as she could stand and then she bolted out with a relieved huff. She had never gone down again and had forgotten the basement even existed. Obviously from the smell of it, so had Aunt Sarah.

She eased herself up and squirmed on the cement floor, trying to get comfortable. A pain shot from her butt to her back.

Voices sounded on the staircase. She lay back down and closed her eyes, wanting them to think she was still unconscious. Multiple footsteps moved down the stairs. Even through clinched eyes she spotted the beam of the flashlight they shined in her face. It took all her strength of concentration not to squint.

"She's still out," the black man said in a deep gruff growl. "I gave her one good wallop."

"You'd better hope she doesn't have a concussion or something."

The slur of Samuel D. Whitaker's voice sent a new chill down her back. She wished she could peek out at them, but if she stayed perfectly still, they might say something they wouldn't say if they knew she was awake.

"I didn't mean for you to hurt her," said a woman's voice. Janie's heart nearly stopped. She couldn't believe her ears.

"What'd you expect?" Ralph asked. "She came sneaking around and stealing my stuff. Jinx had no choice."

"Technically this is her house, and she owns what's in it. You could be in one big shit hole if something happens to her," Whitaker said and paused before asking, "Is she gonna be okay?"

"Who gives a shit?" Jinx said. He lumbered farther down the stairs.

She could almost feel him breathing over her. He gave Janie's shoulder a kick. She flopped to her other side and stifled the urge to moan. In this position she could open one eye without them noticing.

"Quit it!" Thelma said. "I only helped you 'cause Jerry and I thought she had some money worth getting. I didn't mean for this to happen."

"What are you going to do with her?" Whitaker asked.

Ralph said, "We don't know. She done gave us what we wanted. Now that we've got the gun, alls we gotta do is open a new case. We could let her go, maybe release her somewhere in the heart of the city where she would have to fight to get herself back together. Maybe some no-account would mug her or kill her without us having to do nothing." He barked out a laugh. "By then, we'd be finished. You got enough evidence now, right, Sammy?"

More footsteps approached her. "How do you think she came by that gun?" Thelma asked. "Did she steal it from where her mama got murdered or find it here?"

"What's it to you?" Ralph said. "She had it and now we can re-open the case and get me off. I want what's coming to me. They gotta pay me my money for all them years when I weren't supposed to be in no jail."

"I don't know," Whitaker said. "It may not be enough." He paused. "Depends. Are your prints on the gun?"

"What do you think?" Ralph screeched. "I yanked it out of her pocket. How was I suppose to know it was there? Do ya think I should've let 'er shoot me and then ask questions?"

"That's the problem. With your prints on the gun, we're gonna need more. She's gotta confess and sign that paper," the lawyer said, ignoring Ralph's outburst.

"Let's get out of here. It's cold," Thelma said. A dim figure climbed back up the stairs, but the others stayed.

"How the hell we gonna get her to sign? She refused to do it before when we asked nice," Ralph said.

Jinx answered. "I've got ways. Thanks to that chick friend of hers, we know where she lives. There's this guy down in Savannah I can contact. He owes me. He'll find her house and her businesses. All we gotta do is threaten her friends. She'll sign. Trust me, Red."

It took all Janie's strength not to groan. *Damn Thelma!* The sound of Jinx laughing rang in her ears like a fingernail scraping a blackboard. She didn't want to think about what that goon might do to Sue Anne or Steven. Suppressing a strong urge to jump up and strangle him, she held herself motionless.

"I'm getting out of here," Thelma hollered down the stairs. "I want my cut in this. Don't you even think about doing nothing without me. Remember it was us that brought her to you."

Us? Was Nelson in on it, too? In her desperation to get finished with everything here, she had made a fatal mistake—one she had not made in a long time—she trusted someone she didn't know. Janie bit her lower lip in anger at her own foolishness.

"You got her car, ain't ya? That's more 'en the rest of us." Ralph yelled back up at Thelma.

"No way. I ratted her out. There's nothing stopping me from ratting you out if you aren't careful." She left.

"Don't like the sound of that chick," Jinx said.

"She'll be okay. We just gotta keep her happy. She's nervous 'cause she didn't count on this," Ralph said.

"Don't like nervous people. They do stupid things."

"You two shut up. The sound of you is making me nervous. We need to go about this the right way. Just get her to sign, real nice like, Ralph. Then we let her go. Do you hear me? When I come back here, I expect to have that paper in hand."

"Sure thing, Sammy."

"And, if she doesn't wake up soon, we might need to get a doctor," Whitaker added.

Jinx mumbled, "I'd as soon let her die."

They exited up the stairs and rammed the door shut.

Silence.

Janie lifted up on her elbow. A pain shot across her opposite shoulder where Jinx had kicked her. What a jerk.

She had no doubts that once she signed whatever they wanted her to sign, they would kill her. And, not a soul would miss her. Marlene probably thought she had disappeared again. Her one hope rested with Sue Anne, who might come poking around, but by then it would be too late. She had to figure out how to escape, and if that wasn't possible, how to sign the stupid thing without getting killed. She couldn't let Ralph get away with this. She would lose everything she had strived for if Ralph won. Her stomach tightened with dread.

She butt crawled a few feet backwards, hoping to find something sharp to cut the ropes. A knife, a saw, something. Too bad she hadn't explored the basement more as a child. After a few moments, she was exhausted but continued the slow process backwards. She hit up against something on the floor behind her. *Damn, a paintbursh.* She pushed it aside and crawled a few feet farther until she reached the back wall. Once against the wall, she leaned on it to try and stand up. But, her quads collapsed. She couldn't quite get herself on her feet. Instead she kept sliding down. Thinking of all the miles she used to run back in the day, she couldn't believe she allowed herself to get so weak.

Focus, Janie!

She edged to her left closer to a group of shelves full of jars. Granny Jennings used to can applesauce and sometimes peaches. Perhaps she would find a screwdriver.

I have a screwdriver!

She twisted around, trying to get into her coat pocket. Ralph had grabbed the revolver out of her pocket. But maybe he left the screwdriver. She turned her body sideways and pushed up her legs, but it was hopeless. She couldn't get to her pocket. She would have to find another way.

She resumed the butt-crawl. Having no idea how long she had been struggling like a snail across the floor, she continued to ease herself along the edge of the wall, thinking that time must be crawling by about as fast as she was. Once she reached the shelves, she backed up to them and finger searched, trying not to knock anything to the floor. Her hand rubbed across the smooth surface of jar after jar. Finally, she hit on a round object. She had no idea what it was but the edge of it seemed sharp. Maybe this was a lid from a Mason jar.

She clasped it and edged herself back. The light from the high window had darkened. Either the sun went behind a cloud or nightfall had come.

Once back to where she had been originally tossed, she began to work at the rope. The first challenge was to get the implement in the right position without dropping it. If she could untie her hands, she could get the screwdriver and maybe force the lock on the upstairs door. But every time she tried to situate the object just right, it tumbled to the ground and nearly rolled away. She cursed under her breath in frustration, trying over and over again. Finally, she nearly got it placed exactly where she wanted it when she heard a noise from the staircase. *Damn!*

The door opened and footsteps moved down the stairs preceded by a flashlight.

"Are you awake?" It was Ralph.

"No thanks to you," Janie answered. "What do you intend to do with me?"

He moved closer to her. She inched the implement up the sleeve of her coat and held it there, praying he wouldn't push her around. It could easily roll out. God knows what they would do to her if they found it.

"I brought you some water," he said, and put a straw up to her lips.

She sipped through it, wishing she could spit it out all over him but she needed to drink. When she stopped and licked her lips, water ran down her chin.

"I said what are you going to do with me? You can't keep me down here forever."

Ralph turned away from her. "In a little while, we'll bring you something to eat. You may as well make yourself comfy."

She stared at him. "Hope you liked the pen 'cause you're going right back."

He ignored her.

"When they find me, they'll lock you away and toss the key in the Chattahoochee. You haven't got a prayer this time, not like last time."

He stopped in his tracks. "What's that supposed to mean?"

"Just what I said. They didn't have a murder weapon. All they had was circumstantial evidence. If you hadn't run from the cops and acted so guilty, you would have probably gotten off. But you were too dumb. And, boy, you're being really stupid this time. I can't even believe it."

"The cops were shooting at me. And you told them all them lies about me on the stand. Besides, who are you to act so high and mighty?"

Janie chuckled. "I didn't tell them everything. If I had of, you'd still be in the pen or maybe they'd have stuck a needle in you and been done with it."

He slapped her.

Her face burned. "You don't have to be stupid this time. You've done your time. Surely you don't want to risk going back. Let me go, and I'll get out of your life forever. I'll go back to where I came from. All I want is for you to leave Marlene alone once and for all. Haven't you done enough to her? Just let her be and I'll go. That's all I want. Then, you can disappear and I'll forget about all this." She circled her head around to indicate her current predicament.

"You're the stupid cow to come sneaking around 'ere like you done. You and Marly always acted better n' me, but she's nothing but a bastard and you're nothing but the kid of a crazy whore."

Janie's body tightened all over. "Lies."

He laughed. "You think I'm lying. Your ma told me everything, she did. She told me how she got pregnant with Marly and had to marry your daddy and him not even being the father. Him not ever knowing it neither —"

"Why would she tell you such things even if they were true? She'd never trust you."

"She had no choice. 'Cause she wanted me to kill her ex-lover. Paid me money to go after some sorry low-life named Jonathan something or other. He started calling her after your daddy died 'cause he wanted to see Marly. Your ma went crazy-like. Screaming and all. I promised I'd take care of the guy. She paid me three hundred bucks and gave me a letter with all the details. I saved that letter she done wrote me. I still got it. Never know what ya might need."

"Shut up. I don't believe a word you're saying. Why should I? All you know how to do is lie."

He grabbed her by the shoulders, letting the flashlight drop to the ground. She turned her face from the smell of onions on his breath and prayed the implement wouldn't fall from her coat sleeve.

"I'm telling the truth. I scared off the bastard, roughed him up some and she married me. She had to 'cause I done kept the letter and told her I'd tell the police if she didn't. With me 'round, she ain't never heard from that Jonathan again, and I didn't have to kill him like she wanted.

She weren't happy though. She was madder than a mountain lion when I told her I didn't kill him. She wanted him dead."

Silence.

He released her and picked up the flashlight.

"Nothing you say will make me believe you." But she did believe him. Everything started to make sense. "And what's the point of telling me all this now? If you don't let me go, you're going straight back to jail no matter what Mom may or may not have done. There are people who'll come looking for me and then you'll be in real trouble. Is that want you want?"

"I ain't going nowhere. Jinx'll see to that, and I'm gonna clear my good name and then we'll see who's so high and mighty."

"Suit yourself."

He walked up the stairs. "We'll bring ya some food later."

Once alone she worked at the rope until her fingers ached but couldn't tell if she was making any progress. The implement just wasn't sharp enough or strong enough. She would have to find something else in this basement, something sharper.

After what felt like days, the basement door opened again. Ralph came down with a tray of food. Her eyes had adjusted to the dark well enough to see him carefully negotiating the stairs.

She pretended to sleep when he rested the tray next to her. She didn't want to talk to him ever again. He nudged her shoulder with his toe where the big guy had kicked her. She moaned.

"Get up. You gotta eat something."

She didn't move.

"Look, Janie, I know you're awake. Jinx wants me to cut your throat, but I ain't gonna do that. You're my step kid, after all even if you betrayed me. Alls you gotta do is sign that letter Sammy'll bring you. Okay? Then, we can all disappear from each other's lives, like you want. I got nothing against you or your sister."

"Go to hell," she said without rising.

Moments later, he made his way back up the stairs, taking the tray with him.

Chapter Thirty

"How are you feeling today?" Dr. Averett asked Marlene. They sat in his office. He removed his glasses, a puzzling habit—better to see her or not to see her?

"I'm okay."

She studied the strange oil painting behind his desk, trying to figure out what the picture represented. Blobs of color mingled with one another to form shapes that Marlene couldn't quite discern. As she examined the colors—reds blending into yellows with a splash of purple—she saw something she had not seen before. A large yellowish hue emerged from behind the hill shape in the background. She wrinkled her brow.

"Something troubling you?"

She sighed. "You act as though you understand me even better than I do. I suspect you know what's troubling me."

"Perhaps," he said, "but I wonder if you do."

What a strange thing to say. Of course, I know what's troubling me. She glared at him and turned away with a tired sigh.

"Let's talk about going home. You've been here going on six days. I'm pleased with your progress. How do you feel about going home?"

"We've been through this at least once already." Her voice was sharp.

"But how do you feel about it today?"

She moved back her seat and cleared her throat. "If I didn't know better, I'd think my bills weren't being paid."

Dr. Averett smiled but didn't respond. The moments stretched into an annoying silence. They must teach psychiatrists how to maintain quiet. It takes a special skill to know exactly how long to wait before saying something. Ten seconds, fifteen seconds...

She returned her gaze to the painting. The yellow hue had disappeared. She blinked twice, but she couldn't see the hue. Perhaps light from the window presented some sort of optical illusion. She shifted in her seat, no longer in competition with her doctor to break the silence.

"There's something I must tell you before I leave the hospital," she said in a voice she barely recognized as her own. "It has to do with my stepfather."

"Go on."

"It all began when I was eleven years old on my birthday. I had lots of friends from school over for a party. Mama brought home a bakery cake from the Sweet Shoppe, my favorite, and she covered it with eleven candles. I remember the day so well because it was my first birthday party after Daddy died. All during the party Ralph stared at me real funny as if he wanted something, but I couldn't figure out what. I pretended he wasn't there, but his gaze followed me everywhere." She paused and took a breath. "That night he entered my room and stood over my bed. I faked sleep until he finally left. But the next night he came back.

"'You awake, Marly?' he whispered in the darkness like a tiny breath of wind.

"Again, I acted like a possum, barely breathing, and prayed he'd leave. He did.

"But he came back every night for a week, watching and breathing heavier and heavier. His panting got so loud I thought he might pass out on top of me so I finally lifted my head. That's when he crawled in bed beside me."

She stopped talking and studied the painting. Slowly, as she opened the lid to her past, she watched the yellow hue reappear. When she began again, everything poured from her lips—ugly memories she had tucked away, hoping to forget. She told the doctor how Ralph had threatened and abused her. How dirty she felt afterwards, but how she was afraid to stop him.

"How do you feel about Ralph now?" the doctor asked.

"I loathe him," she instantly replied, expressing her feelings without guilt. "But I also feel sorry for him because Mama treated him like a second-class citizen. He never quite measured up. Eventually he gave up trying. Back then, though, I also feared him," she added. "When I was old enough to run from him, he'd tied me down, and I felt helpless, alone, and scared."

"How did he tie you down?"

Marlene tightened her clasped hands resting in her lap. "Mainly with threats. He told me he'd hurt my mother, but even worse, I was terrified he'd turn to Janie. If I kept him happy, everything in the house would stay calm and smooth. It was my choice. He made that clear."

"How long did this go on?"

"Until I left home. I actually did run away once. I was fifteen, and I took Janie with me. We ran away to Aunt Sarah's. But, he dragged us back with more threats. I was too scared for Janie to runaway again."

"What about you? Weren't you scared for you?"

"I'm not sure, maybe at first. I can't remember." She paused and looked away.

"What is it?"

"When I finally left home to live with my aunt, he went berserk. He brutalized Mama. He made good on his promise to hurt her. Then after it was all over, Mama yelled at me. She told me it was all my fault and cursed the day I was born."

"So you blamed yourself for what Ralph did to you and to your mother?"

Nodding, she said, "I realize now, as an adult, looking back, I wasn't responsible. But, if you grow up thinking there's something wrong with you—it's your fault all the bad things are happening around you—it's hard not to believe that. I used to pray to God to let me die and let it all end. But then Mama died."

"What happened after that?"

"I went into a shell. It was like my last chance to redeem myself, to say I how sorry I was to Mama or to yell at her for hating me, I don't know. But, I couldn't do anything. I suppose it was the final straw for me. I'd hit a brick wall." Emotion lodged in her throat.

"Do you want to yell at her now?"

Sobbing, she lifted her head and nodded.

"I was paralyzed with fear for Janie. The thought of Ralph touching her nearly drove me insane. Mama made it clear I was responsible for Janie. At Daddy's funeral, Mama told me to take care of my little sister. When Mama married Ralph, I picked out the yellow dress Janie wore to the wedding. I was more her mother than Mama ever was."

"But you were too young to be her mother."

"I know, but I didn't know that then." She stopped before adding, "I left Janie in the hands of a monster. Guilt overwhelmed me, but I tried to deny it, pretend everything would be okay. I turned my back on both Janie and Mama."

She wiped her nose on a tissue the doctor offered.

"Go on," he said.

"I've never told anyone this..."—she paused—"After I left home, Janie turned on me. She hurled abuses at me for leaving. Janie acted out a lot as a teen, but what could I do?"

"What did your mother do?"

She shook her head. "Mama couldn't handle Janie by then. Janie told me Ralph had disappeared. But, I suspected he was still around. Neither of them could handle her wild rebellion."

"I see."

"Then one day Janie told me Ralph was abusing her. And what was worse she shrugged it off like it was nothing." She stopped and stared at the doctor, heat rising to her face.

"What do you mean Janie shrugged it off like it was nothing?"

Sighing, she continued, "Janie told me it was natural, she said, 'With you gone and Mom worthless, who else is there?' Then she laughed. The sound of Janie's laughter still rings in my ears. After that I suffered nightmares, but I never said a word to Aunt Sarah." She paused. "I've never forgiven Janie. I blame her as much as I blame Ralph."

My God! Had she actually said those words?

"Tell me how you felt toward your mother then?"

"I loved her," Marlene answered quickly. Tears streamed down her cheeks again. "And I hated her. I became the woman I hated."

"Do you still hate her?"

She took a deep breath. "My mother was who she was, a weak, self-centered woman who probably should've never had children. Janie and I both suffered but in different ways. I tried to shoulder everything. Have you ever seen those African women who carry bundles on top of their heads? In middle school I saw pictures like that in the *National Geographic*. The women's faces were weathered like the bark of a tree and pain poured from their eyes. That was me." She paused. "Janie, on the other hand, was like the birds she used to rescue as a child. If she couldn't change things, she ran away. Just like now." Marlene shook her head. "Janie always runs away. For a long time I resented her more for that than anything else. Leaving the way she did after the trial was worse than plunging a knife into my heart."

"How so?"

Tears fell onto her lap. After a few minutes, she expelled a deep breath. "All that time I had protected Janie. In some ways I must've blamed her for what happened to me. If Janie had not been there, I might have run away from Ralph for good. But, I stayed for her and suffered his abuse because of her. Then when she left, I felt betrayed. Like it was all for nothing."

"Did you ever consider telling your Aunt Sarah about Ralph?"

"I couldn't. I was too ashamed."

"What were you ashamed of?"

"Ralph used to tell me how pretty I was, how much he liked my hair and my skin. Somehow I suppose I thought I'd encouraged him. And then when Mama said it was my fault, I know that sounds crazy, but I thought it was. I wasn't sure what I'd done, but I caused everything that was happening to me and to my family."

"Do you think that now?"

"Perhaps," she answered, looking back down at her hands.

After a brief silence, she said, "There's one more thing I need to tell you. It has to do with the day my mother died." He waited.

She told him how she'd come home and found Janie in her mother's room. "Mama was already dead. I could tell by her face. A gun was lying on the floor near her bed. I must've screamed because Janie shook me and told me to be quiet. She ordered me to leave. She said for me to go back to Aunt Sarah's and pretend I didn't see anything. I've never seen her that frantic. I kept screaming and asking what happened to Mama and where was Ralph. But, Janie pushed me out of the bedroom and sat me down in the kitchen. She gave me a stiff drink of something. I have no idea what, but it was very bitter and it settled me down." Marlene choked, trying not to cry again. "Janie made me promise never to tell anyone what I saw, and I never did, not until this moment."

"Do you think Janie had something to do with your mother's death?"

She shook her head. "No, I think Ralph killed Mama and Janie saw it."

"Why didn't you tell the police what you saw?"

"Janie frightened me because she was so desperate, and I wanted to help her. It was like we were bound together again."

Dr. Averett blinked. "Marlene, did you ever wonder if Janie killed your mother?"

"Why would she? No! I can't believe that."

"Can't or won't?"

Silence.

Marlene took a deep, shaky breath. "I don't know."

At the end of her story, her shoulders sagged, but she felt cleansed, scrubbed raw like a newborn baby. Dr. Averett had asked gentle questions without making her feel dirty or foolish or responsible.

The psychiatrist glanced at the clock. "You've come a long way today, Marlene, and you still have a lot of work left to do, but I think you are ready to go home."

* * * *

The next day, Peter drove Marlene back to the house they shared as husband and wife. When he parked the car in the driveway, she blinked twice. The house looked larger than she remembered. She had been gone ten days but it felt more like ten years. The bushes along the front had filled out in preparation for their spring blooms and the jonquils were up. Everything screamed, *Welcome Home*. Her stomach clenched, but she reached for the car door and got out.

Peter unloaded her suitcase and the box of books and wilted flowers she had collected while in the hospital. When she walked up to the door, Amanda threw it open before she could reach for the knob. Her friend grabbed her in a whopping bear hug, bringing tears to Marlene's eyes.

"I'm so glad you're back. We both are." Amanda choked, nodding toward Peter. "He's been worried sick," she whispered in Marlene's ear.

She entered the house as if for the first time and wrinkled her nose from the strong Pine Sol smell.

Amanda said, "Your aunt was here. She scrubbed and scrubbed. You'd think the place had been inhabited by a gang of hobos."

Laughing, Marlene said, "She's always been that way. But, God it feels great to be home."

Just then Nellie came out from behind the couch, looking nervous.

"Hiya, baby," she said, lifting the cat to her face. A soft purr drummed in her ears.

"She's missed you, too," Peter said.

Too? Does he miss me as well?

"Hey, y'all, come on. I've got a huge lunch ready," Amanda called.

Peter left the suitcase and boxes in the foyer, and they followed Amanda into the kitchen. Soon they were all talking and laughing as if she had never left, and the tension in the air lifted. For the first time in her married life, Marlene could be herself without pretense and without a drink.

After Amanda left, Peter started fiddling around the kitchen like a nervous housewife.

Confident in her new self, she asked him, "So what are your plans?"

He placed a stack of dishes in the sink. "That depends on what you want." He sat down next to her. "Dr. Averett said you need some time."

She thought about Nick and how talking to him had helped smooth the way for her to open up to Dr. Averett. Nick had been so easy. Peter was so hard. Maybe he knew her too well. He had been around before her mother died and then during the trial. She had started drinking before they married. Perhaps Peter's timing was all wrong. That thought made her sad. She gazed at his worried face.

"'By time' I suppose he meant, time alone?" she asked.

Peter shrugged. "I'm not sure. But, I get the impression from you that you want to be on your own." He turned away and in a choked voice said, "Why did you do this, Marlene? After all we've been to each other, why couldn't you let me help you?"

"It's not your fault, Peter. There were things I could never tell you. Could never say to anyone except a doctor. It wasn't you. It was me. I'm the one with issues. I'm working through them with help from Dr. Averett. You did more for me than you'll ever know by leaving. It showed me that life couldn't go on as usual—"

"Not if you tried to kill yourself."

"Believe me. If I did try to kill myself, I didn't realize it. I'm sure I hated myself enough. But, killing myself wasn't my conscious intent. So, please get that out of your head." She paused and took a deep breath. What she was about to say took every ounce of her courage. "I don't want you to come home. I need to be by myself. I need to find out what that feels like."

He twisted his hands in his lap. "Are you saying you want me to move out permanently?"

"Yes."

"Are we talking divorce?" His voice cracked on the last word.

"Let's take one step at a time. Dr. Averett says I need to find out how I feel about myself. I can't love another person until I do that. Please."

"How long do I wait for you to find yourself?" She detected anger in his tone.

"I don't know."

He rose from the kitchen chair and walked directly out the front door without turning around.

Just as he shut the door, the telephone rang.

"Hi, Marlene. It's Nick."

Chapter Thirty-One

Janie had no idea how long she'd been lying on the cold basement floor. At some point they had untied her hands so she could eat, but she hadn't put a bite of food in her mouth since when? Her mind registered nothing.

At first she thought she ought to eat to maintain her strength, but when escape looked impossible, she had decided the best thing to do was to die right here on the floor of the basement. One day someone would find her skeleton and wonder about the person left there to rot.

They brought the letter to sign, and she spit in their faces. Jinx kicked her again, but Ralph stopped him before he battered her to death.

"Give her time," he said.

Days and nights ran together. She slept and listened to the drip from a pipe nearby. If starvation didn't kill her, the mold growing in this Godforsaken place clearly would.

She had several regrets. The first was Sue Anne. She imagined her worrying, fretting and wondering. *Would she believe I'd abandoned her, that I didn't love her?* That thought brought a chill to Janie and nearly gave her strength to rise.

Her other regret was Marlene. Her sister would never be free of Ralph. Janie hadn't finished what she set out to do. Instead, she had made everything worse. Ralph might win his plea. He might get vindication for

Mom's murder. In the end, he would triumph. Her eyes flew open. Hatred filled her heart and gave her a burst of energy.

Her stomach rumbled. She grabbed the slice of bread from the food tray sitting next to her and stuffed it into her mouth. Then she swallowed the milk in one gulp. She gagged, her stomach lurched. She turned from the tray and vomited. Breathless, she collapsed once again. *Hopeless. It's hopeless..*

When they first untied her hands, she searched for the screwdriver, but it was gone. Apparently they had found it that first day. Discovering her pockets empty nearly drained her of the sliver of hope she had left.

Her thoughts wandered in a state of delirium. The cold tomblike darkness brought back garbled memories like flashes from someone else's life.

She saw herself skipping from movie theater to movie theater, looking for the raunchiest film in town, anything to avoid a farewell scene with her sister the day Marlene left to go live with Aunt Sarah.

She had huddled in the dark theater on the back row where she sneaked puffs from a cigarette and watched the skinny women stroll before the camera. Their tiny bikini's covered the barest details, leaving little for the imagination. Kevin Bacon and Nathan Lane pretended not to notice. She did, too.

A sound on the staircase brought her back to reality. She lifted her head.

"Aren't you gonna eat?"

It was Thelma. She had not seen Thelma since that first day, whenever that was. She lifted up, blinking from the flashlight beam in her face.

"I tried to eat." She motioned to the vomit on the floor behind her.

"I'll clean that up. But, Janie, you'd better sign that paper. If you'd just do it, they'll let you go. I promise."

"What makes you think I'd believe you? You're nothing but a lying bitch as far as I can see." She glared at her former friend and turned her head away from the light.

"I know what you think, and I'd think the same thing, but I didn't know they were going to do this to you. They told us if we helped, we could get some easy money. Jerry's plan was to blackmail you and them, one against the other. Until they promised more." Thelma paused and sat down next to her. "I'd have never done any of this had Jerry not made me."

"Nobody makes you do anything, Thelma." She spoke in barely a whisper. "That much I know about you. What about Nelson? Was he in on this game with you?"

"Not at first. But Jerry found out he was helping you. He followed him, and he caught him and you talking. He told Nelson he'd better give him a piece of the action or he'd come after him. Jerry's pretty mean when he sets his mind to it. Once Ralph told us his plans, Nelson wanted a cut, too, you know, we all did. That's all. Nelson doesn't know about you being here. Nobody knows 'cept them three upstairs and me and Jerry. That's it."

She shook her head, frustrated with herself for ever trusting Thelma. Even in high school her wayward friend was only out for herself.

"So, now that you know what they're up to, why are you helping them?"

Thelma looked away. "I thought I could get you to eat and maybe sign that paper for your own good. I came over here today to talk them into letting you go. They said all you gotta do is sign and then we can all get out of this hell hole." She paused and looked around as if anyone could hear her. "Look, there's going to be lots of money. Ralph stands to get millions. All you gotta do is sign, and I'm sure they'll cut you in— Ralph even said so. There's going to be more than enough for all of us."

"They'll have to kill me before I sign that paper."

"What about your friends in Savannah? They'll find them and then you'll be sorry you didn't sign when we gave you the chance." Thelma's voice had turned cold.

Her stomach turned. Bile crawled up her throat. "My friends don't know anything about my life here."

"Jinx said he's got a buddy down there that'll hurt people if you don't sign. He's gonna, and then you'll have no choice. He's got connections. That lawyer is holding him back, but he can't hold him forever."

"Go to hell."

Thelma got up and lifted the tray. "I'll be back to clean up that mess."

Tears filled Janie's eyes. Eventually they would find Sue Anne or Steven or someone else, and they would threaten them, or worse still— hurt them, until she signed. If she died first, that would take care of everything. Except Ralph would win. She had to find a way to make sure Ralph didn't win.

Thelma came back with a mop and cleaned up the vomit. Before leaving again, Thelma said, "They said I could untie your feet." She used a knife to cut the ropes. "That better."

"Why?" Janie whispered without moving.

"We asked them, Whitaker and me. See, I'm looking out for you whether you believe me or not. We told them if you were more comfortable, you'd be more likely to sign. Ralph told me to go on and do it. Figures you're too weak to do anything. If you tried, he said Jinx would catch you, and that'd be that. So I wouldn't try anything if I were you, Janie."

She would have given anything for the strength to yank that knife out of Thelma's hand. The woman must have seen her looking at it because she moved out of her reach and headed toward the stairs.

"Think long and hard. This could be over and done with if you'd just sign. And think what you could do with the money."

Janie flopped back down onto the floor. Her mind went in and out of consciousness.

Her thoughts returned to that day after the movie. She had delayed as much as she could and had finally meandered toward Briardale Lane long after nine o'clock. She entered a graveyard quiet house. Smells from the previous night's roast beef dinner floated in the air. She had crept close to her mother's room and had pressed an ear to the door. Whimpering sounds, silence and then a quiet moan.

She shook herself out of the past, determined not to let herself falter. She had to stay awake and not drift back in time.

She rose on one elbow. She could barely sit up. They were right. She was too weak to escape.

The light from the far window glared at her as if there might be some sunshine outside. Her thoughts took her back to bright sunny days, running in the backyard with Marly, chasing after the badminton birdie.

She gathered what little energy she had to stand, inch by inch. Everything in her head circled around. She swayed and nearly toppled to the ground. Quickly, she moved over to the wall to keep from collapsing. How long had it been since she stood upright?

Her shoulder, hips, and abdomen ached where Jinx had kicked her. Her mother's words rang in her ears. "Get me a drink, honey, just a little something." Janie's tongue ran across her dry parched lips. She needed a drink, but not the same kind her mother had craved.

They had left a pitcher of water by the staircase. If only she could walk that far. She eyed the staircase—about ten feet away—but, like a mirage it seemed miles from her reach.

She moved one foot in front of the other, crouching and holding her stomach. She brushed away cobwebs as she shuffled forward. Her legs tingled like they might give way at any moment. She fell on all fours. She was about six feet away from the jug of water. Six short feet. *You can do it, Janie!*

Crawling, her knees aching, she pushed forward toward the jug. Finally she was inches away. She sat cross-legged on the step and caught her breath. Her heart thundered as if she had run a marathon. Victorious, though. She had made it.

With trembling hands, she tilted the jug and swallowed the tepid water. Nothing had ever tasted so good. Water dripped down her chin and inside her blouse.

She drank more.

Chapter Thirty-Two

Marlene and Amanda sat at the kitchen table, drinking freshly brewed Starbucks. Nellie curled up in a ball on Marlene's lap, not having left her side since she returned home. She stroked the cat's soft fur.

"Aren't you supposed to go to Pilates today?" she asked her friend, stirring Half and Half into her coffee.

"I'm not going anywhere this week. It won't hurt me to miss a Pilates class or two. But, if you keep cooking for me like you did last night—God, that shrimp quiche was to die for—I'm going to have to go on one hell of a diet."

The doorbell interrupted them. The clock read 10:15 a.m. Marlene dislodged Nellie, who squawked in protest, and opened the door to a tall woman with a mop of curly red hair.

"My name's Sue Anne DiAngelo. I'm looking for Marlene Tetford."

"I'm Marlene. How can I help you?"

Amanda walked up and stood behind Marlene.

"Look, I hate to bother you, but I didn't know what else to do. I'm a friend of Janie's. May I come in?"

"Of course," Marlene said, stepping aside and introducing Amanda.

"I'm really sorry to come barging in like this, but I drove like a bat out of hell this morning from Savannah. I aim to find Janie if it kills me."

"My goodness," Amanda exclaimed. "We've been worried sick about Janie."

Marlene shot her a puzzled look.

"Well, Jack and I have," she explained. "My husband knew Janie a long time ago when she was a teenager. We just couldn't believe she would disappear without even saying good-bye."

"Disappear?" Sue Anne said. "So, you've not heard from her either?"

"I'm afraid not," Marlene answered, leading them back into the kitchen.

While she poured coffee into the mugs, Sue Anne talked.

"I came here, hoping she'd be here. Praying you'd know what happened to her."

"I wish we could help," Marlene said without enthusiasm and added, "So, how well do you know Janie?"

"Janie and I go way back. She may have mentioned me?"

"We don't know anything about Janie's life," Marlene said, her voice tight.

"Actually," Amanda interrupted. "I did know Janie was living in Savannah and has several beauty salons, right?"

"How did you find that out?" Marlene asked with a deep scowl.

"Janie and I talked a lot that night you were in the hospital. It helped distract us from thinking about you." She paused before adding. "She didn't let much slip, but enough. She's one private lady, that's for sure."

"Janie has fifteen salons in and around Savannah. She's quite successful," Sue Anne said, tasting the coffee and setting it down. "I'm going out of my mind because I know she had some bad experiences growing up here. She never told me what all happened—not the whole story, that is, but I figured it was awfully bad. You could've knocked me over with a feather when she told me she was coming back here three weeks ago. She would have never returned, unless she had to. I'd bet my Mama's last dime on that."

Marlene cringed and spilled some coffee on the table.

"Sorry," Sue Anne said, staring at Marlene. "I didn't get the impression it was 'cause of you, honey. She worships you, and I know for a fact that she hated staying away from you even though she couldn't come back here. She never talked about anyone else from Atlanta except you." She paused and drank some coffee. "She promised me she wouldn't stay long. Then it kept stretching out."

"That was probably my fault," Marlene said. "I was in a bad way for a while."

"Yeah, so I gathered. You doing okay now?"

"Lots better." Marlene poured more coffee into Amanda's mug.

Sue Anne continued, "Janie called me every night—"

"Why did she come back if she hated this place so much?" Amanda interrupted.

"She said she was coming here for some tests at Emory."

"Janie's not sick," Marlene said. "She's never sick."

"She's been having some pain in her gut," Sue Anne said. "And she saw her doctor in Savannah before she took off for here. She told me he ordered tests at Emory, but, now I'm not so sure."

"So, is Janie sick?" Amanda asked.

"I don't know. I contacted the doctor's office, but they won't tell me diddlysquat—patient confidentiality and all that. Then, I called Emory and they wouldn't tell me anything either. But finally this nice girl told me they didn't have her name in the computer. She ended up telling me 'cause I started balling like a baby. I just couldn't help myself. It was all so frustrating." Sue Anne turned away from them, clearly getting emotional again. When she faced them again, her enormous blue eyes were full of tears. "I didn't know where else to turn."

"Wait, honey," Amanda said, taking hold of Sue Anne's hand. "Let's back up a sec. You said Janie called you every night. Why don't you just confront her? Find out why the devil she came back here and what she's up to."

Big tears fell down her cheeks. "That's just it. I haven't heard from her in six days. I've called and texted her a hundred times and left voicemail messages, desperate messages for her to call me. It's not like her not to call. But, I haven't heard a peep, nothing."

"Me, either. I've called and called," Amanda said. "She was supposed to come to our place for dinner, and she didn't show without calling or anything. That seemed weird to me. I thought she didn't return my call 'cause she was embarrassed. Maybe she forgot about our dinner plans or something. I even told her on one message not to worry, but to please call."

Marlene shook her head and took a deep breath. "Look, I've known Janie longer than either of you. Disappearing is not unlike her. She has the amazing ability to tune out bad things—anything that doesn't suit her. And, I'm sure my near-death experience wasn't in her game plan. Running away is typical Janie."

"You keep saying that, but I don't believe it. Not this time," Amanda jumped in. "Something has happened to her. I just feel it in my bones."

Marlene frowned. "The last time I saw Janie was a day or so before I went into Ridgeview. I'm not exactly sure because the days sort of ran into each other. She promised me she wouldn't disappear again. She said she wanted to be near me to help me get through all this. She sounded so genuine even I believed her—"

"You see!" Amanda said.

"Until," Marlene added, "she disappeared again. She did this when she was seventeen. Walked out and never once contacted me until three weeks ago. What am I supposed to believe?"

Sue Anne got a tissue from her purse and wiped her nose. "I can see why you think she'd just vanish. But, trust me. She'd never leave her business. She's worked so hard. Steven, her assistant, needs her for a closing on some property she's been trying to sell. He's pulling his hair out, not that he has much, poor thing. We simply don't know what to do. Besides, I just can't see her leaving me."

"Y'all were real close, then?" Amanda asked with raised eyebrows.

Sue Anne nodded, crying again. "She's my life. I will do whatever it takes to find her."

Amanda shot Marlene a questioning look.

She shrugged. *God! Janie with a female lover. What else don't I know about my sister?*

"How long have y'all been together?" Amanda asked, unable to curb her curiosity.

"Twelve years." She looked from one to the other. "I can see y'all didn't know this about Janie. I mean, about us and all."

"It doesn't matter," Marlene said. "Let's try and figure out what could've happened to her. If she's in trouble, and I'm beginning to think she might be, we must find her. Tell us what you've done."

Sue Anne straightened up and swallowed. "Like I said, I contacted Emory. Then, I called all the other hospitals to see if she was a patient. I thought she could have had an accident or something—maybe she got knocked in the head and had amnesia and her cell got lost—who knows? But I came up empty."

"Where was she staying?" Marlene asked.

"I don't know," Sue Anne said, shaking her head. "I got the impression she was moving around because she asked me to mail her a package, but it wasn't to a hotel."

"Where did you mail it?"

Sue Anne gave them Thelma's name and address.

Amanda rose. "Let's go. We'll find this Thelma person and see if she can help us. That's a start. Then, we'll go to the police."

"Wait," Marlene said. "I know a policeman who could help us. He was the detective who worked Mama's case. Let me call him." She unearthed his card and punched in the number.

When she hung up, she told Amanda and Sue Anne that he said he'd call the precinct and see what can be done.

"Meantime, let's go," Marlene said, and grabbed her purse and keys. "I'll call Mark on the way. He can help with the police as well. Believe me, if something has happened to Janie, I bet my stepfather is involved, and it's best to let the police handle him."

They arrived at Thelma's house thirty minutes later and found no one home. Sue Anne freaked out when she saw Janie's car parked on the street.

"What's her car doing here?" she implored. "She's gotta be inside."

Sue Anne peered through the windows while Marlene and Amanda searched outside where they found no sign of Janie. Sue Anne kept asking why her car was there and she wasn't. Amanda tried to calm her with sensible answers but nothing made too much sense to any of them.

Mark arrived.

"I've called Harlan Daniels, and he connected me to his replacement at the Dekalb County police. The guy balked at first saying there was nothing they could do until we filed a missing persons report. I told him we'd submit all the paperwork he wants, but time was of essence if she's indeed been missing for six days."

"It may be more," Marlene said. "I can't remember the day she came to see me."

"You told me you saw her the day before you left Piedmont," Amanda said, "And that was the day before our dinner. So it must have been six days."

"Either way," Mark said, "Detective Melani said he'd meet us at the house on Briardale Lane. I think Daniels put some pressure on him."

"No! She might be locked up here," Sue Anne said, pulling at Marlene's sleeve. "Her car is here."

Mark walked to his car. "While I was on the phone with Melani, he got a tip he thought might be connected. An anonymous caller informed them that a young woman was being held against her will at 409 Briardale Lane."

"Oh, my God! That's our address!" Marlene said, running along behind Mark, her heart racing in panic. "We've got to hurry!" Images of Ralph brutalizing Janie filled her head.

Chapter Thirty-Three

Janie woke up still on the staircase, the water jug empty. Her stomach bulged as if she'd eaten a full meal. Urine trickled down her leg while tears fell from her eyes.

She clutched the wall and stood up again. Although sticky, cold and dirty, she moved up the stairs, resting after each step. The top seemed higher than a mountain peak in the Rockies. The old planks under her feet creaked. A mental picture of Ralph and Marlene flashed before her. She had watched them through a tiny hole in the bedroom door. The first time she'd witnessed them, it had made her stomach queasy, and she had flown down the stairs to vomit in the commode. But after that initial shock, she had gone back to simply watch, fascinated. She couldn't understand why Marlene hadn't stopped him.

Not long after Marlene moved away, Janie had snatched Mom's gun. If Ralph ever came near her, she'd planned to shoot him dead center in the heart. She creaked up another step and her head throbbed with regret. If only she had pulled the trigger when she'd had the chance. Missed opportunities. Her life had been full of them. She climbed another step, determine not to die regretting another missed opportunity.

Her mother's dead face flashed before her. The blood, the gun, the ruined room, full of empty liquor bottles and dirty clothes. She could almost smell the rancid decay. Or, maybe that odor came from her own rotting body.

Once they had buried her mother, she'd vowed to make Ralph pay. She had watched them lower her mother's coffin into the cold earth striped with rays of sun saluting a woman who spent most of her days in darkness. In those moments of bravado Janie had no doubt she could beat Ralph. But her life's mission was crumbling and the clock ticking. She had to get out of this dungeon.

She wondered how Marlene was doing. Was she still in the hospital? Janie regretted not being there for her. She'd failed her again. She sucked in as much air as she could. She would not fail her this time. Her knee buckled and she collapsed, falling down three steps. Panting, she sat there, trying to regain her strength. If she failed Marlene this time, it would all be over. She may as well just die right here and forget this climb. *I won't!* As long as she had any breath left in her lungs, she'd move forward. She pulled herself back up. Her knee throbbed but she climbed back up those three stairs. She continued one small step at a time, her mind recalling the time she'd swum one hundred laps. She'd told herself, just swim one lap at a time and soon it would be over.

Finally, she reached the top of the stairs and leaned on the firmly latched door. Her memory told her it was a hasp without a padlock, not a bolt. This basement door was at the back of the entrance to the kitchen behind the wall next to the washing machine. No one ever went in or out. Mom kept the hasp latched to keep out the demons she imagined down below. Without a padlock, it could be opened.

She placed her ear to the door.

Silence.

Perhaps they had left the house or they were upstairs or maybe in the living room. If they were in the kitchen, she would have heard voices. She leaned all her weight against the door, but it didn't budge. Had they untied her sooner, before she had become so weak, she could have pushed through the flimsy lock. But now she barely had the power to breathe.

She sat close to the door and leaned on it. Perhaps if she worked the door, little by little instead of trying to barge through, she could escape. But that could take hours. She had no idea how long they would leave her unattended.

She bit her lip to stay awake. They had no pattern in their comings and goings. Her eyes drooped and her heartbeat slowed. *Come on, Janie. Don't fade out again.*

Her mind travelled to her life in Savannah. On the weekends, when she wasn't working, she and Sue Anne took day trips. They had visited most of northern and central Florida, Orlando being one of their favorite places. Sue Anne was like a little girl as far as Disneyworld was concerned. She never tired of going there.

Janie leaned on the door with all her weight. It gave about a quarter of an inch. She held her breath and tried again. Nothing this time. Resting, she lifted her face to the window above the stairs. A beam of sunlight glowed. What were people doing outside today? She had no idea what day it was. She sucked in more air to give her strength and leaned on the door again. It moved. This time less than before, but it moved. A crazy thought entered her mind. Maybe the sunlight had given her a bit more energy. Didn't sunlight nourish plants? She looked up again at the light, willing it to penetrate her body. Took another breath and pushed. Nothing. A tear rolled down her cheek, either from the exertion or from the hopelessness of it. Her shoulder ached, but she pushed again. *I simply won't give up.*

Footsteps raced outside the door, stopping her efforts to wedge the door open. The backdoor slammed shut and a voice shouted, "Ralph Cooper!" Someone sprinted closer to the basement and stopped. Heavy breathing, panting.

She tried to rise when the doorknob turned. "Help," she mouthed, but nothing came out. She wasn't even sure her lips moved. "Help," she croaked. This time the word came out, but with so little volume it sounded like a whisper.

The presence outside the basement door dashed off, crushing her hope for discovery. A window broke and something thudded to the floor.

Although desperate to know what was happening, she couldn't muster the energy to push through the door any more than inch by inch like a mouse moving a boulder. Her mind screamed, *Get me out of here*, but no words came out. Instead, she waited and listened and tried to stay awake. After a few minutes of silence, she eased herself up and placed her ear close to the doorjamb.

Heavy footsteps, at least two people sped into the kitchen. Quickly, she banged on the door. Her fist was so weak it sounded like a quiet knock. The footsteps flew past her and down the hall toward the front of the house. She caught snatches of murmuring and heavy breathing but couldn't make out the words. A crash sounded like a piece of furniture falling or a door being bashed open.

Something was happening outside this prison. Would Ralph and his conspirators abandon her? If they did, she wasn't sure she could scratch her way out. A glimmer of hope rose inside her, giving her the strength to push once more. The door creaked. The old, rotten wood slowly bent to her weight. The nails holding the latch groaned.

Then the unmistakable sound of the blast of a gun shattered her ears. She squeezed her eyes shut. Snatches of red appeared before her clenched eyes, images of blood everywhere. Her mother's contorted face, dried blood stuck to her cheek.

She trembled inside. Footsteps raced by again, this time they headed away from her.

"Hold it!" someone shouted from the front door.

Another loud blast from a gun.

Silence. She waited. Nothing.

Finally she unfolded herself to release the cramps in her legs. She inched herself into a standing position, still listening.

More silence.

Suddenly, the click of the lock released and the doorknob turned.

She grabbed the rail for balance and held her breath.

Chapter Thirty-Four

On the way to Briardale Lane, Both Marlene's car and Mark's became bogged down in noon traffic. Marlene wished she had a blue light on her hood so she could race past these people going places that didn't matter. Mark was ahead of them, but had made no more progress than they had. She gripped the steering wheel and tried to erase the image of Ralph's angry red face from her mind. If she was going to help save Janie, she had to stay calm and clear-headed.

A gentle rain began to splash on the windshield.

"Do you need more heat in the backseat?" she asked Sue Anne.

Sitting with her arms crossed over her chest, her coat collar turned up, and her eyes swollen with tears, Sue Anne shook her head. "Tell me about why Janie would be held against her will by your stepfather?"

Marlene stared straight ahead. This was the last thing she wanted to talk about. "I wish I could answer your question. I do know that my stepfather thinks Janie knows something about our mother's death—"

"He killed her," Sue Anne said. "What else is there to know?"

"Yes, but—" She guided the car around a corner, hoping to miss some of the traffic while Mark went straight. "I don't know the entire story. Janie found Mama before I got there. Something happened that only Janie knows. During the trial it was clear there were holes, and

Ralph thinks Janie has the answers. He always has. He hounded me while he was in prison and has never given up."

"But why would he hurt Janie?"

She drew to a stop at a red light and remained silent. Why would Ralph hurt any of them? Why had he killed Mama? She had no answers.

Amanda flipped the heat vent toward the backseat and added, "I can't believe Janie knew something and didn't tell the police. I heard her testify. She told the court how he attacked your mama."

"And he did. If Janie hadn't told them what he did to Mama, I would have," Marlene responded.

Amanda turned to Sue Anne. "Is that better now back there?"

"I'm fine, really."

After a moment of silence, they breezed through the back streets nearing Briardale Lane when Sue Anne said, "I love this part of Atlanta. The old streets look so cozy."

"Atlanta's no more beautiful than Savannah," Amanda said.

"Savannah has its charm, but it's a different charm. Besides, the weather is brutal in the summer. In Savannah it's either hot or hotter."

Marlene laughed, grateful for a brief distraction.

"So how did you and Janie meet?" Amanda asked.

Sue Anne bit her lower lip and gazed out the window before she said, "I'd just come off a bad relationship. A friend asked me out to eat, and Janie was with her. They weren't a couple or anything, just friends. But that wouldn't have mattered to me. One look at Janie and her haunted eyes, and I was a goner—totally sunk. I was like a kitten with a ball of yarn. I couldn't leave her alone. Finally, she agreed to go out with me and, well, there ya have it."

"Had Janie been with girls before?" Amanda had a hard time curbing her curiosity. Marlene shot her a warning look. Amanda shrugged.

"If you're asking if I was her first female lover, I think I was. Janie wasn't one to share much about her past, even with me. But, my gut told me I might have been her first. In any event, it didn't take us long to fall for each other. We live on Tybee Island now. It's the beach front close to Savannah."

"Are you from Savannah originally?" Amanda asked.

"No. I'm actually from Mobile, Alabama."

"My Lord have mercy! I should've known! Another real Southerner." She reached back and patted her leg. "I'm from Mississippi."

"My parents never accepted my lifestyle. I had to leave when I finished at Auburn, and I've only been back for quickie visits. But, I love being in Savannah especially ever since I've been with Janie—" Sue Anne's voice cracked.

"It's okay, honey. We are gonna find her and then everything will be all sunny again. You just wait and see. Now, Marlene, can't you go any faster?"

A tear trickled down Marlene's cheek. She wanted to know Janie the same way Sue Anne did, but she realized she never would. Even if they found her alive, she had lost Janie a long time ago.

Amanda reached over and squeezed her shoulder. "Don't you fall apart on me, too," she whispered.

Mark's car appeared in Marlene's rearview mirror. She had made the right choice but neither had arrived too fast. As they approached Briardale Lane, she gasped. There had to be a dozen police vehicles in front of the house.

Marlene pulled up behind one. The house had been cordoned off.

They jumped out of the car and approached the nearest police officer.

"What's happening?" Sue Anne asked, her long strides reaching him first.

"You ladies can't go any farther."

Mark walked up. "This house belongs to this young woman. And I'm her attorney. Tell us what's going on."

"We've got the suspects surrounded."

Gunshots sounded from the back of the house. Marlene gasped and grabbed Amanda's arm. "My sister might be in there."

She and Sue Anne tried to push past the police officer, who held them at bay. "It's not safe for you to go in there. We'll let you through as soon as we can. Meantime, you must stay behind this line."

272 | JOAN C. CURTIS

Another shot was fired. Marlene thought her head would explode and her heart would jump out of her chest.

Finally, a group of police came around the house with a black man, a woman, and another man—none of whom Marlene recognized—in handcuffs.

"Where's Ralph?" she implored Mark out of desperation, knowing full well he had no idea.

He held her back and shook his head. "Please stay here. It's not safe and if I let something happen to you, Sarah would never forgive me. I'm going to find Detective Melani," he said, releasing her arm.

Marlene, Amanda and Sue Anne grasped hands behind the police tape and waited. Then Marlene spotted Officer Daniels walking with a man in a business suit. He motioned for Marlene to stay back. Mark approached them.

A siren blasted from around the corner and an ambulance skidded to a stop, double parking next to the police cars and blocking the street. Two paramedics flew out of the ambulance with a stretcher.

"My God." Sue Anne released Marlene's hand but remained behind the tape. Her face looked deathly white. "Please, God, not Janie."

Moments later, Mark returned with Officer Daniels.

"Come over here."

They walked away from the commotion. Amanda was practically carrying Sue Anne.

"I'm sorry to have to tell you this, Marlene, but Ralph is dead."

Tears sprang to her eyes. She couldn't explain why if she had to, but she couldn't help herself.

"What happened?" she choked.

Mark put his arm around her.

Daniels said, "Once we barged in and surrounded them, I guess he decided he couldn't go back to jail. He shot himself before we could stop him."

"And Janie?"

He shook his head. "They can't find her. They're still searching the house."

"She has to be there. Why would they all have run and Ralph kill himself? She has to be there." Panic filled her voice.

"They're looking. Calm down."

Suddenly, a thought hit her. "Did they look in the basement?"

"I'm sure they'll look everywhere," Daniels said. "They're professionals."

"You don't understand," she protested. "It's hard to find. The door is hidden." She broke away from the officer. "Check the basement!" she screamed to the other police detective and raced toward the house.

Mark, Sue Anne, Amanda, and several police officers tore after her. She flew to the house directly to the kitchen until she reached the hidden door.

"Wait!" one officer shouted.

Mark grabbed her by the arm.

"Let the police go in first. You stand back," Officer Melani said with his gun drawn.

When they opened the basement door, Janie collapsed to the floor.

Chapter Thirty-Five

When Janie opened her eyes, she took in the Laura Ashley floral design in the curtains and the comforter. A beam of sunlight came through the diaphanous drapes. She was wearing a celery green, lacy nightgown looking as if it might have belonged to Granny Jennings.

Everything from the moment she fell through the basement door until she reached the hospital seemed a blur. When Sue Anne grabbed her, she realized she had been rescued, but she passed out immediately afterward. Images of emergency room people in green hospital garb, buzzing around her like a swarm of bees flashed in her mind.

Her eyes drooped but stayed open. She spotted Aunt Sarah sitting at the foot of the bed.

"You're awake, thank God. How are you feeling?"

Her mouth felt as if it were stuffed with cotton, but she said, "I'm coming back to life."

"Don't try and talk too much. You're still very weak." Her aunt brought her a cup with a straw. "Here, drink a little of this Gatorade. It will help you regain your strength."

She sucked on the straw. The liquid tasted cool, refreshing and salty.

"Can you hold the cup?" Aunt Sarah asked. "I want to get Sue Anne. She's been out of her mind with worry."

She grasped it by the edges with both hands, her lips not leaving the straw.

A moment later, Aunt Sarah returned with Sue Anne by her side. Sue Anne rushed over to the bed, bringing with her the sweet smell of jasmine.

"Life has come back to your cheeks, my angel," she said with a wide smile and a kiss on her forehead.

Janie pushed herself up. "I'm sorry to have caused so much trouble."

"You! Don't be silly," Aunt Sarah said, arranging the pillows behind her. "You had no idea what Ralph and those criminals were up to. No one did. Thank God, Sue Anne came up here and started rustling the trees." She gave Sue Anne a pat on the shoulder.

"Looks like y'all have all gotten to know each other. How long have I been out of it?"

"Not long," Sue Anne answered. "At the hospital they pumped you with fluids and gave you some nourishment. After two nights, they released you, and you came here to your aunt's house. You were conscious the whole time but very groggy from the meds they gave you. You're doing great, really." She shot her another big smile.

"Why don't y'all catch up a few minutes? I'm going to make Janie some broth and call Marlene. She wanted to know as soon as you woke up," Aunt Sarah said, moving toward the door.

"How's Marlene doing?" Janie asked. "I hated not being able to see her again after she went to Ridgeview. I told her I'd be back the next day." She coughed. Everything ached. She was sure she had bruises where Jinx had kicked her, maybe even broken ribs. A big bandage encircled her ribcage.

Aunt Sarah turned back around. "She's doing quite well. She told me she didn't even have an urge for a drink with all that's been going on. That's really amazing. My only concern, well—"

"How about your bringing Janie up to snuff on all that later," Sue Anne broke in and sent a warning look to Aunt Sarah.

"Of course. I'll get your soup and call your sister."

After she left, Sue Anne turned to Janie. "Don't you ever do anything like this to me again, ya hear, my sweet?" She shook her finger at her.

Janie smiled. She sipped more of the Gatorade, never having realized how good it tasted. "Sorry."

"I'm just kidding, but I must say, you scared the blue blazes out of me. I can't even begin to tell you."

"You'll have to tell me cause I have no idea what happened from the time y'all saved me from that rat hole to this minute."

Sue Anne rubbed her arm. "Okay, sweet one, I'll try, but Marlene can tell you more because she knows more about it all."

As Sue Anne told her about coming to Atlanta and searching for her at Emory and all the hospitals and how she finally ended up on Marlene's doorstep, her eyes kept roaming Janie's face. "I'd thought I'd lost you," she said with choked words. They embraced.

"Tell me more," Janie said, falling back on her pillows. Sue Anne told her how they raced to Thelma's house where they found her car but no Janie.

"By then I was fit to be tied. I just knew that something horrible had happened to you and couldn't understand why your car was there. But, Marlene kept her head. The police learned through an anonymous tip that you were being held prisoner at the house on Briardale Lane."

She scowled. "But who could have tipped them off?"

"Beats me. But between that tip, your Uncle Mark and some detective friend of Marlene's, they acted fast. We all flew to your rescue. At first the police couldn't find you, but Marlene remembered the basement and ran to you like a woman possessed. Thank God!"

Janie thought about how she and Marlene had made up stories about ghosts living in the basement. They had concocted ghouls coming up through the floor and witches flying into the window. Her sister had never ventured down there. Marlene had a fear of spiders and the cobwebs running from the floor to ceiling kept her far away from the basement. For the most part, they had both forgotten about its existence. Apparently, though, Marlene remembered it when she needed to.

"I don't know how much longer I could've survived," Janie said, thinking of those final surges of energy to get up the steps.

"You were nearly dead when we got there. I can't imagine you any worse off. Were they trying to starve you?" Sue Anne asked.

"They offered me food, but I couldn't eat. I don't think they meant for me to die down there, at least Ralph didn't."

At the mention of Ralph's name, Sue Anne looked away.

"What?"

"Why did they hold you captive? What did they want?"

Before she could respond, Aunt Sarah returned with a bowl of soup on a tray complete with a yellow jonquil in a bud vase. "Lunch is served, and Marlene is on her way," her aunt said.

She began eating the soup, grateful not to explain everything to dear, sweet Sue Anne. After a few bites, she said, "When I have more energy, I'll try and tell you everything, okay?"

Sue Anne touched her cheek. "Don't worry. I'm glad it's over."

She ate more soup and then asked Sue Anne, "What's going on with Steven?"

"I told him what happened. Naturally, he was shocked, as we all were. But, he said he could delay the closing for another week. My guess is everything can wait until you're well enough to come home."

"I'll call him later today."

"No, you won't," Aunt Sarah said. "The doctor told us you need to rest. He said to let you sleep as much as possible."

"I'm already feeling better," she protested.

"You've just woken up from a horrible nightmare," Sue Anne said. "We can't even imagine what you went through." She shivered. "A few days of rest in this paradise won't kill you."

"Where are you staying?" Janie asked, continuing to sip the soup.

"Right here. Your aunt has been wonderful." Sue Anne turned and gave Aunt Sarah one of her radiant smiles.

"It's the least I could do," Aunt Sarah said. "I'm glad to have both you girls here as long as necessary. And Sue Anne is a great help. What a wonderful cook!"

"Did she make her famous gumbo?"

"That's on tap for tonight. I got all the ingredients at the Dekalb Farmer's Market yesterday, and Mark is already drooling at the mouth," Aunt Sarah said.

Footsteps approached and the door opened. Marlene stood in the threshold. With her hair pulled into a ponytail the way she had always worn it as a teenager, she looked twenty years younger. Her face was radiant and her eyes clear. She beelined directly to Janie and gave her a big, long hug.

Tears filled Janie's eyes. She melted into her sister's embrace and soaked in the smell of Lever 2000 and Baby Shampoo— what she used to call the Marly smell.

"You scared me to death, little sister," Marlene whispered.

"We'll leave the two of you to talk," Sue Anne said, taking hold of Aunt Sarah and easing out of the room, closing the door behind them.

Marlene grasped Janie's hand but sat in the chair next to the bed. She wore a pink sweater that brought out the color in her cheeks. Janie couldn't remember her sister looking so beautiful and so much like their mother.

"I want to know everything," she said. "What happened to Thelma and Ralph? Did the police arrest them?"

Marlene looked down, a frown creased her brow. "Thelma was arrested and so was that lawyer and the ex-con."

"Samuel D. Whitaker and Jinx," she filled in.

"I have no idea. I didn't really pay attention to their names. But, I recognized Thelma from that time you were arrested in high school. Oh, yeah and her husband, he was one of those kids, too. They picked him up as well."

Janie nodded. "Good, but—"

"But, what?"

"I just wonder what will happen to the children. Thelma's got three kids."

"I'm sure they have family who'll take care of them. That's not your worry. Thelma should have thought about that long before she got herself tangled up with kidnapping you."

It seemed the kids always suffered from the parents stupid mistakes. Was there no end to it? Visions of Sherri's happy little face when they had played hide-and-seek brought a wave of sadness over her.

"And what about Ralph?" She prayed they had tossed Ralph back in prison and thrown away the key.

"There's no easy way to say this, so I'll just say it. Ralph is dead."

Janie sat up. Her head spun like a merry-go-round. "Whoa," she said, sliding back down, still so weak. "Did I hear you correctly?" *Ralph dead!*

Marlene nodded. "He shot himself. The strange thing about it was he shot himself with the same gun he used to kill Mama. That long-lost missing gun. I suppose he had it all the time."

Janie looked down, not wanting Marlene to see the guilt in her eyes.

"I guess I always thought you had it," Marlene continued. "I don't know why I thought that." Her sister paused and bit her lower lip. "It's funny how your mind plays tricks on you in times of stress. I thought I had seen it, but apparently I must've imagined it there. Ralph must have hidden it in the house somewhere, probably in the basement. That's what Officer Daniels thinks. I guess we'll never know."

"Officer Daniels? The policeman from Mom's death?"

"Yes. He stayed in touch with me while Ralph was in prison. He's been very helpful, and he made the police take action to find you. Without his help, I don't know what we would've done."

The sound of the gunshots while on the staircase rang in her head. One of those shots had taken Ralph's life. A sense of relief flooded her, but she didn't know how to express that to Marlene. Instead, she squeezed her sister's hand.

"Thanks for finding me," she said.

Marlene's eyes filled. "I thought you'd just gone away again. You could've died down there, and I'd have never known it. I'd have gone on believing, imagining that you had abandoned me again, probably feeling rather mad at you."

"It's okay and perfectly understandable of you to think that. Aunt Sarah says you're doing great."

Marlene eked out a smile. "Yes, I finally feel human. Once I broke down and opened up to Dr. Averett, I began to heal. I couldn't tell anyone about Ralph. I'd kept it inside me for too long and it was eating me alive."

Janie nodded.

"And what about Peter? Have y'all kissed and made up?" she finally asked.

Marlene took a long, deep breath. "Peter and I have a lot of work ahead of us. Our marriage was built on a lie. I have to tell him about my life at Briardale Lane before we can move forward. But—"

"I know. It's hard."

"Peter is difficult to talk to. And, well, I've met someone—"

"No way," she cut in. "Peter is your soul mate."

"He is, but we've had a very rough patch, and there are so many tangled up emotions. Whenever we talk, he gets all tense and so do I. But, when I talk to Nick, it's so easy."

"So, it's Nick, is it?"

"I met him in the hospital. He totally understands where I'm coming from and he listens to me."

Janie looked closely at her sister. She couldn't imagine Marlene without Peter.

"Look, I'm definitely not one to give relationship advice—"

"Speaking of which. Boy, was I blown out of the water when I met Sue Anne. I had no idea. You've always been a mystery, but I thought I knew you—apparently not."

"Marly, let me finish," Janie said, laughing. "As I said, I'm not the best person to give advice, but it seems to me it's too soon for you to make big decisions. Give it some time. My guess is you and Peter will learn to talk again and rebuild your relationship."

Marlene nodded and added, "I adore Sue Anne. You've very lucky."

"I know."

After a brief pause, Janie said. "I need to go to the bathroom. Can you help me?"

Later, after Marlene left and Janie closed her eyes, she considered everything that had happened. Ralph was dead, killed by his own hand with the gun that killed Mom. How ironic! And appropriate. He would never bother Marlene again. It was over.

What's more, Marlene looked like a new person. She spoke with confidence and wanted to put her life back together. Her sister's body was healing while her own was deteriorating.

She let out a long, tired sigh. She'd done what she'd set out to do.

It was time for her to go home.

Chapter Thirty-Six

Two months later, Marlene, laden with groceries, raced into the house to catch the ringing phone.

"Hello," she answered, dropping the bags to the floor.

"Marly?"

It was Janie.

After Janie and Sue Anne had returned to Savannah, she talked to Janie on the telephone at least once a week.

"I spoke with Aunt Sarah about coming there." She unloaded the milk and yogurt into the fridge as she talked. "She suggested September. How's that?"

Silence.

"Janie?"

"I'm here. I was just checking my schedule. I had hoped y'all could come sooner. It's often very busy here in the fall."

"Apparently Aunt Sarah can't get away before then. Why? Is there a problem?"

Silence.

"September is fine. Just name a date," Janie finally said.

After she hung up and put away the groceries, she made a pot of coffee and fed Nellie who had materialized under her feet.

She walked from the kitchen to the back porch with a steaming cup in one hand and a stack of coupons in the other. She had been separated from Peter for almost three months.

They had settled into a distant routine, each avoiding that dreaded subject—the future. She fingered through the coupons and made her plans for the next weekly trip to the grocery store, but her mind traveled elsewhere. An image of Nick appeared. Last week she had told him they should call it quits.

"I'm not ready," she had said. "I need to give my marriage another chance."

Nick hung his head and took her hand in his. "Whatever you decide to do, I'll be there for you. If you and Peter get back together, I want to be your friend. You've helped me a lot since I've been home, and I'd hate to lose that. Besides, Jenny likes you." He grinned.

"I'll always consider you one of my best friends," she told him.

They'd parted on a positive note.

Not having a man in her life was a new experience for Marlene. She had married Peter when she was barely twenty, and he had been the only person she had ever seriously dated.

She gazed at the sprawling backyard, covered now with overgrown grass and bushes begging for pruning. It would have been a great yard for children. In fact, she imagined a sliding board and a seesaw in the far corner, and they could've hung a swing on the large oak tree near the driveway. When they bought the house, she considered fencing it in just in case she got pregnant. That seemed an eternity ago.

When she finished with the coupons, she opened the textbook sitting at her fingers. Marlene had returned to school to pick up her studies. Even though she had completed two years at Georgia State before she married Peter, she began anew because so much had changed in the field of finance. Marlene took a deep breath and gazed at a chart representing the flow of supply and demand in the global economy.

* * * *

The following week, while Marlene was loading the dishwasher, Peter called.

"I've got to see you about something," he said. "Do you have some time this evening?"

"I'm supposed to go see *Midnight in Paris* at the dollar movie with Amanda. Jack's out of town, and we've made special plans for a girls night out."

"Can you reschedule?"

"Is it that important?"

"Yes."

An hour later, Peter stood in the living room where he used to live. He looked younger and more attractive than she had seen him in months. His hair was neatly combed but longer, as she liked it, and his eyes shone with the same brilliant intensity she had noticed the first time she saw him sitting in his office at Lawton & Brady so many years earlier. Her heart fluttered. *My gosh, I've really missed him.*

"I'm sorry to ask you to change your plans with Amanda, but I believe you'll understand." His voice sounded tense, businesslike.

"What is it? You're scaring me. Is Aunt Sarah okay?"

"Sarah and Mark are fine." He glanced around the room as if he would like to be anywhere else. He cleared his throat and clasped and unclasped his hands. "Sit down," he said.

She moved to the couch, and Peter followed her, taking both her hands in his and staring into her face.

"Janie is dead."

She blinked, not sure she heard him. Then she gasped, her hands began to tremble, and a pain shot across her chest.

He took her in his arms. She appreciated the warmth of his embrace and the familiar woodsy smell of his aftershave. She was breathing fast, afraid to speak. The reality sinking in. *Janie, not Janie.*

Sobs erupted from deep inside her. Tears tumbled down her cheeks. A deep hollow pain opened up in her gut as if someone had taken a knife and removed a part of her.

She had just gotten Janie back. This wasn't fair and couldn't be true. Peter handed her a handkerchief from his pocket.

"But it's not possible," she managed to choke out. "I-I just talked to her."

"She died of cancer," he whispered, his breath next to her cheek.

Pulling away, he continued, "Sue Anne called me this afternoon. She had my number because I'm to execute Janie's will. She was quite broken up, of course, but she did say Janie died peacefully and mercifully. It was ovarian cancer. The doctors never held out much hope. The cancer was painful and cruel, but Janie held up well. She was very brave." Peter spoke in a low voice.

Marlene had trouble concentrating on his words, remembering Janie's face, her huge eyes and half smile.

"But, why didn't anyone tell me?" she asked.

"Janie didn't want you to see her that way. Neither of them thought it would be this soon. They thought she'd have a few more good weeks. But, once it started, well, apparently it went fast. She went into a coma two days ago and died early this morning. It seems she's known about the illness for some time. It's what brought her back here in the first place."

"I don't understand. How could she not say anything? She wanted us to come visit, but—" She was sobbing again by now, remembering Sue Anne telling her Janie had come here for tests at Emory and how she had discounted that. Janie couldn't be sick because she was never sick. Janie knew she would be dead by September, but she didn't tell her. *Oh, God!*

Her stomach tightened and she took a deep breath to try and control her emotions. But inside everything shuddered and sent waves of chills throughout.

Peter withdrew an envelope from his pocket.

"She left this for you when she was here last winter."

"She was so young," she croaked, trying hard to understand.

Peter nodded and released her hands. "There's something else. I'll be right back."

She watched him through the window and fingered the envelope in her lap with her name written on it in Janie's handwriting. Janie had touched this envelope. Another wave of sadness fell over her and more tears tumbled from her eyes.

"She wanted you to have this." He handed her the small music box.

She immediately recognized the Russian-made, antique box as belonging to Mama, a gift from their Great Uncle Willis whom Marlene had met once as a child. She clasped it and the letter to her chest and moved away from Peter. Everything inside her ached.

He walked up behind her. She turned to him, and they embraced.

* * * *

For two weeks Marlene stared at Janie's letter. She couldn't touch it. As soon as she opened it, her connection with Janie would end and a vital piece of her would be ripped out. Losing Janie was like losing the last vestige of her past. Hers wasn't a pretty past, but it was the only past she had. Her world shook beneath her.

Peter had returned every afternoon after he had delivered that awful news. She cherished his strength, but she didn't lean on him as she had in the past. She had no desire for crutches, neither in the form of Peter nor in a bottle of whiskey. Though she grieved, she would survive.

Peter seemed different. When he touched her, a flutter travelled throughout her as when he had touched her for the first time. His incredible eyes penetrated her with deep yearning. But, after a brotherly embrace, he backed away.

Janie's memorial service was held in Savannah. She rode down with Aunt Sarah and Mark. They had reminisced about good times—Janie always playing with her widely curly hair and once rescuing a lizard which she brought to bed with her. How Mama had screamed when she saw it, but the lizard survived. They recalled her rebellious teen years and her inability to ever help around the house. They shared brief moments of laughter.

Peter drove down alone. Mark offered to drive everyone, but Peter said it was better for him to come on his own. Marlene missed having Peter in the backseat with her, but had he been there, the trip down might have been more somber.

Finally, on June 4th, Janie's birthday—her sister would have been thirty-seven—she drove to Briardale Lane.

She walked past the for-sale sign posted on the front lawn, up the narrow walkway and through the front door.

Once inside, the memories tugged at her in every direction—her mother sitting on the big chair near the window, Ralph sprawled out on the floor the day he tried to pin her down.

She stepped over to the couch that faced the Jennings grandfather clock, reached up, opened the face of the clock and wound it. The tick, tock had soothed her the day she left this house to go live with Aunt Sarah. Maybe it would soothe her today.

Perching on the couch, she placed the music box on the table in front of her and pulled the letters out of her pocket. The sight of Janie's uneven handwriting wrenched her heart and brought new tears.

Dear Marly,

By the time you read this, my ugly disease will have won the battle, and I will finally be at peace. I've felt like a failure ever since Mom. Actually I blamed myself for her. I was the one taking care of her, and it was with me that she died. At first I was mad at her for that, but later I felt guilty. Then when I saw the same thing happening to you, I couldn't believe it. I'm so glad you have come full circle. But before I exit this fine world, I must set some things straight. There are things you must know.

The enclosed letter explains a lot, but before you read it, I want to tell you what happened the day Mom died.

First, you must know Ralph never touched me the way you thought he did. In fact I fabricated that impression just to hurt you. I'm sorry. I was an angry and confused kid. I somehow thought if I could lure Ralph to my bed, I could get rid of him. I had planned to kill him. Can you imagine that? A person who cried if her sister stepped on a cricket was contemplating murder. I actually dreamed about the way I would kill him. It became an obsession. The problem was I couldn't get him to go along with my plan. He came home, gobbled down some food, and then left. I suppose Mom still gave him money. I never found out about that. She drank more and more. Even though I got her out of bed, combed her hair, and helped her put on makeup now and then, she continued to empty bottle after bottle of booze. I had trouble keeping a supply in the house. If Mr. Sosbee at Scott's Liquor Store hadn't been so kind, I could have never done it. He never asked for an ID, but of course he knew I was too young to buy liquor. I suppose he really pitied all of us, but he didn't help, he just prolonged the inevitable.

The day Mom died I got home early about nine-thirty a.m., not late like I told you and the police. When I got home, Ralph was there, eating cereal in the kitchen. Once again I flirted with him. Mom called from the bedroom, but I ignored her. Ralph seemed more interested in me than usual. I know this will cause you pain so I won't go into all the details.

He finally decided to follow me to my room where he basically raped me. I fought him with all my strength, but the more I fought, the more excited he got. I'd hidden Mom's gun under my bed for just that moment. When he got on top of me, I screamed but managed somehow to snatch the gun. I pointed it toward his face. But my hands were shaking so hard, I couldn't hold it straight. Just as I was about to pull the trigger, Mom walked in. She yelled. I froze and dropped the gun. Ralph got up, picked up his clothes, and walked out of the house. I was too ashamed to look at Mom. She stood there for what seemed like hours but must've been only a few minutes. Then she picked up the gun, returned to her room, and closed the door. That was the last time I saw her alive.

After Mom left my room, I dressed and ran as far from that house as I could. It wasn't until much later that I found Mom and realized what happened. I got everything nearly done by the time you got there. I know you saw me before I stashed everything, but I counted on the shock to help you erase the memory. By the time you remembered it all, it was too late.

Marly, I'm sorry for everything I did. My hatred for Ralph consumed me. It controlled me. I had to get away from him and everything that reminded me of him. I finally returned here after so many years to remove him from our lives once and for all. I came to finish what I couldn't do when I was seventeen.

Try to understand why I did what I did. It was the only way I could punish Ralph, the only way I could punish myself, and the final way I could protect all of us. I hope God will forgive me.

Love,
Janie

Tucked inside Janie's letter, Marlene found a blue piece of stationery with pink flowers surrounding the edges. She opened it and saw the delicate upward slant of her mother's handwriting. With her heart pounding and her hands trembling, she began reading:

Girls,

What can I say to you, my pretty ones? I want to tell you so many things, but my mind's in a muddled mess. I love you, that's for sure! But I doubt you believe that. I doubt anyone does. This afternoon I dreamed about your daddy, and he told me to stop tormenting his babies. And, by the way, Marly, Malcolm was your daddy more than any man could've ever been. No, he may not have conceived you, my sweet—I'll finally confess that, but he was your daddy. Never doubt it, honey.

Ah, this is hard for me. Anyway, back to the dream. Your daddy was angrier than a wet hornet. You remember what a sweetheart he was, so even-tempered, never yelled at me like Ralph. In my dream he shook me and screamed at me until tears ran down my face. When I woke up, I knew what he wanted me to do.

I'm sorry I was such a rotten mother. Gosh, I tried, but I just didn't have whatever it takes to be a mother. God knows I didn't! Why did God let me have children and not Sarah? She would have made a perfect mother. But I was the one who had the kids, and I blew it. My only excuse was I was too young and stupid to be a mama.

Tonight just knowing it'll all be over gives me strength. I wish I could squeeze you and smell you just one more time. I hope you will forgive me for not protecting you from the evils in this house and for deserting you. I know you both are old enough to take care of yourselves now, and you've got Sarah who always does what's right. I know you will survive.

Your mama did this out of love and someday, please find it in your hearts to forgive me.

Your loving mother,

Eloise

Marlene folded the letters and placed them carefully inside the envelope. She lifted the lid to the music box. When Beethoven's "Ode to Joy" began to play, the old clock chimed twelve and welcomed in a new day.

Music filled the room like the sound of applause after a tragic play.

ABOUT THE AUTHOR

Joan Curtis authored four business books published by Praeger Press. She is also published numerous stories, including:

Butterflies in a Strawberry Jar, Sea Oats Review, Winter, 2004

A Memoir Of A Friend, Chicken Soup for the Working Woman's Soul, 2003 and Flint River Review, 1996

Jacque's Story in From Eulogy to Joy, 2002

The Roommate, Whispering Willow Mystery Magazine, April 1997

A Special Sort of Stubbornness, Reader's Digest, March 1997,

My Father's Final Gift, Reader Digest, November 1994

Her first place writing awards include: Best mystery manuscript in the Malice Domestic Grants competition, best proposal for a nonfiction piece in the Harriette Austin competition, and best story, Butterflies in a Strawberry Jar in the Cassell Network of Freelance Writers Association.

"I write about characters who remind me of myself at times and my sister at times, but never fully so. My stories are told from a woman's point of view. Characters drive my writing and my reading."

Having grown up in the South with a mother from Westchester County New York, Joan has a unique take on blending the southern traditions with the eye of a northerner. She spent most of her childhood in North Carolina and now resides in Georgia.

MuseItUp
PUBLISHING

MuseItUp Publishing
Where Muse authors entertain readers!
https://museituppublishing.com
Visit our website for more books for your reading pleasure.

You can also find us on Facebook:
http://www.facebook.com/MuseItUp
and on Twitter:
http://twitter.com/MusePublishing

CPSIA information can be obtained at www.ICGtesting.com
Printed in the USA
LVOW08s2035210815

450936LV00001B/1/P